THE
Rancher's
HEART

ANNE CARROLE

THE RANCHER'S HEART Copyright ©2016 by Carol Aloisi

Published by: Galley Press
Cover by: Rae Monet
Edited by: Dori Harrell (Breakout Editing)
Cover Copy: www.blurbcopy.wordpress.com
Formatting: www.formatting4U.com

For more information on the author and her work, please visit http://www.annecarrole.com.

Hearts of Wyoming series

Book 1: *Loving a Cowboy*
Book 2: *The Maverick Meets His Match*
Book 3: *The Rancher's Heart*
Book 4: *The Loner's Heart* (coming 2017)

Acknowledgments

Thanks to Denise M. and Regan D. for their enduring friendship and unwavering support through too many years to count, no matter my endeavor, and to my author friends Tina G. and Monica H. for their input and inspiration. And special thanks to my wonderful and generous readers, without whose support none of this would matter.

Chapter 1

The judge, clothed in his ceremonial black robes, banged his gavel.

She had won. Except Cat McKenna didn't feel like a winner.

Kyle Langley, the lawyer she'd inherited along with the ranch that had been in her family for generations, leaned over from the chair next to her. "Smile," he said, his voice low. "It's good news."

The judge rose, and her lawyer nudged her with his elbow and stood.

So did the two people across the aisle.

Cat scrambled to her feet just as the judge turned to exit. Unfortunately, the purse she'd slung over her chair slid loose and tumbled to the ground with a thud.

Her phone skidded along the wood floor, and her wallet, lipstick, pen, and eyeliner pencil spun under her chair. A crumpled Kleenex, recently used to wipe her son's perennially runny nose, and a partially wrapped stick of gum stayed where they landed. But to her mortification, the tampon she'd stuffed in her purse, just in case, had darted out and rolled right to the bottom of the judge's bench. The judge, probably eager to leave, hadn't broken stride as he exited the courtroom.

1

"I wasn't worried," Kyle said as he stuffed papers into his brown leather briefcase, ignoring the chaos on the floor. He was in his forties, married, no children, all business, just the type of lawyer her late father would choose. "We had over a century and a half of law on our side."

She sat back down and bent under the table to retrieve her stuff and heard the click of Kyle's briefcase.

Jamming her belongings back into her leather bag, she was glad for the distraction. She certainly didn't want to look toward the other side of the room at the tall, broad-shouldered man or the pretty female lawyer who represented him.

She had known Cody Taylor all her life and yet had barely spoken two dozen words to him before or after the incident the summer following high school graduation. Today wasn't likely to change that. There was no love lost between the Taylors and the McKennas—and that was an understatement.

Bending further under the table, she struggled to reach her phone. She'd get the tampon once the courtroom was vacant. Not that she was hiding under the table or anything.

The ding of boots on the wooden floor grew louder, while the tap of high heels grew fainter. As those polished, if worn, leather boots came into sight, she pulled her head out from under the table only to stare, crotch level, at a pair of tailored black pants. Warmth slithered up her neck.

She forced herself to look up, past the large silver buckle decorating a trim waist, past the dark suit jacket covering a white shirt and what she remembered as a load of hard-earned muscle, past the shiny burgundy tie, straight to the set of sterling-blue eyes drilling into her from under a black cowboy hat. Those eyes had caused many a friend's heart to break, back in the day.

"How does it feel to steal somebody's land?" He asked the question in the deep-throated growl of a provoked guard dog.

The warmth turned to heat, smothering her face, searing her throat, and clogging her windpipe. It didn't feel good at all.

"Now Mr. Taylor, that's not fair." Kyle jumped to her defense.

"No. I want to know, Miss McKenna. What does it feel like to take land you know is not yours, was never meant to be yours?"

At the challenge, Cat rose on legs that weren't as steady as she'd hoped. She was five seven, but Cody, a full head taller with shoulders at least a foot wider than hers, made her feel small.

Despite the anger storming across his face, he was a testament to God's handiwork. A face sculpted by angels, no doubt to take a woman's breath away. High cheekbones, firm jawline, straight nose a little on the large size but symmetrically placed, mahogany-brown hair, and those arresting blue eyes. He was tall, dark, and ruthlessly handsome, with hatred emanating from every pore of his body. Directed at her.

Kyle had assured her that she had a legal claim to the land in question, and the judge had agreed. She had done this for her son, for the future of the McKennas.

She dug deep for a dose of courage. "The law is the law, Mr. Taylor," she managed to answer in an even voice, reciting the words Kyle always said in answer to her questions.

"If you have a problem with it, I suggest you take it up with the legislature," Kyle added.

Cody's eyes squinted as if he was looking through a rifle sight aimed straight at her. "The act allowing my forefathers to claim that land was also the law."

"I guess those who passed that bill assumed landowners would be aware of the boundaries of their spread and guard it," Kyle replied. It was the same logic he'd used to persuade her to file the claim.

"We wouldn't need so many laws if people just did the right thing in this world," Cody said, reaching down to the floor.

A second later he placed her phone on the table. His expression, equal parts disapproval and disgust, caused a dump truck of remorse to fill her, making it hard to breathe. Turning, Cody Taylor walked away, back erect, head high. As sanctimonious as a newly ordained preacher.

Cat pulled in air to reinflate her lungs. "He's right, you know," she whispered, giving a soft voice to her apprehension. "The land was never meant to be ours."

"Your family ranched it for more than a hundred years. In this state, for an adverse possession claim, you only need to prove ten. They should have enforced their borders, and none of this would be an issue. In this day and age, you have to know what's yours and defend it. The Taylors didn't, and they lost," Kyle lectured.

"By the way"—Cody's deep voice boomed from the back of the courtroom—"when the hell are you going to move your cattle? It's past birthing time, for

God's sake." The bang of doors slamming shut echoed in the chamber.

"Am I supposed to be moving the herds? Will didn't say anything." She felt the erratic pulse of panic rise up. One more thing she should have known to do. But why hadn't Will Springer, her range foreman, said anything?

"Taylor's trying to rattle you," Kyle opined. "Still, I hope you're considering my recommendation to put Pleasant Valley up for sale. You're not a rancher, Cat."

Cat slung her designer bag over her shoulder. How true. She knew as much about ranching as their barn cat, and here she was trying to run hundreds of head of cattle on tens of thousands of prime acres. "I'm thinking about it." But it would be betraying everything her father had worked for. Everything her ancestors had worked for.

Cody Taylor's family went just as far back as her family, hence the court proceeding. It couldn't be right, taking land, just by using it, that wasn't deeded to you, but apparently it was legal.

Putting his hand on her back, Kyle guided her down the center aisle framed by empty wood benches.

"You think your father would have had any qualms about filing an adverse possession claim if he'd had the survey done and discovered it after *his* father had died?" He opened one of the large double doors and held it for her.

"Of course not. Only I'm not my father." Thank goodness. But her father would have known whether to move cattle or not.

They headed down the corridor, and the clicking sound of her heels against the old hexagon-shaped tile echoed off the marble walls. Cat trailed slightly behind the fast-walking Kyle as she tried to collect her thoughts.

The ranch was hers now. She was responsible for making the decisions that would ensure its success or cause its failure. Assuring she had water rights was critical. Because keeping the ranch intact for her son was the one way she could prove she wasn't completely useless. Selling it would be admitting she'd failed—failed her son, failed her father.

"You'd better learn how to be like him when it matters if you are going to run Pleasant Valley. Because on issues of land or cattle, it will matter."

Cat didn't miss the doubt in Kyle's voice. Something about her lawyer always had Cat on the defensive. Maybe it was his condescending tone. Or the feeling that she had to ask the right questions, or he wouldn't tell her all she needed to know.

"I still don't see why we couldn't have offered the Taylors a compromise, like giving them back their land but maintaining our right to the water. Lord knows that family is hurting enough." It had felt like she'd kicked a wounded animal.

Kyle stopped so short, Cat almost stumbled into him.

"You didn't spend all of this money asserting your claim to that land in order to give it back." With his eyes narrowed and his mouth pinched, Kyle looked a little like a lizard. "If you own the land up to that creek, there will never be a question as to water rights. And that will be important whether you stay or sell."

"And likely why one of my forefathers co-opted it before the Taylors knew they owned it." There had been a dark history back in Wyoming's early days. One of rich ranchers lynching poorer ranchers, of land grabs and hired guns, and the McKennas had been in the thick of it.

"As best I can piece together, the Taylor that filed the original land claim died, and his widow and children inherited it. If your ancestor began running cattle on it and the widow didn't know any better, that's just tough luck."

What Kyle didn't say was that the Taylors' ancestor had been murdered and the murderer had never been caught. The Taylor version of history had always laid blame for that murder at the McKennas' door.

"And the Taylors kept using their side of the creek, and we used our side, only it wasn't ours."

"Your family's fortunes would have been vastly diminished if they didn't have clear access to that creek."

"Survival of the fittest, right?"

"Now you're sounding more like your daddy." Kyle smiled his approval, but it only made Cat's stomach feel hollow, like the victory they'd just claimed.

"Still, it doesn't seem right." And those arresting blue eyes and deep voice had accused her of as much.

And then Cat remembered. She'd forgotten to retrieve the tampon.

"Can I buy you a cup of coffee?" The pretty blond lawyer, younger than he was and waiting on the sidewalk, had apologized more than once already. Cody Taylor didn't need to give her any more chances.

It wasn't her fault. She just happened to be the unlucky "first year" to get the assignment at the yellow pages law firm he'd contacted.

He shook his head. "Got to get back to the ranch. I appreciate all you've done, Melissa. It was pretty much a lost cause to begin with." But he'd hoped the daughter would show more integrity than the father ever had and grant him back the land when she'd found out her ancestors had stolen it, regardless of what the law said. Instead she'd taken him to court to legalize the claim.

Cat McKenna had always intrigued him, from a distance, at least. And not just because she had inquisitive brown eyes, or long, rich coffee-colored hair that made a man want to run his fingers through it, or because wearing short skirts and high heels in a school filled with ranch kids, she'd been more princess than barrel racer. But because she'd been the girl in high school who had included a special-needs student at the table where all the cheerleaders held court and had led a fundraising drive when a fellow student's house had been damaged by fire. She'd seemed to be the exact opposite of her hardheaded, tight-fisted father. And then there was that other matter everyone had been talking about for the last few years. But he should have known better. She was a McKenna, after all.

Melissa leaned in and rested a hand on his arm, bringing him back to the present. She smelled nice, like flowers. She looked nice, even if she was suited up. But like Cat McKenna in her New York–style outfits and high heels, Melissa wasn't really his type. He liked women who wore jeans, weren't afraid to get their hands dirty, and enjoyed being outdoors. Natural women who didn't use makeup or high heels or fancy clothes to look good.

"Now that the case is over, well, I was hoping we might get together. Sometime." Melissa bit her lip as a strand of chin-length blond hair swept across her pretty face, blown by the spring breeze that whipped down the dusty main street of the county seat.

He hadn't been out with a woman in a while, and if he didn't feel like he was in the middle of a tornado these days, he might have taken a second look and asked her out before now. But life had him off his game. Else how could he explain his miscalculation of Cat McKenna. She might have the looks of an angel, but it appeared she had the heart of a demon, just like her father.

"If I get out this way, sure." *Leave it vague, Taylor. Don't lead the lady on, but don't close the door either.* It was always a thin line to walk. "Again, thank you. We'll pay the fee in full, but it may be a little at a time, like we discussed."

"I told you I thought I could get the firm to classify this as pro bono work."

She'd removed her hand from his arm.

"The Taylors don't take charity. We'll pay. Eventually." Cody just had to figure out how, given all the other bills piling up.

"Let me know, then, when you're in town." She wiggled her slender fingers in a wave and then hip-swayed down the thinly populated sidewalk toward her office, her heels tapping a beat on concrete.

And he didn't feel a thing. Yup, definitely off his game.

Cody walked across the street to the parking lot and wondered how the hell he was going to break this to his father.

Bumping along in his battered pickup as it sped up the gravel drive leading to the small white-framed ranch house, Cody felt the usual relief at being home and dread at what he'd find waiting for him. Today the dread overwhelmed the relief.

There would be no way to put a good spin on this outcome. He'd known it was a long shot. The McKennas had been beating the Taylors for over a century now. But if his family had held claim to those water rights, it would have been the McKennas who would have lost.

For some reason, fate had this outcome in store for the Taylors, and there was no use imagining what could have been. Cody was too pragmatic to indulge in what-ifs. He dealt in what-is. And these last few years, what-is hadn't been even close to good.

He parked the truck on the grass, worn almost bare with tire tracks, and headed up the steps to the house that had seen better days, letting the squeaky storm door slam behind him. The small kitchen's counter was stuffed with canisters, a toaster, coffeepot, and microwave. A white refrigerator bulged out from the wall, and an oversized wooden table and benches his father had made in better times took up the rest of the limited space.

He breathed in the scent of stale coffee as he set the vials of pills from the pharmacy on the table, along with the bag of groceries he'd picked up from Albertsons. Dishes were still in the sink, the coffeemaker light was on, and the pantry door, its maple sheen long since dulled, was open.

"Mom," he called out. Where was she? But he knew where to check. She'd taken over his room, while he slept on the couch, leaving his father alone to stare at the ceiling of the master bedroom.

After shutting off the coffeemaker, Cody sauntered down the narrow hallway, where the walls always seemed to close in on him. He sensed that feeling was about more than just architecture.

A peek in his room confirmed his suspicions. His mother was curled up on the bed, asleep. An empty beer bottle on the bed stand. She lay with the crumpled cotton blankets low on her thin legs, and her graying hair, once a deep brown, straggled out of the bun she no longer took care in pinning. Loosening his tie, he continued down the hall to the man in the rented hospital bed, a man he didn't want to face.

The sight of his father, with tubes streaming from his arm and surrounded by pumps that kept him barely alive, always jarred Cody. This last year it had been hard to watch the once sturdy and vital man he'd looked up to decline in health and vigor, bit by bit, day by day.

Apparently hearing him come in, his father opened eyes that showed exhaustion. Sadie, the oldest of their two border collies, was stretched out next to him, with her black-and-white head resting on his legs. She raised her head for just a minute before deciding she needn't have bothered.

Until his dad had taken to bed, their two dogs had slept in the kitchen and hadn't been allowed on the furniture. But once Zeke was laid up, Sadie had refused to leave his side except for a trip outside to relieve herself. Her son, Mikey, had taken over all the herding chores.

"Well?" Zeke Taylor's voice was labored, like his breathing.

"We lost." Cody didn't believe in sugarcoating hard truths. Best get them out and deal with them.

His father scrunched his eyes closed, as he did when in pain. Given the hospice worker had come by that morning, Cody doubted his father was in physical pain.

"She's no better than her father."

The last was a rebuke meant for Cody. Though the legal side might have been a lost cause, he'd taken a risk that Cat McKenna would do the right thing. Guess he'd always been a sucker for a pretty woman.

"I agree."

Zeke shook his head. "The thought of Joe McKenna's face when she came back with that kid—imagining it is the only thing that gives me any pleasure where that family is concerned."

The whole county had been talking about it at the time. After a few years away at college and then working as a teacher, Cat McKenna had returned home, unwed and with a toddler in tow. Wagering had been fast and furious about when McKenna would throw his daughter out. But the old man hadn't. And Cat had been home for almost two years now, though he'd rarely caught a glimpse of her until the proceedings. And her old man had been dead going on six months already. The McKenna ranch was starting to feel the loss. Cattle weren't getting moved. The herds weren't being added to. He'd heard she'd lost a lot during the calving season.

Cat McKenna had been handed everything she needed to successfully continue Pleasant Valley Ranch, and she didn't have a clue what to do with it. He knew what he would do if he had just half of the money and a few thousand acres of McKenna land instead of the hundreds of hilly acres the Taylors laid claim to over a century ago and the mountain of debt they'd recently incurred. Cat McKenna would probably run down the enterprise until it was no better than the Taylors' spread. But the Taylors had an excuse. Cat would have none.

There had been little sign of a cowgirl in Cat McKenna back in high school, and that had undoubtedly galled her sonless father. Frilly, flirty, giggly. She'd had a soft tinkling kind of laughter, if he remembered correctly. And she'd always worn a skirt. A short skirt with high heels showing lots of leg. Nice legs. He'd always been a leg man, so he'd noticed. Noticed her legs today peeking out of a tight, above-the-knee skirt. With high heels. Even if he preferred cowgirl boots to heels and jeans to short skirts and women who knew their way around a barn, it was still worth a look.

"So that's it then." The resignation in his father's voice was worse than hearing the judge's pronouncement. It wasn't just resignation. It was defeat. And he'd heard it and felt it too often lately.

"There's no grounds for appeal." And no money either. There'd been a glimmer of hope before, given the Taylors had been paying taxes based on the deed, which included the land in question. But under the law, it didn't matter. And there was no recourse for reimbursement. One wondered sometimes in whose interest the laws of this country were made.

"Where's your mother?" Zeke asked in a barely audible whisper.

"Sleeping." No sense mentioning why. His father knew.

Zeke closed his eyes again. "Leave her be then."

"You need anything?"

"I'm okay. You go. Expect your brother could use some help."

"Right." Cody could almost feel the load on his shoulders getting heavier as he slipped from the room, Sadie trailing after him, apparently seizing her moment to be let out. Once down the hall, he bent down and patted her, and she looked up at him as if to say *do something*. How he wished he could.

For once in his sorry life he didn't feel like working. He'd begun to question for what purpose. Maybe they should up and sell the land. Likely Cat McKenna would buy it. Her father had tried to buy it many times before. But even as Cody entertained the idea, he knew he could never do it. That would really be admitting defeat. And the Taylors might be failures, but they weren't quitters.

Chapter 2

"Mommy." The little blond-haired boy, clad in denims and a T-shirt, ran at full four-and-three-quarter-year-old speed right into her arms—or more like her knees—as she stepped from the light-blue Honda Civic the same age as her son. It was the one material object she could call her own, or almost her own, once she paid off the loan in a few more months.

Closing the car door, she scooped up her wiggling child and planted a kiss on the boy's sticky cheek, hugged him close, and breathed in the clean scent of baby shampoo.

It was all about Jake now. Keeping the ranch going for him so he could decide what he wanted to do with it.

That was another thing she had inherited, but never necessarily wanted, from her father—the dream of Jake running Pleasant Valley Ranch. That possibility had been the only reason Joe McKenna hadn't thrown her out when she returned home, a toddler in her arms, unwed, unwanted, and unemployed. And Jake was the only reason she had returned, given her father's initial reaction to the news of her pregnancy.

Swallowing her pride for a man who had never

taken pride in her had been difficult, but that had been her cross to bear, and Jake had certainly made that cross lighter. If she could have continued to teach and live her life as a single mom in the city or suburbs, she might have made peace with the fact her father wanted nothing to do with her. But when every municipality in three states had started laying off teachers, that proved no longer possible. Unable to make the rent with no job prospects in sight, she'd done the one thing she'd vowed never to do—she'd asked to come home, and to her relief and surprise, her father had agreed. Within an hour of their arrival, her father was carrying Jake in his large arms, showing him around the barns, and ignoring her, as if she'd just been the interim step.

She'd given Joe a grandson, and he was willing to disregard the circumstances. Cat refused to think about what would have happened if her child had been a girl.

Joe McKenna felt he would live forever, no doubt. Certainly long enough to see his grandson take over the ranch. His will gave her child, or children, should there be more than one, the ranch when the age of eighteen was reached. Her mother, Cat, and Kyle Langley had been named trustees until that time, with a modest provision made for the two women in Joe's life.

Joe had been under no illusions about what his daughter felt about ranch life. She'd undoubtedly confirmed that the moment she'd accepted a scholarship at the University of Colorado—and left.

Still in her arms, Jake leaned back from her embrace. He had such dark-brown eyes, like his father, along with the blond hair. He'd be a heartbreaker when he grew up, just like his father. That was, if she didn't instill good values in him. There was no better place to do that than on a ranch where nature dealt regular lessons in humility and livestock required daily care and tending.

So she'd accepted a low-paying job in the county seat as a preschool teaching assistant, helped no doubt by her last name, a job she'd had to give up to take over Pleasant Valley.

"I want to ride my horsey," Jake announced.

She hadn't approved of the pony her father bought Jake for his two-year birthday. She'd insisted she be out there when he "rode" it. She didn't doubt her father would have taught Jake how to shoot a gun if he thought she wouldn't find out, so eager was he to make Jake into his own image.

"Well, it's almost supper, and I have to find Mr. Springer and ask him something about the cattle. How about after dinner?"

"Will's in the barn, Mommy."

Cat didn't like Jake calling his elders by their first names, but Will had encouraged it. She set Jake down and held out her hand for him to take, but in true boy fashion, he blew ahead of her, toward the barn, like tumbleweed on a gust of wind.

How was she to run this huge operation when she knew nothing about cattle? And didn't care to know.

Will Springer, the range foreman, was in the building they used for sick animals and birthing problems. He was bending over, checking a young calf with stains of yellow diarrhea marring its rear. Weathered and gray before his time, given Will was still in his early fifties, he had the look of a man beset by burdens. Only Cat hadn't a clue what they were.

All she knew about him was that he was divorced—something that happened a long time ago—and having been hired by her father, had worked at Pleasant Valley for close to five years now.

Given Cat's inexperience in ranching, she needed a *ranch* foreman, someone who would essentially take the place of her father in directing all the operations, including the range, breeding, land management, and the remuda of horses that were becoming less essential to the operation.

Will Springer had already informed her of his expectation of becoming the ranch foreman, or *ramrod*, as it was known, but for reasons Cat couldn't articulate, she had hesitated in naming him.

"Scours," Will said by way of explanation for the calf's presence.

Cat looked at the diarrhea-ravaged animal, and her heart shuddered. They'd been beset by this plague all birthing season.

Jake crouched near the calf to get a better look. "Feel better," he cooed.

"Don't pet him, honey. You could get sick too," Cat warned. Jake didn't move away, but he didn't touch the calf either.

Will rose as the calf rested on the bed of straw. Her range foreman was of average height, slim, and sported a baseball-type cap with the name of a tractor company written on it, instead of a traditional cowboy hat. A blue-and-white bandanna swaddled his neck.

"Will, I wanted to ask you if we should be moving the herd, given birthing season is done," she said, parroting Cody's words.

"Sure. We can do that."

18

"Why haven't we?"

"Thought you'd want to brand them before we move them to the north pastures for the summer and breeding."

Cat felt her face flush. Of course they would have to be branded. "When do we do that?"

"When you say the word."

"You were waiting for me to say the word?" Why hadn't he told her? Why did she have to ask?

"You're the boss."

"Let's brand them then."

Will nodded. "We have to move them to the pastures we use for branding."

Cat tried to school her features so as not to show her irritation. "Then let's move them."

"We should set up the fencing for the branding operations too."

"Okay."

"Then we have to put out a call for help. We can't do the whole operation with just the crew we have."

Cat was overwhelmed. "Let's move them, set up the fencing, and then we'll take the next step."

"Okay," Will plunged his hands into his pockets. "It all takes time. We are already behind, and we have this scours problem to clean up."

"I understand that, but we need to get started," she said, losing the battle to hide her irritation.

"Thought you was waiting on something. Figured you knew about branding." Will's eyes held an accusation.

"Yes, well, I should have." She spun around. Jake was still cooing to the calf, but he wasn't touching it. She'd make sure his hands were washed, and no boots past the mud room. "Come on, Jake. I'm sure dinner is ready."

"I want to ride my pony."

"I'll take him," Will offered.

"Thank you, but we'll do it after dinner." Cat didn't trust anyone else with Jake when he was on a horse. "Come on now." She held her hand out to Jake.

Her son reluctantly rose and sullenly toddled over. Taking his hand, Cat left Will in the barn and wondered if the calf would survive. Dozens hadn't.

She was so out of her depth it wasn't funny.

"I was waiting for you," her mother said as soon as Cat stepped barefooted into the kitchen, lit by the late-afternoon sun. She had left her high heels and Jake's boots by the door, and they both had washed their hands at the tub-sink her father had installed in the mud room at her mother's insistence.

When an extension had been put on the old Victorian-era house, her mother had made a point of having a southern-facing kitchen to catch the most light. That, along with its spaciousness, gave the room an airy yet warm feeling. The modern kitchen never looked messy, even when her mother was setting out a spread for twenty. Very unlike when Cat did the cooking and why, perhaps, her mother had held on to the meal-preparation chores.

Granite sparkled. Stainless steel gleamed. Tile shone. It was a gourmet's delight in that kitchen, and the food that came from her mother's six-burner stove tasted as good as any four-star restaurant. Lydia McKenna took great pride in her culinary skills and had squeezed all her creative juices into making mouthwatering food. Too bad Joe McKenna had never appreciated the effort and skill that went into his wife's creations. Cat couldn't remember Joe ever paying Lydia a proper compliment, beyond leaving an empty plate for the dishwasher.

Lydia stood now before the stove, a blue apron covering a pair of khakis and a white blouse as the smell of fried chicken wafted through the room and the pan on the stove sent a sizzling hiss through the air. Time had been kind to her mother, and given her robust figure and use of color to keep her hair a rich auburn, Lydia McKenna looked at least ten years younger than her fifty years.

More so now than ever. It had been amazing how much her mother had blossomed since her father's passing. It was like a switch had been flipped and the real Lydia McKenna had come out. Social, outgoing, fun loving. The transformation from dutiful and duty-filled wife to social butterfly had been nothing short of astonishing.

"I needed to talk with Will first. That smells good." Cat snuck a peek in the pan where honey-browned pieces of chicken crackled in oil.

"I'm hungry," Jake announced from behind her. Not that he would eat the chicken without some major cajoling. He'd been such a good eater when he first started tasting food. But just at the halfway mark of his third year, he'd gotten finicky.

"I'll put on some mac and cheese for Jake." Cat looked down at her son. "You need to use the bathroom before you eat, young man. Do you need me to help?"

"No." Jake shook his head for emphasis, his

blond bowl-cut hair fanning out as he headed off to the powder room.

"Call if you need me."

"He'll do fine." It was no secret her mother thought she coddled Jake, just as her father had thought it. "Thanks for agreeing to eat early. I have choir practice tonight. And I already made the mac and cheese. It's in the keep-warmer."

Cat said her thanks as she got the bright floral dishes her father had always hated out of the cabinet. She set them around the table and arranged the silverware with a rose engraved on the handles. When her mother turned down her offer to help with dinner, Cat sank into the chair at the table, grateful to be able to sit for a minute and not have to think.

Lydia stared at her, a frown marring her brow. "What's wrong? Your text message said we won the case, but you look like we lost the whole ranch."

Her greatest fear.

"We did win. But…" What could she say? How could she voice her concerns to her mother, who was obviously depending upon her to keep Pleasant Valley successful, or voice it to anyone at the ranch? They were all counting on her. No one had apparently told them what a long shot they were betting on.

"Must have been a blow to the Taylors, what with Zeke being so sick and the bills rolling in. Joanne Littleton said she didn't give Zeke but another month. Poor Mamie. Our husbands might have been enemies, but I don't hold anything against her. Joanne says Mamie's taken it hard. Drinking, she says. Says that's because they're going bankrupt too." Her mother gave a sympathetic shake of her head.

Joanne Littleton was not only the town gossip, but the town's pessimist. Every town had at least someone who always thought the sky was falling. But what if this time she was right? What if losing this lawsuit was the last straw for the Taylors? Cody's expression as he called her a thief camped out in her mind.

"How bad off is Zeke Taylor?"

"Bad. Big C. No hope."

Cat didn't know what was worse—knowing your father was going to die, or finding him dead in the barn without warning. Both were bad. One had you dreading the inevitable every day as you planned for the worst, and the other left you in shock without a plan.

"Did you know we were supposed to move the herd after birthing and brand the new calves?" She folded her arms on the table and rested her head there. Even if she didn't know the answers to things, she at least had to know what questions to ask. She never asked for this responsibility, never wanted it. At a young age, she had accepted her father's verdict that she would never be fit to run a ranch, mainly because she didn't have a certain male organ hanging between her legs.

She'd gone on to other things, hoping her success in school, in dancing, in cheerleading, in being a proper young lady would make her worthy of at least some of his time. It hadn't. If she hadn't had her mother to lean on, she'd probably be screwed up—at least, more screwed up. Cat never was quite sure she'd actually escaped those emotional scars or had just gotten real good at burying them.

"Well, come to think of it, we've always had the branding before Memorial Day weekend, when I go visit Uncle Len. But you know I don't know a thing about ranching. That was Joe's area," her mother said.

"Cody Taylor had to tell me. More like shout it to me as he was leaving the courtroom." Before seeing him in court, she had only caught glimpses of Cody since she'd been back. In a grocery store, driving down Main Street, at one of the town's many parades. She found it easy to pick him out of a crowd, given he was so tall, with a smile that sent any red-blooded woman's heart pumping. Only today, there had been no smile.

Lydia turned the black knob on the stove, and the sizzling in the pan dampened. "Well, that was mighty nice of him to tell you at least. But why didn't Will mention it?"

Cat let out a sigh. "Exactly." She listened for the flush of the toilet and the sound of water that said Jake was washing his hands.

"I assume that's what you talked to Will about? What did he say?"

"He was waiting for me to give the order."

And that response had scared the bejeezus out of her. Because if the remuda foreman and the breeding foreman were also waiting around for her orders, what else had been neglected? She hadn't a clue.

"I told you that you need someone who can take over the whole thing, a ranch foreman. All the big outfits have 'em, only your father never felt the need. I'm sure once Will has the title, he'll feel comfortable making the decisions."

"I'm not so sure. And how will I know he's making the right decisions? I'm a teacher, not a rancher. The most I know about cattle is they have four legs, four stomachs, and they chew cud. I never wanted to know more." She'd always tried not to get too familiar with the animals, knowing their fate. That meant distancing herself as much as possible. She might have been raised on a ranch, but she was as far from a cowgirl as any city-born female.

"The men will help you. That's why you have them."

Jake came running into the kitchen and slammed into her knees, grabbing her arms with his cool, still-wet hands. Kissing him on his head, she breathed in his little-boy scent. "Here, sit in the booster seat. Grandma made you mac and cheese already."

Jake scrambled up the chair next to Cat's, which had been fitted with a blue plastic booster seat, as Lydia set a bowl of elbow macaroni covered in cheesy orange sauce in front of her son. Cat noticed a few pieces of chicken coated in the melted cheese. Her mother sent her a wink. Jake picked up his fork and dug in, oblivious to the deception.

"If the men are going to help, why did Cody Taylor have to tell me what to do with my own herd?" That had been nothing short of humiliating, no doubt what he intended.

"For all Joe's hard feelings against the Taylors, he did admire the sons, if not the father."

"Sons he wanted." Cat had grown up in the shadow of the son her father never had. For an imaginary person, it was a big shadow, made bigger by the fact her father's rival had two boys that, as her father said many a time, would have made any man proud. Of course, that was before that fateful summer evening.

"Yes, your father wanted sons. Lord knows I tried to give them to him."

Her mother's expression softened to a wistful melancholy. No doubt she was thinking of the many miscarriages Cat had heard about time and again in the story of Lydia and Joe's marriage.

"But despite what you may think, he loved you. As much as he was capable. He just didn't want you saddled to this ranch. He knew how difficult ranching is. He just didn't think it was for you."

Her father had judged her lacking, but her toddler son was deemed fit?

"Know where I can rent a Cody Taylor?" If Cody Taylor was running Pleasant Valley instead of her, the ranch would be so much better off.

Her mother gave a snort. "You renting him for a good time or for ranch foreman?"

"What?"

"You're talking about renting a man, and he's a fine-looking one, you've got to admit. Half the girls in the county have set their caps for him—the other half just haven't met him yet. Zeke was a good-looking man in his day. But his sons, both of them, are something out of central casting."

"Mama!" Cat had never heard her mother comment on the physical attributes of any man. Never.

But Cat couldn't deny what her mother said. Today she'd had an up-close encounter with Cody Taylor, and his masculine essence had overwhelmed her—as it had once before. Cody was all cowboy from his Stetson to his boots, polished no doubt for the occasion. She had tried not to look at him during the hearing, but she couldn't help stealing glances as they had waited for the judge.

He'd been a hound dog in high school, taking

everything a gal was willing to give. Based on the gossip, that had been a lot. He'd been fun loving, up to mischief, and dangerous—a heady combination for seventeen-year-old females, including her. But being he was a Taylor, she'd only been able to *imagine* a night with Cody. Until that summer, of course.

Today he had sat stoic and unflinching as the judge read the verdict. He'd grown into the kind of man her daddy would have admired, if he hadn't been a Taylor. Unyielding, standing up for what he believed, and never backing down from a fight. A man who knew his business and kept to it. The kind of man Joe would have preferred to be his only child.

Not the child who, in his own words, had gone wild in the city and gotten herself pregnant without a ring on her finger and no hope of ever being made an "honest woman."

"I may be beyond my prime, but I've still got eyes and a beating heart. I know a fine man when I see one."

Well, Cat was in her prime—at least age-wise. Yet she hadn't been with a man since Jake's father. For most of the time, she'd been too tired and exhausted being a single mother and major breadwinner to date. Didn't mean she didn't long for someone to hold her, whisper in her ear, make her feel she was desired.

She was sure Cody Taylor could do that for a woman. She'd heard as much from Angie Jean and Cyndi Lynn and a handful of other high school friends who had numbered among his conquests. Though not recently. Most of her friends from high school were either married or had moved away after college. If it hadn't been for her childhood friend from another town, Mandy Prescott Martin, and her newest friend, Libby Cochran, she'd have had no social life to speak of when she'd returned to Pleasant Valley. Now that both were recently married, that social life had pretty much dried up. Maybe it was for the best, since she was busy doggie paddling in a sea of ranching.

"Daddy would turn over in his grave if he heard you talking like that about a Taylor." Especially Cody.

She wondered if Cody ever thought about that night. Ever regretted it. Ever blamed her.

"Your daddy ain't here. I've come to grips with the fact I'm a widow. And one that will be thinking for herself now, thank you very much. You need to start thinking for yourself and stop worrying about what he would do or say. There's no gain in that. So if you don't know what to do about the ranch and you don't have faith in anyone here, you best find someone you do have faith in, and fast. There's lots of people depending on you, including that little one right there." Her mother pointed at Jake, who, with all eyes on him, took the opportunity to send a noodle flying through the air off the end of his fork.

That noodle was soft, limp, and clearly expendable. And though Cat might feel the same way, she needed, as the old song said, to pick herself up, dust herself off, and start again.

The two-and-a-half-year-old colt shook his head as if giving a silent answer to the question of the saddle in Cody's hand. The sorrel was a beautiful specimen of a quarter horse, and should be, given his lineage could be traced back to Mr. Gun Smoke. At fifteen-and-a-half hands, Smoking Gun was muscular and quick. So far he'd shown a lot of cow since Cody had worked with him, but he was far from trained. A half a year more and Cody would try him in the three-year-old futurity. At least that had been the plan.

With so many bills adding up, he might have to sell the colt that had resulted from his initial foray into horse breeding. All the time, all the work at getting the right bloodlines, would end up with him settling for less than half what the colt would bring as a three-year-old.

Aid for his father was not cheap, and their meager health insurance only paid for the basics, not the chronic care his father needed. Not that selling Smoking Gun would have a prayer of clearing all the debt they were buried in, but it might have to be done.

"He's beautiful, son."

Cody turned around. His mother stood by the fence. She looked tidier, her hair pinned back, her dress changed. And he hadn't noted any slurring in her speech. Maybe she'd truly just been tired. He could hope.

"He is at that." Saddle in hand, Cody ambled over to where his mother stood, a spring breeze bringing a late-afternoon nip in the air as evening settled. The sun sparkled low in the sky and soon would be painting the horizon in purples, pinks, and oranges.

"Your father told me the news." His mother leaned against the rail, her slight weight settling on the bony arms she'd rested on the wooden plank.

A soft wind brought the familiar pasture scents of earth, horse, and manure and ruffled the hem of his mother's faded print dress.

"There wasn't much of a chance to begin with. But at least I can say we tried." He set the saddle on the ground near the fence.

His mother nodded. "You'd have thought his daughter would be different, considering what she's been through. Her mother's a decent enough woman. How she stood being married to that SOB, I'll never understand."

Cat McKenna had stood in that courtroom looking like she'd stepped out of the pages of a fashion magazine, with her burnished-brown hair falling on her slim shoulders, a muted purple blouse, short black skirt, and those high heels emphasizing a pair of long, tanned legs as she bit her lip and looked at him like he was going to strangle her. He'd thought about doing that...and something else.

"Well, not much has changed since he died, so I guess Cat McKenna isn't any different." And much less of a rancher. "Dad okay?"

"Sleeping." Her eyes looked sad, exhausted, defeated. Like he felt. "I'm sorry I wasn't awake when you got in. You could have woken me, you know. I'd have gotten you something to eat."

She looked at him like she was expecting recriminations. He was plum out of them today.

"I wasn't hungry, and you looked like you could use some rest." That was the truth.

Mist formed in her tired eyes, eyes that once sparkled with sass and mischief. "What are we going to do now? Zeke said we don't even get any money. I don't understand how this can be?" She rubbed her hands together like she was trying to wash them clean. "Seeing him so disappointed, watching someone you love, have always loved, shrivel up before your eyes, you don't know what it's like." She blinked, no doubt trying to stop the flow of tears. He prayed it worked.

"I do know what it's like, Mom. He's my father." Why people always assumed he didn't feel anything was a wonder to him. He might not display emotion for all to see, but that didn't mean it wasn't killing him inside.

She nodded and then captured him in a hug. "Thank God you're made of sterner stuff."

He didn't feel so stern. He felt downright whipped as his mother's spindly arms encircled his neck. He caught a stale whiff of alcohol before she released him as quickly as she'd embraced him.

"He'll bring a pretty penny, I wager." She nodded toward Smoking Gun.

"That's what I'm hoping." No sense burdening her with the possibility Smoking Gun would be sold sooner rather than later.

She stared up at him with such hope he could have sworn he glimpsed some of her old sparkle. "If we can hang on, I know you'll get top dollar for him. If we can just make it until we sell the calves next year."

"I'm hoping." The timing of going grass-fed, which garnered more per head but meant a smaller market, couldn't have been worse. It changed calving time until late spring / early summer, and that meant a year without income until they could get in synch with the new calendar. Decisions made before they learned of his father's cancer.

Her nod was a solemn one, like she understood the odds. "Hungry or not, supper will be in fifteen minutes. You told your brother yet?"

"Yup. Jace isn't any happier than you or me about it." His younger brother had big dreams, rodeo dreams. But his dreams had been curtailed because of their father's illness.

"Don't be late tonight. Your father will appreciate company." And then his mother walked away, head bent, shoulders stooped, steps unhurried.

Cody turned around and took a long look at the colt that held the hope of the Cross T Ranch, knowing it wouldn't be enough.

Chapter 3

Cat sat on the back of her father's bay horse, named Custer after the general, as the horse picked its way along the bank of the creek that provided water for the ranch. *And which wasn't intended to be yours.* She'd never been horse crazy like most of her friends, but she did know how to ride, one thing her father had actually spent time teaching her.

She'd taken a detour to the creek after she'd overseen the movement of a portion of the herd to the pastures to the west of the house. Will had used ATVs instead of horses to move them, but since she was just watching, she'd chosen to do so on Custer, even though her legs and butt would no doubt ache afterward since it had been a while since she'd been in the saddle.

Once the branding was completed, the herd could be moved even further to the northern pastures, and the bulls would be let lose to begin the process all over again. Time on a ranch, she'd learned, was measured by the breeding cycle of cattle.

This part of the creek had cottonwoods scattered along its banks, which provided shade and, as she'd come to find out, an obstacle to soil erosion, before the land opened up on both sides to grassy meadows. The meadows on her side were used in the winter months because this expanse was near the house and water. Having provided sustenance during the winter, the grass was, by this time of year, decimated and would need replenishment, and Cat could only hope the farmers contracted to till this land knew what they had to do, because she sure didn't.

The effects of last year's drought was still in evidence, as the creek was flowing under capacity despite decent snowfall in the mountains, thankfully, this winter. The creek, named Crystal Creek for the quality of its water, was the only water source for both ranches and thus the cause of much acrimony through the decades, even before this latest battle. Pleasant Valley would not have been so pleasant without access to water.

Movement caught her eye, and she looked over her shoulder to see a rider on a horse moving toward the creek on the Taylor side. A dog was trailing behind. It had been days since the judge's ruling, and she hadn't seen Cody Taylor—but she had been thinking about him for some crazy reason.

He'd called her a thief, pulling forth memories of when she'd been much younger and had slipped a piece of candy into her mouth from the bin in Miller's Feed Store. After she'd swallowed it, she'd told her father so he could pay for it. Instead of paying, her father had labeled her the same and told Mr. Miller he would bring her back to pay him out of the small sum she'd made from chores. She remembered Mr. Miller's you're-a-naughty-girl scowl as he'd looked down at her from behind the counter. She remembered, too, the red face of her father as he snatched her hand and dragged her out of the store. But most of all, she remembered the shame.

The rider got off, his long legs hitting the ground. Given the height, it could very well be Cody. If it was him, it wasn't likely they'd exchange any words. Or get any closer than the creek that kept them separated and always would.

Her father had been envious of Zeke Taylor on one account only—his sons. Yup, if Pleasant Valley was in the hands of Cody Taylor, the ranch would be thriving.

Maybe he'd be interested in working for her.

As soon as the thought sprang into her mind, she quashed it. Really, what could she hope to prove by asking him to manage her ranch? He'd not only turn her, a McKenna, down, but likely laugh in her face.

Only she needed someone like him.

And he needed money, or so her mother had reported. If she offered a job, maybe it would ease her conscience. At least she could say she tried.

Before she thought better of it, she reined her horse and headed for the creek, where the rider stood staring in her direction.

"You're trespassing on my land, Miss McKenna. Or are you trying to lay claim to this side too? Because I warn you, I'll be enforcing our borders in earnest."

Cody Taylor stood in a gunfighter's pose, holding the reins of the horse beside him. His dog, a tricolor border collie, sat in a rigid pose beside him, eyeing her. She took in the rifle that was strapped to the back of his saddle. It wasn't uncommon for people to ride armed in this country, what with coyotes, wolves, bears, and assorted game, but given his words, she might have been scared. Odd that she wasn't.

Maybe she was overestimating him, but there was something about Cody that had always been more attractive than ominous. Something beyond those arresting blue eyes, that muscular build, those long legs that gave him such a commanding height, and that handsome, too handsome, face. Something that was warming, not frightening. Something that made her feel protected rather than threatened. Like she had felt that night long ago.

"I'd appreciate it if you could call me Cat since we've been neighbors, if not friendly ones, for all our lives. I just wanted to know how your pa is doing."

He looked at her with those steel-blue eyes for a few long heartbeats before his gaze roamed from her face, down her body, and slowly up again. Something sizzled inside of her, as noticeable as water dancing on a hot fry pan. What was it about this man? She wished she knew so she could get rid of it.

"He's hanging in," he said curtly, as if doubting her reasons for asking. "Am I to believe this is a social call?"

His no-nonsense tone made her sit up straight, like a teacher had called on her when she wasn't sure of the answer. "Actually, it's a business call."

His eyes narrowed, and this time she did feel like a target, only she wasn't sure what ammo he was using. Courage, she reminded herself. *You need help, Cat McKenna. He can help you. The least he can do is say no, and then you are no worse off than before.*

"Unless you are planning to give me back the land you stole, I can't think of any business we would have to talk about, Miss...Cat." He pretty much snarled her name. "And if you have any ideas we would be interested in selling our land because of my father's illness, get yourself some new ideas."

Cat took a deep breath. Nothing like being put in her place, but then he'd put her in the wrong place.

"No." She pulled on the reins to raise her horse's head as it tried to go for the sweet grass Cody's horse was docilely chewing. "I came to ask if you'd come work for me as ranch foreman. Oversee the whole operation." She took a deep breath. "I'm not a rancher, and I need a good manager." It was hard for her to admit some things, but not being a good rancher was too obvious to try to hide. No doubt she'd been the talk of many a gathering for being so late to move her herds. She wasn't fooling anyone.

"You're kidding, right?" She caught a smile teasing his lips. He had a very sensual mouth, with a little indent at the center of his upper lip. He hadn't shaved, or maybe it was just a normal shadow, because his jawline was outlined by stubble, creating a bad-boy look. She'd always had a thing for bad boys in high school…and this one in particular.

But her schoolgirl infatuation with Cody had been more like having a crush on the likes of Hugh Jackman or Bradley Cooper. Clearly unattainable, nice to fantasize about, and someone she could imbue with all sorts of romantic characteristics because she really didn't know him and never would.

"I'm as serious as can be. I need help. You're someone who could help me. And I pay well."

He snorted. "I bet you can pay real well. But some people can't be bought. Why in the Lord's name would you think I would consider working for you? A

McKenna? The same McKenna who stole my land and didn't even care to compensate me for the taxes we've been paying on it all these years. Despite the fact you can 'pay well.'" He shook his head in disbelief, and Cat felt her cheeks warm.

It hadn't occurred to her to offer to pay the taxes. She hadn't even thought about it. It would have been a nice gesture. She hardly knew what to say.

"Cat got your tongue, Cat?" His half smile was mocking, and her heart sank at his sneer. "You've already got a good crew of men to help you."

Well, she'd already humiliated herself. Why not go with the truth?

"They need direction. I need someone who knows what to do and who can teach me."

Cody gathered up his reins, and Cat watched as he mounted his horse. Smoothly, in one motion, and yet it looked like he had hardly put his weight on the animal. And what a horse. Shiny paint coat, nicely formed head, large withers, intelligent eyes. And not the least bit agitated. Just beautiful.

"Sorry, Princess. I helped you once and got slammed for it."

So he did remember. And the use of the nickname he'd planted on her back then confirmed it, bringing with it the heat of embarrassment.

"And now I'll ask you again to get off my property." He touched the brim of his hat, this gentlemanly gesture belying the sting in his words.

"Think about it," she managed to get out before she reined the horse around to splash through the shallow part of the creek. Seemed she would need a plan B.

Cody waited for the slow burn of anger as he watched Cat McKenna guide her horse across the creek. It didn't come. Instead he found himself watching her tight little jean-clad backside as she rode away. He couldn't remember seeing her in jeans but once before, and never on a horse. If he didn't know better, he might have thought she actually was a cowgirl instead of a ranch princess.

He reined the horse around and headed back. The more he rode, the crazier the whole idea seemed. What in the hell had the woman been thinking? That he had so little to do on his own spread he might as well run hers? Did she think the Cross T was such a pitiful operation he didn't need to bother himself with it? Or was it charity? Or maybe a way to soften him up in order to wheedle his land out of him—as if he would ever sell to a McKenna.

Where was the naïve girl he'd protected that night? And had gotten a black eye, figuratively and literally, for doing so?

He'd been right from the beginning. She was a princess—used to getting her own way and useless in running a ranch. And yet she'd inherited one of the biggest and wealthiest ranches in Wyoming and didn't have a doggone clue what to do with it.

The anger finally came as the land opened up into prairie, the grasses waving across the horizon as the plains stretched out flat and wide, touching the blue cloudless sky.

He nudged his paint into a gallop and let the wind blast his face.

Fifteen minutes later, his anger still percolating, he drew near the house, reining his horse to a walk.

His dog, Mikey, dashed ahead, barking, and Cody's heart stopped as dread washed through him. There, parked in front of the porch, was an ambulance. Without the lights flashing.

The funeral was five days later. Five long days. His father's lungs had filled with fluid, and he had passed before the paramedics had been able to even reach the ranch. It probably wouldn't have mattered, considering the directives in his father's living will. Zeke Taylor had known his days were short—he just didn't know which day would be the shortest.

The worst was that his mother had been home, had watched as life seeped out of the husband she had loved for thirty-two years, helpless to do anything as she waited for the ambulance. And Cody hadn't been there to spare her.

He'd walked into the house amid the chaos of death, past people he didn't know, and back to the room where his father's body lay on the bed, covered by a thin white sheet. Sadie sat next to him, standing guard.

Cody had been unable to move past the doorway, unable to process the scene, wanting to deny it as his mother wept over the body of her husband, her thin frame visibly shaking from the force of the sobs. The tubes had been removed and dangled off the side of the bed. Jace was there, tears falling as he tugged at his mother, trying to pull her off so the paramedics could take his father away. Not to the hospital but to the coroner.

The pressure on Cody's chest had forced him to gulp for air. There before him was the ashen, lifeless face of the man he'd loved, the man who had taught him how to ride, how to rope, how to train a horse, lasso a steer, how to vaccinate, castrate, breed, and nurture a herd. The man who had taught him to ride, fish, catch a ball, swing a bat, throw a football. All the things a father taught a son, his father had taught him. But most of all, he'd taught him how to be a man. Responsible, tough, decisive, persistent, determined, a risk taker even if the risks didn't always end well. As if his father knew he wouldn't be around for the long haul.

He understood why his mother didn't want to let go. He didn't either. To do so was to admit the hopelessness, the defeat, the failure—and the loss.

The two male paramedics had stared at him, their eyes holding a silent plea. They'd seen this too many times before, no doubt. And they were looking for someone to take charge.

Despite the force holding down Cody's chest and squeezing his lungs, he'd walked in, gathered his mother into his arms, where she sank against him like dead weight as he held her. After giving the command for Sadie to stand down, he nodded to the paramedics, who commenced moving his father's body onto the stretcher.

At the funeral home, before they closed the casket for burial, he'd stood while his mother pressed her lips to cold flesh, watched as his brother touched his father's hand, and waited for them to leave the room before he too bent over the casket and looked for the last time at the man who had always been his rock, had always been there for him, and now wouldn't be.

He too had touched the cool, blue-tinted flesh, just to remind himself that all this was real. His father had gone to his reward. Only the empty shell remained. But as he had stood there, staring at his father's lifeless body, it felt as if someone had punched him in the midsection, pushing all the air out of his lungs.

Now, back at the house, things seemed surreal, like he was watching himself go through the motions. His mother's sister, Lucille, fluttered around him and his brother, and her husband, Tom, patted Cody and Jace on the back and said he'd be there for them. But as much as Cody appreciated the offer, he knew there wasn't much help the man could give. Uncle Tom was an oil-field worker and didn't know much about ranching, and Cody knew extra cash was at a premium for everyone in the family, not that Cody would have asked for a handout anyway.

Lucille and Tom had three children, two boys and a girl, and they had all taken off from work to be in attendance. Cody was grateful for their presence, knowing that his cousin Quentin had to fly in from Texas, where he'd recently bought into a business, and Michael, the youngest, had to pull strings to get off, since he had just been promoted to detective in Laramie. Cody's cousin Emily, the oldest, was married, with a baby.

He was grateful to see them all, but not under circumstances like this.

His aunt Lucille, however, did offer something helpful—to take his mother to stay with her in Laramie for a few weeks.

As people floated into the house, surrounding his mother with heartfelt condolences, Cody watched from the distance of the corrals. Mikey sat by his side, while

Sadie stretched out on the ground at his feet, as if all the energy had been drained out of her. His father had bought Sadie home as a pup, had carried her on the horse out to the north pastures each morning until she was old enough and strong enough to make the trip herself, had praised and cajoled her into being the best herder they'd ever had. When she had her litter of pups, his father's rancher friends had taken one in hopes they, too, would get a Sadie. Zeke had picked Mikey to remain, saying he had the most intelligent eyes. Mikey had proven his father had good instincts.

Cody reached down to pat Mikey's head and wished the feeling of dread that had been his constant companion since he'd learned about his father's illness had abated with his death. It had only gotten worse. What the hell was he going to do now?

He and Jace had inherited the ranch, with the proviso his mother be allowed to live in the house. And with the ranch came a mountain of debt that couldn't be cleared by selling the herd or the horses. Unfortunately, when they had made the decision to go to grass-fed, it necessitated a change to a later calving and selling season. Grass-fed was an effort to gain more profit per head by selling directly to high-end restaurants and natural-food stores through a co-op arrangement. They'd planned to sell the calves born this July the following year instead of this fall, as they would have done if the calves had been born in March and April. Now, in retrospect, they couldn't have done more to bury themselves even further in debt. That meant one thing. The ranch would have to go.

The absence of any clause putting restrictions on a sale meant his father died knowing that.

And that hurt most of all.

Over a century and a half, Taylors had ranched their land in the shadow of the richer, more successful, and seemingly entitled McKennas. And not a one of his ancestors had succumbed to the easy way out—selling. Despite rustlers, droughts, blizzards, recessions, and depressions, his forefathers had held on to the land and turned it over to the next generation of Taylors. And now Cody Taylor would have to betray them all, most of all his father.

He had to find a way out of the mess.

"Can't we get a loan?" Jace asked, coming beside Cody as if he had read Cody's thoughts. His brother leaned on the wooden fence rail, a plastic plate full of Aunt Lucy's chicken and dumplings in his hands. The meaty aroma made Cody's stomach grumble, though his insides were too scrambled to eat.

Jace still had a boyish look despite his twenty-two years. Cody figured it was the round face he got from their mother's side. Or maybe the fact that, as the younger brother, he hadn't had the weight of the family's fortunes, or lack thereof, on his shoulders for as long as Cody. Not that Jace didn't do his part. But his brother's heart wasn't in ranching. He had other dreams, rodeo dreams. He'd probably be happy to sell.

"Who's going to loan us money when we don't have enough collateral to pay them back? This place is already mortgaged to the max. We might as well sell everything ourselves and save the sheriff the trouble." And his mother the humiliation.

I need help. Cat McKenna's words bounced around his head but failed to land. Cody needed help too. Too bad she was a McKenna. He might swallow

44

his pride if it was for anyone but a McKenna. Anyone but her.

He looked over at the two-and-half-year-old colt that he'd hoped was the future of the Cross T—horses requiring less grazing acreage than cattle and therefore better suited to a modest ranch like the Cross T. Smoking Gun was to be the seed money that would have allowed him to add more brood mares and pay the stud fees for top-notch stallions. The horse was the symbol of his dreams, the antidote to the high cost of raising a modest herd of cattle on limited acreage.

Selling Smoking Gun before he reached his third year, before he could be trained and shown at one of the futurity events, meant significantly less money and giving the glory to someone else. But what else could he do? How could he sustain the ranch with no money to buy feed, pay vet bills, or the two mortgages? And that wasn't counting the medical bills that lay strewn across his father's bureau. The sad fact was even selling Smoking Gun wouldn't be enough.

"Maybe it's for the best. This ranch feels like an anchor around our feet." Jace looked out over the pastures, as if he was taking a last look at the place they'd always called home. "I could rodeo. You could train horses for someone. We'd get by."

"And what about Mom?" Cody reminded, not yet ready to concede defeat despite the odds.

Mamie Taylor was a good mother. A good rancher's wife. She'd help with the herding when needed. She canned from the garden she tended. She believed in a bit of fun after a hard day, playing hide and seek with her sons when they were small, assuming the catcher position during a softball game with their dad when they were older. She baked, cooked good comfort food, and rarely complained. She loved her husband and her sons fiercely. But it was no secret she drew her strength from the man she had married. The younger daughter of a divorced mother of two, Mamie had left a difficult life in Laramie for life with Zeke Taylor. Zeke had been a fighter, a protector, with a tender heart and a bucketful of spirit—enough for the two of them. And though Cody could understand why his mother might reach for the bottle given all that had happened, he saw it for what it was—a weakness.

I pay well.

"How bad is it?" Jace asked.

Jace had a right to know, though Cody hated to burden him. He named the figure that Melissa, who had probated the will, had given him.

Jace's low whistle was lost on a gust of wind that snatched the empty plate right out of his brother's hand and sent it flying through the corral. "Will selling everything even pay all of that?"

Cody wished he could have spared Jace. But he wouldn't treat him any less than an equal partner in all this. Besides, how could Jace understand the right decision if he didn't know the facts?

"Expect we'll find out, but I doubt it."

"Can't we declare bankruptcy or something?"

Public failure. A humiliating end to the Taylor legacy.

"Let's think first about the 'or something.'"

"I think I'll go get me a beer. Actually, I could use something stronger. You want anything?" Jace asked.

Cody shook his head. He doubted he could keep

anything but water down, the way his stomach was churning.

Jace gave Cody a bleak nod and then shuffled away like a man with a lot on his mind.

* * *

"I rodeo. You find a horse trainer spot. Mom lives with Aunt Lucille. And we sell the ranch." Jace was tucking into the leftover chicken as they sat at the kitchen table, the evening sunlight streaming in the dirt-dusted window as they discussed, again, their situation. They'd spent a hard day working with the herd and training the colt. Sadie laid her body against the screen door as if she knew no one else would be entering. Mikey sat at Cody's feet, hoping, no doubt, for a bite of food to make it to the floor. His father had a strict rule about feeding the dogs from the table, and for the right reasons. But Cody wasn't above letting a piece of chicken free from his fingers, as he did now. Mikey gobbled it up. Sadie barely noticed.

The day after the funeral, the house was surreally quiet. His mother had gone willingly to Laramie with her sister after the rest of the relatives had cleaned up, packaging up the leftover food and putting it in either the fridge or freezer.

"Aunt Lucille's isn't a permanent solution. And I checked with Melissa, who called a real estate agent. We would have to declare bankruptcy to clear the debt. And we'd have nothing left for any of us."

And not owning up to their obligations was not the Taylor way. He didn't want to be the one who changed that.

"Let me go on the rodeo circuit then. If I'm good enough, I can clear a hundred thousand, enough to pay off the medical bills at least."

There was his brother, dreaming again.

"Only fifteen guys out of, what, hundreds, get a chance at that kind of money, and they have to rodeo all year just to make it into the finals. They work years to be good enough to get there."

Discouragement wrapped around his brother's young face like a bandage. "Then I've got nothing."

I pay well. Cody had been thinking about Cat McKenna's offer half the night. If it wasn't a McKenna doing the asking, if it wasn't Cat, he'd have already swallowed his pride and said yes. Should he let a McKenna defeat him or use them to save the place? It would certainly be an ironic twist.

One his father would have said no to. And his mother too. That was how much they both begrudged the McKennas. It was from years of McKennas draining off more than their share of water and no way to stop them, years of standing in the shadows of McKenna success and being seen as less by comparison.

"If I had a way of making some money, enough to pay those bills and hire someone to take my place, could you run the operation? I'd still be around to advise, but I wouldn't be doing the work, because I'd be working for someone else."

Jace frowned as if Cody had just asked a dumb question. Maybe it was a dumb question. Maybe it was a dumb idea, but looking at the numbers, Cody was plum out of options.

"You know I'm just as good a rancher as you are."

He wasn't, not yet, but Cody wouldn't argue.

"But who would you work for around here that would pay you that kind of money? You plan on striking oil or something?"

"Or something. Cat McKenna asked me to work for her."

Jace sat back in his seat and pushed his dark hair from his brow, revealing a look of pure, wide-eyed shock. "You're shitting me."

"I'm dead serious."

A low whistle passed Jace's lips. "Dad would be pissed as hell."

"Maybe, but I think he'd take it a whole lot worse if we had to sell to pay the bills."

"Why would she want to pay you to work for her?"

Cody hadn't been sure of her motive, but he understood her need. "You remember her from high school?"

Jace's smile wasn't exactly angelic. "Yeah. Who could forget her in high heels and short skirts? She looked like something out of a New York magazine right here in little old Wyoming." Cody didn't like Jace smacking his lips. But he ignored it. Cat was two years older than Jace and out of his league.

"Exactly. The woman has no sense when it comes to running a ranch. She hasn't moved her herd since birthing, and from what I hear, scours is decimating her calves." Cody raised his eyebrows.

"And she doesn't get the connection?" Jace asked in pure cowboy wonderment.

"Exactly. Thing is, she at least realizes she doesn't know shit. And her being a ranch princess, she isn't likely to solve that problem herself."

Jace snorted as he leaned back on his chair and balanced on its back legs. "Probably doesn't even know how to ride."

An image of Cat's jean-clad backside hugging her saddle flashed through his mind. She certainly had the assets of a cowgirl, if not the expertise. "She was riding a pretty bay down by the creek the day Dad died. That's when she saw me and rode over to ask. But she's also not one to get her hands dirty. It would ruin her manicure, I expect."

Jace chuckled as he came down on all four chair legs. "Still, she must be pretty desperate, and arrogant, to ask you after what she did."

That was what Cody was still trying to figure out. Why him? It wasn't like they were on good terms before the court proceeding. And certainly not after. "I imagine it took some courage."

"Or maybe she's trying to make amends."

He was not interested in scraps from the McKennas' table. "Hell of a way to do it."

"But she'd pay you that much?"

"Only one way to find out."

Chapter 4

Cat stepped out of the barn and into the bright sunshine. It always amazed her how things could look so normal despite the troubles someone was going through. Another calf with scours. Birthing season had been marred by a number of still births, some cows that wouldn't let their calves feed, a few calves that wouldn't nurse, and now scours. The list kept growing, reminding her of when she'd been young and one of the barn cats had kittens, and each day another kitten would die until there was only the grieving mama cat. She never did figure out what caused their deaths, whether man made or genetic, but she had tried so hard to save them, sleeping overnight in the barn, feeding them milk by hand, and all to no avail. Was that how it was going to be with the ranch? A slow, one-by-one death until there were no cattle left and no clue why?

She heard the growl of an engine a few heartbeats before she spied a beat-up old pickup bumping along the road leading up to the ranch. Probably someone looking for work. She'd put an ad in the local paper just yesterday for a range manager, but no one had called yet. Seemed this ranch hand was a little casual about the application process. But she'd hold her judgment until she met the man. Maybe he was just the eager type.

Curiosity turned to surprise when the black pickup stopped a few feet away and the tall, handsome cowboy driving the rig stepped out. The morning sun sparkled above Cody Taylor, casting his lean body in bright rays and his face in gray shadows, but she recognized that build, those wide shoulders, that narrow waist, those long, jean-clad legs. Despite his good looks, you'd never see him on the slick pages of a magazine advertising something. He was too rugged. Too masculine. Too…male.

She took a deep breath to tamp down the sudden uptick of her pulse. He was just a man, a man she was barely on speaking terms with—his choice.

And a man who had lost his father only a week or so ago.

The McKennas hadn't gone to the funeral despite being neighbors for more than a century. They would not have been welcomed. Out of respect, her mother had sent a flower arrangement, taking care it was not too big or showy. As Cat recalled, the Taylors hadn't sent anything when her father had passed, but then the McKennas could afford to be gracious.

"Cody, I am surprised to see you here." Her voice took a little upturn at the last word. Somehow, seeing the man had sent her heart racing to catch up with her pulse. Like she was excited or something, but what had she to be excited about where Cody Taylor was concerned? That he'd come to work for her? Unlikely. That he wanted to sell his land? Only meant more for her to worry about. "It at least gives me a chance to say how sorry I am for you and your family's loss. Your father was a respected rancher in this county." Too formal, maybe, but how did you pay your respects to a man who thought of you as the enemy?

He kept his gaze on her as he swaggered forward, his long legs closing the gap in no time, until she was staring into a pair of eyes the deep-blue color of a summer's day after a storm had cleared.

He didn't answer at first, just perused her from top to bottom. She knew she must look a sight in soiled jeans, a dirt-stained blouse, and strands of hair escaping from her ponytail and straggling around her face, thanks to the spring wind that had whipped up off the mountains. Not to mention no makeup. She'd been up since early morning cleaning barns and nursing calves, and she was plum wiped out. She futilely smoothed back a wayward lock of hair and stared straight into his eyes for confirmation of her state of disrepair. His expression revealed nothing.

"Thanks. But this isn't a social call."

Gruff, to the point. And no mention of the flowers they'd sent, of course.

She glanced past his perfect lips, down his thick, tanned neck, to the hollow of his throat where his shirt was unbuttoned and a wisp of hair peeked out, before scanning the rest of him.

Cody looked like he had been equally hard at work before venturing into enemy territory. His boots and the bottom of his jeans were dirt spattered, and his plaid shirt, neatly tucked into his jeans, was faded, but on him it looked authentic. And attractive. And like a man who worked hard with his hands. Very hard.

"Business?" she asked, returning her gaze to his.

Would he actually sell the ranch? Did she want to buy it? She hadn't discussed the possibility with Kyle, since the lawyer had been so sure there wasn't a chance of it happening. "Care to step into the house, then?"

He looked so somber, so stoic. Selling would be hard for him. It would be yet another kind of death he'd have to deal with. The death of dreams, of the future as well as the past.

She knew about giving up on dreams. She'd done so when she'd had Jake, though he'd inspired a new kind of dream. She'd done so again when she'd taken over the ranch instead of pursuing her own passion for opening up a preschool for children. That was all she'd ever wanted to do, work with children. Not cows. Not horses. Kids.

She started toward the house and listened to his boots scuff across the stones in an ambling gait. As they crossed over the threshold and the thud of his steps echoed on the plank floors, she wondered when, if ever, a Taylor had entered a McKenna household in the history of Carbon County. It was a notable event witnessed by no one but Cody Taylor and Cat McKenna in the twenty-first century.

"Mommy." Jake scooted out of the kitchen doorway and rushed down the hallway headlong into her knees, grabbing her around the legs and holding on tight. He lifted his jelly-smeared face up to hers.

She had to laugh.

"You look like you've been having some toast and jam for breakfast."

He nodded, his little-boy smile wide and bright.

She scooped him up, enjoying the weight of him

in her arms. "Let's say we both go into the kitchen and wash up." She turned back to Cody.

He'd removed his hat and held it in his hands as a strand of his brown hair, cut short on the sides, left longer on the top, fell casually across his brow. An uncharacteristic smile was on his face as he looked at Jake. Something pinched in the vicinity of her heart.

"Jake, this man is Cody Taylor. He's a neighbor of ours." It was the easiest way of introducing him. Likely her son would never set eyes on another Taylor if the family was really selling.

"Howdy, partner." Cody's tone had lightened considerably, and those blue eyes sparkled with amusement.

"Howdy!" Jake shouted back with childlike enthusiasm and waved his jelly-streaked hand in a friendly gesture.

In a heartbeat, her mother appeared in the kitchen doorway, wiping her hands on an apron that covered her cotton print dress.

"Did I hear right?" Her mother was frowning, though clearly curious as to what brought a Taylor to this historic moment. "Cody Taylor. I haven't laid eyes on you since you were in high school with Cat. Two years older, right?"

"Yes, ma'am." Cody's fingers, holding the brim of his hat, moved the Stetson in a clockwise direction.

"I was sorry to hear of your loss. Zeke was…a good man." Her mother's smile was friendly, if tentative. "How is your mother doing?"

"She's doing all right. Thank you for the flowers. And I'm sorry for your loss too, Mrs. McKenna." The Stetson stopped moving.

Her mother nodded. "It's the passing of one generation and the start of a new generation taking over. Maybe some good can come out of it."

She reached out for Jake, but Cat shook her head. "I'll clean him up. Cody, the study is here," she said, nodding her head toward the doorway on the left. "I'll be back in a minute. Just make yourself comfortable."

Jake in her arms, she followed her mother back into the kitchen. Cat couldn't wait to find out the reason a Taylor had come calling on a McKenna, leastwise without a gun in his hand.

"He's come to offer his land?" her mother asked as soon as they cleared the kitchen doorway.

Cat headed for the kitchen sink. Grabbing a paper towel, she wet it at the faucet.

"I don't know. Could be. Hold still, Jake. Let Mommy wash your face."

Like most little boys, Jake was determined not to let that happen. But she managed a few good swipes with the wet paper towel before she set her wiggling son down. "You'll need to use the potty before we head for school."

"I'll take him to school. Looks like you've been up for a while. Besides, you'll have to see what that man wants. Your father would have loved to be here when a Taylor walked into the house to give up his ranch."

"I'll stand right outside the bathroom door, Jake." Cat took up her post against the wall of the bathroom that was right off the kitchen and waited as her son performed his personal chores, ready to step in if need be. "We don't know why he's here."

"Why else?"

Cat hadn't told her mother about her impetuous offer of employment. "I said something to him the other day."

"What?" Lydia's frown deepened.

Cat knew her mother didn't hold a grudge against the Taylors like her father did, but that didn't mean Lydia trusted them any more than Joe. "I asked him if he'd be interested in working for me." Realizing her son was finished, she reminded him to wash his hands.

Her mother's silence was more censure than any words.

"I need help. He can help me. You said to find someone I had faith in."

Her mother brushed her palm against the side of her throat to hold the back of her neck. "I can't believe this, Cat. What would your father say?"

"You said I had to stop thinking about what Daddy would say. First and foremost, Daddy would want me to save the ranch. I'll wager he, as well as our ancestors, made many a bargain with the devil to do just that." As evidenced by the abandoned oil wells in the northern pastures.

"If you'd asked him, I think he would have preferred the devil to a Taylor."

That was probably true.

"Look, Mom. I've signed up for almost fifteen years of ranching or more before my son will be able to take over. And I haven't a clue what the questions are, much less the answers. Cody is knowledgeable, and he might just need the job."

"I'm hoping he's smart and wants to sell. You try to convince him to take that path, Cat. For your father's sake and my peace of mind. How do you know he doesn't hate us, just like your father hated them? We just won that case against him. I can't even fathom why he would want to help us out." Her hand moved to the front of her mouth as if the possibilities were too horrible to voice.

"I trust his knowledge, but I'm not stupid enough to turn my back to him. I know exactly what I'm getting, and I won't be tempted to let my guard down for any reason. And of course, I will pay him what it's worth to me, so he should have no cause to ruin things for either of us."

"He's here to sell the land. I know it. I can't imagine anything else. A Taylor isn't going to be a McKenna's savior, and it was reckless of you to even mention such a thing. Sometimes, Cat, your judgment…"

She didn't have to finish. Cat saw it in her mother's eyes, heard it in her voice. The rebuke that was always just under the surface. A rebuke for not being good enough, strong enough, moral enough, or wise enough not to have been taken in by a charmer.

She'd never change her parents' opinion of her. She'd given up trying.

"Well, I did. And I'll stand by my offer if he's fool enough, or desperate enough, to take it. It's the least we can do, and I mean the very least, given all we've taken from them."

Cat entered the bathroom as her son exited, in order to wash her hands and tidy up at least a bit. She stared at her reflection in the mirror. Her skin had a sheen of perspiration, her hair was coming loose, and her eyes had dark circles under them. Not a pretty picture. The days of getting her nails done, styling her hair, and wearing pretty clothes were behind her.

"If you mean the land…." Her mother continued, coming to stand in the bathroom doorway.

Cat held up her hand. "I know. It's the law. But it's not right. You know it and I know it."

Cody looked around the well-appointed oak-paneled room Cat had called a study. It reeked of money, from the soft leather chairs, to the Native American rug, to the large oak desk that squatted almost dead center in the room, to the bookcases holding Native pottery and assorted books with titles related to the history of the West. He pulled out one on gunslingers and began to thumb through it, scanning familiar names like Tom Horn, Bat Masterson, and Ben Thompson.

Yup, the McKennas had done well for themselves, slaking their thirst and the thirst of their cattle with Taylor water. The thought dredged up anger he'd been trying to keep in check, knowing he would meet with Cat today, knowing he'd be entering enemy territory, knowing he'd be offering to help the one family he'd sworn he'd never lift a finger to aid.

Since reality had hit, he'd realized he'd do anything to keep his own ranch, and this time that meant helping a McKenna.

He'd been shocked to catch her working and not playing the princess. She'd been turned out in a soiled top and jeans, fatigue clear on her face. And even though her dirt-speckled jeans had been studded and her dusty boots better suited to dancing than barn work, she looked damn attractive. There was something about a hard-working woman he found sexy.

He shook his head, trying to clear it. He needed to get laid. He'd been too consumed by the ranch and his father's illness to give a thought to his own needs. But now all he wanted was to feel the curves of a female body under his, to bury himself inside a wet and willing woman, and feel alive again.

Putting the book back on the shelf, he looked toward the doorway and listened for the sound of footsteps. Closing his eyes, he reminded himself that he still had time to change his mind. Time to walk right out the front door and never look back.

In the second it took to open his eyes, Cat was in the doorway, holding a tray of coffee cups and fixings. She'd taken time to clean up. Her long, thick hair swung loose across her shoulders and disappeared down her back. It looked like she'd brightened her cheeks and lips some. Those brown eyes of hers looked darker. And she'd changed her shirt to a clingy turtleneck that outlined her well-developed curves. She'd put on a clean pair of jeans that looked more designer than western, emphasizing those long legs, and she'd even changed her fancy boots for an equally fancy clean pair. And his only thought was that they'd likely fit well together.

Yup, he needed to get laid.

"Let me help you with that," he said, remembering his manners. He reached for the tray. His fingers brushed hers, and a little jolt shot through him. She glanced up at him, and he was captured by a pair of warm brown eyes that shimmered for a split second like heat on pavement before evaporating like the mirage it probably was.

He had to stay calm and cool so he could

negotiate this just right and get what he needed. That meant no thinking of Cat McKenna as a woman.

"On the desk okay?" he asked. She wasn't his type. Mainly because she was a McKenna, but also because she was too...high maintenance. Too frilly. He liked his women hard on the outside and soft on the inside. He liked knowing a woman could take care of herself, but wanted him. He was here precisely because Cat McKenna didn't know the first thing about ranching even though she'd been raised on a ranch. And that said it all about the kind of woman Cat McKenna was...and that kind of woman was certainly not for him. Not to mention that getting involved with any woman beyond a one-night stand was out of the question.

She nodded, and he set the tray down on the highly polished wood surface.

She stood just off from the desk, looking at him like he was something she'd never seen before. Well, likely a Taylor in a McKenna's house was something she never expected to see. Neither had he.

"You want to fix your coffee, and then we'll sit and you can tell me to what I owe this honor?"

He caught the hint of sarcasm.

God, this took a heap of pride swallowing. But he wasn't begging. She'd asked him, not the other way around.

"Just being neighborly. Figured you came on my land—I'd come and pay you a visit."

They sat in the leather chairs that flanked the desk, each holding their respective cups of coffee. He took a sip. The hot brew was strong and aromatic, just the way he liked it.

He watched as her lips drew in the warm liquid, lips that grew shiny from the moisture. Soft-looking lips, pliable, kissable. He forced himself to look somewhere else. She was off limits for so many reasons, they didn't bear listing.

Time to get it over with. He set down the cup on the wooden side table, leaned forward, and placed his elbows on his denim-clad knees so he could look right into those magnetic brown eyes of hers, eyes filled with questions. He'd definitely caught her off balance. Maybe that would give him an advantage.

"Last time we met, you asked me to work for you. That offer still stand?"

Her eyes widened like a camera aperture expanding to catch more light. "You're interested?"

"Maybe. Depends upon the particulars. First off, what exactly do you want me to do, and how much authority will I have to do it?"

She leaned back in the chair and stared. Maybe she hadn't been serious about hiring him. Probably was a spur-of-the-moment request. He should have realized that. She'd likely been relieved when he'd turned her down. He was making a fool of himself.

"I want you to do two things. Manage the ranch profitably—make sure we do the right things to bring a good price for our beef without hurting our future. Our herds have been diminished some with that September drought last year, and birthing season has had a few casualties already. I need someone to tell me if I'm going in the right direction and then help me get there. And that sort of gets to the second thing."

She bit her lower lip as if hesitating. Leaving it reddened. God, she had a kissable mouth.

"Which is?"

"I need someone to teach me the ranching business. Not how to brand a steer or castrate bulls. I've got ranch hands to do that, gratefully. But when to do it, how to supervise it. What to feed my cattle so the calves don't get so big we can't birth them. What's the cost-slash-benefit of maybe going grass-fed? What are the things I need to be thinking about? I need to understand the business end of things."

He leaned back. He hadn't expected she'd even have that much of a grasp on things. She must have been studying up.

"Those are some good questions. Why do you think I'm the one with the answers?" Given they were sinking under a mountain of debt and hadn't yet completed the process of transitioning to grass-fed didn't exactly spell recommendation. But what he could do with a spread like Pleasant Valley's, with the land they had. He'd always dreamed of running a big operation. But in his dreams, the Taylors had bought out the McKennas and the ranch was owned by him, lock, stock, and barrel.

"My daddy always said you were a good rancher."

Now that was something he never expected to hear. Especially after that night. He settled farther back in his seat. He wished he knew if that was just some bull she was throwing, or a real compliment.

"I appreciate that. But you do remember what my last name is, don't you?"

"Not likely to ever forget." Slowly a smile spread across her face, and her eyes twinkled. She was even prettier when she smiled. It dimpled her left cheek and brightened her face. She should do it more often.

"What I do know is that I need a good ranch manager to teach me, and so far none of the foremen have given me the confidence they are the one."

"But I have?"

She sighed even as her lips, moist from the coffee and looking way too enticing, held that smile, a really beautiful, light-up-the-sky-on-a-spring-day smile.

She'd always been a looker in high school. But she was a Barbie doll kind of girl, and he was no Ken.

"You're blunt, to the point, forthright. I don't think you'll ever make the mistake of thinking I know more than I do." She stared at him from under her thin, perfectly curved brows, looking for confirmation or denial, he wasn't sure.

"And that's a good thing, is it?" Maybe she was tougher than she looked.

"Yes. I need someone who will tell it to me straight. But I also need someone who will take the time to teach me."

He admired her frankness. He liked people who didn't sit on ego. After today, no one could accuse him of that.

"How long would you need me?"

She waited a heartbeat, and he could almost see the wheels turning in her head.

"How long could I have you?"

"Till the end of the year. If the money's right. That would be after the October sale and your herd was moved back to the winter pasture. Should give you enough time to look for someone longer term. That's about all I could spare from my own spread."

She took another sip of coffee. He watched, fascinated, as her tongue swiped the corner of her mouth, as if to get the last drop. He could give her tongue. So deep she'd choke on it.

"And that's another reason I think you're a good choice. You won't be afraid that by teaching me you'll be out of a job. You want to go back to your ranch. Still, I'm surprised you're willing to chance this, Cody."

"Money is a powerful motivator, Princess." No use standing on useless pride. The whole county likely knew the Taylors were close to bankrupt.

"You must want to keep your ranch as much as I want to keep mine for either of us to consider getting in bed with the other." A pretty pink blush rose from the top of her turtleneck and suffused up her slender throat to her softly sculpted cheeks. "I was speaking metaphorically, of course."

He couldn't help the smile that claimed his mouth or the pure zing of lust at the notion. She. Was. Not. His. Type.

"Maybe. Maybe not. You've heard of a Freudian slip, I'm sure."

His gaze fell on her chest, where two nipples poked the fabric of her top. Was she cold? Or turned on? He forced himself to raise his gaze to her rosy cheeks, matching the shade of her lips, and making her look as inviting as a sparkling creek on a hot summer's day.

Too bad the water had been poisoned.

Cat rose. She'd seemed to have lost control of their conversation. One thing she could not let Cody Taylor believe was that she was in any way attracted to him. She wasn't. Not beyond the superficial tug of a handsome face and a hard body. That was all there was to it, she assured herself. Really. Nothing more.

"Definitely not the case here. This is strictly business. Nothing, and I mean nothing, more."

"No need to sound so defensive. I believe you."

But those teasing eyes of his said otherwise.

Likely because he was used to women falling at his feet. He still thought he was the stud he'd been in high school. And likely with good reason. But she'd learned a hard lesson where "studs" were concerned. And she needed to remember it. Every time she looked at him. Every time she was near him. Every time she started to imagine him naked…

"What would you need to do this?" she said, channeling her best school-teacher tone.

Cody named a price. It was high, though not higher than she'd been prepared to pay. But that was the dollars-and-cents price. What other price would she pay for having a man like Cody Taylor around every day? A man who still thought he was God's gift to women…and actually might be. *If you like that sort of man…*

"And I want you to loan me a ranch hand of my choosing to work on *my* ranch as a replacement but still paid for on your books. Plus the authority to hire and fire the crew."

She folded her arms. The hired hand was an unexpected demand, but at least it had snapped her out of her carnal thoughts. It also proved he needed her help as much as she needed his. But considering she'd be taking him from his own work, it wasn't an unreasonable request. Actually, it was a pretty creative solution. She'd been wondering how he could afford to leave his own spread. And she'd been thinking about what would make it worth his while so this could work for both of them.

"Oh, and our calving season is coming up later this month, so I may need a few hours here or there to help Jace out."

"I thought cows calved in late winter and early spring." One of the few things she thought she knew.

He crossed his leg over the other knee, stretching the denim fabric across his well-formed thigh, and placed his arm along the back of the chair, revealing a silver-toned watch at the edge of his shirt cuff. His boots, though scuffed and worn, were a rich black-cherry leather and a high-end brand Cat recognized, having gone on enough shopping trips with her best friend, Mandy, who was obsessed with boots. Apparently Cody didn't skimp on quality.

"Not if you go grass-fed. Birthing follows the natural order of things. You breed them to calf when the grass is high and plenty. That's more like late May or early June than March."

"Sounds better than the wicked cold and wet during our season." The idea appealed, given the heartbreaking loss of more than a few calves this year. By the end of this March, she'd almost made up her mind to sell. Almost.

"And my other requirements?" His gaze seemed to drill into her as if he was searching inside her mind for the answer, cracking the air with intensity…and something else. Something akin to electricity.

She swallowed over the huge rock that seemed to be blocking her breathing. This was a negotiation, and she had to keep on topic despite the male filling the room.

"As for hiring and firing, my three current foremen—Will Springer, who is range foreman; Charlie Oakley, who takes care of the remuda of horses, such as it is; and Jim Smith, who handles the breeding program—will take orders from you, but you can't fire them without my approval. Everyone else is fair game—both for firing and working on your land. Any major changes, you need to consult with me before implementation so I can understand the reasons."

"Deal." He thrust out his hand for a shake.

Before when his fingers had brushed hers as he took the tray, something close to lust had sparked inside of her. No telling what a full-on handshake would ignite. Still, she needed to prove to herself that she wasn't affected by him, never would be.

He was, after all, a Taylor. And the kind of guy who flitted from woman to woman. So far he'd eluded settling down, no doubt by choice, since she knew plenty of women who would be more than happy to share Cody Taylor's burdens. She'd already been burned by that type of man. No need to add to the carnage.

She slid her small, slender hand in his larger, firmer one and stared directly into his eyes, daring herself to feel anything.

He held her hand tight as heat suffused through her body. Her belly tingled. Her heart raced. She pulled back her hand.

So much for that experiment.

He put his hat on his head, ready to take his leave, and she hoped he hadn't noticed her body's response. But when he hesitated, she felt her cheeks flush in anticipation.

"Just so you know, Princess," he said, coming close enough to whisper the words in her ear. She hated that he called her *princess*. She knew it wasn't a compliment. "Work boots will serve you better than those fancy dance boots, and your designer jeans are going to end up in the rag pile, so I suggest you try some western jeans made for work."

With that he breezed past her, and before she could follow, she heard the door slam shut.

What had she gotten herself into?

Chapter 5

Cody made sure he was at the ranch by 6:30 a.m. the next day, just in case Cat McKenna woke up thinking she could change her mind and renege on their bargain.

He'd spent an unsettled night trying to understand what the hell had happened to him in that study. One minute he'd been asking for a job, the next he'd been thinking about jumping her bones. And that would never do. Besides not being his type, she was two things that should keep his pants zipped—a McKenna and his boss.

Nonetheless, he'd lain in bed half the night thinking about only one thing, Cat McKenna—her carnal curves, her silky hair, those rose-colored lips, and the golden-brown eyes that missed nothing and showed everything. Including that she was attracted to him.

Could he be attracted to her? Was that what that zing of lust, like electricity dancing on a wire, had been all about?

He'd known plenty of good-looking women—and in the biblical sense. But they were always women who knew how to handle themselves. They enjoyed the things he did, like camping, hiking, riding, and rodeo. Most had grown up around cattle or horses or both. All had been used to hard work and taking care of themselves. None would have needed him to tell them when to move herds or brand cattle.

He parked his pickup next to two other rigs, no doubt belonging to the ranch hands who lived off the place. He hadn't even bothered to ask how many men he'd be overseeing. That in itself would be different, and a reason he might not have been the best pick for the job. On his spread it had always been Jace, him, and his father, and maybe a local high school kid during the summer months. And it hadn't been until this past year, when his father had landed in bed, that Cody had the full responsibility of running things.

His father. Cody felt the hitch in his heart, not only from the loss of the father he loved and respected, but from knowing his father would have seen this as a betrayal.

I'm just trying to keep the land.

Jace had understood that, even if he'd been shocked. They'd both agreed not to burden their mother, who was safely ensconced at Aunt Lucille's for a few weeks, with the news, and hoped to hell Laramie was too big to catch gossip from the outskirts, because people in their little town would surely be talking about this now and for years to come.

This was right up there with the discovery a few years ago that the elderly Pinchot sisters had been making ends meet by providing phone sex via a 900 pay-to-call number when a neighbor, a senior citizen himself, had realized the dog barking in the background on his phone call was the same one barking at his fence. Or when the US Marshals had led the local preacher's wife away in handcuffs for running some sort of Internet scam. Or when Cat McKenna had returned home an unwed mother and hadn't been thrown out by her daddy.

He found himself smiling at the thought of little Jake. He was a cute, rambunctious tyke who looked nothing like his grandfather and not much like his mother, for that matter. The boy must have taken after the father, and that had Cody more than a little intrigued. Like what kind of man had gotten Cat McKenna into bed and then left her and a son any man would be proud to call his own? A jackass, no doubt. One of those amoral city types. Rumors had it the guy had been her professor. Others said he'd been a minister. Still others that he'd been some wealthy married man. Whatever the case, he'd walked away from the very things Cody Taylor wanted in life—a good woman, a family, and yes, money. If that last one made him shallow, sue him.

He put the truck in park, retrieved the insulated lunch bag he'd packed with some leftovers from the funeral gathering, and exited into the dawning light of a new morning. And a new beginning, he hoped.

Cat walked out of the barn, looking at the dusty ground as she processed the reaction of her foremen to the announcement of the new ranch manager. A cool morning breeze sent a chill through her. She'd had second thoughts as soon as she'd shaken Cody's hand, and her foremen's reaction had her praying Cody wouldn't show up that morning, that he'd reconsider and relieve her of having to tell him she'd changed her mind.

A barn cat scooted across her path, causing her to halt midstride. She looked up and caught sight of a broad, hard chest matched to a pair of intense blue eyes that sent her startled heart racing.

Mere inches from her, the sun's dewy rays spotlighted his very fine body clad in a lightweight ranch jacket that was blowing open to show a workingman's shirt stretched across muscle and a worn pair of denims hugging some well-defined thighs. Leather boots and a Stetson rounded out his gear, while an insulated lunch bag dangled from his large hand. His clean-shaven face emphasized his strong jawline and high cheekbones, and the shadow cast from the brim of his hat gave him a too-dangerous appeal.

"You're deep in thought," he said, that low voice triggering a wave of sensations she had no explanation for. At least none she was willing to admit.

He was like man candy—good to look at, maybe taste, but not good for her.

His gaze traveled over her like he was looking for…trouble. She hadn't had time to get new boots or jeans, as he had advised—or rather instructed in a not-so-subtle fiat. In fact, she wore the dirt-speckled boots from yesterday and another pair of high-end jeans that already sported a slight tear from a barbed wire. When faced with the daunting prospect of running the ranch, she'd felt entitled to splurge on expensive jeans since she had given up her preferred wardrobe of skirts, dresses, and sleek pants more suitable for a teacher than a rancher.

But she had bigger problems than clothes he found unsuitable.

"Lot on my mind," she said and frowned. "You're here early."

How could she tell him this wasn't going to work? And what reason would she give? That she was afraid she was attracted to him? Or should she look weak and blame it on her foremen?

Which one was less humiliating, given the all-business look in his eyes?

"Anxious to get going on my first day. By the way, I forgot to ask—how many men work on the ranch?"

One more than she needed. No, that wasn't true. She needed a ranch manager. She just didn't need him.

That wasn't true either. She needed him. Problem was she couldn't let herself want him—totally different issue.

"We have six wranglers in addition to the three foremen. According to Will, my range foreman, at this time of year, four to five are generally with him on the range, one works on repair, one with Charlie on the remuda, and Jim works mostly alone, since his work is done largely on the computer, figuring out which heifers to keep, buying and selling the bulls, determining how big an insemination program we'll need to supplement. Then there are the two farmers who we contract to tend the planting. In the fall we hire on more hands for the processing phase, and during calving season we might take on one or two more for a few weeks." She tried, unsuccessfully, to stifle a yawn.

"What's gotten you out here with the roosters?" he asked.

"Scours."

"How many?"

"It seems to run in dribs and drabs. We get one fixed up, and then there's another. Sometimes they don't make it." The calf Jake had cooed to being one of the latest heart-wrenching casualties.

"Have you moved all the cattle?"

"Some. Some are still in the near pastures."

"Where is your scours coming from?" he asked.

His serious expression made her feel like she was taking some type of oral exam…and failing.

She shook her head. "I don't know."

His mouth flat-lined like a teacher disappointed in his pupil's answer.

"Maybe I should ask your range foreman."

Will Springer had been the most vocal against a Taylor coming on board, telling her she was going to ruin the ranch. Without Cody, that was a sure bet. With Cody, maybe she had a chance. And Will hadn't threatened to quit, at least.

"About that."

A loud bellow came from the stable pens.

"I'll check out the scours situation." He nodded in the direction of the pens.

It would be nice to have someone who could tell her what she needed to know. And despite the whole feud thing, Cat believed Cody would be brutally honest. He'd tell her the good, the bad, and the ugly and not expect her to ask questions when she didn't know what questions to ask. Maybe she needed to buck up, handle her awakened-from-dormancy crush—because that's all it was—and take advantage of this unusual opportunity.

"You should know my foremen aren't too pleased

about you coming to work for me. They are in there waiting to meet you."

He raised an eyebrow.

"It's not that they don't think you're a good rancher. To a man they said you were. But they don't think a Taylor is going to do right by a McKenna."

"It is hard to believe." His grin caused his eyes to crinkle. He was handsomer when he smiled, if that was possible. And he didn't look quite as foreboding. Maybe her concerns weren't over his integrity, but maintaining her own.

"You'll have to prove yourself," she said, going bold.

"And what do you have to prove, Princess?"

That I'm not affected by a handsome face and a take-charge attitude. "That I can be a rancher, I expect."

"So we've both got something to prove. And if you thought one of those men in there was up to the job, you wouldn't have approached me. You said that yourself."

She swiped a hand across her brow. "Do you give me your word, Cody Taylor, that you will put the best interest of this ranch first and foremost?"

He shifted his weight as he looked straight into her eyes. Her pulse blipped.

"The honest answer is yes in all matters except those that in any way involve our ranch land. I will never stop believing the McKennas stole that land from my family, despite what the law says. And I'll always blame you for not being better than that."

Those words bit like an icy January wind.

"Then how can I trust you if you don't like me, us?"

He shrugged his shoulders. "Because I'm not an anarchist. I respect the law. And you are paying me a lot of money to do right by you. I respect that too. Either you think I can be trusted, or you don't. I've been as honest with you as I can possibly be. But either you've given me this job because you believe I can help you, or I don't take the job. I will help you, Princess. But you've got to believe in your decision, or it won't work."

He'd been forthright about his reasons, about his feelings. She needed to be the same.

"You've been honest with me. Now let me be honest with you. I'm not sorry how things turned out regarding the creek. Without access to that water, we'd have to shut down our ranching operation, I expect. I can't change decades of history or law."

She felt like she was channeling her daddy.

His jaw bunched, but his face remained impassive.

"Hard to hear, but good to know. Have we cleared the air?"

She nodded.

"Good. Now you can tell me why you are still in fancy boots and jeans, which, by the way, have a tear in them. Those items are made for going out prowling. They aren't for the type of work you're going to be doing, and that rip proves my point."

"I didn't have time to get anything else." And why she felt the need to defend her choice of clothes was the wonder—even if he was right.

"Go tonight then. Pete's Western Wear. Off Main Street in Rawlins. They're open till eight. Get a pair of sturdy denims. They may not make your butt look as good, but they will hold up."

He thought her butt looked good?

"Is that an order?" She could easily stop at the western store when she picked up Jake, but she didn't like taking orders from Cody…about clothes anyway

"Yes, Princess," he said.

"I'm not a princess." A princess would not be mucking about with a calf that had scours.

This time his smile was broad, and she immediately regretted letting him know he had gotten under her skin.

"You're a ranch princess. Can't deny it. Better own it." He winked. At her.

Instead of anger, a seductive warmth gushed through her like a geyser blowing off steam.

"Let me introduce you to our foremen." She turned on her heel and led the way to the barn before he could see the heat climbing up her cheeks. At least she hoped it was before.

Cody followed Cat and tried not to be distracted by how nicely she filled out her jeans, or the little wiggle she had when she walked, or the sway of her ponytail against the tanned skin of her neck.

Only two of the foremen were in the barn, and neither Jim nor Charlie hid their doubts. Jim, whose dark, handlebar moustache and deep voice invoked an Old West cowboy, went so far as to say that Joe McKenna was probably looking down and spitting nails, but he did so with a smile and a hand extended in friendship. A hand Cody shook. He'd gotten Charlie talking about horses, and once they started trading cow pony stories, Cody knew he'd found a kindred spirit.

Cat joined in, mentioning that they used ATVs now

more than horses. A frown formed on Charlie's face. Clearly some weren't happy about the move. Cody was a horse man all the way. What was the fun of ranching without horses? Plus, horses were key to the future of the Cross T, and large ranches moving to ATVs, drones, or helicopters would not support that future.

As they talked, he couldn't help stealing a few glances a Cat. She had a natural beauty with a tanned complexion, big brown eyes, rosebud mouth, and sun-kissed cheeks, and despite the fatigue on her face, was more attractive than when she'd been all trussed up in the courtroom.

He was curious as to how her foremen treated her now that she was running Pleasant Valley and not her father. She had big shoes to fill. And her earnest expression, bunched hands, and stiff stance told him she knew it.

When her body went rigid and her gaze centered on the back entrance, Cody turned to look. A man sauntered in from the rear of the barn, looking both peeved and curious. Most likely the range foreman, Will Springer. The man who had wanted to be ranch manager.

He looked to be in his fifties, with a paunch hanging over the large silver buckle on his pants, work boots cladding his feet, a blue-and-white bandanna around his neck, and a baseball cap where one would expect a cowboy hat. Will looked more trucker than cowboy.

"Will," Cat called out in a voice about an octave higher than usual. "Come meet Cody Taylor."

Will continued walking forward, staring straight at Cody, his eyes narrowed, his mouth tight.

"Mr. Springer." Cody nodded and extended his hand.

Springer stopped, looked at Cody, and hesitated.

Cody kept his hand out, aware the other men were watching.

Finally, Springer clasped Cody's hand, gave a sharp yank, and pulled it back. It was a start.

"Got to set up the branding pens," he mumbled. He turned and walked back out.

Cody watched the man's purposeful exit. Someone he would definitely have to be careful around.

"I'll give you a tour of the barns," Cat said as they all watched Will disappear out of the back of the barn. He wondered how much Cat liked her range foreman. She hadn't given him the ranch manager job.

The barns were in good order, clean, stocked, and well laid out. The birthing area and the clinic-like space for health issues looked sanitary. Cody examined the calf that had scours and tried, somewhat successfully, to get more fluid into it. But he was concerned that Cat didn't know the answers to some of his questions, like whether they had been providing electrolytes in the fluids.

While good hygiene was being practiced in the barns, the near pastures used for birthing were another matter. The grass was too short, the pen muddy, and the cattle that remained were too many for the size of the area. Supposedly, Will had already moved some of the herd to the branding pastures, but Cody couldn't help wonder if the whole herd had been crammed in there, and for how long. The state of the pastures could explain the outbreak of scours. Ample grass supply for the cows and good sanitation were important for the health of newborn calves.

Cat didn't comment on the pastures, which made him wonder if she even knew what good pasture management was. He mentally put that on the to-be-taught list.

Today, with her jeans dirty, her hair tied back, and a cowgirl hat on her head, she *looked* like she belonged to a ranching family, albeit the pretty side. But she *acted* more like a tour guide than an owner, showing him buildings and enclosures without any enthusiasm or pride. He would expect both from a seventh-generation rancher.

Ending the tour, she took him inside the house to the study, where they'd hammered out the agreement the day before. She sat at her father's desk and started tapping the keys on the computer. A wisp of hair fell free of her ponytail and brushed against the smooth skin of her cheek. She blew a breath to keep it from her mouth. A mouth that, for some reason, he found distracting today.

She hit another button, and the printer hummed to life. When she turned her attention to him, he was caught by the worry that wrinkled her brow and tightened those distracting lips.

"I don't think it is going to be good news." She pulled the sheet from the printer tray and handed it to him.

He perused the sheet, looking at the columns. He pulled his cell phone from his breast pocket and used the calculator app to compare some of the numbers. He checked the figures again.

She had reason to worry.

He looked up and into a pair of dark eyes that held a mountain of concern. Reviewing these figures, he now understood just how desperate she needed his help. And what a mess he'd taken on.

"By this count, you've lost almost ten percent of your calves."

That loose strand of hair fell across her brow, and he had to restrain himself from reaching over and brushing it from her face. Instead, she tucked it behind her ear as she nibbled her lip. "I take it that's not normal."

"It's high. Did you guys vaccinate? Or did you have a lot of cases of pneumonia?"

Cat drew back into the embrace of the chair. "I think we vaccinated. How many did the Cross T lose this year?"

"Ours haven't calved yet—remember?"

"Oh. Right." Her frown deepened, but she looked as bereft of answers as he was.

"I'll talk to Springer about this. Maybe he has some insight. If you've vaccinated, scours is most likely due to poor pasture management."

"What do you mean by poor pasture management? Are they ingesting something they shouldn't?"

"Cows aren't the most sanitary of creatures. They'll eat right where they just dumped. You've got to keep moving the herd so they aren't standing in their own filth. That can facilitate scours. Once it takes hold, it can go through your whole herd. Most ranchers have a birthing area and then move them to a pasture set aside for the nursing cows and their offspring. Then they rotate them into different pastures."

"I'm sure Will is doing all the right things. He's been on the ranch for the last five years."

Cody straightened. "Except, despite my telling you to move them, you still have some of your cows and calves in the pastures you used for birthing." Hard to believe that the herd hadn't been moved up closer to the summer pastures by now.

"Will said we needed to brand them first. He just started to move them to the pastures we use for branding. Those pastures on the other side of the house, farther from the creek." She bit her lip.

She did have a nice mouth. One a man could enjoy kissing.

"He should have done that before now. Question is why he didn't."

"It's my fault."

"How so?" Cody leaned his hip against the desk.

"He said he was waiting for me to give the order. I don't know about branding times. I don't know about pasture management." She raised her eyes, and her look was one of pure defeat. "You see, this is why I need a ranch manager. I know nothing about running a ranch. Absolutely nothing." It was almost a wail.

"You at least know what you don't know, and that's a start, Princess. And your range foreman knew. You pay him to know. And you pay him to tell you what you don't know." Anger at Will Springer bubbled up inside of him. How the man could call himself a range foreman and risk a herd "waiting for orders" was beyond the pale. "Let's take a ride out there and see him."

"It's not far. About six miles from here. I'll drive."

"How about we go by horse, and you can show me some of the range afterwards. But before we go, I've something else to discuss."

She nodded, but by her frown, he guessed she was a tad worried.

"I typed up our agreement last night." He didn't like formalizing things, and with anyone but a McKenna, a handshake would have sufficed. "Look it over and sign it. Tomorrow will do." He placed it on the desk.

"If I have any issues?" She scanned it.

"We'll talk. But you won't. I typed up exactly what we agreed to. I only want what is mine, Cat, not a penny more." Unlike the McKennas, who grabbed all they could get. "Being a McKenna, you might not understand that."

She looked at him as if he'd wounded her. Sometimes the truth hurt.

As they prepared to head out to the new pastures, Cody learned that not only were ATVs the transportation of choice on this ranch, with the exception of when they relocated the herds, but her father had been thinking of getting a helicopter to do that work.

Cat had even suggested he try an ATV.

He would be damned if he was going to ride around on an ATV as a matter of course. Those vehicles had their place when you had to haul something or pick up a lame calf in an area that a pickup couldn't get to, but he preferred to do his ranching from the back of a horse. Tomorrow he'd be sure to bring over one of his own horses and board it at Pleasant Valley for the duration. For now, he insisted they ride four-legged transportation.

From atop a chestnut cow pony he'd picked out, Cody watched as Cat gracefully slid a leg over the back of her bay quarter horse. The horse had great lines. And so did the rider. If she weren't so prissy…and a McKenna…he wouldn't mind those legs wrapped around his waist.

"Why do you have a remuda of horses if you're using ATVs?" Cody asked, as much to distract himself as to learn about the operation.

Cat shrugged. "Dad had only recently gone to ATVs. And we still need horses for some of the work, as well as pleasure riding and the hunting parties we occasionally host. I came across an analysis for that helicopter when I started to go through his papers."

"Well, unless you plan on taking flying lessons, I'm assuming a helicopter is off the table?"

She nodded. "I'm not a fan of flying to begin with."

"Good, because I'm probably going to ask the hands to ride horses from now on. Just seems that horses are the enjoyable part of ranching."

Cat didn't say yes or no to his proposal as they nudged their horses into a walk and headed for the pastures.

Cody decided to make conversation to avoid getting distracted by the way Cat kept her seat in the saddle, her body moving back and forth in time with the horse's leisurely movement, reminding him too much of a different activity and leisurely motion.

"Given how you feel about ranching, I'm surprised you ride."

She turned her head to look at him, frowning again. She looked much prettier when she smiled.

"It's the one thing my father spent time teaching me," she said. "The only thing."

She didn't sound pleased.

"You never took up barrel racing, did you?" he asked. He was curious at her seeming disdain for ranch life. He loved living and working on a ranch. He loved being outdoors, he loved training horses, and he loved working cattle. He might, at times, hate the weather conditions and the financial unpredictability of ranching, but being his own boss and working in and with nature made up for a lot.

"No. And I wasn't a rodeo queen either."

"You don't like living on a ranch?" It seemed a waste to have someone who didn't appreciate the outdoors, the livestock, or the lifestyle being gifted with so much of it.

"No." No hesitation there.

"Then why not just sell out and be done with it? Sell to someone who would appreciate it." It galled him she wasn't grateful for what she had, particularly when she had been given so much.

She bit her lip before answering, as if studying what to say. "I'm not selling for the same reason you're not selling. I owe it to my ancestors. I owe it to my son. So far, he's proven to be all cowboy. The ranch was left in trust for him with provisions for any other children I may have. I'm just a caretaker, keeping it going until he's old enough to take over."

Cody chewed on that piece of news. He hadn't heard that the ranch had gone to the little boy and not to her. They rode in silence for a bit, Cody enjoying the natural beauty—land and otherwise.

"You resent not being left the ranch but having the burdens of it all the same?"

She squared her shoulders. "Having the burdens of it, yes. But I'm happy my son was left the ranch.

This way a McKenna that values it will have it. That is, if he does grow up to like ranching."

Cody didn't remember hearing if the boy had the McKenna last name, but he had McKenna blood all the same. "You want him to like it?"

She shrugged and sat up straighter in the saddle. "Ranching is a good life for those who enjoy it. I'm going to do my best to see that he does. But if he doesn't…" There was a long pause. "If he doesn't, I want him to be able to follow his dreams, and then I'll be the last of the McKennas to run this ranch. Ironic, wouldn't you say?" Her jaw tightened.

Cody didn't know what was ironic about it, but he wasn't about to ask. It was hard to hear that she didn't like ranching. Ranching was all he'd ever known and all he ever wanted to know.

"I guess you'd be teaching if you weren't ranching, huh? You like teaching?" He didn't know where teachers got the patience, but he was glad there were people in the world who had it. Kids needed good teachers. He hadn't appreciated his until he was out of school.

For the first time on their ride, she smiled, and when she did, her whole face lit up as if she had just been told she'd won a million dollars. "I love teaching. It's very satisfying to help a child read their first sentence. See the light bulb turn on as they learn to add and multiply. To help them make sense of the world." She turned toward him, her face still glowing. Maybe it was just from the breeze, but he doubted it. "I was homeschooled until high school. But I've never wanted to do anything else but teach kids."

A long silence stretched between them before she

added, "And now, for the next fifteen years or so, I'll be working with cows." The smile faded, and she took a deep breath. "That's life."

Cody had learned well enough that sometimes life didn't work out as you planned.

It didn't take more than another minute to reach the herd, and Cody didn't like what he saw as they walked their horses among the animals. Most of the cattle were strewn across the pasture, some by themselves, which was never a good sign. Herds that were healthy and content generally kept together.

He scanned the pasture, but nary another cowboy in sight.

"Should I get on the walkie-talkie?" she asked, turning around in her saddle so she could see him.

Cody pulled up his horse. "Let's take the opportunity to check out the herd first. Then we'll call. Follow along, and tell me what you see."

Cat didn't see anything except pasture and cows, but clearly Cody expected her to take notice of something. "Well, the herd is spread out, so I guess that's good. They aren't all huddled together, and they can have their own patch to eat."

"Might seem like it should be, but it's not a good thing."

Cat felt the heat climb up her neck, like when she'd given the wrong answer in a class. "Why?"

"Cattle herd. They should be together. Loosely, but together."

Cody headed his horse for the water trough, where some of the herd were standing but not drinking. Cat followed.

"What do you see here?" he asked without answering her question. He actually looked angry.

She stared down into the large water trough, where water was trickling in. Water from their mutual creek. Was he worried about how much water they were using? That had always been an issue, with the Taylors accusing the McKennas of siphoning off too much. Was there to be a showdown already? Cat's head ached.

"What am I supposed to see?"

"Not enough water. You're not pumping water at a rate that will keep the trough full."

"I'd think you'd be happy that we weren't depleting the creek."

He shook his head, and the frown deepened. "That's a separate issue, and one we've never won. This is about having enough water to satisfy the number of heads you're managing."

"Shouldn't Will know this?"

"Exactly."

The sound of an engine came from somewhere over the ridge. It grew louder as they both sat on their horse and waited. Finally an ATV came bounding into the pasture. No doubt the man on it was Will.

The cows looked up as the ATV stopped at the outskirts of the pasture, and the engine died near a lone cow resting in the shade of one of the few trees. The lanky man jumped out and sauntered over to the cow and appeared to check her out.

"Why do you think he did that?" Cody asked, sounding more and more like a school teacher. Obviously he wasn't asking because he didn't know.

"Something's wrong?"

"Right. Cows don't lay down until they've eaten their fill, and at late morning it's unlikely she has."

One right answer.

"What do you think is the matter?" Her hand fluttered to her hair to tuck that wayward strand behind her ear. The breeze had picked up as they had gotten closer to the mountain, and she was glad her hair was in a ponytail. She only wished she'd thrown on a jacket, given the cooler temperatures.

"Could be anything from foot rot to pneumonia to scours. You seem to have more than your fill of that going around."

After checking the cow, Will Springer ambled over, leaving his ATV where he had parked it. From everything Cat knew, her father had trusted Will. Perhaps because Will had been a good sergeant to her father's lieutenant, rather than the person who gave the orders.

"You found it." Will gave a clipped nod in greeting

"How many head you got up here on this ridge?" Cody launched right into his questions.

"About five hundred, including calves."

"Where's the rest?"

Will waved his hands toward where he'd just come. "Another five hundred are over the ridge. The rest are still in the east pastures near the house and creek. I expect you've seen them."

"Seems water is coming in slowly today."

Will held his gaze on Cody. "I was just coming to check on it. We've been having some problems."

"When are you planning to brand?"

Will seemed surprised at the question. "That's up

to Miss McKenna here." He nodded toward Cat. "That's her call."

Great.

"Guess I'll be telling you for the foreseeable future." Cody said. "And I'd like to wait a bit to make sure the calves are healthy. Seems we have more than a few cases of scours to clean up. But no reason not to move all of the herd. Not like you don't have enough pasture."

"All right." Will looked at Cat as if for confirmation.

"Yes, Will. Cody will be giving the orders for now. I'm here to learn."

Disgust rode his face like a rider glued to a bull, a mean bull.

"What's wrong with the cow?" Cody asked.

"Foot rot. I'll take care of it," he said somewhat defensively.

"Good. Miss McKenna and I will ride on to see the rest of the herd. Tomorrow, I'd like to meet with you in the morning, before you come out here, and go over some things. I'd also like to meet the rest of the crew."

"One's riding fence. The other two are putting salt out in the pasture by the creek."

"We'll find them. When we ride back, let me know if you are still having trouble fixing the water supply. Oh, and since we will be delaying branding some, no need to put up the railings just yet."

Will mumbled an "all right," and Cody reined his horse around, nodding for Cat to follow, and headed for the ridge.

"I don't like it," Cody said as they headed back. He'd taken a good look at the other pastures, met the three young men who seemed to be hard at work, and hadn't liked what he found among the cattle. If Will Springer was the range foreman, he was doing a piss-poor job at range management. Cat was likely to lose several more from her herd if conditions didn't improve. And it didn't take a rocket scientist to understand what needed to be done. It was a simple matter of better pasture management and assuring an adequate water supply. And Pleasant Valley had enough of both.

By the time they rode back through, whatever was wrong with the water supply seemed fixed, but the downed cow was nowhere in sight, and neither was Will Springer.

"Tell me why and what you would change," Cat said.

At least she was interested in learning.

Cody launched into a lesson on the benefits of grass management. "Do you know if the farmers have prepared the winter pastures for planting yet?" The type of grass was as important as the quantity.

She shook her head. "I guess you think I should know all these things you've been telling me, but honestly, until six months ago, I had no contact with the ranch hands or the herds."

It boggled his mind that someone could owe her livelihood to something and not take an interest in it. And considering this was one of the finer ranches in the county, it was all the more of a wonder. He could have done amazing things with the assets this ranch possessed. This setup was only something to dream about, as far as he was concerned, and yet it belonged to a woman who didn't appreciate it and a boy who might sell it.

"Guess you're going to need a lot of hand holding, Princess. We're going to need to spend time each day on some aspect of ranch management, maybe an hour or so, so you can understand what I'm pointing out as we encounter things."

"You've made me realize how much needs correcting—only I haven't a clue yet what to do to correct it."

"First step toward true wisdom is understanding what you don't know. My father used to say that." Cody felt a twinge near his heart.

What would his father think of him tutoring Cat McKenna? Helping her with her ranch? Hell, Cody wasn't sure what *he* thought about it. Except she paid damn well.

As they rode in tandem, he discussed the importance of having the right mixture of grasses, the benefit of grazing intervals, and how to assure healthy soil. This was especially important in grass-fed cattle, but it bore out regardless.

He'd become a convert to grass-fed cattle ranching two years ago after attending a seminar on the subject, and, except for the timing issue, his experience had been nothing but positive. Breeding had gone well, the heifers had wintered over, and there had been less need for hay. Of course, it had been a milder winter than most. The real test would come with the later calving season.

Though Cat's herd was destined for the commodity market, there was still some value in grass

93

feeding and managing the pastures for optimum consumption. From what he saw, the winter pastures had been overgrazed, and the summer pastures were going to suffer the same fate if they didn't institute better management techniques. Tomorrow he'd get ahold of the farmers and make sure their grass mixtures were optimized. And he'd work with Will to come up with a systematic grazing scheme that assured herd migration and good, nutrient-rich grazing. And ample water. As for moving the calving season, maybe he could talk Cat into giving it a try. But first he'd have to teach her the basics.

"Working a ranch and running a ranch are two different things. Roping a cow is in the how-to-be-a-cowboy lesson. Learning the best techniques for grazing cattle to assure optimum weight gain is in the how-to-be-a-rancher lesson. I'm going to teach you how to manage your land and herds for the best possible financial outcome."

By the time they reached the barn, he was staring into a pair of tired brown eyes, pretty as they were.

"We can continue this discussion tomorrow morning. I'm going over to talk with Jim about the breeding program and get the low-down on the bulls he'll be breeding to your stock. I'm going to suggest, too, that we do a real count and not rely on just a paper count. I need to know exactly how many cattle and calves you've got and, more importantly, how many you've lost these last few months."

A frowned formed on the lovely Miss McKenna's face. "If we've lost more than we thought, there would be no one to blame but me." Resignation tinged her tone.

"This isn't about assessing blame, and even if it were, I think Mother Nature and your range foreman would bear most of that burden."

There was something about Will Springer that just didn't set right with Cody. Anyone who worked cattle would know the basics of herd location, scheduling branding, when to turn out the bulls, and assuring ample supply of water. Cody was finding it hard to swallow that Will Springer was waiting on orders. Especially if the man had hopes of being foreman over the whole outfit. But maybe that was the way Joe McKenna liked it.

"No more today. Tomorrow will be soon enough. That's an order from your ramrod. Give you time to get some decent clothes too. And say hi to your little guy."

She gave him a rueful smile. "I'm not sure how I feel about taking orders from you."

"Easy to get rid of me. Don't sign our agreement."

Chapter 6

A week later Cody looked out from the barn at two range hands who were saddling horses, not revving ATVs, to ride out to check the fencing in the summer pastures. Will had long since departed from the group that morning, riding an ATV like a man on a mission.

Cody wandered over the corral, kicking up dust as he walked.

Cat had signed the agreement without changes, and since then, Will Springer aside, Cody had made some progress. He'd sectioned the herd, worked out a pasture rotation plan, tutored Cat on what grasses they should replant in the winter fields, began taking inventory, and switched the ranch hands to horseback for the majority of their work. All except Will Springer, that was.

Cody had also selected a ranch hand to begin work over at the Cross T. Duane Wilson had been a year ahead of Cody in high school, and they'd been friendly, if not friends. Cody knew his family, good ranchers all, and felt comfortable Duane would be an asset.

Opening up the gate to the corral where several

horses grazed, Cody realized that, today, at the start of a new week, he felt settled in his role. The depth and breadth of Pleasant Valley would take some getting used to after facing the limits of the Cross T all these years, but the prospect invigorated him. It was too early to tell if Cat was up to the challenge though. She asked good questions, and she was always taking notes like a reporter following a story, but it remained to be seen if she could retain the knowledge and acquire the insight to run a major commercial enterprise like Pleasant Valley. From exasperated sighs and forlorn looks, it was clear Cat McKenna's heart wasn't in it.

Cody checked the water troughs. Clear water from the creek filled the tub.

So far, she'd accepted his suggestions, including changing out her designer clothes for dependable western wear. And her butt still looked good.

Strolling over to where Comanche grazed, the horse lifted his head and looked at Cody as if questioning if the horse was in the right place. Cody ran his hand down his horse's neck.

"Enjoy the luxury of this ranch while it lasts," he said.

One thing Cody hadn't done was set a date for branding, and, with the days rolling by, that needed to be decided sooner rather than later. He also wanted to talk to Cat about moving the date for turning out the bulls to better follow nature's schedule. This might improve calf survival rates by allowing more pasture births and reducing scours. There could be ramifications, however. The calves next year, born later in June and July, would not be ready for sale to feedlots come fall. They'd have to be wintered over for sale the following spring or finished out in the pastures and sold in late summer as eight-hundred-pound yearlings, before weanlings flooded the fall market. Feeding all those older yearlings was costly, and it was this very transition period that could yet prove the ruin of his own ranch.

Cross T would be facing calving season soon. He hoped his brother was up to the challenge.

Satisfied Comanche and the rest of the horses in the corral were taken care of, Cody headed back to the gate.

It had been a wonder how easily he could forget the issues at Cross T. Jace was handling things and didn't appear to want or need his big brother's advice, though Cody offered it anyway over the dinners, mostly grilled food, sometimes accompanied by bowls of canned soup, they shared after putting in a hard day at their respective ranches. Duane was proving to be a worker and didn't seem to mind taking orders from a younger Jace.

So much had happened and was going to happen, it seemed ages ago they'd buried his father, rather than almost two weeks. Yet it was hard to accept that his father was gone from this earth. More like he was on some hunting trip and would return any day now. Cody hadn't had time to grieve. Not that it mattered, grieving, that was. Things couldn't be changed, no matter how much he'd want it otherwise.

Play the hand you're dealt, his father would have said.

He'd talked to his mother and his aunt Lucille, and from what he could tell, his mother was doing okay. She'd even gone with his aunt to her office to help out one day when someone had called in sick. No one mentioned any news about the McKennas, so maybe small-town gossip hadn't traveled to Laramie. When his mother came home there, there would be some explaining to do. He'd played the hand he'd been dealt, and this coming Friday when that first paycheck hit his bank account, he knew he'd be glad he did.

Cody looked at his Seiko watch, the one his father had proudly presented to him for his high school graduation gift. His mother had told him how his father had insisted on going to the jewelry store himself to pick out just the right one, even though she couldn't remember when Zeke had gone to a jeweler, except to get their wedding rings. It may not be one of them Rolexes, but it was priceless to Cody.

Cat would be waiting for him, no doubt, in the study with a list of questions she'd gotten in the habit of producing each morning. Apparently she spent her evenings poring over information or website links he'd leave for her. Though she seemed determined to do her best for her little boy, there was no denying she was a ranch princess, not a rancher, and she had a long way to go. Maybe too long.

He sauntered out of the gate and toward the house. Felt like rain was in the air. Probably tonight.

He couldn't help wondering about the boy's father and why that man wasn't doing something for his son's future—not that little Jake would want for much, given the McKenna money. But a boy needed more from a father than just the bills paid.

Jake's father, whoever he was, had something Cody wondered if he'd ever have—a child. A family.

His hands were full keeping things going while

paying off piled-high debts. No way he could support another mouth to feed, much less a family on what they made from the Cross T. It hardly supported the needs of one family, much less two—or three if Jace ever walked down the aisle.

Even before his father's illness, it had been clear there would never be enough money to support a wife and children. There hadn't been enough to go around then, and now finances were worse.

How could he ever ask a woman to marry him "for poorer," knowing that was exactly what life would be? How could he ask her to give up thoughts of having children when that's what he too wanted?

And here some clown had thrown away a potential wife and a child when money would not have been a consideration.

Had Joe threatened to disown Cat or shown the bum the door? Cody would have fought Joe McKenna with every fiber of his being for rights to his child and the mother of that child. He would have made Cat his wife and claimed Jake as his son.

But he wasn't that guy. Cat wouldn't have gone for someone like him. She'd made that clear a long time ago.

And he would never want to date a ranch princess who worried about her manicure and mussing her hair. He needed a woman who was independent, didn't mind getting her hands dirty, and didn't need anyone to tell her what needed to be done. A woman who had grown up on a ranch and embraced the life, not one who had run from it.

Of course, more than a few women in Wyoming would fit that description. But he could only date them, and how did a man do that knowing he could never put a ring on a finger? Right now it was a moot point because he wasn't dating, period. And from what he could tell, Cat hadn't dated anyone in the two years she'd been back—and he'd checked around.

Cyndi Lynn Spencer, nee Logan, had once been a girlfriend of his, if a few weeks in high school wearing his ring on a chain around her neck made her a girlfriend, and he knew she and Cat were still friendly. It had taken nothing more than an ice cream at the Dairy Doodle, when he ran into her on Saturday as he was doing errands, to get her talking. After mentioning she was now separated from her husband, Cyndi Lynn said she'd just been talking to Cat about getting together, seeing both were at loose ends. She also said she didn't know anything about the man who had fathered little Jake, only that Cat had gotten pregnant during her last year of college.

Cody figured that must have been a tough time, but it hadn't changed the fact Jake was the one who lit up Cat's world. She took mothering seriously. Her child seemed always first in her thoughts. She'd expressed more than once that she felt guilty if she wasn't there when he got home from preschool and that she missed taking him in the morning and picking him up, that chore now falling mostly to Cat's mother. Preschool would end soon, and Cat fretted about whether Jake would miss his school friends or find enough to do on the ranch during the summer, given she'd be tied up with duties.

Cody opened the front door to the McKenna house, as he'd been instructed to do for their morning meetings, and stepped inside.

Hell. Ranches were like amusement parks to kids. But he couldn't help wonder what Miss McKenna did for fun these days.

* * *

"We need to set a date for branding."

Cat looked up from the computer screen, and her breath hitched like it had been taken by the wind. A whirlwind named Cody Taylor.

Every morning now, Cody met with her to go over the day's schedule and answer the questions that had filled her head from the night before. And every morning a sizzle of electricity pinged through her as she took in the tall, slender man dressed in thigh-hugging jeans, a wrinkled shirt, worn boots, and carrying a hat in his hands. His face was shaven, his dark hair combed, and his eyes seemed to sparkle with mischief—or interest. Cat could never tell.

"What day did you have in mind?"

"We've slowed the scours outbreak, and the afflicted calves seem on the road to recovery. Another week should do it."

Cat looked back at her computer screen at the breeding charts. Maybe if she didn't gawk at him, this unsettled feeling would go away. "My mom is taking Jake over Memorial Day weekend to visit my uncle and his wife in Montana. She goes every year. I've been going with them, but not this year." No way could she take time off. Not now and probably not ever. She felt a little heaviness in her heart.

"And?" Cody sauntered over to the edge of her desk. If she looked straight ahead, she'd be staring crotch level at a pair of jeans faded in interesting places.

"My mom will need to be here. She handles the food, cooking, and coordinating." Cat kept her focus on the computer screen. "You want everyone to get fed."

Cody chuckled. It was a low chuckle, like wind through tunnel. "I take it you don't cook, Princess?"

At that remark, Cat did look up and got caught in his line of sight. His eyes crinkled at the edges in laughter, and his mouth was cocked in a half smile.

She had to stop allowing her emotions to be tossed about by a handsome face.

"No one can cook like my mother. If you want people to heed the call, you'll need her to supply the food." Her father had always said that in order to get the neighbors to help, he had to bribe them with the promise of her mother's cooking.

"Well, then how about we set it for the Thursday after they get back. I'll have to rotate the herd to a further pasture before then, but I'll just drive them back that morning."

"Sounds like a plan." Cat focused back on the monitor and away from the man who was making her heart skip. She needed to keep her mind on her work. Her reaction just proved it had been too long since she'd been on a date.

She'd dated a few times when Jake had been a toddler and she'd been able to get one of the teachers from his day care to babysit. But those times had been few and far between, and none had progressed beyond a first date. There was always something wrong. Too pushy, too self-absorbed, too quiet, too much like Jake's father.

She glanced back at Cody, who looked at her as if waiting for an answer. By all accounts, Cody had been a player like Jake's father, and no doubt still was. Why did that type of man attract her? It was as if she was looking to be disappointed.

"Did you say something?" she asked.

"No. But you seemed deep in thought."

Not any thoughts she wanted to share. *Focus on the ranch.*

"If we delay the branding until after Memorial Day, how will that affect the date we turn out the bulls?"

There was so much to learn that most days she felt overwhelmed, and yet Cody seemed to have all the answers at his fingertips. And no doubt was judging her because she didn't. There were so many variables to account for in cattle ranching that it made her head swim. People who thought you could just buy a few cows, breed them, turn them out, and let nature take its course before you sold them were so wrong it wasn't funny. And despite living on a ranch for most of her life, Cat had been one of them.

She'd never realized all the things her father had dealt with. From types of grasses, to types of cattle, to types and quantity of hay, to which cows to cull and which ones to breed, to which ones to winter over and which to sell now, when to rotate the herd, when to breed, how many gallons of water per head to pump, there was nothing but decisions to be made. And when she added in the physical labor that left her near exhaustion and the weather that held constant surprises, it was no wonder her father hadn't always been in the pleasantest mood.

She'd snapped at Jake the other day when he wouldn't listen to her exhortations against climbing one of the few trees that shaded the house. She'd told herself the short temper was because it was a safety issue, but really, she didn't seem to have any patience after making decisions all day long. She'd vowed to gain some, at least where her son was concerned.

"I've roughed out a plan to move breeding time to a more natural schedule. There are lots of benefits to later birthing times and being more in synch with nature. I'd like to review the proposal with you once I have it finalized."

"Can the ranch afford to take such a step, now, this year?" Didn't she need a better handle on the current state of affairs before she started messing with things? "I mean, you said yourself that we are too big an operation to go totally grass-fed."

"The way I figure it, selling calves in January or early spring instead of October, or carrying them through as yearlings, the ranch will still make money. But I admit that the Cross T, being a smaller operation and having gone this route, is likely to suffer this year, given we won't be selling stock until the new calendar year."

She peeked at him using peripheral vision. The corners of his mouth had turned down as his brows drew into a frown.

"That's hardly an endorsement. Frankly, I don't feel confident enough to make that decision."

He set his butt on the desk and draped a leg over the edge. Great. Now his firm rear end was in her sight line. And it was a fine one.

She had to stop lusting after this man. It was an

exercise in frustration, and she was already overflowing with that.

"Is there anything you like about the idea?" Asking questions when she asked a question was what he did when he was in teaching mode, helping her think things through.

That was one of the things, the many things, she liked about Cody. He was patient when he was in teaching mode. He was smart. And a problem solver. When things went wrong, like the pipes feeding the troughs clogging up, he assessed the cause and initiated the solution. He knew more about raising cattle than any of the men working on the ranch, with the exception of maybe Jim Smith, and he'd already made a friend of her son, who tagged after Cody whenever he was in sight. Remarkably, Cody didn't seem to mind. In fact, he seemed to enjoy her son's attention.

And he sure was nice to look at.

She swiveled in her chair to fully face him and took a deep breath, trying to ignore the uptick in her pulse. "I like the idea of being in synch with nature. Birthing when the grass is high instead of when the wind is blowing and snow is falling. Maybe it would get rid of these scours outbreak. And with so much grass available, maybe supplements won't be as necessary, and maybe the calves won't be so big as to cause the mothers trouble during delivery."

"And what scares you about the idea?"

You scare me. Every time I look at you, it feels as if I'm testing biology.

"Less money coming in and a payroll to meet. It's a change, and I'm just not sure now is the right time." She'd answered honestly. About the ranch.

"And what questions do you still have?"

"Whether it will actually improve our survival rates. Whether it will be worth it."

"I ran some numbers last night, and I think it will be worth it. I have to finish up the count today, but I can review them with you this evening or tomorrow morning. I think you'll be convinced."

His tone shouted confidence, and as his smile broadened, his eyes twinkled. At her. Her heart did a little stutter beat, a pitter-patter dance. For a moment, she let herself believe they were twinkling *because* of her.

She shouldn't be attracted to him. Really, she shouldn't. She didn't want to be. He was exactly the type of guy to stay away from because he wasn't in it for the long term. And he didn't think much of her. Something his frowning face indicated every time he asked her to answer one of his many questions.

So what was it about him? It was more than a mere physical attraction, although that was uncommonly strong. It had to be the man's sheer confidence about what he knew and who he was. The way he took on problems, faced them down, and then did whatever needed to be done. The way he managed the men—firmly but with an openness and a readiness to listen, something her father had never shown. It was his confidence, in his knowledge, in his world. All of which she lacked.

And he didn't talk down to her. He took the time and exercised the patience to teach her.

"You already ran the numbers?" When had he found the time?

"I brought my laptop so I can show you. It's in

the truck. By the way, you need to invest in a computer program designed for herd management. Given the size of the Pleasant Valley herd, I'm surprised you don't have something already."

Seemed the computer age had met ranching. Who knew? Certainly not her father, who had been challenged when it came to the computer or the Internet. Cat had offered multiple times to teach him, but her father had refused. She suspected he didn't cotton to the idea that his daughter could actually teach him something. Pride could be a foolish thing. "Tell me which one, and I'll buy it."

Cody named a program. "I'll set it up, teach you how to use it, but you're going to have to update it regularly. You'll need it when I'm gone, because, honestly, I haven't seen much from your range foreman." Cody rubbed his jaw as if it hurt. "Maybe I'm not looking hard enough, but you definitely need to see what other candidates for ranch manager are out there."

She'd come to that same conclusion, which was why she'd asked Cody for help in the first place. "Dad liked him." She had withdrawn her original ad for a range foreman since Cody had said he would help until the end of the year. She had time.

"Will takes orders okay," Cody offered, as if searching for something good to say.

She'd seen some tension between Cody and Will over orders, but Will had gone along with what Cody asked, at least as far as she could tell.

"So you think you'll finish the count today?"

"By end of day. Then we'll know what we are up against. And you'll have more facts on which to base a decision."

Given his voice had just gone flat and his words sounded clipped, Cat wasn't expecting good news.

Great. Her first six months and she was already failing. She felt exhausted, and the day had just begun. She was so tired of ranching...

"Maybe we should discuss all of this over dinner. Maybe at the Granville House?" She bit her lip, wondering if she was being too forward. A change of scenery just sounded like a good idea.

"I..."

"We'd use the ranch account since we'll be doing ranch business." It was important to get that issue resolved. For the ranch, of course. Decisions had to be made, and if she was asking him to spend so much time on these issues, the least she could do was treat him to a nice dinner. Right? It was business, after all, strictly business.

His eyebrow arched. "All right."

"I'll call and make a reservation." Was she too eager? Before she lost her nerve, she pulled out her desk drawer and grabbed the plastic gold card that sat on top of a sheet of paper. "Here," she said, holding it out to him. "This is the ranch credit card. It's for the foremen, and now you, to use when you need to buy something for the ranch. Will, Charlie, and Jim are all able to sign. I've already added you to the list. You can use it tonight for dinner."

Had he flinched? But he took the card, and his fingers brushing against hers sent a frisson of pleasure rippling inside her. She really needed to start dating again if a man's touch, if this man's touch, caused all this turmoil. Question was, when would she find the time? Or the energy? Or the man?

"Before we'd head out, I'd need to go home and change, since I'll be out with the herd the rest of the day. I can be back here by seven."

She hadn't thought about his need to change, but of course he would have to. The Granville House was definitely in the category of "nice" restaurant. She supposed she could have chosen the little café that sat like a relic from the fifties on the side of the highway leading to Laramie, but she'd wanted some place quieter. *Some place intimate?* She rejected that thought.

"As you suggested, I'm meeting with the farmers this afternoon and going over the schedule we made out for them. Any words of wisdom?" she asked, to clear the disturbing thoughts clouding her mind.

He looked down at her as he crossed his arms over his chest. "They work for you. You have to get used to giving orders, Cat."

True, but she hadn't much experience giving orders to anyone over the age of eight. At least, not to anyone who had listened.

She took a deep breath. "See you at seven, then."

Chapter 7

Cat swung open the front door only to feel like she'd been hit with the effects of a stun gun and the current had knocked her senseless. She grabbed the doorjamb for balance.

As if he hadn't a care in the world, Cody Taylor, dressed in shiny cowboy boots, black pressed pants, and a crisp white shirt with the collar unbuttoned and the teensiest bit of hair peeking out, leaned casually against the doorframe. With no cowboy hat on his head, his full head of dark-brown hair was burnished with flecks of gold from the light of the waning sun, and an errant lock casually dipped over one brow.

Cody Taylor cleaned up nice, real nice. Shaved, polished, and pressed, he looked yummier than a hot fudge sundae on a sweltering summer day.

Smile lines crinkled at the corner of those sterling-blue eyes as his mouth twitched up in a smile, as if he knew she liked the view. And she did. Or at least her body did, if the heat flashing through it was any indication. Her mind, well, she was still trying to control her mind. Keep her thoughts on the moment. On business. But honestly, she was going to lose that battle any second.

"Ready?" He cocked his head and shifted his gaze in a leisurely perusal down her body.

Another flash of heat.

It had taken her a full hour just to decide what to wear.

A businesslike skirt and blouse? Too reserved.

A breezy sundress? Too casual.

An ass-grabbing black dress? Too much like a date.

White pants and a cotton top? Too mom.

In the end, she settled for a sleek black skirt, high-heeled sandals (he could definitely handle the height), and a silky fuchsia blouse with a little lace inset. She'd stuffed a black cotton sweater in her leather purse in case the restaurant or the night was too cool.

Not trusting that her voice wouldn't betray her, she simply nodded in answer to his question. She'd already said good-bye to Jake before her mother had swept him into the tub for a bath. Thank goodness for her mother's help.

Her mother. When Cat had mentioned they were going out to dinner, her mother had christened the evening a date, and no amount of argument otherwise could change her suspicious mind.

"You can talk business right here in the study," her mother had scoffed. Lydia still hadn't accepted the idea that Cody Taylor was working for Pleasant Valley. Or that he wouldn't guide her to ruin.

It was business. She had a lot to talk about with Cody. She'd only suggested dinner because if she was going to ask for more of his time, she could at least make it pleasant. But for a few minutes, she could pretend, couldn't she, that she was on a date? After all, it had been how many years since...

Too many. And she felt older, used up, as if her best years were behind her. At the age of twenty-five. Her friends had told her if she didn't use it, she would lose it. She hoped that wasn't possible, because it might already be too late. Tonight wouldn't change that, of course.

But getting ready earlier—choosing her outfit, styling her hair, putting on makeup, including a little glitter eye shadow she hadn't used in forever—she'd felt younger, hipper, and yes, eager. So what? Pretending never hurt anyone, and as long as Cody Taylor never knew what she was thinking, what was the harm? Really?

How the hell had he ended up here? Cody looked around the dimly lit dining room at linen-wrapped tables, gleaming-white dishes, silver forks, knives, and spoons, and lit candles, and felt like a dog at a feline party.

More so for the "cat" sitting across from him, looking sexier than any woman had a right to look in a skirt and heels that elongated those centerfold legs. Hell, he'd had to keep his chin from dropping and his mouth from drooling when she'd opened her front door.

She'd stood there with her hair all fluffed up, skin glowing, lips the color of ripe plums, and those brown eyes of hers intriguingly feline. He tried to look casual, but with his body suddenly on alert, he doubted he succeeded. Made him want to grab her arm, pull her close, and kiss her like she'd just welcomed him home after a long leave.

So much for her not being his type. Physically, she'd be any red-blooded male's type. Too bad she was a princess.

Take the place she'd chosen for their business dinner. He'd never been in the Granville House, but he'd sure heard about it. From the menu to the way it was decorated, it shouted expensive—just like Ms. McKenna.

Those French-named entrees would have really made him feel like an alien if it weren't for the plain English descriptions that followed. Not that he hadn't gone fancy a time or two, but he didn't think chicken stew would taste any better because it was called *coq au vin* or vegetables go down any easier when they were called *ratatouille*. At least the filet mignon was a cut of beef he knew. And the prices...well, he was sure glad he'd be getting paid this week, because no way would he take a woman out, even if she was his boss, and not pay the bill. Especially a woman named McKenna. And yeah, pride was a bitch.

Not that he was intimidated by any of it. It would take a heap more than French words and astronomical prices to make him feel uncomfortable in his own skin. But he also wasn't someone who would pretend he ate like this every day. He didn't, and he didn't care who knew it.

"Can I get you something to drink? A bottle of wine?" the friendly waiter asked. At least people hadn't left their western neighborliness at the massive oak door that fronted the place.

Cody had already scoped out the list of microbeers. He ordered a Dry Dock.

"A bottle of Châteauneuf-du-Pape for the table,"

Cat chimed in. "I take it you'll be ordering beef." It wasn't really a question, and she hadn't waited for his answer. Was he that much of a stereotype? *Guess so.*

After the waiter scurried away, Cody snagged the wine list and scanned it for the wine she'd named. "Hell. That bottle of wine is more than I've paid for a meal." There went groceries for the week. What some people spent money on seemed more than just wasteful. It seemed sinful.

"I wanted to express my gratitude."

She didn't know it yet, but she wasn't paying. Of course, dressed as she was, he couldn't help but think of a few ways she could express gratitude that would be a lot more gratifying for them both.

"It's been over a week now," she continued. "But already I feel I'm learning a lot. Even though I've lived on a ranch most of my life, I never, ever realized all that went into raising a good cut of beef. Or how hard my father must have worked." At this last sentence her, brows drew in.

Cody settled the linen napkin on his lap and rested his elbows on the table. "Ranching is hard work. But people generally think about the physical labor. They don't realize all the variables you have to factor in, plan for, and navigate. Much you can't control, like the weather and the topography, but a lot of it you can. Like what grass to plant, how to rotate the cattle, how to use and replenish the land to maximum benefit, assure adequate water, stock the right breed for the climate and the land, hire the right ranch hands."

She really was a beautiful woman. A stunner, his father would have said. And tonight sitting across from him, looking like the princess she was, it was hard not to fantasize that they were together…in the biblical sense.

He gave a mental shake. He needed to focus. They were here on business. Though he thought it unusual she had wanted to discuss it over dinner. At the Granville House.

He'd taken a long shower to assure every trace of cow and manure was erased. He'd even slapped on some of Jace's aftershave, though he didn't usually go for the stuff.

The waiter came back with a small basket of bread in addition to the bottle of wine, and a glass, not a bottle, of beer. After pouring some wine for each of them, the waiter took their orders with comfortable efficiency and exited, leaving Cody to stare into a pair of whiskey-colored eyes that caught the candlelight and left him feeling a hunger that had nothing to do with food. If he wasn't careful, he'd lose himself in those eyes. And then she'd know what he'd really like to do—and it wasn't talking cattle over dinner.

The thin gold bracelet on her arm sparkled under the candlelight as she slathered butter on a piece of bread, her fingers long and elegant and clearly not used to the punishing work of ranching.

What would happen if she knew he was thinking about undressing her and leaving her in nothing but those stiletto heels that made her legs look like they went on forever? That he'd like to stand her up against the wall, wrap her legs around his waist, and ease on in? Princess or not.

"So did you finish up the count?"

The question snapped that image into oblivion. Because he had finished the count. And the result was

116

not good. Neither were his suspicions as to the reasons. Suspicions he'd have to keep from her until he was sure.

Cat didn't like the way Cody's brow furrowed or expression hardened. For a brief moment it seemed he'd eyed her like she was the filet mignon he'd ordered for dinner, feeding her fragile ego, and now he looked ready to wrestle someone to the ground. The news couldn't be good.

She took a bite of bread as she mentally prepared for his news.

"I went out today just to double-check, but there's no getting around it. You've lost one hundred thirty-eight head."

Considering they could fetch up to seven hundred dollars a head even with lower prices for cattle these days, that was big money. She felt her stomach churn, and just like that, her appetite disappeared.

"How? Why?"

He shrugged, but his tense body and narrowed eyes looked anything but casual. "That's what I've got to find out."

Cat sat back in her chair and closed her eyes. "Already I've ruined Pleasant Valley. Dad hasn't been gone six months. He knew I'd be a failure. I've proved it in record time." She could feel nausea hollowing out her belly. She took a gulp of wine, hoping it would settle her stomach and relax her nerves.

"Cat, look at me." Cody's voice rumbled the command.

She didn't want to, but she opened her eyes. Concern stared back at her.

"I don't know what is going on, but I am certain you aren't to blame for this."

"But I didn't move the stock. Didn't rotate on time. They all have the scours, it seems. Birthing didn't go well…" She could have gone on, but he cut her short.

"Even given all that, the number is too high for it to be birthing and scours issues alone, even if that is what it says in the count book. Hell, your whole herd should be infected at these rates, and it isn't. And if you lost so many in birthing, why don't you have more orphans or more cows without calves? Doesn't make sense that they would go out in near equal numbers."

His Adam's apple bobbed as he tipped the glass of beer to his lips.

"What, then?" She wished he would wrap his arms around her and make all this go away.

He set the drink on the table, his strong fingers fondling the glass in an absentminded fashion.

"I'm going to find out. That's why you brought me here. That's part of what you pay me to do."

And then it dawned on her. "Rustlers?" She took another gulp of wine.

He shook his head, a little too quickly. "I don't know. But I will find out. And sooner rather than later."

"Shouldn't we call law enforcement?"

His thumb stroked the smooth surface of the glass, up and down. His silver watchband gleamed in the candlelight. He had big hands, strong and rugged.

"I don't have anything to show them, and mostly, they can't be bothered. I hate to break it to you, but since time immemorial, ranchers have pretty much been on their own when it comes to rustlers. Only nowadays, once we catch them, we turn them over to the law rather than hang them. I'm not sure that's progress."

He winked, and her body felt like a blow torch brushed it.

"Going after rustlers is dangerous," she said. To cool down, she took another large gulp of wine, draining the glass. The dry grape taste left her wanting more.

The ranch was so large, it would be easy for anyone to come onto the property unobserved if he were up to no good.

A sheen of moisture appeared on Cody's lips after he took another sip of beer. Setting the glass down on the table, his thumb resumed its hypnotic stroking. "I'm going to search for evidence. Once I find it, we can decide what to do next. I'm not looking to get my head blown off, but I'll be damned if I'll let someone steal their way to an income."

The wine seemed to settle her nerves, and she poured more before the waiter could. By the time her dinner came, she started alternating forkfuls of food with sips of wine as Cody threw a ton of numbers at her. He showed her several spreadsheets and some study done in Nebraska on changing to a more natural grazing and breeding program. Dancing before her as she sipped her wine were per cow, calf, and yearling numbers on hay, purchased feed, grazing days, feeding labor, calving labor, pregnancy rates, weaning rates, ADG rates from wean to grass, feedlot, and slaughter weights. Numerals swirled in her head like leaves caught in a whirlwind. He insisted the numbers bore out the conclusion that moving the calving date would make them more money despite the timing issues of cows coming into estrus, the cost to winter over yearlings, and the uncertainty of the weather.

The thought of changing things up, however, started her stomach churning again, and she left half her meal on the plate.

She'd already made a mess of the ranch. What if this didn't work? After all, her father had never made the change. There had to be a reason he hadn't. And she had people depending on her, workers and family. The McKennas had wealth, but much of it was tied up in the land, invested in the ranch, or in saved in accounts intended for the future, her son's future. Payroll and expenses had to be met out of the proceeds from the ranching operation.

No longer interested in her meal, she begged off dessert and sat back to wait for Cody to finish.

She was glad she had ordered the wine. She was feeling more relaxed, although Cody had stuck mostly to his beer, having taken just a few sips of the wine. But he seemed to enjoy his steak, only complaining that it was an awfully small portion. He'd made up for it with a piece of flourless chocolate cake.

He seemed as comfortable in the upscale restaurant as he did in the barns, and she admired him for that. The only place she felt comfortable was in a classroom full of children. Cody Taylor was the genuine article. If only she could claim the same.

"What's your decision driver?" Cody asked as the waiter set the check, encased in a leather folder, next to him on the table.

"I don't know." The effects of the wine were

kicking in. Why had she drunk practically the whole bottle? She was feeling light headed just when she needed to be clear headed.

Leaning to the left, Cody pulled out his wallet. "You need to define that, or you won't be able to make a decision. What are the main factors?"

"I just learned that we've incurred almost $100,000 in cattle losses, and you're asking me to accept that moving this date is going to give me higher weight calves or yearlings, or whatever you call them, even if the pregnancy rates slip and the weaning weight goes down? It's a lot to take in." She felt off balance. Definitely the wine.

"So it's purely money that drives your decisions." The disdain in his voice was unmistakable.

"Not totally, but the ranch needs to make a profit."

He took a look at the bill and frowned before he slipped a credit card into the leather folder, only it wasn't the ranch's credit card.

"What are you doing? Where's the ranch credit card?" she asked, afraid he had lost it.

"In my wallet, where it will remain. I don't take out a woman, even if she is my boss, and make her pay for both our meals. Call me old-fashioned, but that's me."

"I wouldn't have ordered that wine if I thought the ranch wasn't paying." Cat felt horrible. She could only imagine the price of the check. "I can't let you pay. I invited you."

"And I accepted. And I knew under what terms I was accepting."

"Terms you decided without consulting me." She

tried to focus, but she could feel herself drifting. She'd obviously had too much to drink.

The waiter scooped up the folder with his credit card. She wanted to call him back, but she didn't want to risk a scene, and she hadn't brought her own credit cards with her, secure in the knowledge that she had already taken care of the matter. Only she hadn't.

"I will give you the money in the morning. How much was it?" She was embarrassed at her extravagance in ordering the wine, which she had meant as a friendly gesture and which now sank the Taylors only deeper in debt. All for his stubborn pride. But she couldn't deny that something inside of her felt a little happy at his gallantry. However shortsighted.

Cody shook his stubborn head. "Not telling and not taking. Now as to the ranch making money, what about those oil wells on your property and the hunting parties you host in the fall?" Out of the corner of her eye, Cat spotted a young blonde, someone she recognized, headed toward her and Cody, though the image was a tad blurry.

"Your lawyer is here," Cat managed to get out right before the woman stopped at the table. And turned her back on Cat to face Cody.

"Cody, I didn't expect to see you here. And certainly not with her." Arms crossed, the woman directed her statement, and her whole body, at Cody. Dressed in a black suit with a subdued print blouse, the lawyer had undoubtedly come straight from work. Cody's lawyer looked like one of those California blondes—bleached, buoyant, and beautiful.

"Melissa, you remember Cat McKenna," Cody said and drained his glass of beer.

"I'm hardly likely to forget," Melissa said as she glanced back at Cat. "Ms. McKenna."

"Ms. Meyers."

Melissa returned her focus to Cody and waited for the explanation.

Cody cleared his throat. "I'm working for Pleasant Valley at the moment. Earning some extra money."

"I told you…"

Cody held up his hand to stop her and shifted in his seat. "If you want to talk about it another time, we can."

Melissa exhaled a huffy breath. "Call me, then?" With a clipped nod toward Cat, she turned and strode toward a man with glasses who stood near the exit. He looked to be in his thirties and was dressed in a dark suit, as if he too had come from some white-collar job.

Now she wondered if there had been, or was, anything between Cody and his pretty young lawyer. The thought rankled.

"Now about those wells." Cody wiped his mouth with the cloth napkin and set it on the table. A five o'clock shadow outlined his strong jaw, and he looked more handsome than usual…and that was pretty handsome.

"Those wells are played out," she said, trying to stay focused, though the effects of the wine combined with Melissa's visit were making that difficult. "And hunting parties are not bankable income." A hiccup rose in her throat. "Dad always made sure"…hiccup…"the ranch made money, regardless. With the losses and these changes you're proposing"… hiccup…"you'll assure that my first year running things, I'll lose money"…

hiccup…"a lot of it." *I'll be failing.* She hiccupped again. Cat took a deep breath and held it.

"You okay?" Cody was actually laughing.

She nodded. She may have lost her dignity at the moment, but she wasn't about to lose the ranch…not yet anyway.

"It's not losing if it will make you more money in the coming years. That's called an investment, Princess."

Cody just didn't get it. Did he "get" Melissa? He called Cat a princess, and yet Melissa seemed just as princessy. Was that even a word?

She exhaled and hesitated to be sure the hiccups were gone.

No more hiccups. But always more decisions.

"You said yourself the move to later calving may cost you the Cross T because of unforeseen circumstances. What if we have a drought? Heavy snows? I'm not willing to risk it. Not this year."

His face was expressionless, but there was a hard line to his jaw as he picked up the wine bottle and nodded toward her glass. She shook her head. She'd already had too much. He poured the last of the wine into his glass and took a big gulp.

He may not like her answer, but it was her ranch, or more accurately, Jake's ranch.

"Guess you just made your decision."

"Guess I have." She felt relieved actually, even as the room seemed to tilt.

"Not much of a vote of confidence in your new ramrod. But you're the boss."

Cat took a deep breath. There went the evening.

The silence inside Cody's battered truck weighed heavy on him. He'd put in a lot of time working out the numbers to see if moving out the birthing date would be good for the enterprise, and his analysis proved it would be. And she'd said no. Not because she'd found errors in his analysis. Not on the merits of his argument. But because she was either too scared to make the decision or didn't trust him. Either way, it didn't say much for Ms. McKenna or him.

And why did it matter?

He shouldn't give a rat's tail what happened at Pleasant Valley. By the time any plan to change the breeding schedule showed results, he'd be back on the Cross T.

He shifted the truck into fourth gear. Maybe he was just standing on useless pride. Being right didn't mean squat if the other person didn't have confidence in you. And it was clear that Cat McKenna had a long way to go before she had confidence in him. He shouldn't be surprised by that.

But he was.

They still hadn't said a word to each other when he pulled into her half-moon driveway and parked in front of the house's stone steps. Cat reached for the door handle, probably anxious to put distance between them.

"Wait. I'll help you," he said, jumping out of the cab. His mother had taught him manners, after all.

With a few long strides, he was around to her side. Pulling open the door, he reached for her and firmly wrapped his fingers around her wrist. She stepped down, landing close, very close, to him. So close he could feel the heat of her body and smell the fragrance of her floral scent. So close he could see the glint in her eyes from the house lights as she looked up at him with something akin to…desire. He'd dated enough women to recognize that look.

Question was, what *should* he do about it versus what he wanted to do about it?

She pulled her hand from his grasp, relieving him of answering that question. Turning, she moved up the steps with an unbalanced, wobbly stride. Before he could caution her, she stumbled. His hands grabbed her from behind as she fell back against him.

She huffed as she twisted in his arms to confront him face to face, body to body. But this time when she looked at him, what she wanted was evident. She wanted him.

Hell.

Without hesitation, she wrapped her arms around his neck and rubbed her body against his. In a breath, she locked her warm lips to his and pressed against him so he could feel every curve, every angle, and she had nice ones. Like a spark igniting dry brush, a three-alarm blaze erupted within him, flames licking against his insides.

He'd had a burr under his saddle for Cat McKenna since high school. One he thought was removed when she left for college. Apparently not.

Her fingers traveled up the back of his neck and ran through his hair. As she deepened the kiss, the moan from deep in her throat almost brought him to his knees. It was as if she couldn't get enough of him. She opened her mouth wide, and he slipped his tongue inside. She tasted like wine, felt like silk, and he lost himself in the moment. Lost himself in the feel, the taste of her.

He'd waited years to kiss Cat McKenna. From the first time he'd met her in high school coming down the hall, he'd wanted to taste her. But she was a McKenna and off limits. And then that evening when he'd found her camped out on some friend's ranch, looking like bait in a sea of sharks, he'd wanted more from her. Even though he knew it could never happen.

His hand traveled to cup her soft breast, and his thumb brushed across her hard nipple. She leaned into him, kissing him as if she wanted to devour him. This was the closest thing to sex he'd had in a long time, and every part of his being wanted to be devoured. By her.

His body was at attention, while his mind was in free fall.

He had to stop.

She kissed him like a woman who wanted hot sex, and with a frenzy that had him wanting to give it to her.

But she was likely drunk, and he was taking advantage. Of his boss. His McKenna boss.

He pulled back, broke the kiss. Looked at her. The light from the overhead porch lamp cast a shadow over her brow, but it didn't hide the glow and the hallelujah smile that spread across her face. Damn.

She didn't move from his arms.

Not that he wanted her to move, but reality was, they'd crossed the imaginary line that had kept McKennas from Taylors and bosses from subordinates, and he'd done it knowing she wasn't sober.

He was a better man than that. Maybe.

"Time to go in," he whispered against her ear.

Turning her toward the stairs, he placed his hand at her back to guide her up the steps.

Without protest, she climbed, her steps a little wobbly.

Reaching the stoop, she fumbled in her small purse for her key, finally producing it. He took it from her hand, put it in the lock, and turned it.

"I enjoyed that," she said, looking up at him as if she wanted more of the same.

So did he, but he needed to squash those feelings with the force of a bug hitting a car grille at eighty miles per hour.

"Come morning, I hope you still feel the same." Only she wouldn't. And he would.

She blinked at him like she didn't understand. "Stay," she breathed.

She was tempting, all shiny silk and smooth flesh. It wouldn't take much to push her inside and have at it in the study. But he wasn't that guy, however much his body urged him to be.

He leaned over and brushed his lips against her warm forehead. Then he pushed the front door open and walked back down the steps.

"No regrets, Cat," he called back, even though he already had them.

Chapter 8

Cat hid the next day. She insisted on taking Jake to preschool so she wouldn't be around in the early morning. After dropping Jake off, she'd run some errands, none of which were essential but would keep her away from the ranch. She'd run into Cyndi Lynn Spencer who, having recently separated from her husband, reiterated she was anxious to go out on the town with Cat. She suggested this coming weekend, and Cat agreed.

She had to do something after throwing herself at Cody the night before. The memory of their kiss burned through her like fire following a trail of gasoline. She'd obviously been out of commission too long, and just being with a man had her losing her mind. And control.

She'd woken up that morning with a throbbing head that felt like it had been overstuffed with cotton balls. Yet her memory of the night before had been all too clear.

As was the fact he had kissed her back. At least initially.

She managed to avoid seeing him the rest of the day by sending word she needed to get some paperwork done. A lame excuse she was sure Cody had seen right through. Then she called the two friends she cherished most in this world and cajoled them into meeting her for dinner at the café where they held their monthly get-togethers to catch up on one another's lives.

This wasn't the day scheduled for their monthly dinners, but her girlfriends had come anyway, for which she was grateful.

Cat slid into the café booth across from Mandy Martin and Libby Cochran. Both had married the loves of their lives. Libby was the proud mother of a seven-month-old baby boy named Shane, and Mandy was due in about six weeks, although looking at the size of Mandy's belly as it rubbed against the edge of the table, Cat wouldn't be surprised if it was sooner.

"How are you feeling, Mandy?" Cat asked as she took a menu from her friend's hand. Mandy looked the picture of mother-to-be health, with a rosy glow to her complexion and a shine in her green eyes. Long brown hair waved down her back. She wore a blousy top, one Cat had seen on Libby not too long ago, maternity jeans, and a pair of embossed leather cowgirl boots, one of many from Mandy's ever-expanding collection. Hopefully, her feet wouldn't grow due to her pregnancy, or Mandy would have a storeful of cowgirl boots to get rid of.

"Good, except this baby seems to be a night owl, keeping me up half the night." Mandy rubbed a protective hand across her stomach. "We're coming into full-on rodeo season in a few weeks, and I could certainly use a good night's sleep."

Mandy headed up her family's rodeo stock

company, and the struggle to lead the business after her grandfather died had led to fighting the man who would become her husband. Their romance could have been a novel, what with all the twists and turns they went through before they found their happily ever after.

"And how's little Shane doing? I half expected to see him tonight," Cat said to Libby.

Libby had gotten her figure back in record time, a situation she credited to breast feeding in the early months. Cat had breast fed Jake, but it had still taken her a good year to get down to her prepregnancy size. But there Libby sat in form-flattering jeans and a cotton T-shirt, looking more like nineteen than her twenty-five years.

"Shane's growing like a weed. Dad and Chance are watching him. With things slow on the circuit this month, it's been nice having Chance at home for more than a day or two," Libby said, brushing a lock of her blond chin-length hair behind her ear. Libby's husband, Chance, was a star saddle bronc rider to whom Libby had been married *and divorced* when she was a teenager. The fact they had found each other again was nothing short of a romantic miracle.

"Now tell us what couldn't wait until our regular monthly dinner?" Mandy said, giving Cat an *I know something's up* look.

Cat had been friends with Mandy since they'd competed in county fairs, and they'd been supporting each other through everything from fairground competitions, to the unexpected death of Mandy's father, to Cat's relationship with Jake's father, and much, much more. Mandy had introduced Cat to Libby after Libby had interviewed for a public relations job at a rodeo where Mandy was representing the suppliers' interest, and the women realized they had a lot in common. They'd been meeting once a month ever since.

A perky waitress who had tied her brown hair up in a bun came to take their orders. She wasn't their regular waitress, so the friends had to actually voice their menu choices instead of saying "the usual." Once they ordered, Libby and Mandy stared at Cat, arms crossed and *spill the beans* looks in their eyes.

"I think I may have done something horrible."

"What?" Libby asked as she pulled her cell phone from her purse and placed it on the table in plain sight.

"I've hired Cody Taylor to work for me," Cat blurted out.

Libby's mouth dropped open, and Mandy fell back against the padded booth. It took a moment for either of them to speak, while the din of the café's diners buzzed in Cat's ear.

"Well," Libby finally said. "That's a surprise, a shock really, especially after you told us you won your court battle. But it's not horrible. Horrible is when you kill someone, not hire someone."

"My question is," Mandy began, leaning forward now and looking Cat straight in the eye, "what in heaven possessed you? Your daddy must be…"

"Turning over in his grave, right?"

"Well, yes." Mandy didn't mince words.

Cat shook her head in resignation. "I need help. Cody needs money. He wouldn't have done it otherwise, because his poor father is definitely going end over end in his grave."

"I'd heard that Zeke Taylor had passed. I don't

know what is happening. We seem to be losing the older generation before their time." Mandy had lost her father over a decade ago in a car accident and lost her grandfather a year ago.

"Just because both your fathers, who are no longer with us, might object to helping out each other, doesn't mean it's horrible. Just unexpected." Libby always looked on the bright side.

The waitress set down two glasses of cola and a decaf coffee and then wandered over to the next table without a word. This night none of the women had shown an interest in the craft beer menu the café was known for. Libby was a mother now, Mandy was going to be, and, after last night, Cat had no desire for alcohol.

Cat looked from Libby to Mandy, screwed up her courage, and took a deep breath. "I find myself..." This was tough to admit. "I find myself..."

"Attracted to him?" Mandy had the nerve to smile. She'd known all about Cat's high school crush on Cody. "That isn't news, and certainly not something to be upset about. You're human. He's a good-looking guy."

Libby patted Cat's hand. "I'm guessing working with him isn't helping."

"Question is, what do you want to do about it? Fight it or give in?" Mandy typically got to the point.

"Fight it, of course. But now I'm working with him every day. Part of our bargain is he has to teach me the ins and outs of running the ranch, so there is no ignoring him. And believe me—I've tried." Cat took a slug of soda, enjoying the carbonated sweetness. It may not be good for you, but sometimes you just craved a taste.

Three hamburger platters piled with french fries

were set before them. Conversation was suspended until the waitress set the ketchup on the table and asked if they wanted anything else. They all answered no, and the waitress turned on her heel to take care of the next customer.

"Guess your brain got hijacked by those pheronomes, or whatever they are called," Libby said.

"Pheromones. It must have. I was trying to do a nice thing. I figured it would be a win-win for both of us. I didn't count on..."

"Did something particular happen?" Mandy asked, stirring her decaf coffee filled to the brim with cream and sugar.

Mandy sniffed out secrets better than anyone. There was nothing to do but confess. Cat took a deep breath.

"I let him kiss me."

Libby gasped. "Already?"

"Actually, I'm pretty sure I initiated it." Confessing felt like a huge boulder had been lifted from her chest. "And I liked it. Too much."

"Well, God did a good job of making sure we'd be attracted to the opposite sex so we'd procreate," Mandy said. "I mean, look who I ended up with—my sworn enemy!"

"He was also your first crush," Cat pointed out.

Mandy shook her head. "It was complicated, just like your feelings for Cody."

"Only there is no way it can end well with Cody Taylor, for so many reasons. What am I going to do?" Cat wanted to let out a wail.

"Don't ask me," Libby said. "I'm the last one to give relationship advice."

Mandy leaned forward. "If the fact he's a Taylor hasn't turned off your motor, I'm not sure what could. Does the fact you're a McKenna clog his carburetor?"

Cat fiddled with her fork. "He kissed me back. At least at first."

"Maybe that was just an impulsive reaction," Mandy opined.

"And then he pulled back as if he realized who he was kissing." Cat laid the fork down. Unfortunately, she hadn't been drunk enough to forget that moment. Or the humiliation. "I may have asked him to stay." She could feel her cheeks flush.

Mandy glanced sidelong at Libby before speaking. "Did he?"

Cat shook her head. "But he told me no regrets. I wasn't sure if I wasn't to have any or he didn't have any. I may have been a little bit inebriated." She took a bite of burger, hoping the familiar charcoal taste would distract her from the little tingle that went through her body as she remembered being in his arms, feeling his hard body next to hers, enjoying his kiss. She might have had a little too much to drink, but she'd been fully in that moment...and enjoying it.

"Was this a date?" Mandy asked.

"Not exactly. It was a business dinner. But it...well, I may have pretended to myself that it was a date. It has been so long since I've dressed up for a man." She sipped her drink. "He insisted on paying though, so I'm not sure what it was, to tell you the truth."

"What do you want it to be?" Libby had almost finished her burger but hadn't touched her fries. Maybe that was why she was so darn thin.

"As much as I am attracted to him, I cannot afford a casual affair with anyone, and certainly not my employee, not a Taylor, and especially not a guy who loves 'em and leaves 'em. Been there. Done that." Having polished off the rest of her burger, Cat reached for a fry.

"You could always fire him," Mandy said. "You are the boss. You don't have to give him a reason."

"He has actually been helpful. Not only am I learning a lot from him, but we've been losing an inordinate amount of cattle, and he's got some ideas as to why. I think I need him." Although how she was going to face him, she didn't know. She stabbed several fries with her fork.

"Maybe you're just attracted because you're a lady in distress and he's you're knight in shiny armor," offered Libby, the romantic one.

"That still leaves me attracted to him." Or maybe she was just horny.

Libby sighed. "Then you'll have to be strong, although believe me, I know as well as anyone how difficult that can be. I had such good intentions regarding resisting Chance, and look what happened." Libby's face positively glowed with her beaming smile.

"And I'm hardly one to give advice on resisting someone," Mandy chimed in. "Maybe, instead, you should explore the possibilities. It might be good for you."

Had Mandy lost her mind? Although the thought of exploring things with Cody Taylor warmed her from the inside out. Having finished her own fries, Cat snagged one from Libby's untouched pile. "I'm in no position to explore anything. And what if it got serious?"

"If it's the Cody Taylor I remember from your high school days, you won't have to worry about it getting serious. Didn't he date just about every girl in your class?" The mother-to-be, having cleaned her plate, also took a fry from Libby's.

Cody Taylor had run through the girls in her high school like he was thumbing through a directory. Which was why he was bad news for her. In so many ways.

Mandy leaned forward. "How long has it been, Cat?"

Mandy knew exactly how long it had been.

Libby patted Cat's hand. "It might do you some good. You might not be so susceptible to a man's kiss if you...you know."

"I can't believe what I'm hearing." She'd come for advice, but not this advice.

Mandy snagged a whole forkful of fries from Libby's nearly empty plate. She was pregnant, after all. "The fact he's a Taylor means it is unlikely you will feel like taking it further after...you know. And the fact he's Cody Taylor means he won't want to take it further."

Cat folded her arms across her chest. "I'm going out with Cyndi Lynn Spencer this weekend. Her divorce is going to be final, and she wants to go to Laramie, where we won't see anyone we know."

"For mindless sex?" Mandy's smile was almost feline.

"No!" Cat took a deep breath. "To find a guy. A nice guy to date. There has to be at least one such creature still left in Wyoming."

Chapter 9

Cat knew it would be impossible to avoid Cody for more than twenty-four hours, even though she spent the following morning in the study trying to figure out the new ranch management program she had downloaded that morning based on his recommendation. And Cody hadn't come by. She'd wanted to ask him several questions on its use, but she'd deciphered it on her own via the help screens. Definitely safer that way, and besides, she needed time to figure out what she would say.

She'd been practicing all morning and most of yesterday. Should she apologize for kissing him? She was definitely wrong to cross the line between boss and employee—people in corporations got fired for what she had done. But he hadn't exactly fought her off either.

Cat leaned back in her dad's office chair and touched her lips, remembering the ferocity with which he devoured her mouth and made her want more. That kiss had started out gentle on her part, but it had quickly escalated, and she had lost her mind, literally.

The thought brought heat to her cheeks and made her shudder. *Stay.* Kissing him had awoken every female part of her body, and now none of those parts were ready to go dormant again.

And yet he had walked away. Kissed her on the forehead like a brother and taken his leave. *No regrets.* Her or him? She had a ton, but she suspected he had none. Despite the fact she had initiated the kiss, he had been in control. In control of his feelings, his responses, his actions. While she had been totally out of control.

She'd just have to confess—she'd made a mistake, crossed a line, and she would have to live with the consequences. One of which was she had to start dating so this type of impulsive behavior didn't happen again. It was beyond time, and the lack of any man in her life was undoubtedly responsible for her attacking the first man who had paid her the teeniest bit of attention. She was tired of being on the shelf, afraid she was going to pass right by her expiration date.

Only finding a man, a good man, was not all that easy. And where to look in a rural county where the single male population was already well known to the single female population—and familiarity wasn't always a good thing.

It didn't help that the only man who flamed her fire in the last four years was a tall, lean player cowboy whose last name was Taylor and who thought she was some high-maintenance princess, despite all the hard work she was putting in. It reminded her too much of a father that diminished her accomplishments and never valued her efforts, and a lover who hadn't really loved her.

She didn't want a man like that. She didn't want a

man who was commitment phobic and just looking for a good time. She didn't want a man like Jake's father, who had played her for a fool. She'd been naïve then. She'd have no excuse now.

At the sound of the knock, she thought about running and hiding, but her conscience told her to answer it.

As drops from a spring sun shower pelted the porch roof, Cody removed his damp hat and waited for someone to answer the door as the smell of fresh, wet earth and rinsed air filled his nostrils.

She'd avoided him yesterday, no doubt embarrassed by her behavior, but he could assure her she should not be the least embarrassed. That kiss she'd planted on him had opened up some possibilities that, until now, he'd rejected. She knew as well as he did that there could never be anything permanent between them, based on their last names and circumstances. She was a ranch princess. He was a working cowboy. She was well off and land rich. He was in debt and land poor. But the spark between them had ignited an inferno of lust that had spread through him with the speed of a dry timber fire. That she initiated that kiss meant she was anxious to explore possibilities too, didn't it?

It had been a long time since he had felt something that intense. That sexual. And it had taken willpower not to crush her against the door and take what she had been offering. Ever since then he'd been fantasizing about her. About kissing her, holding her, undressing her, and... He combed his fingers through his hair. In fact, he hadn't been able to think of anything else.

Usually he was good at compartmentalizing. He'd gotten real good at it over the last year. Real good at not thinking about debts and disease and death until forced to. Real good at focusing on the moment and what cow he had to doctor, what fence he had to mend, and what step he had to take to get through the day. Real good at not thinking about any woman, not thinking about sex, not thinking about the release that would let him know he was still alive. Real good at denying he was still a man with needs and desires, a man who loved a woman's soft skin, gentle touch, and warm body.

But one kiss from Cat McKenna and it came back harder and stronger than ever.

Would she be open to a mutually satisfying relationship? Because he could guarantee that it would be. And nothing to fear that it would amount to anything. She would never consider someone like him, and given his financial situation, he couldn't consider her, even if she was his perfect match. And she was far from that.

She had to be as frustrated as he was, since she was stuck on the ranch day after day and their one-traffic-light town didn't afford much beyond the supply store, a mom-and-pop grocery, a drugstore, an ATM machine, a western-themed memorabilia shop, and the café on the highway out of town. The county seat wasn't much better. You pretty much had to go to Laramie, an hour away, for anything resembling nightlife.

The shower was a passing one, already diminishing to a soft patter.

He was glad it was stopping, as his plan was to take Cat out into the pastures and teach her about moving cattle, a basic need for anyone who worked a ranch. It would give them ample opportunity to clarify things.

It amazed him that someone could own all these beautiful acres and not appreciate what she had. He tapped the knocker against the door again. Now or never.

Seated on Custer, Cat pulled up alongside Cody and surveyed the small herd that grazed nearby.

"I brought you out here so you can learn about herding." Cody was riding his own horse, the paint he'd been riding that day at the creek. He'd trailered the horse to her ranch and had already set the gelding up with a stall in Cat's barn. Apparently Pleasant Valley horses weren't good enough for him. He'd also brought the tricolored border collie. The dog he called Mikey now sat at the side of Cody's horse like a soldier on duty.

She had almost forgotten the pleasures of riding. Being outside and enjoying the peace of wide meadows and gentle breezes—at least if the weather was good.

Though she'd been dreading the encounter, so far he hadn't brought up their kiss. When she'd opened the door and he'd stood there, hat in hand, his hair tousled, his jacket damp, and his jeans clinging to his legs and cupping his groin, she'd felt a surge go through her like lightning hitting a wire, though his bland expression gave away nothing. He informed her, in the same authoritarian tone he'd always used, that she would be working the range today and should be ready to mount up in an hour. After she'd closed the door, she stood for a moment and fought the urge to run away from her mistakes. Instead, she'd closed out the management program on her computer and headed upstairs to change into the kind of attire he would consider appropriate: jeans, a T-shirt, and her new pair of sturdy barn boots.

Mounted on her horse, she'd straggled behind him most of the way out to the pasture so there would be little opportunity for conversation, all the time worried he would rein in his horse, as he had now, and ask her what the hell she'd been thinking the other night. With the sun shining high in the dense blue sky, the mountains framing the far reaches of the ranch, the grass high and plentiful, she could almost forget she had planted a kiss on his lips, pressed her body against his hard one, and asked him to stay.

Cody stared back at her now, the sunglasses doing a good job of obstructing her ability to read his face. In her ear she could feel the pulsing of her blood. Maybe this was it. The moment she would have to confess that she had been an idiot.

He removed his glasses as if to get a better look at her. Confronted with his scrutiny, the embarrassment from her earlier behavior bloomed inside her.

Maybe she should bring it up now. First. Apologize. Blame the booze.

"What do you see today that is different from the other day, Princess?" He turned away from her and swept his gaze from edge to field edge.

She was certain he didn't mean *princess* as a compliment, but today she could ignore it if he was willing to ignore last night.

She looked over the pasture dotted with cattle. All were grazing peacefully. They looked content, like stereotypical cows.

"They are all grazing. None are lying down yet. They are loosely bunched together."

He sat his horse so comfortably, effortlessly. He looked like he'd been born to the saddle, and he had been. Strictly speaking, so had she. But for most of her life she'd run away from ranching. On a brilliant day like today, with a soft breeze off the mountains, a sky now clear and sunny, the fresh air scented with earth and grass, and temperatures in the sixties, she wondered why.

"And the calves?"

Twisting in her saddle to get a panoramic view, she scanned the herd. The calves stood by their mothers. Some nursed. All looked normal.

"No scours?"

"Do you know why, Princess?"

"We nursed them back to health?"

Cody had her take a rotation, just like every other cowboy, tending to the sick animals, and eventually new cases had ceased.

"Partially. The other part is pasture management. You left them too long in the birthing pasture. Herds need to rotate."

"That's a lesson I won't forget." She'd had to learn it the hard way instead of from her range foreman, who should have known.

"We need to move them again."

"But they haven't been branded."

"We can't wait for the calendar to work out. When it's time for branding, we'll herd them in. We don't want the pasture overgrazed. Remember the pasture scheme I showed you?"

She looked around. She didn't see any other hands in the pasture.

"Is someone coming to move them?"

"We're it. The hands have already moved the rest of the herd. We're moving what is left."

She swallowed. Hard. "Just you and me?"

"This is a small bunch. Not more than thirty. We can do it."

"On horseback?"

He chuckled. "I don't recommend getting off a horse when a herd is on the move. You've heard of stampedes, I'm guessing."

Stampedes?

"Shouldn't we have more cowboys then?"

"There may come a time when you have to move them yourself. You need to know how."

As he leaned on the saddle horn, Cody talked about a cow's security zone, warned against approaching them from behind where they couldn't see you, and pointed out that, once on the move, the side was the best place to be so you stayed in their peripheral vision. He was all business, and her fear that he might bring up their intimate moment dissipated.

If he was willing to ignore what had happened that night, so was she.

"We want a low-stress approach. The way to move cattle quickly is to take it slow," he summed up. "I'm going to scope out the leaders and gently pressure them to the open gate over there." He pointed to the gate leading to the new pasture. "Imagine a triangle, with the tip of that triangle at the gate and fanning out from there. That's the path we are going to try to get them to take."

"How?" She'd never herded cattle. She'd only *watched* the cowboys move them, from the safety of the sidelines.

"You are going to walk your horse side to side across the back here, like windshield wipers, slowly moving forward with each pass. I'm going to be at the far edge of their security zone up at the front. We are going to move them slowly, exerting just a little pressure to move them forward," he said. "Mikey here is a trained herding dog." He looked down at the dog.

Mikey's ears pricked up at the sound of his name.

"He will patrol the side border."

"What if one of them leaves the herd?"

"Good question, Princess. At this point, we are going to ignore the straggler. We aren't moving them far, just the next pasture, and this pasture is enclosed, so we don't have to worry about them getting away."

"Do I yell or whoop?" Wasn't that what they did in westerns?

He smiled. "Nothing but calm, quiet voices. The goal is to move them without panicking them."

Cat shook her head. "But I don't know anything about moving cattle." And she certainly wasn't ready to be tested.

"Hence the lesson, Princess." He straightened and tightened his rein. "I'm going to give the cattle a lot of room as I ride to the front. Mikey will follow me. Don't worry about him. He knows what to do. Just back and forth behind the cattle. I'll wave forward if I want you to come closer, and wave back if I want you to give them a wider berth. Just watch for my hand signals."

Before she could say another word, he was walking his horse in a wide sweep toward the gate. The cattle didn't pay him any mind.

She watched him as he rode. Watched his firm

butt. Watched his broad shoulders. He would make someone a fine husband if he ever decided to settle down. And given his reputation, it was a big if. Not that she'd heard talk lately of his exploits, but from whom would she hear them? Maybe she'd ask his old girlfriend, Cyndi Lynn, about him on the trip to Laramie.

Even if he was ready to settle down, what would it matter? She wasn't interested in him that way. He'd just been convenient the other night. She'd been starved for male companionship. She was seeking to remedy that. She just needed to get back out there so a man with long legs, dark hair, and a voice that made her want to crawl inside his clothes wouldn't faze her in the least.

She watched Mikey dutifully follow Cody. If she couldn't find a man, maybe she should get a dog. Dogs were loyal. Dogs were obedient. Dogs provided unconditional love. Her father never allowed dogs in the house, so she had never wanted one. Wyoming winters could be punishing, and she couldn't have stood to have a dog outside in freezing weather. But Jake would surely like one. Especially if he got a look at Mikey.

Once Cody was up ahead, he turned and looked back at her. She supposed that meant she should start to ride her horse back and forth. She nudged Custer into a walk, and they picked their way along the back of the herd. After her second pass, she looked toward Cody, and he waved her forward. She moved her horse a little closer, and as if there had been some signal, several in the herd began to mosey. Another pass and they were beginning to bunch together as they strolled forward.

A straggler munched grass, and she watched as Mikey trotted over toward the animal. The cow fell in line.

In the space of a few minutes, the lead cow reached the gate and passed through. The others followed, slowly, but they followed.

No fuss. No muss. Who knew?

As she marveled at the ease with which the herd moved, she heard the whir of an engine. A split second later an ATV topped the small hill in front of the old line shack, which sat at the edge of the new pasture near a copse of cottonwoods, and then headed toward the gate.

In that tentative moment, the cattle reacted. The dozen or so that hadn't yet headed through to the next pasture turned, as if programmed, and charged toward her, away from the sound. Focused on the oncoming herd, she heard the slam of the gate shutting and Cody yelling something over the din of hooves and engine.

Her mind clicked in. This was a stampede, and Cat was going to be in the thick of it. She had to get Custer away before the cows literally knocked the legs out from under him and Cat found herself on the ground. Heart pounding, adrenaline pumping, she kicked against Custer's sides. The horse lurched into a full-out gallop, and Cat headed the horse toward the pasture's edge and away from pounding hooves and wailing cattle.

She cleared the herd's path just as the line of cattle reached her, and she didn't rein in her horse until she arrived at the far side of the meadow. Behind her the engine ceased its noise, and all she heard were pounding hooves, Mikey barking, and lots of hollering.

From a safe distance Cat surveyed the damage. About a dozen head of cattle were scattering in her pasture as they came up on the barbed-wire fence that surrounded it. Cody had apparently been able to close the gate on the other dozen or so cows that had made it far enough into the new pasture to be captured there.

Cody was yelling at the ATV driver who, Cat was sure, was none other than Will Springer. She couldn't hear his words, but if tone accounted for anything, Cody was angrier than a bull that had been speared.

As Cody continued to yell, the ATV engine roared to life again, and rider and vehicle sped away, disappearing over the hill and out of sight.

The cattle in Cody's pasture milled around in a confused tangle of bodies. Cat watched as Cody trotted his horse to the gate, pulled the rope from over the post, and swung open the gate. Horse and rider moved through, Mikey following. Cody closed the gate from atop his horse and headed toward her.

She could see, even from some distance, the deep frown and utter disgust that rode his face. Mikey trotted behind, head down.

Horse, rider, and dog pulled up alongside of her. "You okay?" he asked as he leaned forward in the saddle, his brow furrowed.

"Other than being scared to death, you mean?"

The frown turned into a smile as he wiped a sleeve across his brow, his other hand holding the reins. "Yeah. That was pretty intense. But you had good instincts. Others might have tried to run with the herd, which is a recipe for disaster for your horse, and maybe you. Running to the side, out of the path, kept you both out of harm's way."

That almost sounded like a compliment.

"Was that Will?"

Cody nodded. His mouth pulled tight. "He could have caused real harm coming over the hill that way when he knew we were moving cattle."

"He knew?"

"Will had helped earlier when we moved the rest of the herd. I told him of my plan to have you help me move the remainder." Cody thumbed back the brim of his hat. Sweat dampened his brow. "If you ask me, that man is not only worthless, but a hazard."

Cat took a deep breath and hoped Cody wasn't about to ask her if he could fire Will. Despite what happened, Will had been working at Pleasant Valley long enough to deserve the benefit of the doubt and a second chance. Even though Will had been cool to her ever since she'd hired Cody as ranch manager, he still did his job, even if it wasn't all that well. He'd been used to taking orders from a man who knew how and what to order, and it had to be an adjustment to now work for the clueless daughter and her hired Taylor ramrod.

Cody turned his gaze to the cattle that had taken up residence at the far end of the pasture. They milled around, still agitated.

"I think we can leave these dozen or so cows, and I'll move them later. Give them time to calm down a bit. Let's head back." Cody tightened his reins, ready to bolt.

"You don't want to move them now?"

"It will take time for them to calm down. See how tight they're bunched. They don't trust the situation anymore."

"Shouldn't we wait and try to move them?"

He leaned back in the saddle, unbuttoning the cuffs of his shirt. He pushed the sleeves up to his elbows, revealing tanned forearms dusted with dark hair. The stainless-steel watch encircled his left wrist, and he checked it for the time. "Your son will be home from school soon. We'd better head back. There will be plenty of opportunities to move cattle."

She nodded, touched that he'd thought about Jake. She did like to be at the house when he got home from preschool. It was one of the benefits of working at home.

"Why that cussed man insists on ATVs, I don't know," Cody said, reining his horse around.

"You'd think the cattle would be used to them by now."

"They're okay with them as long as the damn things don't come out of nowhere and charge toward them. He claims he forgot we were moving cattle and was coming to check that the gate was closed."

Seemed reasonable. "You don't believe him?"

"I don't know what to think about Will Springer." He pursed his lips. "But you did pretty well, Princess."

"That sounds almost like praise."

The corner of his mouth twitched up. "Almost."

She felt like a child who had just won a trophy for a sport she'd been failing. A feeling she'd tuck away to pull out when she was alone. She'd actually done something right. On horseback and with cattle. She wondered what her father would have thought of his daughter, the one he so frequently discounted, working cattle.

A feeling akin to elation washed over her.

"That was kind of amazing," she said, watching the cattle as they milled.

"Now you know how to move a herd."

Was that a smile gracing his lips?

"I think I need to do it a few more times before I can make that claim. And without a stampede in the mix."

"You did better than I expected. For a princess anyway."

"A lot of people seem to have low expectations of me."

"Including you." He nudged his horse into a walk. "Why is that?"

She shaded her eyes, more to conceal her emotions than anything. "Years of being told what you can't do?"

They reached the gate leading to the range and home. Cody leaned over and unhooked the chain so they could pass through.

She nudged Custer. Horse and rider moved past Cody and through the gate. Mikey followed. Maybe that was why she'd shied away from anything to do with the ranch. It had been made clear to her from the beginning that ranching was not for her. But maybe it was. She'd never given it a fair shake. Now she had to.

Cody trotted his horse up beside her, looking like a cowboy model, with the brim of a Stetson shading his eyes, the breeze ruffling his shirt, and thighs wrapped around his horse. The memory of kissing him, how he'd held her, how he'd feasted on her mouth, how he'd kissed her neck and come back for more, caused her pulse to pick up and her belly to tingle. While she'd been working the herd, she hadn't thought about the other day and that inappropriate kiss.

Now was as good a time as any to clear the air. A dose of humility certainly would dispel the strange feeling that wrapped around her when Cody was near.

She took a deep breath and focused on the horizon. Cody's horse kept pace with hers. It might be a long ride back. "Cody, about the other evening."

She stole a glance in his direction. His eyebrows arched, and his expression held interest. Why did he have to be so handsome? Look so good?

"I...I was drunk and..." she said, hesitating as his brow furrowed. She had to just get it out. "I don't know what got into me. I'm sorry. It was a mistake. A huge one." She could feel the heat climbing her neck, and it wasn't from the sun.

He stared at her, and her pulse pounded.

Say something. Anything.

"Forget it." His tone was clipped and matter of fact. His knees nudged his horse, and before she knew it, horse and rider loped ahead.

That was what she wanted. She wanted him to forget it.

So why did she feel so deflated?

Chapter 10

"Hey, Jake," Cody called to the little tyke as Cody came out of the barn, Mikey at his heels. Jake was riding one of those pedal cars across hard-packed dirt still damp from the earlier rain.

"Hi, Mr. Taylor," Jake said as he stopped the car. "I'm waiting for mommy. We're going to ride my pony. Who's that?" Jake was up and out of the car, eager to meet his new four-legged friend.

Within a heartbeat, Jake had his arms wrapped around Mikey's neck and was hugging him as Mikey panted in place. Mikey was a good dog and would never harm a child, but Cody couldn't help wondering if Cat had taught her son to ask before petting a dog. It was just common sense.

Cody looked toward the house. *It was a mistake.*

Yeah, on both their parts.

Cody crouched down and focused on Jake. "This is Mikey."

"He's your dog?"

The awe in the little boy's voice tugged at him.

"Yep."

"I want a dog," he said matter of factly, not loosening his grip one iota on the animal.

A boy should have a dog. But the boy did have a pony. "You want to help me saddle your pony?"

The little boy released his grasp on Mikey and faced Cody. "Yes."

Cody rose and reached his hand down, and little Jake slipped his tiny one into Cody's. Something choked Cody's windpipe as he walked with the little guy. Something that pulled up a need Cody knew had always been there but had rarely seen the light of day. Something elemental and private and strong. The need for a family of his own. A child like Jake. A wife like…

In the barn, Cody saddled the pony while instructing Jake on everything he was doing. On how to loop the cinch, how to assure the pony hadn't bloated his belly, how to check that the saddle was on tight. Then he put on the bridle, instructing Jake in looping it over the ears and getting the bit between the teeth. The little guy gave Cody his rapt attention, though Cody doubted Jake would remember or understand much of it. Still, it distracted Cody from thinking about Jake's mother.

It was a mistake. She meant it. And it was probably for the good. After that kiss, he'd actually been thinking about asking her out. On a real date. Sure it had been more like fantasizing, but he'd found himself practicing lines. He'd just been ready to discuss a mutually beneficial arrangement when she'd launched into her apology.

That had snapped him out of it.

Once the pony was tacked up, Cody led the small horse out of the barn and toward the corral, Jake and Mikey following.

He glanced toward the house. No Cat.

He checked his watch—almost dinnertime.

"You sure your mother said she was coming out?"

Jake nodded. "Can I just sit on him?"

No harm in that, Cody guessed. "Let's do it in the corral." Cody opened the gate, and like a pied piper, Cody led the horse, Jake, and Mikey into the confines of the fence. Closing the gate and slipping the rope over the post, Cody moved the entourage toward the center of the pasture.

"Come here, partner." Cody picked up Jake, who was lighter than a bag of feed, and set him on the pony. "All you need is a hat, and you'll look like one of the cowboys," he said as he fitted Jake's feet into the stirrups. "Hold on to the horn."

If Cody had a son, he'd be riding by himself already. Growing up on a ranch, the first thing a father taught his son or daughter was how to ride. Heck, his mother had pictures of him riding in front of his father as young as a year.

Cody glanced at the house. Still no sign of Cat.

"I'll take you around," he said.

Jake's smile was all the reward he needed. With his hand holding Jake's leg and his other holding the pony's rein, he walked the pony around the corral, while Mikey sat in the middle of the corral, on guard and no doubt tired from his herding chores.

Cody had ridden at a gallop the whole way back from working the herd. He'd had the saddle off and his horse rubbed down and turned out to pasture by the time Cat had ambled in on Custer. Still feeling the burn of her remark, he'd left her to do her own horse and gone to check on one of the hands who had just finished setting up the fencing that would partition the branding pasture.

He'd been trying to "forget it." Only he wasn't making much progress.

"What are you doing!" The words were said in a loud shriek by a voice he recognized.

Turning toward the sound, he saw Cat crawling through the fence railings.

"Jake wanted a ride. Said you were coming. Thought I'd entertain him in the meantime."

Cat looked wild eyed as she stomped toward him. "He's not allowed to ride his pony with anyone but me. And certainly not without a helmet."

A helmet? "You've got to be kidding me," Cody said. "What kid wears a helmet?"

She stood there with her hands on her hips, her hair blowing with the evening breeze, and a scowl on her face. "Kids with mothers that care!"

She reached for Jake. Jake shook his head.

"I want to ride, Mommy. You promised."

Cat took a deep breath. "I said after dinner, Jake. Not now." Her tone was even, but Cody could see it was a struggle. With her eyes bright, her cheeks flushed, and the wind blowing her hair about her face and across a pair of tight pink lips, she looked worked up and damn attractive. He'd like to work her up...

"But Cody was walking me. We were enjoying ourselves."

Cody couldn't help but chuckle at the tyke's words.

Cat threw him a look that could sear fur off a hide.

She huffed. "Yes, well, we will enjoy ourselves too. After dinner." She reached for her son again, but Jake pulled back.

Cody had to admire the little guy's tenacity.

"Jake, it's time to go in. You can ride your pony later. With a helmet," she negotiated.

"I don't want to wear a helmet. I want a cowboy hat like Mr. Taylor's. I'm a cowboy."

Cat shifted her narrowed-eyed gaze to him. "See what you started."

This time Cody held back the laughter that bubbled at the back of his throat like the effervescence from a gulp of beer. She was as mad as a cow that had its calf taken away. He turned to Jake. "Jake, cowboys listen to their mothers. Always. After dinner, buddy." He reached toward the boy, and Jake, somewhat chastened, allowed Cody to lift him off.

Instead of setting Jake down, he held the boy in the crook of his arm and looked up at the cherub face. Something inside him turned on. Something needy and emotion filled. But it wasn't something meant to be. Ever.

"Now you're going to listen to your mother. About riding your pony and wearing your helmet. That's the cowboy way, young man. You won't let me down on this, will you?"

Jake looked into Cody's eyes with something akin to worship, and Cody's heart turned over. "No, Mr. Taylor."

"Good man. And call me Cody."

He set Jake down and looked back at Cat.

"Thank you," she said with enough reluctance that Cody was certain she wanted to bash his face in, but she was holding back because of the boy.

Cody touched the brim of his hat. "Forget it."

"Are we going to Aunt Lucille's this weekend? Mom was asking," Jace said as he ladled out a two bowls of canned soup from the pot on the stove and set them on the table next to paper plates filled with the burgers and buns Cody had grilled. "I think she's missing us," Jace added, making it plain they had to go.

Cody sighed inwardly as he procured two beers and a bottle of ketchup from the fridge and set them on the table before he sank onto the kitchen chair. He was bone tired, and all he wanted to do on his one weekend a month off was sleep.

He glanced at the dirty pots and bowls piled in the sink.

Sleep was a luxury he wouldn't have been able to afford anyway, given the demands of the Cross T. "Any cows look ready to calf?" he asked. Come another two weeks or so, they wouldn't be able to leave so readily.

Jace shook his head. "You can check for yourself, but I'd say no, based on the size of their udders."

Cody would check for himself, but if what Jace said was true, he'd be visiting his mother this weekend, ranch work or no ranch work. "Then I guess we'll be going."

Jace took a sip of beer before tucking into his burger.

Cody alternated between bites of burger and slurps of soup. It wasn't exactly the gourmet dinner he'd had at the Granville House, but it at least filled his stomach. Cody tried to push back thoughts of one wavy-haired princess, but they kept crowding his mind. *It was a mistake.* So was working for Cat McKenna. He'd been prepared for the fact she was a McKenna, but he hadn't been prepared for the gut punch of lust when he'd kissed her. Or the feeling he was missing something important when he held little Jake's hand.

Still, the money had already come in handy. He'd managed to work out payment arrangements with the hospital, the home-nursing service, the doctors, and his lawyer's office. Based on his budget, he'd be able to make minimum payments on the credit cards and make the mortgage payments. As far as he could calculate, if nothing else went wrong, they had a chance of hanging on until he could sell the soon-to-be-born calves next winter. And he might not have to sell Smoking Gun until the horse had attained that magical three-year mark.

He just needed to keep his focus on matters at hand and not get distracted by brown eyes and long legs.

"You don't seem enthusiastic." Jace's expression was serious.

"About what?" Cody set down the bottle of beer he'd been nursing.

"Seeing Mom."

"I just don't want to lie to her about working for the McKennas, and I don't want to tell her the truth either." She wouldn't understand. Hell, he didn't understand. A lot of things.

Like why Cat McKenna had kissed him like he had rescued her from a burning house and then blamed it on booze and claimed it as a mistake. Which annoyed the hell out of him. Because it felt like something she'd been wanting to do for a while and had just gotten the courage, liquid as that courage may have been. Nope, it hadn't felt like a mistake.

And fool that he was, he'd actually been working out a plan so they could be alone together for some mutual satisfaction.

He needed to follow his own advice and forget it. It was the sane thing.

Too bad sanity didn't hold much appeal when he saw her every damn day. How could he forget a woman who kissed like every man's fantasy and looked like…a princess?

But that was the kicker. She wasn't his type, so why was he so attracted to her?

Because once she kissed him, his "type" no longer seemed to matter.

He needed to find his type. Fast. An independent-minded woman who would be satisfied with a little lovin' for a night and not ask for more.

"Don't tell Mom," Jace said.

"Huh?" Cody snapped out of his thoughts. He took a slurp of soup. It was already on the cool side.

"Don't tell Mom. Unless she already knows, why bother? I'm not going to say anything."

"She'll find out sometime. I'd rather she hear it from me."

"You think she's going to be less mad because she heard it from you?"

Jace had a point.

"And the money has been nice. You said so yourself. We'll actually be able to pay the mortgage. And Duane is working out."

"At some point I'll have to tell her, but I suppose it can wait." Maybe Cody could wait until his mother announced she was coming back.

Jace took a long slug of his beer and tipped back

on two legs of his chair. "How's it going over there? Working for her?"

Kissing her. Watching her. Thinking about brown wavy hair, tanned skin, and curves he wanted to sink into.

"It's going."

"She still playing the princess?"

Only when she kisses you like she wants to drag you to bed. And tells you it was a mistake.

"She herded cattle today. Did pretty well." After her initial complaints, he hadn't expected much. Then she'd surprised him. Including getting out of the way of a stampede.

Jace came down on all four legs of the chair. "Really? I thought she didn't like ranching?"

Cody shrugged. "Guess she's coming around."

Years of being told what I can't do, she had said. Being Joe McKenna's daughter must have been hell. And bringing home a child without a husband couldn't have made it any easier.

Just like working with her every day wasn't easy. He needed to nip his attraction in the bud, or he might find himself locking lips with her again. And then what? That was the problem. There was no reasonable next step.

"You want to hit some bars when we're in Laramie?" Cody asked his brother. "We can go Saturday night, take Mom to dinner, then head out. If our cousin Michael is around, maybe he'd like to go with us."

"I could sure use a good time," Jace said, tipping his chair back again.

It had been a long, hard slog for both brothers

since his father had fallen sick. And fun had been sorely lacking.

"Me too."

"We'd have to stay over. Can we afford time away?" Jace looked hopeful.

"I'll see if Michael has any room for us in that apartment of his. He might be working that night, but I don't think he'd mind putting us up. We can ask Duane if he wants to earn a little extra cash and stop in and check on the animals Saturday night. We'd leave to come back Sunday at the crack of dawn."

Jace lifted his bottle in a faux toast. "Sounds like a plan."

Chapter 11

"So where should we go?" Cat asked as she and Cyndi Lynn exited the Primp and Pamper Salon and Spa and stepped onto the sidewalk and into the fading Laramie sunlight. It had been Cyndi Lynn's idea to treat themselves to a salon and spa day, and since Will Springer was minding the ranch and her mother was minding Jake, Cat had jumped at the chance.

With her long hair trimmed and styled into a cascade of wavy layers, her body massaged, her nails painted for the first time in months, and makeup applied, she actually felt ready to face a night of small talk and tall drinks in hopes of finding that elusive "good guy" she knew was out there somewhere. Caught up in the moment and with scented oil and calming music filling the air, she'd even gotten a bikini wax knowing she had no intention of having an intimate moment with a stranger she'd meet at a bar. But she had to admit she felt feminine…and much more confident.

"There's the Starlight Lounge," Cyndi Lynn offered as they walked down the main street of the shopping district, past storefronts displaying shoes, western wear, antiques, and knickknacks. "They have karaoke, which might be fun."

"Isn't that the place with those pink stools and purple tables?" She doubted any red-blooded son of Wyoming would be caught dead in the place.

Cyndi Lynn nodded.

In celebration of her divorce being final, Cyndi Lynn had gone for a complete makeover, cutting her thick auburn hair into a sophisticated bob that made her look like she'd stepped out of the pages of one of those hairstyle magazines. She'd had a facial and a massage, had her makeup done, and apparently had waxed everything available to be waxed. In tight black jeans, red cowgirl boots, and a satiny red camisole, Cyndi Lynn, at a petite five feet two inches, looked ready for action.

Cat had decided to dress up in a short white skirt, a pink silky top, and a pair of high-heeled sandals that gave her more height than was probably wise if she was on the prowl. But the heels made her feel sexy, and right now, she needed that boost. And by the appreciative glances of the few men they'd passed on the sidewalk, it might have been worth it.

She couldn't help but wonder how a certain cowboy would think she looked.

She had to stop thinking about him. That was what today was supposed to be about—forgetting Cody Taylor.

"You think we'll find the kind of men we are looking for at the Starlight?" Cat asked, trying to be diplomatic. The sun was setting on a picture-perfect day, and the air was cooling. She should have brought a sweater or a jacket.

She wondered how Jake was doing. If he was still running around or headed for bed. She pulled her phone out. No messages—a good sign.

"Good point." Cyndi Lynn slung her oversized pocketbook, larger than a small girl should carry, over her shoulder.

"I saw online that the Tipsy Bull is going to have live music tonight. We can get a booth, eat, and be there when the festivities start," Cat said.

Cat had almost had a heart attack when she'd seen Jake riding his pony without his helmet, Cody by his side. Cody didn't have children. He didn't understand how one misstep, one accident, could change a child's life forever.

"I've never been in there, but I've heard it's… lively."

Cody had clearly thought she'd overreacted. Typical Wyoming cowboy logic. He'd probably ride a bull without a helmet.

"Just what we want. Are you nervous? I mean about getting out there again?" Cat asked as they walked along Grand Avenue toward the bar.

At least Cody had convinced Jake to listen to her. He seemed to have sway with her son. And she didn't know how she felt about that. Heck, she didn't know how she felt about Cody, period.

"Honey, I'm so nervous that if a guy asks me to dance, I might just pee my pants."

Cyndi Lynn was nothing if not blunt. She'd always been one to speak her mind.

"Me too." Cat confessed. "It's been long, way too long." And impulsively kissing Cody Taylor that night had proved it. Why else would she have wrapped herself around that man and asked him to stay? Drink couldn't explain away everything.

"Well, I was married for the last three years. What's

been your excuse?" Cyndi Lynn asked as the Tipsy Bull's awning came in sight. "I have hardly seen you since you've been back. And that's almost two years now."

What was her excuse? Cat stopped just outside the entrance to the bar. "I could say I was too busy being a mom, but the truth, Cyndi Lynn...I was too scared. Still am. But it's time to get over it."

Cat pushed the bar door open and stepped into the beginning of a new phase of her life. Dating.

Mamie Taylor spoiled her boys. And neither Cody nor Jace were of a mind to do anything about it. They had offered to take her out to dinner, but Mamie had insisted she would cook for them all, borrowing Aunt Lucille's kitchen to make her mouth-watering pot roast with all the fixings and a German chocolate cake for dessert.

Cody was happy to see a spark in his mother's eyes as she fussed over the two of them. The visit with her sister had worked its magic. He hadn't even detected liquor on her breath when she'd greeted her boys with a hug and a kiss on the cheek.

Aunt Lucille and Uncle Tom had joined them for dinner and then discreetly disappeared to another corner of the house. Michael had generously offered up his place so they could stay over, but as Cody had suspected, being the newest detective, Michael was pulling night duty for the foreseeable future and couldn't join them for dinner, much less an evening of bar hopping.

Cody and his brother entered their aunt's cozy den with their second cups of coffee, and their mother followed them into the tidy paneled room outfitted with a brown leather sofa, two matching recliners, and a big-screen television. Cody could finally relax. Nary a word had been spoken about the ranch, and even though his mother seemed a bit on edge, he knew if she had caught wind of him working at Pleasant Valley, it would have been the topic of conversation the moment his foot hit the porch step.

Checking his watch, he was glad to see it was just nearing eight thirty. Plenty of time yet to sample Laramie's nightlife.

Mamie sat on the edge of one of the recliners, holding the beige ceramic coffee cup in her hands, and looked directly at Cody. "I have something to discuss with you boys."

He should have known.

"What is it, Mom?" Jace asked as he sat down next to Cody on the sofa.

Cody leaned forward, elbows on his knees, and steeled himself for the inevitable.

Mamie, looking years younger in a print dress Cody had never seen before, smoothed back her hair, though no strands had yet escaped the bun.

"You know I have been helping out in Lucille's office when they've needed someone."

The heaviness in Cody's chest that had made it hard to breath eased.

"Well..." She hesitated. Looked from one boy to the other. "They have offered me a permanent position. With benefits."

"A job?" Jace asked, not hiding his surprise.

From the smile his mother was trying to hold back, Cody guessed she was pleased about it.

"What would you boys think if I accepted it?

Lucille has offered to let me stay here with her since she has the room, what with her children out on their own. I'd pay her some money toward expenses and food, even though she says she doesn't want any." His mother bit her lip and looked up at them from under furrowed brows. "It would mean you boys would be on your own at the ranch. I could come on a weekend and clean the house for you."

"Mom, you don't have to do that. We are capable of taking care of ourselves," Cody said and tried not to think about the sink full of dishes and the dust bunnies rolling across his bedroom floor. They'd have to get in gear and take care of the house, like they should have been doing all along.

"You boys wouldn't mind me living in Laramie?" She looked at Jace, having taken Cody's offer as agreement.

Jace was frowning. Cody side-kicked his leg.

"No, ma'am," Jace said.

"If this is what you want to do," Cody added. "But you shouldn't feel as if you have to just for the money. I've worked things out, and with some luck, we'll make it until we can sell the calves this winter."

Mamie shifted back into the embrace of the recliner. "I enjoy working. And I like making a little money." The pride in her voice was palpable. "They pay good, and as I said, I get benefits, so if anything were to happen to me, we wouldn't be…well, we wouldn't be so bad off, like with your father. And Jace can be covered under those benefits." She turned her gaze on Cody. "You're too old now."

Benefits were the least of his issues. "If you enjoy it, then go for it."

"I just…the thought of going back to the house… without your father…" She swiped at her eyes. "I'm not ready."

Cody wondered if she would ever be ready.

"If you two could, well…" She fingered the hem of her dress, and her thin arms and dainty wrists reminded Cody how delicate she was. "Pack up your father's things. Don't get rid of them. Just put them away?" She turned a tearful glance their way. "I would be grateful."

"Sure, Mom," Jace answered.

Cody wasn't looking forward to that chore, but if he could spare his mother the heartache, he would.

In the next breath, she raised her chin and added, "I'm not drinking. Haven't had a drop since…it's been weeks."

"That's great, Mom," Jace said.

"Proud of you," Cody added. He knew it took a dose of humility for his mother to admit drinking was a problem. She must have wanted the job badly to use her sobriety as an argument in favor of the plan.

She clasped her hands in front of her. "Then it's settled. And you'll visit. Once a month would be good, more if you can spare it, but I know we are coming up on the new calving season."

Nothing to do but agree.

"I've been able to add a little money into the bank account. It will help with the bills. I don't need much for myself. I did buy a few dresses for work, but I shouldn't need to buy much more…"

Cody held up his hand. "There is no need to account to us for what you see fit to spend." She was his mother, and he had no right to dictate to her.

She rubbed her hands together, and her smile beamed a warm glow through him. "You two are the best sons a mother could ask for."

He doubted she would feel that way if she knew where he was working.

In a heartbeat, her brow furrowed again. "But I haven't seen any money taken out of our accounts. I know there are bills to be paid, and the mortgage."

Jace looked at Cody. Cody looked at his mother. "I've been paying them from my own account. We're up to date on the mortgage, both of them. I have worked out payment plans with the hospital, doctors, and the nursing service, and I've been making minimum monthly payments on the credit cards and our feed-store account."

Mamie took a huge breath. "I should have known you'd have it well in hand, Cody. But where have you gotten the money, if not the ranch?"

Where indeed.

"He's working odd jobs. We both are."

"Really?" She looked thoughtful, "Well, I guess between calving and branding, there are certainly ranches that need help. Just don't neglect the Cross T, boys. If we can hold on through the winter, I know we'll be okay."

"Yes, ma'am," Cody said.

"What if I take over the payment of the secondary mortgage? I've done my own figuring, and I think I should be able to swing that, seeing you boys have worked out the other bills." His mother looked so serious and determined to do her bit.

"Sounds like a plan," Cody agreed.

She opened her slender arms. "Come. Give me a

171

hug. If we stick together as a family, we'll make it. Family is everything."

The boys rose in unison. Cody suffered through his mother's hug, feeling he was betraying that family.

Cat drummed her fingers on the plastic tabletop as the waitress set down two drinks, a cosmos for Cyndi Lynn and a chocolate martini for Cat. Now that dinner was finished, the waitress cleared the dishes before heading back to her station.

"Here's to dating again," Cyndi Lynn said, raising her glass.

Cat clanged her martini glass against Cyndi's. She was only having one drink, since she would be driving home. It would be fruit juice mixed with ginger ale after this. "It's terrifying out here."

The place was filling up, and the prospect of distinguishing princes from toads was ratcheting up the anxiety already tumbling her stomach. It was that fretful feeling that made her regret having scarfed down a grease-laden burger and equally oily fries, even if they'd tasted yummy at the time.

Cyndi Lynn set her elbows on the table as she hugged her glass. "I think I stayed with Ray longer than I should have because I didn't want to face this."

"I know what you mean. Especially since everyone else seems to be married or hooked up with someone." Libby and Mandy had already found their happily ever after. That left Cat the odd person out.

Cyndi Lynn leaned in closer. "Ray was getting into bad things. I wanted no part of it."

"Bad things like?"

"Drugs." Cyndi Lynn sat back at that

pronouncement. "Not illegal. Not yet, at least that I know of." She swirled her cosmos, some of the liquid lapping over the side and spotting the table. "He was in a bad accident about a year after we were married. They prescribed heavy-duty painkillers. A lot of them. And two years later, he is still on them. And he's on disability, but he's got money, so I don't know what is going on," she said, her voice tinged with worry. "Claims he's in pain without those drugs, but he's a different person now." She raised her eyes to look into Cat's. "Not a nice person, if you get my drift." Cyndi Lynn took a sip.

Cat felt the impact of that confession as if Cyndi Lynn had landed a punch on her. "I'm sorry. I had no idea." And Cat hadn't. Ray Spencer was a big lumbering guy who had played offensive guard on the high school football team, if she remembered correctly. Cat could only imagine what petite Cyndi Lynn had gone through.

"It only happened once, but I wasn't waiting around for the next time." Cyndi Lynn sucked the liquid off her twizzle stick.

"I don't blame you. Have you seen him recently?"

"As far as I know, he's left the state and gone to work for his uncle in Montana. And good riddance. Seems like we both struck out, huh?"

Cat hadn't planned on discussing Jake's father, but since Cyndi Lynn had confided in her...

"Jake's father was a graduate student. A teaching assistant for one of my courses. We hooked up. I fell for him. Found out too late he was already married. Then found out I was pregnant." The short version, but it conveyed the essential facts.

"Ouch."

"Exactly."

"Ray and I didn't have any kids, which I'm glad about. I'm not very maternal anyway."

Cat wasn't sure what being maternal entailed, but she accepted her friend's verdict.

"As you've been living in the area, do you keep in touch with many people from high school?" Cyndi Lynn and Cody had dated once. Cat wondered if Cyndi Lynn would be interested in renewing that connection. And what if she was?

Cyndi Lynn nodded. "Angie Jean married a boy she met at Wyoming State, and they live in Rawlins. Marie Salizar married some guy she met online and moved to Denver. Not too many people have stayed around, unless they are ranchers, like your family." Cyndi Lynn fluffed her new hairdo. "You know Cody Taylor is still around. I saw him the other day and made sure he knew I was single again, not that he seemed interested."

That answered that question. But it shouldn't concern Cat. No siree. She was here precisely to exorcise any remnants of Cody's kiss. And from scanning the bar area where it was standing room only, there just might be some candidates for that duty.

Like the guy in the plaid shirt and Dockers. Or the one in jeans and a polo shirt. Nice, middle-of-the-road guys. Not just good-time cowboys.

The band was tuning up, and the din had grown louder as more people joined the fray. Soon the race would be on because there were also quite a number of women at the bar. Some with dates. Many, like her and

Cyndi Lynn, without. It would be easier to just sit and listen to the music. Only she'd come here to begin a new phase in her life, and being a wallflower wouldn't accomplish that.

Tonight she needed to at least dip a toe in the old watering hole. A dance or two with a guy would be a nice first step.

"What I wouldn't give to hook up with him again," Cyndi Lynn said, bringing Cat's attention back to the matter at hand.

She should let the remark go. Change the subject.

"You dated Cody Taylor in high school, didn't you?"

Cyndi Lynn's smile said it all. "For three months. He was my first."

Okay, she was pretty sure Cyndi Lynn didn't mean her first date.

"And it spoiled me. I measured every other man, even Ray, by his yardstick—and I mean that in every sense."

Too much information. Cat could feel her cheeks heat, but Cyndi Lynn was oblivious, in the throes of relishing the memory.

Change the subject. Get out before you can't. "What happened?"

"Cody was, and by all accounts still is, Mr. Love 'Em and Leave 'Em." Cyndi Lynn's eyebrows arched. "But, honey, right now I'd be happy with just one night. It was that good between us." Cyndi Lynn took a gulp to finish off her cosmos. Nary a drop was left in the glass.

Cat should put an end to this conversational thread. She really should.

"He's working at Pleasant Valley, you know."

"No way." Cyndi Lynn practically squealed. "A Taylor working for a McKenna?"

"I need someone who knows ranching. He needs some extra money. Seems care for his father was costly."

Cyndi Lynn waved her hand in the air at the nearby waitress and held up her empty glass. Good thing Cat would be driving.

"Sad about his dad. I went to the wake. Cody's mother took it hard," Cyndi Lynn said after snagging the waitress's attention and hand-signaling her order. "How do you get anything done with Cody around? He's as yummy as a chocolate cake smothered in caramel."

Cat laughed. She felt the same way. "He is…well…good looking."

"Honey, it's okay to admit you're attracted to him. I don't know a single woman in Carbon County that isn't. And probably a few married ones too. If Cody Taylor were working for me, we'd sure be doing some extracurricular activities."

Boy, that heat in her cheeks had staying power.

The waitress set a cosmos on the table and grabbed Cyndi Lynn's empty glass. "Anything for you?" she asked Cat.

Cat had barely touched her martini. She shook her head, and the waitress disappeared.

"So are you two, you know, passing the time together?"

The five-piece band launched into Blake Shelton's "Sangria." Cat took a sip of her drink. It was cold, chocolaty, and sweet. And did nothing to cool the warmth spreading through her. Maybe she was hormonal. That would explain her physical reaction to just talking about the man.

Cyndi Lynn was waiting for an answer.

"Hardly. He's a Taylor, he's technically my employee even though he's the one teaching me, we work together, and what did you call him? Mr. Love 'Em and Leave 'Em. Been there. Done that. No thank you."

Cyndi Lynn's *you protest too much* smile said she wasn't convinced.

"I can truthfully say that a one-night stand with Cody Taylor is well worth whatever the fallout might be. As long as you know going in that it's not forever, why not?"

"I'm looking for a good man. No one-night stands. No lying cheats. Just a man that wants to settle down, will be a good father to my son, maybe wants to have more kids, and isn't afraid of working hard."

"Well, good luck with that," Cyndi Lynn said, straightening in her seat. "Tonight, I'm just looking for a good time. I've been through the settling-down phase, and it ain't all it's cracked up to be." She took a large gulp of her cosmos and quickly set the glass down, her eyes wide, and she pressed fingertips to her mouth. "Honey, that one-night stand we were talking about? He just walked through the door. With his brother."

Chapter 12

Cody, with Jace following, pushed into the crowded saloon to sounds of a Blake Shelton song. Even though it was just past nine thirty, the dance floor was jumping, and the bar was mobbed. Having escaped the evening without his mother finding out he worked for the McKennas, he needed a beer. And hopefully a woman, given there were a number of them clustered in the bar area.

He wanted to forget about the Cross T, Pleasant Valley, and one McKenna in particular, and tonight, the Tipsy Bull seemed the perfect place to do that.

She'd torn into him about letting her son ride a pony, like a lioness fending off an attacker. Jake was in sore need of a father who would stand up to his overprotective mother. What was the term? Helicopter parent? The boy needed to learn how to handle the rough and tumble if he was one day going to run a ranch the size of Pleasant Valley.

Yup, Cat McKenna was a woman filled with complications he didn't need. And he was hoping this bar was filled with a lot of uncomplicated women.

It took a while to get the bartender's attention, but once he and his brother had a beer bottle in hand,

Cody took a moment to look around. There was a woman looking his way. Or maybe it was Jace's way. She had short, spiky blond hair and a long tattoo of something running along her arm. He shifted his gaze down the bar, where several women sat in a row, swiveling their chairs now and again to look past him to the dance floor behind him.

"Good crowd," Jace said appreciatively.

It felt good to be out. Among people. Among women.

And a little fun was what they both needed.

The song changed to Maroon 5's "Sugar," and Cody turned to watch the dancers change out, some staying put, some leaving, new couples entering. The group of women from the bar piled onto the floor to dance together. He thought about going over and asking one of them to dance, when a guy in a plaid shirt gave up his bar seat, as did his friend, who wore an insignia-branded polo shirt. Cody and Jace snagged the stools. Now that he had a seat, maybe he'd wait for a slow dance to ask one of those girls.

He swiveled to follow, with his gaze, the two guys who were heading toward a table. A table with two women.

Cyndi Lynn Spencer? And…he froze as brown wavy hair, long legs, and high heels rose from her seat. A confection in pink and white looking like a coroneted princess if he ever saw one. She walked with the plaid shirt, who was about an inch shorter than she was in those heels, to the dance floor.

His mouth dry despite the slug of beer he just swallowed, he watched her. Watched her shake her booty. Watched her shake…everything. A hip bump.

A rocking step. A flirty turn. The back of his neck felt damp. His heart sped up. He was mesmerized.

"Hey, that looks like…" Jace began.

"Cat McKenna."

"Where? Because I just saw Cyndi Lynn Spencer."

Cody raised his chin in Cat's direction. He should turn away. He should leave. He should do anything but stare at her like a panting dog waiting for a pat on the head. But he couldn't.

"Wow," Jace breathed in Cody's ear. "She's even more gorgeous than in high school, and I was in love with her then."

He could do without that confession. "She's out of your league."

Jace chuckled. "You going to tell me she's in yours?"

"Maybe." Cody could feel the burn of irritation as he watched the guy try to twerk her. She moved a step back. Cody raised the bottle to his lips and took a swig.

"Too bad she's your boss." Jace was doing a good job of adding to that irritation.

The music switched to "Lady in Red." More like "Lady in Pink." Cody set his bottle down on the counter and headed to the dance floor.

Dancing with the guy in the plaid shirt, Cat should have been enjoying herself. Instead, she was focused on Cody, not the guy who had been clumsily trying to twerk with her and now was holding her way too tight in a slow dance that emphasized she was at least an inch taller in heels. The top of his head was below eye level, and she could see where he would soon be bald.

Awkward.

Not that she was a height snob. Okay, she was a height snob, but this was her fault. Her need to wear high heels in order to feel flirty.

On the other hand, Dave, as he'd introduced himself, was sweaty, and his breath carried the scent of liquor. This was Wyoming, after all.

When Cyndi Lynn had told her the bad news, she'd resisted turning around and checking Cody out. Instead she'd waited until he was at the bar to glance over. A head taller than most, in jeans and a T-shirt, his brown hair catching the glow from the bar lights, he was easy to pick out in the crowd.

She'd prevailed on Cyndi Lynn not to immediately run over and greet Cody and his brother. The two men who came to their table to ask for a dance had further delayed the inevitable. At least dancing gave her time to think about what she would say to him. It wasn't like she owed him an explanation. It was obvious they were both looking for something, but very different "somethings," she was sure. She was looking for a good man. He was looking for a good time.

So why had he been sitting on a barstool, frowning and staring in her direction?

She turned her head to get another look, and Cody Taylor's face, eyes narrowed, mouth pinched, was up close and personal. Dave didn't see Cody, but Cody tapped Dave on the shoulder. Her partner twisted his neck.

"Get lost," Dave growled. "This isn't a high school prom."

"I'm cutting in, mister," Cody said.

Dave reared back to get a better look at Cody, raising his eyes to take in Cody's height. They stopped dancing. Was Cody going to make a scene right in the middle of the dance floor? Heads started to turn.

"She's with me," Dave said with a little less conviction now that he'd gotten a good look at the interloper.

"She's my girlfriend."

Cat was about to protest, except Dave folded. Just like that, he uncoupled, stepped back, and grimacing, walked away, leaving Cat on the floor with a glaring cowboy. Apparently she wasn't worth fighting for.

Cody immediately filled the void, wrapping his arms around her, pulling her tight, and moving to the rhythm of the music. She set her hand lightly on his broad shoulder and gingerly wrapped the other one around his neck so her fingers barely touched his skin. If only she could ignore the hard body she was pressed against. With her heels on, their eyes were on the same plane. The twirl of multicolored lights flashed on various parts of his face, giving her glimpses of narrowed eyes, a hard jaw, and those lips.

"Why did you say I was your girlfriend?" Not only wasn't she his girlfriend, but he'd ruined her chances with Dave. Not that Dave was anything to write home about, but that should have been her decision, and she hadn't made it yet. Well, maybe she'd made it, but she hadn't told Dave.

Cody's cocksure smile was wide. "How else was I going to get to dance with you?"

By waiting his turn, but she had a feeling Cody wasn't used to waiting for anything.

"What are you doing here?" she asked, trying not to let the hardness of his chest, the musky scent of his aftershave, or how well they fit together, even if she was wearing heels, fluster her.

"Same thing as you, I expect. Looking for a little distraction."

Watching his lips brought back an intense desire to taste him. And that would never do. Yeah, she needed a distraction. From him.

"Cyndi Lynn and I are celebrating her divorce."

He sang along with the music, his breath whispering over the sensitive skin of her neck. Was he flirting with her or just singing? His voice wasn't half bad in a deep, rumbling, sexy-as-hell kind of way. She was doomed.

"Why are you even in Laramie?" she said, trying to hold together the parts of her body that were ready to mutiny.

"Visiting." His breath tickled.

"Who?" A woman?

"My mother is staying with my aunt in Laramie. Looks like it might be permanent. She's getting a job."

He was visiting his mother. Something inside her softened. "So you boys will be all alone at the ranch now."

His half-cocked smile held a tinge of mischief. "All alone."

He twirled them around as the band sang the chorus. "Should be lady in pink." Cody's breath brushed her ear.

Her fingers curled into his shoulder. If she turned her face just a tad, her lips would meet his.

"I like you in heels," he said close to her ear.

"I thought you were a boot man?"

"Heels are a better fantasy."

Fantasy?

"What fantasy?" she asked against her better instinct. She resisted the urge to lay her head on his shoulder, despite the fact it would fit perfectly.

"High heels, long legs." His hand slid down her back and rested at her hip, in grabbing distance of her butt. "Nice curves…"

Was he talking about her? Or a generic someone?

He pressed her close, and her fingers slid across his cotton T-shirt to the middle of his firm back. Her lips were next to his neck, and she could smell his cologne, the same cologne he had on when she'd kissed him. She could easily brush her lips across his skin. Maybe he wouldn't notice.

Cody pulled back, looking her in the eyes. "Don't tell me you don't fantasize?"

She did, but she refused to share. With him.

"What is your fantasy wearing?" His voice rumbled like low thunder next to her ear.

Nothing, and riding a paint horse.

"Does he ever wear cowboy boots, Cat?" he pressed.

Always. "Maybe."

"How about a cowboy hat?"

A black Stetson. "Possibly."

His fingers brushed the bare skin of her shoulder, warming her from the inside out. He nuzzled her neck, and her flesh tingled from the heat.

"We should get our fantasies together sometime."

Desire pooled low in her belly, and the urge to brush her lips along his neck magnified.

"Cat?"

"Hmm?"

"The music has stopped."

Cat stilled, raising her gaze to meet his. It was as heat fueled as she felt.

The music changed to a fast tune.

"Let's sit." He slid his hand to the small of her back, and she could feel his warmth through the thin fabric of her top.

We should get our fantasies together sometime? Like now?

Cat slid into the booth, and despite the fact Cyndi Lynn was still dancing, Cody slid in next to her so they sat on the same side. Just inches from each other.

He draped his arm across the back of the booth, invading her space.

As if signaled, the waitress appeared. "Drink?" she asked, looking harried.

"Beer. Coors." Cody nodded to Cat. "You want to freshen that?" he asked, referring to the half-drunk chocolate martini.

"No, I drove." Thankfully, because she couldn't risk an inebriated repeat of the other night.

The waitress took off.

"You drove?"

"Someone had to. Who drove you?"

"Me. But we're staying overnight at my cousin's. It's a long way back to your ranch."

Cat shrugged. "We wanted to go someplace where we wouldn't know anyone."

Cody shifted to face her. "How that work out for you?"

She had to laugh. "Not well."

He touched his finger to her chin. Raised it so she had to look into his blue eyes. "I think it worked out just fine."

She could hear her heart beat in her ears. Or was that the music?

"Cody Taylor." Cyndi Lynn's squeal pulled Cody's attention, and finger, away. The woman wrapped her arms around Cody's neck in a hug that seemed to go on a tad too long. The familiar-looking young man whom Cyndi Lynn had named as Cody's brother slid into the seat across from them.

Cat hadn't noticed Cyndi Lynn had changed partners.

"Hey, Cat," Jace said by way of greeting before he focused on Cyndi Lynn, who was focused on Cody.

Cat took a good look at Jace since she hadn't seen him, up close, since high school. He still had a boyishness that Cody lacked. The same hair as his brother, but worn longer so it brushed his collar in the back. Hazel eyes instead of blue. Same work-honed physique though.

"Surprised to see us?" Cyndi Lynn asked as she sat down next to Jace with a bounce. Her face was glowing. Perhaps from dancing.

"Didn't expect anyone from town to be here," Cody responded.

Jace wrapped a possessive arm around Cyndi Lynn's waist, but as if she hadn't noticed, Cyndi Lynn reached across the table to pat Cody's bare forearm. "See, you never know."

"Congratulations, if that's the right term, on your divorce." The light caught the side of his face, illuminating his strong jaw and his five o'clock shadow. Why did Cody Taylor have to be so... desirable?

"It's the right term," Cyndi Lynn said with a beaming smile.

Cody tucked both his arms under the table.

Cat felt a hand on her knee. A squeeze.

"I told Cyndi Lynn they could stay over at Michael's if they want," Jace said. He looked way too eager.

"I will be driving home." Cat had too many reasons why an overnight stay would not be a good idea. Tempting. But not a good idea. "Thank you though."

Cody's fingers brushed her bare thigh. Moved higher. Just under the hem of her skirt. Heat slithered along her leg to her crotch.

Too many reasons.

Cyndi Lynn cocked her head at Jace. Then at Cody. "I might take you up on that."

Cody leaned forward, but his hand remained up Cat's thigh. "Jace means well, Cyndi Lynn, but we are staying in someone else's house."

Cyndi Lynn's pout looked authentic.

Now if Cody would just remove his hand so she could think again.

Jace frowned, but he didn't correct his brother. "You're always welcome to visit the ranch, Cyndi Lynn."

Cyndi Lynn's pout turned into a self-satisfied smile. "Why, thank you, Jace." She patted Jace's chest. "You may just see me out there. Soon."

The waitress set the bottle of beer in front of Cody. "Can I get anyone anything?"

Jace ordered a beer. Cyndi Lynn ordered her third cosmos. Yup, Cat would definitely be driving.

The band struck up "Honky Tonk Badonkadonk," and Cyndi Lynn slid her hand up Jace's arm and cupped his chin. "C'mon, little brother."

Within seconds they were heading back onto the dance floor.

"Seems like Cyndi Lynn has her sights on Jace," Cat said. She really should tell Cody to remove his hand.

"For tonight. Doubt she's going to be looking for anything long term for a while. And Jace can't afford to."

"And you?" Why she asked, she didn't know. Maybe it was the way his fingers were brushing the inside of her thigh, causing her to feel more than she wanted. Based upon the tingles settling in her abdomen, she definitely hadn't reached her expiration date.

Cody frowned. Not a good sign.

"And me what?"

"Are you looking for the long term?" She didn't know whether she hoped he'd say yes or no.

His frowned deepened.

"No." His hand slipped from her thigh and emerged at the edge of the table. He took a swig of beer. She shifted in her seat and sloshed her drink around in the glass, the ice almost melted. Of course Cody Taylor was still just looking for a good time.

"And you?" he asked as he fingered the bottle.

Fess up, Cat. He could never be "the one" anyway, so it shouldn't matter. She knew who he was. A leopard didn't change his spots, and the Cody Taylors of this world didn't settle down.

"If you're asking if I'd like to find a man who wants to get married, raise a family, the answer is yes." She wasn't getting any younger. It shouldn't be a surprise.

"And so you came here to find that someone?" He sounded incredulous.

"Well, I'm certainly not going to find him stuck out in Pleasant Valley."

He raised the bottle to his lips. The watch on his wrist caught the light and reflected it onto the wall painted a dark blue. When he set the bottle down, he turned to look at her. "I guess not."

The tune switched to Shaina Twain's "When You Kiss Me," bringing a lump to her throat. This was the song she'd played repeatedly when she was dating Jake's father, so sure he was her happily ever after.

Remorse coupled with a deep soul-searing sadness washed over her as the strains of the love song filled the cavernous room, blotting out the sounds of talk and laughter. She took a sip of her drink, wishing she could wash away the feeling, the memories, the disappointment, knowing it would forever be a part of her.

"Let's dance," Cody said, holding out his hand.

To be held by another man, even this man, might help dissipate the feeling of betrayal the song now invoked.

She grabbed his hand like it was a lifeline, and he slid out of the booth, tugging her with him. When they reached the dance floor, he wrapped his arms around her. But the hollow feeling of utter abandonment didn't disappear. She laid her head on his shoulder, felt the softness of his T-shirt cradle her cheek as his embrace tightened.

She wanted to be held. By a man. By this man, even if he would never be her man. For the moment, this would have to be enough.

189

Chapter 13

One minute they'd been laughing. The next minute she'd pulled away like he'd thrown a lighted match on her, all because he'd said he didn't want to be tied down, and now she was holding on to him for dear life.

Cat McKenna was the definition of enigma. A complication he couldn't figure out and didn't need.

She'd said she wanted to settle down with a man.

And she'd come to a honky-tonk to find him.

Guess he couldn't blame her, since there weren't many places to meet people when you were stuck out in the middle of nowhere running hundreds of head of cattle. And he should know. Not that he was looking for what she was looking for, but he at least had a more realistic chance of finding it at the Tipsy Bull.

And yet, here he was with the one woman he shouldn't be with.

He slid his hands down her sides, resting them on the curves of her hip.

The one woman who had so much baggage, she'd need a train car all to herself.

He nuzzled her, tempted to taste the soft skin of her neck, where a light floral scent tickled his nose.

She tightened her hold on him.

Maybe…maybe she'd be amenable to a different kind of relationship. A mutually satisfying, no-strings-attached, *love the one you're with and get it the hell out of your system* relationship.

"Cat," he whispered against her ear. She cocked her head. "Let's go outside. Get some fresh air. Talk."

Cody wanted to talk?

Cat was only too happy to leave the dance floor and the wrenching song behind. But what did he want to talk about?

Slipping her smaller hand into his larger one, she followed him through the maze of bodies that lined the dance floor and filled the bar area, and they stepped out onto the Laramie sidewalk.

It was dark, and there weren't any people in the vicinity. Just the two of them. Alone. Under the murky glow of a streetlamp.

He leaned against the brick wall of the bar and pulled her to him. She stumbled, and he caught her in his arms and pressed her against his body, engulfing her in his arms.

His embrace was intimate, sexy, dangerous.

She nestled against his hard lines, his hard…everything. Her insides sizzled like steak on a fire as she breathed in the scent of musky aftershave and yeasty beer. She felt the strength of his muscles, the hard lines of his body, the bulge in his pants. Something inside her rejoiced that a man desired her.

"I just wanted to be alone with you," he mumbled as he nuzzled the sensitive area behind her ear.

Tiny flutters filled the empty spaces of her body

as firm lips kissed her neck. Her whole being responded as if it brought to life.

He nipped her ear, sending a yearning low in her belly.

His lips brushed across her cheek, and like a puppet he controlled, she turned her head toward him.

His kiss was warm and powerful as his hand held the back of her head as if she needed tethering, and his lips swallowed her mouth and sucked the oxygen out of her. Lust, pure, potent, and persuasive gripped her.

Like a boa surrounding its meal, she wrapped her arms around his neck and plunged in as passion surged into the empty spaces of her being, filling them to capacity.

She'd only have herself to blame for this kiss.

He made out with her like the randy school boy he'd once been. His kisses were deep, provoking, soul searing, turning on every part of her body like he was pressing levers. His tongue found hers as his hand ran down her back, cupped her bottom, and pressed her closer so there was no mistaking how much he wanted her. And it was a lot.

They were on the streets of Laramie making out like teenagers where any passerby could watch, and she didn't care. Her body didn't care. Her mind could no longer care. And her heart…well, it was outvoted.

"Cat…" He whispered her name as he fed her kisses. Kisses that kept her glued to him, wanting more.

His grip tightened, and he ground his erection against her. She thought her legs would buckle from the heat he was generating.

When he finally pulled back, his eyes were hooded, his hair tousled, his lips moist, and his smile appreciative.

"How about we satisfy each other…you know."

She didn't know.

"I think you and I could..." His voice was soft and sexy, deep and gravelly, like he'd been drugged. "Have some fun while you...you know, wait for the right one to come along. We can go to Michael's and take it nice and slow."

Alarms bells went off inside her head like someone had just pulled a robbery. She struggled to take a step back, but he was holding her tight and trailing soft, tantalizing kisses down the side of her neck.

"Do you mean what I think you mean?" Please say no.

She sought his eyes for confirmation and saw lust staring back at her. Nothing else. Just something primitive, elemental, and purely physical.

"You can feel how much I want you. I can feel how much you want me." His voice took on the urgency of argument. "We're adults. We both know the score."

She knew. To him she was a princess, and he never wanted to be her white knight—just the man who bedded her. She squirmed.

"We've got chemistry. Volatile, mind-exploding chemistry," he continued, seemingly oblivious to her struggles to be free. "We should explore that. Scratch each other's itch."

She was an itch now?

She pushed hard against his chest. His arms dropped to his side, and she took a step back and fought to calm her heart.

His eyes were hooded from lust, his expression hopeful as he remained against the wall, his hands digging into his pockets.

This was what "dating" was nowadays? Scratching people's itches?

"No," she said as firmly as her cracked voice could master.

Then she turned on her heel and headed toward the bar door. She'd have to find Cyndi Lynn and leave. Before she did something she'd regret. Like slapping his face. Or telling him to go to hell. Or worse.

Taking him up on his offer.

She'd driven home alone, Cyndi Lynn having opted to stick with Jace. Cat crawled into bed exhausted and wondered if they'd made it a threesome. She'd spent the next day, Sunday, with Jake, including giving him time to ride his pony. Against her better judgment, she didn't make the boy wear a helmet this time, just kept a death grip on him.

When her mother asked her about Saturday night, her reply was that the evening had made it clear she wasn't ready to date yet. But what had really been made clear was that her expectations about men were unrealistic. She would never find Mr. Right looking in the wrong places. Only she hadn't a clue where to find the right places.

Sunday night, after Jake went to bed, she fired up the computer and tackled the accounting books. Her father had died just after the October sale of cattle, and they were still operating off the proceeds from that sale. Come this October, the ranch would be operating on proceeds from *her* year of raising cattle, and they couldn't afford to lose any more.

And that meant she was in no position to fire Cody, even though she was sorely tempted. Poor choice of words…but perhaps more honest. Because she was tempted to give in to her needs and just go at it with him like rabbits. Why not?

Because she was morally outraged at his suggestion?

Hardly.

Because she thought too much of herself?

Not really.

Because she had too much pride?

That had been disproven more than once.

Because…she might just fall for Cody Taylor.

The truth was hard to admit.

She'd already fallen in love once with a man who had broken her heart. A man who wanted to use her body but didn't want her. No thank you.

Sounded good. Only conviction was missing.

Cody adjusted his sunglasses as he sat atop his horse and contemplated his next move. Not with the horse, but with Cat McKenna.

He'd been a fool. A lustful, out-of-control fool. Maybe she'd accept that he was the one drunk this time. Only he wasn't, and she'd already used that excuse.

Just something about the woman. If only he could figure out what. So he could exorcise it.

She was pretty. Okay, so were a lot of women. Women he'd dated. Women he'd…yeah, a lot of women.

He looked over the pasture, cropped short courtesy of the herd. They'd be moving the herd up into the hills to the summer pastures after branding. The calves would be harder to handle now that they were bigger, but they were also healthier and less stressed. Waiting had been the right decision even if it opened them up to the possibility of rustling.

He still had his suspicions, but he needed evidence.

He nudged his horse and headed in the direction of the barns. He would have to face Cat, and he still wasn't sure what to say.

This time he'd been the one to cross the line...and he'd taken her with him. Oh yeah. She'd been passionate and possessive. When she slid her body against his and wrapped her arms around his neck, his knees had weakened.

And then he'd made the mistake of opening his mouth and saying what was on his mind.

Yup, he'd screwed up last night. He'd not only crossed the line, he'd managed to insult her when, really, he'd only had compliments for her. He wasn't sure what was going on, but he hadn't been able to concentrate on anything or anyone else since Saturday night.

He'd driven Cyndi Lynn crazy making her check her cell phone for a text from Cat that she'd arrived home safely. And he'd spent a restless night on his cousin's pull-out couch with his brother while Cyndi Lynn slept it off in his cousin's bedroom, seeing as Michael was working the night shift.

Jace might have had other ideas for the night with Cyndi Lynn, but Cody had been firm. Cyndi Lynn was vulnerable, and Jace was not going to take advantage. It wasn't lost on Cody that he'd tried to take advantage of Cat, who was just as vulnerable.

His horse trotted, pushing against the bit to go

faster. He pressed his heels against the animal's sides, and the horse sprang forward into a full-on gallop. Warm wind hit his face, and he lowered his head to keep his hat from falling off.

What was he going to do about Cat McKenna, about her curvy body, her welcoming smile, her wanton kisses, and her princess ways? Because he had to do something.

"Cody, Cody, Cody." Jake's voice echoed in the large barn, as did the patter of his footsteps on the concrete. The boy burst down the stall aisle, coming out of God knew where and headed straight toward the tack room, where Cody was oiling his horse's bridle. The boy's blond bowl-cut hair bounced as he roared toward Cody at full speed.

"Hey, cowboy." Cody tried to sound cheerful as he rose off the stool and hung up the bridle. In truth, he was happy to see the boy. It was the woman several feet back, walking at a slow, deliberate pace, that he would have avoided. Only that would be the coward's way out.

Jake launched headlong for Cody and would have knocked into his knees except he scooped up Jake. The boy seemed to weigh no more than a bag of Styrofoam. Jake wiggled and giggled as Cody lifted him, and reached out his small arms.

Cody settled Jake in the crook of his arm, and the boy wrapped his arms around Cody's neck.

As Jake stared adoringly at Cody, something squeezed inside of him. Something that meant family.

"We played T-ball today, and I got a hit," Jake chattered.

197

Baseball. Something fathers taught their sons, parents taught their children, and his father had taught him.

"You like baseball?" Cody asked. Cat continued to walk toward them, but her focus was on Jake. She wore form-hugging designer-type jeans, a white sleeveless top, and a pair of fancy cowgirl boots. She must have gone to town to pick Jake up from school, instead of her mother. Her hair tumbled down around her shoulders. He remembered how silky it had felt in his hand, how soft. He remembered a lot of things.

Jake nodded.

"My daddy loved baseball, and we'd play after chores were done."

"Will you play it with me? I want to get another hit."

Cat stopped a few feet before the tack room door, apprehension in her eyes, as if she feared he would do or say something. Question was, what did she want him to say? He was sorry. Or he wasn't. Truth was, the only thing he was sorry for was misreading her. If she had said yes to his proposal, he wouldn't have been sorry at all.

"Your mother can show you," Cody said, wary about aggravating her.

Jake looked thoughtfully at Cat. "She can't play. She told me so."

"I can play. Just not well," Cat defended.

"We got a T-ball set. Can you puh-lease help me," Jake pleaded, and Cody felt the squeeze in the vicinity of his heart. He was coming to like the little tyke more than was a good idea, seeing as how the boy's mother felt about him.

Cody glanced at Cat for guidance. She definitely looked like a princess today. Just like she had Saturday night. And the funny thing was, he liked the view. He liked it too much. And he'd love to teach the little guy how to play baseball. Might be his only chance to teach a little boy like Cody's father had taught him. The thought was a sobering one, but one he'd been learning to live with. He had no choice.

Cat brushed her hair behind her ear. "Mr. Taylor is busy. It's quitting time soon, and he'll want to head home."

"Actually, I'm finishing up. I'd be happy to help Jake."

Chapter 14

Cat watched from her "outfielder" position as Cody showed her son how to hold the bat, told him not to take his eye off the ball, and demonstrated how to take a few practice swings before actually hitting the ball. Not that she had much to do regarding the ball. The few times Jake had connected so far, the ball had barely gone two yards, and Cat had been able to retrieve it with ease.

Jake's full attention was on the man making her heart ache with need. Both Jake and she needed a Cody Taylor in their life. Only this model had commitment issues and liked his women ranch ready. He wasn't for either Jake or her, and her protective side was worried about Jake getting too attached. It wasn't as if Cody lived so very far away once he went back to his ranch. Only she doubted he would visit Jake if he wasn't working at Pleasant Valley.

Yet, he did seem to be enjoying himself. The two high-fived when Jake hit the ball off the T, and Cody had been encouraging when Jake missed the ball, urging her son to try again. Jake didn't seem to get frustrated like he did with her. He giggled as Cody teased that he'd have to start calling Jake a ballplayer instead of a cowboy. Jake stubbornly asserted he'd always be a cowboy, even if he became a ballplayer.

It was cute, poignant, and heartbreaking because Cat knew this was what she couldn't give her son. That male-bonding experience. She might be able to help him play T-ball, she might even be able to send him to sports camps and let others more knowledgeable teach him, but the relationship forming before her eyes was something particular.

Why Jake's father had so completely abandoned this bright, energetic, eager little boy was something she would never understand. Part of her was glad for one less complication in her life. Part of her was angry that her son was missing out on something special. And part of her could not help but feel grateful to Cody Taylor for stepping in, even if it was just for a brief moment, to give her son what he was missing.

Jake nodded, focused, and swung. The ball flew off the T and over her head. Jake was jumping as if he was on a pogo stick, and Cody was fist-pumping the air.

Her little guy wasn't half bad for his first real lesson.

They'd been out for an hour, and dinner would surely be on the table by now. "Thank Mr. Taylor," Cat instructed her son.

Jake hung his head and kicked at the dirt. "One more," he pleaded.

"No more, Jake." Cody's voice was stern. "You need to listen to your mother, like we discussed."

"Say thank you," Cat prompted.

"Thank you, Cody," her son said.

Cody fist-bumped the boy, and Jake, resigned, shuffled along behind her as she led the way to the house. She was aware that Cody was following them, and she wondered why. He couldn't expect to be invited in.

Reaching the back door, she turned and hesitated. "Thank you, Cody. I'll see you in the morning."

"See you, Cody," Jake said as he pushed the door open.

"See you, partner. I'd just like to talk to your mother for a minute."

Cat felt…trapped as her son ran inside, leaving the door ajar. "Grandma is in the kitchen," she called after him.

Suddenly her hands felt clammy and her neck sweaty. She didn't want to talk to Cody. She wanted to forget Saturday night ever happened and just continue on as boss/employee. Was that asking too much?

But part of her was curious. Would he apologize? Would he try to convince her to accept his proposal? Was it something about the ranch, with nothing to do with Saturday night? She could only hope.

Cody stepped alongside her, close. Too close. Her pulse beat at her temple.

He looked down at her from under the brim of his hat.

She looked up at him, at his strong jaw, at his piercing blue eyes, at the five o'clock shadow defining his face. He rubbed the back of his neck and tipped up the brim of his hat.

"I need to apologize for suggesting…well, for suggesting an arrangement that was completely self-serving. I was out of line. And I can't even blame being drunk, because I wasn't. I was stone-cold sober. I knew exactly what I was asking because it is exactly

202

what I wanted. But I wasn't thinking about you and what you wanted."

"Forget it," she said and hoped she could forget the feeling that zinged through her every time he walked through the door.

He placed his hand on the wall behind her, trapping her. "I can't, Princess. I keep thinking about it. About you."

He was thinking about her?

Her mouth felt dry, and she tried to swallow, but it felt like a ball was lodged in her throat. His chest was inches away from her chest as he leaned into the arm supporting him. His finger brushed under her chin, raising it.

"It's hard, Princess. It should be easy. But it isn't."

The spot on her chin where his finger touched was hot. Flaming hot.

His lips were so close she had to fight the urge to wrap her arms around his neck, press her body against his, and kiss the daylights out of him. She still wanted him. She just wanted better terms.

"But I want you to know, I'm committed to trying. I hope to hell you find what you are looking for, Princess. For both our sakes."

And then, like a cold wind gusting over a lake, he turned and blew down the walk and out of the yard, leaving her heartbreakingly alone.

Kyle Langley stood behind his walnut desk and stared at her, a cat-that-swallowed-a-canary expression on his face. "So have you given anymore consideration to selling Pleasant Valley, Cat?"

He'd phoned Cat and told her he had some things

to discuss with her and had offered to drive out to meet with her. Given her mother and Jake had left that day for her mother's annual Memorial Day weekend visit Cat's uncle and his wife, Cat had decided to drive into Rawlins to meet with Kyle in person. Call her lazy, but it would give her an excuse to get takeout at the pizza parlor in town instead of cooking for a total of one.

Kyle had the kind of neat, sleek office that looked like not a lick of work got done in it. Not a book was unshelved, not a paper was on the desk, not a file cabinet or a folder made an appearance. It was all polished surfaces, angular lines, and monochromatic colors. Ensconced in his meticulously neat office with its polished wood desk, tall bookcases filled with lawyerly tomes and plush carpet, his question was a surprise. She could have answered that over the phone.

She tucked her legs under the ledge of the desk and folded her hands in her lap. "No. I'm not interested in selling."

That was the new truth. Though running Pleasant Valley overwhelmed her at times, since Cody had shown up, she was beginning to believe she could manage it. Under his tutelage, she was getting a handle on pasture management, grass plantings, feed supplements, and even moving herds.

Despite the hard physical work, there were things about ranching she enjoyed. Like wide-open spaces, fresh air, schedule flexibility, and yes, working with animals. It was a treat to ride out to the herd on horseback. It was a benefit to be there when her son got home from school. And she could already see that her son was a happy boy living on the ranch. A happy *cow*boy, as Cody would say.

At the thought of Cody, her heart squeezed. Even after their "talk" on the porch, he'd continued to be attentive to her son, taking time out at the end of the day to coach him on T-ball or, since Cody learned Jake was heading for her uncle's, teaching him to cast a fishing line. Jake looked forward to time with Cody so much, even her mother had noticed how much Jake was coming to dote on Cody—enough to voice her concern.

But overall, life on the ranch was working out, and Cat wanted to preserve it for her son, now more than ever.

Kyle leaned forward, placing his hands on the desk, his now serious expression demanding her attention. "You may change your mind when I tell you the offer that has come my way."

"What offer? I haven't put the ranch up for sale." Why would someone make an offer on property that wasn't on the market?

"True, but an offer has come in nonetheless. I have contacts in Wyoming, and I put out some feelers just in case. A property the size of Pleasant Valley would need some pump priming if you were to sell. Anyway, one of those contacts has struck pay dirt."

"But I'm not interested in selling." Nor did she want to be tempted after finally being at peace with ranching, largely due to hiring Cody.

It amazed her that in the few weeks since Cody had taken charge, so much had been accomplished. Scours had all but disappeared, and the herd was thriving. The loss of cattle had diminished, and there was now a pasture management system as well as a computerized ranch management program. The branding had been scheduled for the Thursday after Memorial Day weekend, and she had enlisted the help of Mandy Martin's brother, husband, and brother-in-law, as well as Libby's husband. She was actually looking forward to the event, which would bring out neighboring ranchers too. Everything was falling into place.

Except, of course, her love life.

"They are prepared to offer you a substantial price for your deeded land along with your BLM leases." Kyle pulled out the padded office chair and sat.

Being near Cody every day didn't help with her love life. Every time she saw him, it reminded her that he was the perfect man—if he wasn't a Taylor and was interested in settling down. It scared her because…she was falling in love with him.

That was the only explanation for the way her heart raced and her head got all muddled just seeing him across a pasture.

"Cat, are you listening?" Kyle asked, drawing her attention back to the matter at hand.

"Yes, someone wants to buy my land." *And it is not for sale.*

"They are offering a lot of money." Kyle named a seven-figure number. Her pulse kicked up, her neck felt damp, and her forehead hurt as a torrent of anxiety flooded through her.

That was far more than the land had been valued for purposes of the inheritance tax, and a sum she couldn't just dismiss. Perspiration seeped through her blouse.

"Why?"

Kyle shrugged. "Your ranch is one of the few intact ranches from its original founding. I suppose that carries value."

She didn't want to think about it. She didn't want to have to make such a life-altering decision—in either direction.

"As a lawyer I am bound to present the offer to you, and as a trustee, I feel bound to tell you that I would vote for this deal."

And as a trustee for her son's inheritance, she was bound to consider it.

"Haven't you been losing a lot of cattle, Cat? Are you really cut out to be a rancher? Wouldn't you rather open that preschool you've been talking about? With this kind of money, you and Jake could go wherever you wanted, invest it in whatever you wanted. As a trustee, I would be very supportive of investing some of the money in a preschool."

Silence loomed over the office as she tried to sort through Kyle's arguments. It could mean a new start. Somewhere that the name of McKenna didn't carry meaning. Somewhere other than an isolated ranch on the plains of Wyoming. Somewhere there would be people to interact with instead of cattle. Somewhere she might meet a future husband and father other than Cody Taylor.

But Pleasant Valley wasn't just a place—it was a legacy.

"Things have stabilized at the ranch since Cody Taylor arrived."

Kyle frowned. "Maybe in the short term, but do you really trust Cody Taylor to do right by Pleasant Valley? How do you know he hasn't been the one rustling your cattle?"

"How do you know about my cattle being rustled?" She didn't remember discussing that with Kyle.

He shook his head. "I ran into Will Springer the other day. He mentioned it."

Did Will suspect the losses were due to rustlers too? He never mentioned it. Still waiting for her to ask the right question before he would tell her what she needed to know. Cody never waited. He anticipated what she would ask and had the answer at hand. Thank goodness for that.

"I have no reason to suspect Cody Taylor. He has been nothing but helpful."

Kyle cocked his head. "Well, he has the neighboring ranch, so he would definitely have access. And don't you find it odd that he is helping you, a McKenna? You may have let a mountain lion into your herd, because being your ramrod would make it a lot easier to rustle your cattle, Cat. Have you thought of that?"

No, she hadn't. Because Cody wasn't like that. She was sure of it.

Kyle slid a piece of paper toward her. "Here's the offer. Take it home. Look it over. Talk to your mother. Get back to me next week. There's no immediate hurry, but they won't hang around for long. They'll find another property."

She glanced at the name on the document. "Who is LEW Consortium? That doesn't sound like a rancher's name."

Kyle waved a hand. "Nowadays for a ranch this size, it is usually run by a consortium of investors who want to own a ranch but can't afford one individually."

"They aren't developers, are they? Pleasant Valley can't be turned into a tract-house development."

Kyle folded his arms across his chest. "I assure you they aren't housing developers."

She folded the paper and placed it in her purse. "I will look it over and get back to you."

"Consider what I said—about ranching and Cody Taylor. He might talk a good game, might sound like he's helping you, but that could just be so he can steal you blind. I don't trust him. And your father wouldn't either."

Kyle Langley knew just what to say to undermine her confidence in her own judgment.

Chapter 15

Cody lifted the saddle off of the sawhorse in the tack room and proceeded to lug it out to the stable area, where his horse was tied and waiting.

For the past few days, Cody had struggled to keep his word and stop thinking about kissing Cat McKenna, touching her, and other things. It should have been easy, what with getting ready for branding at Pleasant Valley and preparing for calving season on the Cross T. It should have been, only it wasn't.

Maybe because he was with her every doggone day. And he looked forward to it. No denying that. Every time he was around her, and even when he wasn't, his mind churned through memories of kissing her and fantasies about other things he'd like to do with her.

Yup, he enjoyed talking over ranch issues a little too much. She was doing her homework about things like feed supplements, market conditions, and breeding. He'd found her huddled with Jim Smith one day talking about the merits of frozen semen versus turning out the bulls, and all three of them had a constructive discussion of bloodlines and hybrids.

But she'd kept it all business, preferring to meet

with him in the barn, or with another foreman or ranch hand in attendance, rather than alone in her office. That was probably wise, given where his thoughts kept taking him. But it wasn't any less frustrating.

Working around the ranch, he felt like a randy sixteen-year-old waiting to catch a glimpse of the girl of his dreams.

Only Cat McKenna was not the girl of his dreams, because he had no dreams, no illusions. He was a bankrupt rancher, and the most he could offer her, or any woman, was a booty call.

And that brought him to Jake. The little guy was clamoring for attention, and Cody was happy to give it to him, even if, afterward, when he was back at the Cross T, he felt hollowed out and lonely.

Maybe it was the loss of his father finally hitting him as Jace and he tackled cleaning out and packing up his dad's things. But Cody was pretty sure that a little boy named Jake and a pretty rancher named Cat had a lot to do with the deep need that overwhelmed him in the wee hours of the morning.

Hopefully, he could clear his mind for at least one night spent watching the herd. Tonight would be the first opportunity he'd had to see if his suspicions about the rustlers were true.

He planned to stake out the herd without letting anyone know. It had been a while since he'd camped out, and maybe it would do him good to be alone so he could puzzle through why he was so interested in Cat McKenna and figure out how he could control the lust that flashed through him whenever he was near her.

He flipped the saddle on his horse, Comanche. He'd brought Comanche over from the Cross T, a nine-year-old paint gelding he'd trained from a three-year-old. Comanche was a fine cow pony, and training the gelding had been what had whetted his appetite for breeding horses.

After cinching up, he loaded on his bedroll and some supplies, tying them to the back of his saddle. Yup, it had been a long time since he'd camped out. He was looking forward to it, even if he'd be spending the night alone.

Cat watched out the back kitchen window as Cody Taylor rode his horse toward the mountains. She glanced at the clock. Where was he going at seven o'clock in the evening? Shouldn't he be heading home rather than heading out? And with a full pack on the horse's rump.

The timer beeped, and she looked around the empty kitchen. Just her. For the next few days it would just be her. Cat had always enjoyed the annual visit to her aunt Cassie and uncle Len in Montana, but she couldn't go this year. Maybe never again, given the demands of the ranch. If there still was a ranch.

Selling would mean she wouldn't be tied down, at least not in the 24-7 way that a ranch tied you down. Of course, if she could permanently hire a ranch manager of Cody Taylor's caliber, it might not be an issue.

Using a potholder, Cat slid the slice of pizza from the oven and onto a paper plate before slumping down in a chair at the table. The aroma of crusty baked dough, seasoned tomato sauce, and cheese filled the room. She gobbled up her slice like it was her last meal, sauce dripping down the side of her mouth and sliding onto the plate below. What did it matter how sloppy she ate? There was no one to see it.

She reached for the toy action figure she'd retrieved earlier from under the table. She rolled it around in her hand. She wasn't used to being without her son and had never imagined how lonely she would feel. She set the toy down.

When her mother had offered to take Jake, she'd thought of all sorts of things she would do with the extra time. Take a long bubble bath. Meet the girls for drinks. Set out on another road trip to Laramie with Cyndi Lynn. She'd even changed into some fancy underthings so she'd be ready to go if Cyndi Lynn said yes. Only she never made the call or any plans, not even for a manicure.

She snorted at the idea of getting her nails done again. The results of her manicure in Laramie hadn't lasted past Sunday. She turned up the palms of her hands and gave them a good look. Reddened skin, calluses, dryness. She felt like hiding them behind her back.

"You're old before your time," she voiced out loud, breaking into the disconcerting quiet that had settled over the room.

She hadn't felt so old when she'd gone out to dinner with Cody. Or when he'd kissed her in Laramie.

After Saturday night and his subsequent coaching of Jake during the week, she'd been so unsettled by her growing attraction to him, she'd alternated between trying to avoid him and finding an excuse to be where he was in hopes of seeing him. Though she'd made sure she didn't see him alone, it didn't stop her craving the feel of his arms around her.

He seemed the embodiment of everything she wanted in a man. Smart, competent, and terrific with her son. In fact, Jake was becoming as starry-eyed about Cody as she felt. And that was a recipe for heartache for them both.

There were so many reasons it couldn't happen.

He might talk a good game, might sound like he's helping you, but that could just be so he can steal you blind.

So just where was he headed on her land?

Cat knew it was a bad idea. Somehow that hadn't been enough to stop her. With a sense of urgency, she'd tucked her hair under her hat, saddled up Custer, and headed in the same direction Cody had taken. Gratefully, she still had a half hour or more of daylight, and if he was heading out to the pastures where he'd moved the herd, she'd have enough time to catch up to him.

And then what?

She'd confront him, she guessed. What reason could there be for him to ride out to her herd on his own time? Her stomach went queasy.

What if he was the one rustling her herd, like Kyle insinuated? What if he'd needed the money so badly he'd decided to take her stock and working at Pleasant Valley was part of the ruse?

A hundred and thirty-eight head was a lot to lose.

And she only had his say that she'd lost them. What if she hadn't lost them? What if Cody had given her a lower count because he intended to help himself to a few of her steers? Wouldn't she have assumed the loss happened before Cody got there, like he surely intended?

Had she inadvertently let a panther in with her cattle? She pondered that unsettling possibility as she rode Custer over the grassy ground.

As time passed and light waned, she looked out over the range as it slipped into the shadows of evening. It had been years since she'd been out on horseback at this time of night. There was something magical about it. Like any minute she'd see fairies dancing over the waving grasses sprinkled with dew.

Pleasant Valley was one of the prettiest ranches in Wyoming, the range stretching out for miles of uninterrupted beauty. In the distance to the right, the thin, slate-blue ribbon of water that separated her ranch from the Taylors' knifed through the gently mounding land, while the mountains, looking like giant purple whales, glowed in the distance under a lowering sun that streaked pinks, purples, oranges, and ever-expanding gray across the horizon.

Looked like rain could be in the offing later.

Wind blew against her face, the air holding on to some warmth and moisture from the day. This meadow had been used for staging prior to calving, but already she could see the grasses shooting back up to create a thin blanket of sage green. This was the rhythm of nature, of regrowth and rebirth. There were worse places she could be. And despite the demanding work, she was coming to appreciate this land and what it took to keep it. Only now she might be selling it all, selling out for a load of money. The thought added to her anxiety.

With the view wide and unbroken, it wouldn't be hard to spot him, especially if he was headed out to the herd. What if he was hiding out, like in the old line shack that was now used for storage of rope and wire? She nudged Custer into a trot.

Beyond confronting him, she had no plan.

Chapter 16

"What are you doing here!" The voice was firm and scolding, but there was no mistaking whose voice it was.

Cat whirled around at the same time Cody Taylor lowered the shotgun he had been pointing at her back. Cody actually looked mad. At her!

She had arrived to find the herd grazing at the bottom of the hills that rolled through the west pastures. She'd dismounted and staked her horse in order to search the ground for any signs that would reveal Cody's whereabouts since, in the dim light, there was no other horse in sight. By the time she'd arrived, the cows were mere shadows as some milled and grazed, others bedded down for the night.

Her hands found the support of her hips, and she stared at the man who seemed to have frozen in place.

"I might ask the same of you. What are you doing here after hours? And with a shotgun, no less."

"Damn it," he said, vigorously shaking his head. "I could have killed you. Damn near did. Sneaking up on someone like that."

If she didn't know better, she'd say his free hand was trembling, but it must have been the low light playing tricks on her vision. "I could say the same about you. I'll ask again—what are you doing here, on my land, after hours and without telling me?"

She prayed she'd believe him. She didn't want to be wrong about him. She didn't want to find out he'd duped her. She'd been deceived by a man before, and it had cost her dearly.

Cody placed his shotgun firmly by his side, shaken by the fact he'd pointed it at Cat before he'd realized just who had followed him. Having tied his horse behind the old line shack and camped out on the far side of one of the small hills that mounded the rocky pasture, he had found a spot to watch the herd unobserved. Only to find someone trailing him. With her hair tucked under her hat and her back to him, he hadn't been able to tell who it was until she'd turned around.

Only then had he realized he could have shot her. He wiped an arm across his brow. Despite the cool air of the higher elevation, he was sweating.

"I'm trying to catch a rustler who I hope isn't scouting right now, because I've certainly blown my cover. I didn't want to risk you telling someone. I don't know who the culprit is yet, but I suspect it's someone who knows Pleasant Valley Ranch pretty damn well. That could mean it is someone working for you."

Her hands were on her curvy hips, and her chest rose as she took a deep breath. He admired her chest. Perky and perfectly sized.

"That description would include you."

Cody felt the verbal slap as if his face had met the

flat of her hand, sparking anger he struggled to control. A man's reputation summed up his worth. And no one had ever trampled on his.

Too furious to speak, he turned on his heel and walked away, toward his gear and the line shack. While the cows lowed in the background, he could feel the steam rising in his blood as his boots crunched along the rocky soil. He didn't deserve her suspicions. He merited better than this. If she'd been a man calling him out as she had, he'd have decked her.

Despite the loss of money he so desperately needed, better to find out now how little she thought of him than to go on fooling himself that she respected him, maybe even liked him. Enough to find some solace in each other's arms. What a fool he'd been to even contemplate such an arrangement with a woman who couldn't hide her disdain for him and the life he valued.

"Cody," she called from behind him, her voice loud but wavering. He kept walking, taking bigger strides to lengthen the distance between them.

Nope, he'd dodged a bullet.

He heard her boots scuffing along the stony ground at a run as she breathlessly called his name.

He was surprised at how much her lack of faith cut him. Anger was one thing. But her lack of confidence in who he was felt more like betrayal. More like she'd knocked the supports right out from under him, sending him into a free fall of emotion. He'd thought they'd gotten beyond mistrust. Way beyond.

The scuffing noise was getting closer.

He turned. Ready to have it out. She stopped just a few feet away, her breathing ragged.

"I'm sorry. I..." There was desperation in her voice.

"You don't accuse a man of stealing and then think you can say a few words and all is forgiven. I may not have much in this world. But I do have my reputation. Yet just now you accused me of something no rancher accuses another of unless it's meant. You either believe in me, or you don't. There are no shades of gray in this."

She came nearer, head bowed but eyes glued on him, approaching him tentatively, like she was afraid he might balk and walk away. Well, she had reason to be afraid of that. But something held him in place. Something made him want to hear from her lips that she didn't believe what she'd said.

"I'm scared, Cody. Down to my very core. I'm not sure if I have what it takes to run this operation, and then you tell me someone is rustling my cattle..."

"It's a theory right now."

"*May* be rustling my cattle," she corrected, her voice breaking. "And that it is likely someone I know. Someone I trust. My trust has been betrayed before."

"What does your gut tell you? Because if it tells you not to trust me, it will be best for both of us to go our separate ways."

"My gut...says to trust you. And I do."

The apology was in her eyes, and he softened. "Why'd you say what you said then?"

"I guess...I guess I wanted to show you how difficult it is to accept that it could be someone working at Pleasant Valley. I want to help find these rustlers," she said, wiping a hand across her cheek. "I want to know who's been taking my cattle."

"Too dangerous. If there are rustlers, you can bet they'll be armed—just like I am. You turn around and head back. I've got a flashlight in my pack if you need it. Light is fading." Cody looked up at the darkened sky just as a huge clap of thunder sounded in his ears. Hell.

Cat felt a drop of rain. And then another. And another. And suddenly it was pouring.

Cody swore an oath.

"You didn't happen to bring a tent, did you?" he asked as water dribbled down the crown of his hat and splashed off the brim.

"No, didn't you?"

Already she could feel the wet and cold seeping into her skin as the rain intensified. She hadn't brought a jacket, much less a tent. She'd been so intent on finding him, she'd just saddled up and rode out.

"No. The old line shack." He pointed to the weathered structure a few yards to the side of the small hill.

"Isn't it filled with supplies?" Wind gusted around her, throwing water on her like someone had dumped a bucket over her hat.

"Seems we have three choices." Cody was shouting above the pelting rain. "Shelter in the line shack, get wet out here, or risk our horses as well as get soaked heading back in the dark and the rain."

Thunder pounded above them. In the distance, lightning sliced the dark sky. The herd milled closer together to huddle against the rain.

"Hell, looks like it will be a head banger. Right now, our best bet is to wait it out in the line shack, and when it stops, decide whether to head back or stay," Cody shouted. Not waiting for her thoughts on the matter, he headed toward her horse, clearly expecting her to follow.

Cat scurried after him, her boots sinking into the muddy grasses.

She easily led Custer to the back of line shack. The horse seemed satisfied to be secured next to Cody's paint gelding and out of the direct line of the wind that had kicked up. She uncinched the saddle and pulled it and the blanket off her horse. Rain pressed her wet clothes next to her skin, making the fabric akin to slime on a rock.

Cody had already grabbed his saddle and his pack off his horse, and she footslogged after him as he strode to the door. He kicked the shack door open and tossed in the pack before carrying the saddle and his shotgun to the far corner. The pack thumped as it hit the floor. By the time she had limped inside under her burdens and kicked the door closed, Cody was shining a flashlight beam around the shack's dirt-spattered wood floor.

"Do you think there are mice in here?" she asked as she tentatively moved farther in and set down her saddle. Vermin were not high on her list of companions. Another crack of thunder, this time louder, sounded above them.

"Definitely." Cody's voice held amusement as the flashlight's beam hit on rolls of wire and loops of rope stacked around two of the walls. The light caught sight of a tattered blanket covering a crude structure on the far side, which had probably been a bed once. "They don't like the rain any more than we do."

The din of the storm had grown louder as the wind pelted raindrops against the roof. They'd made it just in time, though her clothes were soaked. At least the light hadn't caught any moving critters…yet.

"Be careful of the barbs in those wire bails. Don't get too close," he cautioned, motioning to the rolls of wire lined up like coiled sentries.

Cat bit her lip. "We're going to just stand here and wait?" Between the saddles and the fencing supplies, there wasn't much room in the small cabin.

Cody handed her the flashlight as he grabbed his bedroll from the pack. "I'm sitting down." He folded his bedroll in half and dropped it in front of her onto the floor, at the same time beckoning her to take a seat.

"We can't see the rustlers from here, can we?" There were no windows in the shack.

"No. And they might strike in the rain. Washes away any prints." He slid down onto the floor, sitting akimbo. She followed, pulling off her wet hat and setting it to the side. Thanks to her hat, her hair had not gotten soaked, and it tumbled around her damp shoulders.

Their knees touched. A raw chill shivered through her. Her hair might be dry, but the rest of her felt clammy and cold. She scrunched, hugging her knees to her moist chest and away from contact with Cody.

"You're trembling in those wet clothes. You've got to get out of them. You can put on my jacket to keep warm. With that rain out there, no way I can start a fire. All the wood will be wet as a duck in a pond."

"I am cold. But where will you be while I'm changing? There's barely room in here to stretch our legs."

"I'll close my eyes. You'll just have to trust me."

As Cody shrugged out of his jacket, he wondered if Cat was capable of trust, of trusting him. She was a McKenna, after all.

She grabbed the jacket from his outstretched hand. He clamped his eyes shut as promised.

"Glad I've had practice changing in cramped restrooms a time or two," she said as he listened to the clomp of boots hitting the ground and the rustling of fabric being removed.

He concentrated on counting silently so his imagination wouldn't take flight. He got to a hundred and twenty-four before she said okay.

He opened his eyes and caught sight of red lace against creamy skin before the ranch coat was zipped. Like a cherry on top of whipped cream, that visual conjured up mouthwatering thoughts.

He wished he hadn't seen it.

Wished he didn't know she wore nothing but red lace under his jacket. But he was a man, and his mind set to processing the possibilities. Bikini or thong? Cut high or string? Matching bra? With front or back fastening? He had more questions than a lingerie model beginning a shoot. And wasn't that an arousing thought. Jeezus. Who thought he'd ever be jealous of his coat?

The jacket was big enough to cover the essentials, but that left a lot of leg uncovered.

"Feel better?" he asked, knowing he didn't.

She nodded as she tucked her hands into the jacket's pockets. "Your jacket is surprisingly dry."

"Ranch jackets are made for this type of weather."

He scooped up her clothes and laid out her shirt

and pants on the rolls of barbed wire, careful the barbs didn't catch on the cloth. Her flowered scent rose up from the damp fabrics, bringing into relief memories of Saturday night. This was going to be hell.

He turned back around. She was pulling on her boots, but they didn't cover enough of what seemed like miles of shapely legs. He was almost grateful when she tucked those gorgeous gams under her.

"I can't ride home with just your jacket on."

His gaze swept over her, taking in how pretty she looked with her hair tumbled around her shoulders and wearing just his jacket and a pair of cowgirl boots that had never looked sexier. He rubbed a hand under his chin and thought about stripping that jacket and taking a gander.

"When we leave here, you can step back in your jeans, but I'd leave the blouse off and just go with the jacket because without sun, nothing is going to dry in the dark and humidity."

It would cause a stir if they rode back together, especially since it was unlikely they'd be able to start before first light. He wouldn't risk the horses in the mud and the dark. He'd have to think about how to stage things so rumors didn't get started.

"Guess we can't leave before dawn. And the rustlers, if there are any, won't come in the rain." She hugged the coat tighter around her, and the pout of her mouth reminded him too much of kissing her.

"Rain can be a rustler's friend. Wipes away any trace. On the other hand, depends on how bad a rain. If this is a soaker, the ground could be too soft to get a truck up the dirt road that runs up the side of this pasture. But if this is a fast-moving storm, it might work out for them."

"You didn't check the weather report either."

Cody shrugged. "Not since this morning. My mistake, obviously."

As if on cue, there was a muffled roaring sound. Like an engine.

"Seems the rustlers did check the weather and decided it was fast moving enough." Cody felt a mixture of regret and steely determination to get the bastards. He reached for the shotgun. "You stay here."

Chapter 17

Rifle in hand, Cody crouched at the entrance to the line shack and cracked open the door. He angled his head until he could see lights from the beams of the trailer truck highlighting the falling rain and the bleak countryside.

Adrenaline rushed through him as he sighted two shadowy figures moving among the herd, which had bunched up tight against the storm, making things easier for rustlers. He took a deep breath as he poked the gun's barrel through the narrow opening.

He'd originally planned to confront them. He'd even brought handcuffs and rope to tie them up. He figured his shotgun would serve as a motivator. Not that they wouldn't be armed too, but he would have the element of surprise. More than anything, he wanted to know who was doing this.

But Cat was in the cabin, and if things got ugly, she could be in danger.

The most important thing was not to let them steal any more cattle.

"What are you going to do?" She had come up to stand behind him.

He turned to look at her and was caught by the

shadow of worry that now sheathed her pretty face as she leaned over him to peek through the narrow opening.

"I told you to stay put."

"This is my ranch. Those are my cattle." A shaky hand brushed hair behind her ear.

He turned back to the shadowy figures moving farther into the herd, outlined by the beams from the truck.

"I'm opting for scaring them. This time. It's too dangerous to try to take them."

"I can call the sheriff." She waved her phone, which she held in her other hand.

"First off, I doubt you'd get a cell signal out here, and second, they'd be gone before the sheriff could arrive. We are miles from the main drag." But only one mile from the paved road that led out to the highway.

"Do something!" she urged. "They're leading one of the calves away."

Cody looked back out the door. Sure enough a shadowy figure was snaking through the herd with a calf in tow. "Only if you stay back." Cody demanded. She took a step back.

"Far from the door." This time he uttered it as a command.

Hesitantly she plodded back, nearer to the old bed.

He didn't want her any place bullets might fly. He turned back, pointed his shotgun so the barrel was aimed out and toward the empty copse of trees to the right of the herd. The shadowy figures slithered through the cattle, one of them leading an animal. He took a breath. And fired, aiming over their heads. The gun recoiled against his shoulder.

Bedlam ensued. The herd dispersed in a full-out run. The cow being led bolted, causing the man leading it to slip. His partner pulled him up, and they scrambled toward the truck.

Cody crouched on his belly as he heard a shot ring out in response. He couldn't tell where the shot was aimed, and it looked like the rustler who fired it had fired a hand gun, not a rifle or shotgun. They'd probably left the long-range arms in the truck. Cody fired another shot, again aimed at the treetops. It was unlikely they knew where he had fired from, but Cody wasn't going to take chances.

The man who didn't fall reached the truck first. The other one, probably older, moved like he was hurting. Cody wanted to go after them, but with the weather, it was doubtful he could overtake them without risking his horse. Still.

"Stay here," he said looking back at her. "And this time I mean it." He hoped she'd listen. She'd be a sight in just his jacket, even in the veil of shadows.

"What are you going to do?" She came toward him like she was prepared to follow.

"See if I can get close enough to get a license plate." He snatched the flashlight from the floor.

"It's dark. And it's raining."

"Got to try." It was as simple as that. This might be the only chance he'd have of catching these thieves.

"Here, take your jacket. You'll need protection more than me."

Before he could protest, she'd shrugged out of ranch coat and stood there shivering in nothing but a red lace bra that pushed her breasts to overflowing, and a scanty, lacy red string bikini that barely covered her private areas, and a pair of fancy boots. She looked like a fantasy out of a soft-porn movie. His mouth went dry.

Now he knew.

The slam of the truck doors echoed in the night.

"Take it," she demanded, holding out his coat. "Just be careful."

Cat sat in the dark on the bedroll, wrapped in a saddle blanket that smelled like horse. She was cold and damp and raw...and afraid. Not for her safety—for Cody's. Several more shots had been fired before the hum of the truck's motor had vanished minutes ago, leaving only the intermittent whoosh of wind and the chorus of night critters and bugs. Given the relative silence, she imagined the rain had stopped also.

The temperature must have dropped for her to be so rawboned cold, and the scratchy horse blanket didn't offer enough warmth to keep her from shivering. She'd checked on her clothes, and they were about as wet as when she'd shed them.

Where was he? Why hadn't he come back?

What if one of those shots had found its mark?

He'd been commanding...and brave. Protective and fierce.

And never more attractive.

What was it about Cody Taylor that made her want to curl up in his arms like a favored feline and never leave?

She'd stood before him in nothing but her underwear. And he'd appeared stricken into speechlessness by the sight. The thought made her both smile and blush.

Where was he?

Deciding not to wait any longer, she crawled to the door. Opening it slightly, she peeked out. A gust of cooler air blasted her face and sent a chill through her. The rain had stopped, but looking out into the black night, she couldn't see anything or anyone else. If she couldn't see anything, then nothing could see her.

One of the horses whinnied.

Maybe one of the rustlers was still out there. Maybe he was looking for Cody. And wouldn't she be a sitting duck in the line shack.

She rose up halfway and scooted out the door. The sounds of the herd were distant, more distant than before. She guessed the shots, combined with thunder and lightning, had frightened them. No telling where they had scattered. Or how far.

As her eyes adjusted to the murky dark, she could pick out outlines of trees, the contrasts of grays between land and sky.

Not a shadow of a person was moving. Where was Cody? Had he taken off with the rustlers because he was one of them? Her lawyer had put that notion in her head. Risking his life to protect her, Cody deserved better from her.

But what if something had happened to him?

Hugging the blanket, she walked toward the tree line, picking her way among the wet grass, brush, and stones that covered the ground. She'd gone about five yards, when suddenly a strong arm snagged her around the waist and pulled her against a hard body and damp canvas.

She cried out as fear washed over her, tingling her toes and pricking her insides.

"What about staying in place didn't you understand?" a familiar voice growled.

Under the horse blanket was slick flesh, lacy fabric, and a honeyed scent. Cody felt his body respond in full to having a nearly naked Cat against him in the dark. Except this one was squirming for her freedom. Cody released her. And she turned on him.

"Where were you?" she said in a whispered yell as she adjusted the inadequate blanket, leaving lots of leg exposed. "It's been forever…"

Water was still dripping from his hat, his jeans were steamed to his body, his boots had taken on water, and he felt like a wet hide that had just been salted. Only to come back to find her exposing herself to…danger. And wearing cowgirl boots and a too-small horse blanket that revealed more than it covered, he wasn't just talking about the criminal kind of danger.

"I was searching for clues. They hightailed it out of here before I could get a license plate, but I wanted to see if I could find anything around the tire marks, something they might have dropped. What I didn't expect to find was you creeping out into the middle of the pasture. What the hell were you thinking?"

There was no accounting for sense, or lack thereof.

"I thought you might have gotten hurt."

Despite the dark, his eyes had adjusted enough to see the shapely curves of her lower body—from her tight waist to her sweet hips to her long limbs. Cat

McKenna didn't look like his fantasy. She looked better than his fantasy.

Cody raised his gun. "I had this with me."

"But I didn't know what they had." She bit her lip. "I was worried."

She'd been worried about him. He tucked that away.

"No need to worry about me."

He motioned toward the line shack. "It's damp out here. Best hunker down inside."

Wrapped in the blanket, Cat walked back to the shack without another word. She plunked down on the bedroll, and he prayed she'd keep that blanket wrapped around her, even though he itched to turn the flashlight on and take a full gander. Instead he sat down next to her.

He had to figure out a way to get through the night without losing his restraint. The fact she as much as accused him of rustling should have made that easy. It hadn't.

"Did you find anything?"

He pulled out a bandanna from his pocket. It was streaked in mud, and in the gray light, it was hard to tell that it was blue and white. "Just this."

"It could be anyone's, dropped on any day."

"True." But only one man wore a bandanna on a regular basis. Apparently, Cat believed more in Will Springer's innocence than she had in his. Not that the bandanna was a lot to go on, but it pointed in a direction that was hard to ignore. With a lot less evidence, she'd been ready to convict him.

"At least they didn't get any of the cattle," Cat said between shivers.

The only part of Cody that wasn't wet was the part covered by the ranch jacket and his hat. His jeans stuck to his body like a thousand barnacles and felt just as clammy.

"Here, take the jacket back." He shrugged out of the coat. At least the top half of him had been kept dry.

Apparently she didn't have to be asked twice. Red lace and curvy flesh flashed before they were hidden underneath his jacket. She handed him the blanket.

"I'm going to have to get out of my jeans." He looked at her for a reaction, but she merely nodded.

He toed off his boots and shimmied out of his pants, made more difficult by the wetness and weight of the denim. There he was in his skivvies and shirt with a beautiful woman wearing red lace and cowgirl boots, and nothing was going to happen.

"We stopped them tonight, but no doubt they'll be back. And no doubt they have been helping themselves to your cattle all along," he said. He needed to keep on topic and his unruly thoughts at bay.

"If only we knew who they were."

"They pulled out like someone had set them on fire. There will be some terrible ruts in that dirt road. But bottom line, by the time I got within sight of the truck, they were already backing down the road. It was too dark to see the license plate. All I can say for sure is it was two men, one older, one younger."

"You got that close?"

"No. I know that from watching them run to the truck. The older one was moving pretty slow, and he was the one who tripped and fell. The younger one moved out like a swarm of bees was on his tail. I'm figuring that was the age difference between them."

"But nothing to identify them." She hugged the ranch coat tighter.

"No." Except that bandanna, which Cody felt should be pretty convincing. "But at least we know that it is rustling, not something you are doing at the ranch, that's the cause of the majority of losses."

"Who would do such a thing?" She visibly shivered.

"My cousin's a detective in Laramie, and he said rustling is on the upswing in these parts due to the rise in drug use. At the prices a calf commands, it's an easy way to get money. I know you don't want to hear this, but I believe these are people familiar with the terrain and habits of Pleasant Valley. We only recently moved this herd. Someone had to know that."

Cat felt the truth of that statement to her very core. Someone was duping her. And it couldn't be Cody, as Kyle had suggested, since she'd been with him when the rustlers came. Her stomach pitched at the realization that she'd lashed out at the one man who was actually helping her. The man who had risked his life to save her cattle and protect her.

"What should I do?" Not for the first time, she felt helpless. Selling the ranch would relieve her of all of this turmoil, all of these decisions, all of these problems. And relieve Jake from having to face them in the future. But this land had been in her family for generations. Would she be the one to end the legacy? "Should I round up the crew?"

Cody draped the small blanket over their legs. Both of their feet hung out the end, only she had boots on. His boots needed to dry out.

"I think we will have to be a little more subtle than that."

The "we" sounded encouraging. His hair was mussed, and moisture still clung to his long lashes. She could see a scrap of his white underwear peeking out from the blanket, and his shirt hugged his chest. It had been a while since she'd seen a man in his underwear.

"Have you decided I'm not a rustler, Princess?"

He made her sound like she was high and mighty. Given she felt overwhelmed, that was a blatant mischaracterization.

"I never said you were." Though in truth, she had considered it based upon Kyle's suspicions. "I said that when you said it might be someone working on the ranch, that could include you. I don't want to believe that it is one of the hands from Pleasant Valley."

"My question stands."

"I do not believe you are rustling my cattle." She said each word slow and distinct so he would know she meant it. "But do you really think it might be someone from the ranch, even Will Springer, based only on that bandanna?"

"It's more important what you think," he said.

"I don't want to think." A shiver ran through her as the cold nipped at the spots of flesh that weren't covered. "It's freezing."

"Surely not that cold, though the plains cool off at night. Scooch on over here, and we'll spoon."

Spooning with Cody Taylor? "I don't think…"

"Honey, this is strictly utilitarian. Nothing else. Just like that time after high school. You remember that time."

She did. Too vividly. "That was…"

"What exactly was it, Princess?"

She swallowed, the saliva doing nothing to wet her dry throat. "I am sorry for that."

"What part of 'that'?"

"My father. Not standing up for you."

He stared at her, no hint of what he was thinking on his face, making her guilt even more palpable.

"It was easier to let him believe I was the culprit, was it? Guess he died thinking I had tried to take advantage of you. Instead of protecting you."

She turned so she wouldn't have to see his face, look in his eyes. "I did tell him the truth before I left for college. After I came back home, he actually said some nice things about you and Jace now and again." Though her father still thought the worst of her for going to that party. It played into his narrative that she was impulsive and pigheaded.

And she couldn't say she blamed him, since she had gone to a camp-out party on a former classmate's ranch, knowing guys would be there and realizing, too late, that she had put herself in danger. She'd never been with a guy, and when guys several years older with bad reputations had shown up drunk or drugged—she couldn't tell—looking for some action, she'd realized she was in over her head. Almost immediately, the girls she was with had paired up, but several guys, mostly the ones with the worst reputations, hadn't. Yet.

Then she had spotted Cody. She must have looked like a frightened little girl, because he'd immediately sauntered over, told her to act like she was with him and nothing would happen to her. She'd crawled into his bedroll. He'd wrapped a protective arm around her and kept his word.

The other guys had just gotten drunker, more rowdy. Some had brought shotguns to the camp out. The worst of them were getting belligerent.

And then, in the middle of the night, her father had shown up. He'd gotten wind that the camp out wasn't exactly sanctioned by the girl's parents, who were attending a rodeo in another state. And he'd come looking for her. And found her in the arms of Cody Taylor.

He'd called Cody every name in the book, taken a swing that landed Cody a black eye, and dragged her from the scene. She'd been grounded for weeks before she headed off to college. When she'd told her father the truth, he'd said nothing. Just walked away.

"Good to know you set the record straight." Cody lifted the flap of the bedroll. "Get in. It's the best way we can keep each other warm."

Chapter 18

Chilled from the brisk wind and damp clothes and weary from the ordeal, she tugged the saddle blanket from around her and maneuvered into the sleeping bag, hoping that the dark concealed her underwear. At least now they could both stretch their legs.

Immediately the heat from his body engulfed her as she nestled against his warm chest, spooned against his hips, and felt hair-brushed legs rub her bare thighs. He wrapped his arms around her, completing the cocoon. His saddle formed a backstop, and he leaned against it so she could lay her head back on his shoulder. She breathed in the scent of fresh air, damp cotton, and man.

She felt comforted and safe—and she shouldn't feel any of those things.

"Did you wear those red lacy underthings to drive me crazy," he whispered, his breath tickling her ear.

"I…" She fumbled through her mind to try to find some plausible explanation for her choice of undergarments and came up empty. "I like to feel feminine."

He tightened his embrace. "Believe me, honey. You don't need help in that department."

"So you really think it is someone from the ranch who is rustling." She needed to change the subject. "Most everyone has worked at Pleasant Valley for at least a few years, and all of them hired by my father. You are my first hire."

"All the more reason you shouldn't have doubted me." He said it resolutely but not with anger.

"The problem is, I don't have any confidence in my judgment about anything or anyone." And why should she? The one time she'd put her trust in someone, she'd been burned, and badly. And yet there had been signs with Jake's father. She'd chosen to ignore them. It had been easier than facing the truth. "That's why I didn't go with the changes you recommended. I just…I'm just not sure I can be a rancher."

He reached for her hand. His thumb stroked her palm. Lazy, swirling strokes, as if he wasn't conscious of what he was doing…or very conscious.

"There's a lot to learn, but you can do it. Hell, I bet you got A's in school. Made your daddy proud."

His fingers brushed up her arm, and his light touch sent a little tremor rippling through her.

"I got A's, but it didn't make my daddy proud." She whispered the truth and felt the old hurt lodge near her heart.

His fingers were once again fondling the soft skin of her palm, caressing, soothing, bathing her in pleasurable little tingles. She should pull her hand away.

"Of course it did."

"No. The only thing he ever wanted was a boy to leave his ranch to. I've come to realize I was just a side trip he'd been forced to take. Nothing I did made him proud. And much I did made him…well, not proud."

She really should pull her hand away. The connection was too intimate. But she didn't.

"Your father stood by you when you needed him, Cat. Half the county was betting he wouldn't. That took not only love but, for someone as old school as your father seemed to be, I imagine it took courage."

"You're wrong." Her father had not been courageous.

Now his thumb was circling her wrist, lightly touching the area where one would test for a pulse, a pulse that was no doubt jumping impatiently under her skin, if the beat of her heart was any measure.

"You're his daughter. I only knew your father from a distance, but one thing I think our shared family history has shown is that family sticks together."

"He didn't want me to have the baby." A lump lodged in her throat. "He wasn't brave, Cody. He was willing to sacrifice my child for his pride." And she'd never been able to forgive him for that.

He blew out a breath, the warm air tickling her ear. "I'm sorry to hear that. And glad it worked out the way it did. Jake's a fine little boy."

"Thank you." Tears sprang to her eyes. She would not cry. She'd cried enough over the years. "Jake worships you." He'd also worshiped his grandfather.

"I get a kick out of him. Any man would."

Any man but Jake's own father. Who didn't know Jake and apparently didn't care to know him. Not that she hadn't tried. In the beginning.

"My father certainly changed his mind when he saw Jake. I hadn't planned to ever see him or Pleasant Valley again. But after I was laid off...well, that's when I asked to come home...for Jake's sake. My son deserved better than an unemployed, soon-to-be impoverished mother if all I had to do was swallow my pride. So I did."

"And your father took you in."

"One look at Jake was all it took. Now he had someone he could groom into his replacement. Someone who would keep the McKenna legacy alive. But me? I don't think he ever forgave me. I always wondered if he regretted his earlier edict. But I never had the courage to confront him." Nor the inclination to forgive him.

"You know the sad thing?" she said, twisting all the way around to face him. "I didn't care. It was enough for me that he accepted Jake. I didn't care what he thought of me."

"You did what you had to do for your boy's sake. No shame in that. One thing it appears you and your father have in common is tenacity. You don't give in or give up—you get moving."

Her father had always called her pigheaded. Tenacious sounded much better, even if it wasn't how she felt. Not with the issues facing the ranch. Not with the offer on the table.

Cody's hand stroked her arm, as if offering comfort.

Maybe if she said it out loud, told someone, the decision she had to make wouldn't seem so formidable. Maybe he could help her think it through...before she had to discuss it with her mother.

"I've an offer for the ranch. A good offer. I don't know if I can refuse it."

The more she had thought about the money, the opportunity it would give Jake versus saddling him with all the issues and problems of running an operation like Pleasant Valley, the more tempting the offer had become.

He stroked his hands down her hair.

"I imagine it was a good offer. What do they want to do with it?"

Even though they were having a serious conversation, the way he was touching her made her feel... desired.

"They aren't interested in putting up houses, so I assume they want to ranch." She looked back at Cody for confirmation, but his eyes were narrowed in skepticism.

"Who is 'they'?"

"Some consortium. My lawyer didn't really say who was behind it, just that these were investors who couldn't afford a ranch of Pleasant Valley's size individually."

"Princess, the days of investors buying up ranches in Wyoming to actually ranch has pretty much gone the way of the stagecoach. Can't think of a ranch run by investors since the days when those British aristocrats were coming over and taking land. You know, the ones that our ancestors fought for land rights."

"Then why is a group of investors interested in Pleasant Valley?"

"That's the million-dollar, or several-million-dollar, question your lawyer should be answering. I assume you hold the mineral rights to your land. Those of us who have held the land since homesteading generally do."

"You mean for oil and mining and stuff?"

"Exactly."

"I think so. I know we did when Dad allowed those oil wells to be drilled."

"You might want to see if you can find that information, either among your father's papers, or ask that handy-dandy lawyer of yours. See if anyone sent inquiries to your father. If something sounds too good to be true, Princess, it usually is."

"You don't think there is a consortium?"

"I don't think there is a consortium that wants to go into ranching. Would you sell it for mining or oil drilling?"

The thought of the land being pockmarked with more oil wells, or craters from mining, made her stomach turn. Since she had returned home, a slow welcoming love of this land, her land, had stolen upon her. "No. Absolutely not." The answer was surprisingly easy. "I think I finally understand why my ancestors, why my father, was so devoted to preserving it."

"That sounds like a rancher talking, Princess."

Cody nuzzled her neck, sending a wave of sensations through her.

"I'd ask a few more questions of that slick lawyer of yours before I'd make any decisions."

"Why do you call me *princess*?"

He stared at her, looking puzzled.

"I don't like it," she said.

It took him a moment to answer. "At first it was

because your father pampered you, like a princess. And then because, though you know nothing about ranching, don't seem to like anything about ranching, you've inherited a kingdom of a ranch."

So the truth was Cody Taylor didn't respect her. That shouldn't have surprised her. But after these last few weeks, it hurt.

"But," he continued, "since we've been working together and I have seen you knee deep in crud, herding cattle, avoiding a stampede, and giving it your all to learn, it's more about you being top dog around Pleasant Valley."

Pride bloomed inside her at his faint praise.

She felt the soft brush of his fingers down her cheek. "It's more of a compliment now."

And one she wouldn't soon forget. Even if she gave up the ranch. It meant more than he could know. She wrapped her arms around his neck.

"So you think I can ranch Pleasant Valley. Leave it in good shape for my son?"

"Princess, I think you can do anything you've a mind to do. But you have to believe that. My telling you isn't going to convince you."

Chapter 19

She stared through the night's gray curtain into his eyes, felt her heart beat hard against her chest, and wondered if he would kiss her. And knew she wanted him to. She didn't want to fall for Cody Taylor. She didn't want to love him. But it was too late.

She brushed her thumb across his cheek, roughened by stubble.

"You did wear red lace to torture me," he whispered. "There's a price to pay for that, Princess."

A price she was too willing to pay.

He lowered his head. She raised hers.

His lips slowly brushed over hers, warm and firm. As if testing out the taste of her.

His mouth covered hers, and he pulled her tight against his chest, against his body, against the bulge in his underwear. His tongue probed the seam of her lips, and she opened her mouth and invited him in.

This kiss wasn't slow. It wasn't tentative. It was demanding. And fierce. And provocative. As his tongue performed a slow dance with hers, he literally sucked the oxygen from her lungs.

He'd chased away her doubts, listened to her fears, and told her she wasn't worthless. She felt closer to him than she had to any man in a long, long time. She knew she was playing with fire, but she was beyond caring. He pulled desire from where it had been buried deep inside of her, driven there by circumstances.

"You're a passionate woman, Cat," he said when he came up for air.

He made her feel that way, as if she were floating above all her problems, all her concerns, on a soft blanket.

"And you make me ache," he admitted, his breath puffing along her skin. "You've always made me ache."

Always?

"I've tried to stay away from you. From this. I couldn't on Saturday night. I'm going to fail big time now," he said, as if confessing.

She wanted him to fail. Not heeding the red alerts pulsing through her veins, she pressed her lips to his and sank into the kiss. She didn't want him to leave her alone.

His large hands slid down her back and pressed her against his chest. Heat rolled off his body to warm hers as his hand traveled down her bare thigh. He had large, rough, calloused hands that were surprisingly gentle as he caressed her leg.

Her palms skimmed under his shirt and up his chest, passing over smooth flesh and firm muscle as he nuzzled her throat and nipped her earlobe. Wanting to touch him body to body, skin to skin, she fumbled with the buttons on his shirt. Opening the final one, she spread apart the flaps to slide her body against his, hot flesh to hot flesh.

He fed her warm kisses as he shrugged out of the shirt. They were now both in their underwear.

When his hand traveled back up her leg and his thumb latched on to the top of her panties, her stomach bunched into a knot, her breasts tingled, and her nipples tightened. He slid the underwear down her legs, and she kicked them off her feet.

It had been so long she'd forgotten the pure, sensual pleasure that a man she desired could call forth. It was like two ends of a severed electrical wire had finally been fused together to fill her body with surging lust. In the dark shadows of the night, she lost herself.

His mouth wandered down her throat until he stopped to suck her pulse point. She tingled from her scalp to her toes.

With one motion, he threw off the top of the bedroll, causing cool air to dance over her heated skin. Grabbing the discarded horse blanket, he shoved it under her head for a makeshift pillow, then nuzzled the lace of her bra. She arched her back. She knew what was coming, and she wanted it, wanted to feel the draw of his mouth on her breasts. He unhooked her bra as she combed her fingers through the sides of his hair and held his head in place. His warm, wet mouth found her nipple.

"I want to make love to you, Princess," he whispered. "Body melting, too-hot-to-handle, volcanic love."

She'd wanted him from the time she'd seen him in high school, all broad shoulders and wicked smile and burning testosterone. And knowing now that he was caring, and smart, and protective, and good with her son only made the wanting more acute, more urgent, more dangerous.

Her mind was whispering no, but her heart, well, her heart was screaming yes.

"You'd better say something now, or it's happening, Princess."

He trailed kisses down to her stomach, and she was speechless.

"You've been driving me crazy ever since I saw you in that courtroom."

He licked her belly button.

"Actually, since I saw you coming down the hall in ninth grade."

He nuzzled her pelvis, his hot breath teasing her skin.

"You look like every man's fantasy in high heels and short skirts." He lifted his head. "And red lace and cowgirl boots." His warm breath grazed skin.

She was a fantasy? He'd told her that before. She hadn't believed him.

"I've become very fond of princesses. Very fond." He kissed her inner thigh.

Warmth spread between her legs. Her nipples tightened. Her body ached. And her heart beat like it was the drummer in a heavy-metal band doing a solo.

If it was just sex, she wouldn't be so scared. But it wasn't just sex for her. It was more, dangerously more, heartbreak more.

He kissed the inside of her other thigh. Her mind shut down, and her body took over.

"Do you want me, Cat? Say my name. Say who you want, Cat."

He licked. There.

"I want you, Cody Taylor."

His mouth was wet and hot, swirling tongue and sucking lips. Her mind went blank and her body tensed. The coil of lust tightened as if someone was turning a crank with every lick and swirl.

She wanted him, more than she had ever wanted anyone.

Every flick, every tug sent pure, elemental desire spiraling through her, ever higher, ever tighter. He fingered her as his mouth preformed an erotic dance.

Her breathing ragged, her body tensed in anticipation. She arched. A surge of sensation swamped her, and the coil released like an overtightened spring, sending wave after wave of contractions shuddering through her, pulling sensations and feelings that had lain dormant so long, she'd forgotten how wonderfully freeing it was.

Through the haze of release she was aware he'd raised his head. That he was watching the orgasm convulse through her. As ripples replaced waves, her need for him was the only thing that mattered.

"Please. Inside me," she managed to get out.

He slid up and pressed his erection between her thighs. She opened her legs. He slid his arm behind her shoulders as his other hand positioned the tip of his erection. With the first thrust, her body resisted. He pulled back, looked her in the eye, and thrust deep and forceful. He filled her as a groan thundered from somewhere deep inside of him.

"You feel good, honey. Real good," he whispered against her ear.

He felt good too.

She wrapped her legs around his waist and stared

into eyes heavy with lust. He nuzzled the side of her neck, his warm breath tickling her skin.

He moved inside her, setting a rhythmic pace.

"You like it fast or slow?" he asked.

She didn't know, and it had been so long, and she could barely function. "More."

He thrust harder, faster, giving her what she asked for. Her fingers grasped his shoulders, and she hung on. Again and then again and then again, one after the other, he hammered against her like he was knocking down a door, and with each thrust her body clamored for more until he was pounding into her with intense urgency. She tried to meet his thrusts as her heart pulsed in her ears, and he pushed her closer to another orgasm.

It was as if he, too, had waited a long time for this and had lost control. She clutched his shoulders and hung on as a tornado of desire picked her up and sent her sailing. She was aware of his strong arm holding her, keeping her back and head from the hard floor.

The rhythm got faster, the pace more frenetic until she was free-falling through a cascade of contractions as powerful as any earthquake's tremors. With one last convulsive thrust, a deep, elemental groan thundered from his chest.

She clung to him, and he hugged her, his breathing ragged, his chest heaving. He held her as if he'd won some battle and she was his reward. It took a while for his breathing to return to normal, and when it did, he pulled back and looked at her as if he was surprised she was in his arms.

"That was…intense," he said.

He'd definitely rocked her world, set it on a new

axis, and thrown it to a different area of space. Their lovemaking had been both fierce and sensual, altering her sensibilities. But one thing was certain. She was in love with Cody Taylor.

"Extremely," she whispered.

His smile was slow, and satisfied, and sexy as hell. "You mean you don't come like that all the time?"

Truthfully, orgasms had been a rarity during her time with Jake's father. Lovemaking had been planned and hurried and had never contained the power and awe of what had occurred on the dirt-filled wood floor of a cramped line shack.

"No," she admitted. "And you?" Cyndi Lynn had given him such praise, maybe his experience had been like this with every girl. Maybe she was nothing special.

"Never." He playfully touched her nose, and she felt a tingle near her heart. She was so in trouble. "Are you on the pill or something?"

Cat stared up at him. Blinked. The glow dissipated with that question, and the real world intruded. "I have an IUD."

"A what?"

"An IUD. I had it put in after Jake was born, for obvious reasons." It all sounded so clinical, but she was glad she had done it. If even for this one night, it had been worth it.

He released a long breath. "Sorry about forgetting a condom. I haven't been with a woman for over a year, so no worries on that front."

She tucked away that last bit of surprising information.

"I haven't been with a man since Jake was born."

Cody's eyebrows rose as if he was considering the implications of that fact. She knew the implications. No sex, no lies…no life.

"We dodged a bullet then, thanks to you."

Now he was talking about sex being a bullet?

She hadn't expected him to confess undying love and offer to marry her. But something a little more would have been nice. Something that said he at least cared.

Despite her best efforts to resist, she'd given him tonight what he asked for Saturday night. A moment's pleasure. At least with Jake's father there had been a real relationship, however flawed. What did she have with Cody?

It was her own fault. She was impulsive, just like her mother accused. She shifted to face away from him and burrowed farther into the bedroll. No feeling sorry for herself. This was what she deserved. All that she deserved.

"Are you cold?"

She nodded. As good an excuse as any.

"Slide next to me. We can spoon."

She looked over her shoulder at him. "Isn't that how this started?" And there would not be a similar ending. It was too risky. To her heart.

"Yes, but we've gotten it out of our system."

As if she were some bug he'd expelled. Or an itch he'd scratched.

"Scoot on over," he said and held up the bedroll's flap, revealing the outline of a naked man. A muscular, heart-throbbing, naked man with a penis that was anything but flaccid.

How was she going to get through the night after what had just happened? She leaned her back against his chest, ignoring the package bulging against her butt, and prayed for restraint.

Holding Cat in his arms, sleep eluded Cody. Now he knew. All those years of fantasizing, and now he knew the reality. And it was as good as any of his imaginings. Even given the hard, dirty floor of a line shack in the middle of lowing cows.

He'd lost himself in Cat McKenna. And now he needed to find himself again.

There was no future for the two of them. They'd both known that going in. And yet it hadn't stopped either of them.

He breathed in the scent of her hair and smoothed down the strands that spread across his bare chest.

For years he'd wondered about her. From the time he saw her coming down the hall the first day of ninth grade, all legs and limbs, with big eyes, wavy hair, in a simple dress that looked like high fashion on her fourteen-year-old self. He'd resolved then to get to know her so he could ask her to the next dance. Then he had found out her name, and his plans were shot to hell.

All through high school he'd watched her. Watched her as her flats became high heels, her skirts got shorter, her tops tighter, and the boys following her multiplied. But she didn't date. Rumor was her old man wouldn't allow it. For once he'd been in accord with Joe McKenna. Didn't stop the wanting though.

And then that night after high school he'd found her anxious, alone, and out of her element at a camp-out party. A princess in a crowd of bad seeds. He'd offered her protection and had gotten a black eye for his trouble. Her father had found them together, assumed the worst, and punched Cody in the eye before he'd dragged his daughter out of there. And she'd never said a word in his defense.

Cody didn't tell his father when he got home, but Zeke Taylor heard all about it and was mad as hell. Over Joe hitting Cody, over Cody "cavorting" with Joe's daughter. And by the time the rumors had gotten to Zeke, Cody was being accused of almost raping Cat McKenna.

That had been a dark summer for him. Suddenly he was being spoken of in the same league as Bobby Prentiss, and nary a word from Cat McKenna filtered back to him. He never knew if she had told her father the truth or if her father would even have believed it if she had.

The next time he spoke to her was that day in court six years later. When she'd allowed an assault of another kind to go unprotested.

Well, Joe McKenna wouldn't be coming after them this time. Instead, Cody was left with the knowledge that he now wanted someone he could never have. She was a McKenna. He was dead broke. This would have to be a one-night stand. And the really painful truth was that Cat McKenna would want it that way.

When Cat awoke, Cody was nowhere in sight. She stretched out the aches in her back, but it didn't clear the knots of uncertainty in her stomach at what they had done and where it would or would not lead.

Gingerly, she flung back the flap of the bedroll and rose from the hard floor. Retrieving her underpants from inside the bedding, she slid into them. Finding Cody's jacket on a bundle of barbed wire, she put it on. Her jeans were still damp, but she tugged them on, the moist fabric clinging to her legs.

She felt clammy. Inside and out.

Opening the door, she stuck her head out. In the dewy light of dawn, she caught sight of denim and plaid at the side of the shack. Cows lowed in the background as if they, too, had just woken up.

"Good morning, Princess," Cody greeted her as he cinched the saddle on her horse. "Everything okay?"

He didn't look at her, just concentrated on the cinch.

Should she tell him the truth? That she had floated between blissful happiness and sobering reality all night? That life had just gotten even more complicated, and she didn't know what to do about it? Or should she just give in to her urge and kiss him.

"Fine," she said, brushing her fingers through her hair. "And you."

"Everything will be okay once I get us on the road. Sun's just coming up. We should get back before 6:30."

He drew the cinch tight for one last loop and looked up at her for the first time.

She must look a sight, morning never being her best time of day, and particularly having camped out on a dirt floor, wet and cold and…

But he smiled. As if he couldn't help it.

A warm tingling feeling went through her.

He took off his hat and wiped his sleeve across his brow. Set the hat back on his head.

"You ready?"

She took a deep breath. "No."

"No?"

"I don't want to leave here without…without talking about what happened." There. She said it.

"Are you one of those women who likes to talk after?" The smile was still on his face, but it held more dare than amusement. "Guess so."

She dug her hands into the damp pockets of her jeans, hoping to find courage.

He leaned on Custer's belly and looked at her from over the saddle.

"So talk," he said, tipping back the brim of his hat.

"Was this a one-night stand or something more?"

He stared at her an extra beat before answering. "What do you want it to be?"

And there it was. The question to which she had no answer. Or no answer she wanted to share.

"What do you want it to be?"

She could feel his eyes drilling into her as if he was seeking her secrets.

"Does it matter?"

"Yes, it matters. It matters a lot."

"Why?"

Her heart beat in her ears. *Say it. Just say it and get it over with.* "Because I want more."

Cody patted Custer's neck as he ducked under it and came on her side. He walked over to her. Her heart thumped against her chest, so loud in her ears she thought he must hear it. Her palms were sweaty as she watched him, stone faced and unflinching, stand before her, stare into her eyes. He cupped her chin. His palms seemed as damp as hers.

He looked down at her, his heated gaze seeming to burn as it traveled over her face.

"Me too."

Cat felt the tension of uncertainty tighten as Custer trotted toward the barns only a few feet away. So far, there was no sign of movement in the area. Could she possibly get away with it?

She wore Cody's jacket and her damp jeans. Her wet shirt was bunched up in a saddle bag. It couldn't be much more than six thirty in the morning. Though that was when some of the hands showed up, most didn't arrive until seven. Cody had veered off toward his own ranch, crossing the river at a low point, so he could change into some dry clothes.

Before he'd headed toward his ranch, he had drawn his horse close, patted her knee, fingered the brim of his hat in a salute, and told her everything would work out.

She didn't know how. And as she rode on without him, she was more and more certain it couldn't work out, that it would be a recipe for nothing but heartache.

Turning Custer onto the still-muddy path to the barn, she wondered if selling the ranch wouldn't solve many problems—money, flexibility, fear of failure, and her attraction to Cody Taylor. Before she could ponder more, Will sauntered out of the barn and into the sunlight—holding his left arm. Upon seeing her though, he stopped holding it.

"What happened?" she asked. The thought that

Will might have slipped in the muddy pasture trudged across her skeptical mind. She hoped it was a weird coincidence. It was true she had her doubts about him, but she didn't want to think that a rustler was someone she knew.

"Arthritis acting up." His eyes crinkled as he smiled, as if he was the one to blame. "Rain last night bothered it."

"Have you seen a doctor about it?"

"Naw, just getting old." He cast his gaze over her and the horse. "And what have you been up to this early in the morning?"

Cat sucked in a breath and looked Will square in the eye. "Couldn't sleep, so went out for a quick ride to cool my head." Literally true, objectively false.

"Whose ranch jacket is that?"

"Found it lying around." She hated fibbing. "I've got to put Custer away." The horse's coat was still matted from the rain, and he was no doubt starving, not to mention needing water.

"He looks a little scuffed up for just a morning ride," Will observed as he scrunched his eyes to scan her horse.

Cat shrugged.

"Know why Cody's truck is here but his horse is missing?" Will continued.

"Not a clue." She gave Custer a soft kick, aiming the horse toward the barn and away from Will's scrutiny.

"So how bad did it go?" Jace asked when Cody lumbered into the Cross T's kitchen after taking a long hot shower and changing into a dry pair of worn jeans and a cotton T-shirt. He finally felt human again—an unsettled human.

He'd made love to Cat McKenna. And instead of slaking his thirst, he only wanted more. Wasn't natural. Or was it?

Jace was waiting for him at the kitchen table, having already had a good laugh at Cody's expense upon his arrival that morning, no doubt looking worse than a rabbit dunked in a water trough.

Retrieving his mug from the dish strainer next to the sink, Cody poured himself a hot cup of coffee, delaying his response and the slew of questions sure to follow. The mug was one of four his mother had purchased through one of those photo sites a few years ago. Each mug had a picture of the Cross T sign plastered on it. She'd bought one for each of them, the sign having been photoshopped into a different color to distinguish them. Cody's had been blue, Jace's red, his mother's yellow, and his father's green.

Guess that green one will be staying in the cabinet now.

Feeling a little gut-punched at the thought, Cody returned to the table where Jace sat sipping his own cup of coffee in the red-tinted mug. Cody pulled up a chair and plopped his butt down. His brother had already placed a plate of scrambled eggs, bacon, and toast at his place. The smell of cooked bacon had his mouth watering. Jace was becoming a regular hash slinger now that he had to fend for himself.

"Thanks for the eggs," Cody said, tucking into his food. He took a sip of hot coffee, enjoying the nutty taste and the warmth that slithered down his throat.

"You said things hadn't gone well when you

came in earlier. How. Bad. Did. It. Go?" Jace enunciated each word as if Cody might not have heard him. He'd heard. He just didn't know how to answer.

"We saw them."

"We?"

"Cat McKenna was there too." Cody kept his focus on his eggs.

"Wait. You took Cat McKenna with you? To track rustlers?"

He looked up into Jace's face filled with disbelief.

"It wasn't by invitation. She saw me heading out, and curiosity bid her follow." *And you know what they say about curiosity*, he thought. "I almost pulled my rifle on her. In the dim light, I couldn't tell it was her until she turned around." That had shaken him to his core. He'd heard more than a tale or two of people accidentally shooting someone they knew. Someone they loved.

Jace placed a booted foot over his knee. "And you didn't send her right back?"

"It started to rain. And it was dark by then. And she was soaked."

Jace rubbed his hand across his chin as if he couldn't believe Cody had been so stupid.

Believe it.

"Jeez, so what happened?"

Cody took a mouthful of scrambled eggs and a big bite of buttered toast before he answered. Starved didn't begin to describe his empty stomach. And unsettled didn't begin to describe his discomfort. "Two men came in a white truck. No windows in the trailer portion. Guess they figured the rain would be intense but short lived and the perfect cover for their crime."

Jace leaned forward. "So how come you didn't catch them?"

Cody shook his head. Last night was all about opportunities, missed and otherwise, but he'd planned to report only on the one involving the rustlers. "Cat was with me, so I fired in the air, over their heads to scare them. One of them was leading a calf. He dropped the rope, and they both started moving fast, only one of them slipped and fell. Looked like something out of a Chaplin movie."

"And you didn't go after them?" Jace seemed incredulous.

If he had been alone, he'd have ambushed them as they loaded up the cow. But gunfire could have been exchanged, and his only thought was of Cat, alone, waiting, in that cramped line shack. *In nothing but her red lace bra and bikini underwear.*

"Can you at least identify them?"

Jace's questioning was annoying, mainly because it pointed out how inept Cody had been. But what could he have done that wouldn't have risked placing Cat in danger?

"It was dark and raining, and by the time I got near the truck, they were pulling out. There will be some huge ruts in that dirt road."

Jace sat back, ran a hand through his auburn hair, and shook his head. "You had them dead to rights."

"Couldn't risk it."

Jace shook his head, clearly struggling to believe his big brother's clumsy handling of things. Cody tried not to feel defensive.

"So where have you been all night?"

His throat felt dry. He swallowed. Still dry.

"We spent the night in the line shack. It was too dark and too muddy to risk the horses. And before you ask, the line shack was tight for one person, much less two."

Cody drew a sip of coffee and shoveled in the rest of the eggs and a slice of bacon, hoping Jace would drop the subject.

"Sounds real cozy." Jace picked the remaining piece of bacon off of Cody's plate and scooped it into his mouth.

Well, his brother did cook it for him.

"Are you gonna tell me nothing happened between you two while you were camping out, again?" A frown furrowed Jace's brow. "Remember the last time you tried to help her out. You darn near got accused of rape."

He remembered. Remembered her father's fist connecting with his face. Remembered the ache deep inside of him. Remembered the look of disappointment on his father's face. Not only for "consorting" with the enemy, but giving Joe McKenna something to throw at the Taylors.

"Joe's gone."

"Gone or not, Cat McKenna will use you like she used that boy's father and throw you back as not good enough," Jace said.

That wasn't anything Cody hadn't said to himself on the ride home.

I want more.

"She's lost a lot of cattle, and now we know that the size of her loss had nothing to do with ranching.

Someone is stealing from her, and that's something every rancher for miles around needs to be concerned about, including us." He punctuated his point with a wave of his fork.

He'd been surprised by her declaration, since she'd been absolute about not wanting that type of relationship the prior Saturday night.

Sex with Cat McKenna was a balm for his very soul. If he could just keep it at sex and not want more. But he hadn't lied to Cat. He did want more. More of something he couldn't have. Guess he was into torturing himself.

Jace heaved a sigh. "So far, I'm not aware of any cattle gone missing. Duane and I already moved them to the near pasture in case anything goes wrong with the calving."

Cody nodded his approval. Jace was stepping up. Cody couldn't help but feel a little guilt. About last night. About not being there to help Jace.

"Still think we've got another week or so before calving begins?"

Jace nodded.

"Good, because I've scheduled branding at Pleasant Valley for this coming Thursday. I expect you and Duane to be there."

"They haven't branded yet?"

"Place has been mismanaged. I told you that."

"It hasn't been a year yet that she's been running it."

Cody washed the last forkful of eggs down with his coffee. He was finally feeling half himself...but just half. The other half was thinking about red lace and long legs.

"It's not her. At least it's not totally her fault. She's had lots of help from that range foreman. Worthless piece of…"

"Will Springer?"

"That's him. Duane say anything about him?"

Jace shrugged. "Just that he's fair minded and not bad to work for. But he did mention that he doesn't like some of his edicts. Duane likes ranching from the back of a horse."

"Will is an ATV kind of guy."

"Yeah, well, they've got a big operation. Guess it's harder to justify the horse power you need when you can get it from vehicles that don't require food and care."

Cody liked the traditional ways. And saw no reason to change. And besides, he was counting on eventually selling horses to put the Cross T back in the black, and every time a ranch went to a modern conveyance, it cut down a little more of the market. "Save me from progress, will you?"

Jace laughed as he retrieved his brown cowboy hat from its place on the counter. Their mother would have never let a hat beyond the mud room.

"Mom called last night."

Great. Just what he didn't need. "What did you tell her?"

"That you were working late. Out checking on the herd. I didn't say which herd."

"I owe you."

"You can pay me back by keeping at arm's length from Cat McKenna. That woman is trouble. For you especially."

Too late.

Chapter 20

A quick shower, some coffee, and a leftover piece of pizza from the night before should have done the trick, but Cat still felt off kilter. Maybe because she'd had earth-shaking sex with a man she'd fallen for. And it scared her. She thought about calling up Mandy or Libby and asking them what she should do, but it was still early morning. If Libby was up, she'd be busy with the baby, and if Mandy was up, she'd be getting things ready for a rodeo.

As she led first one and then another of the horses from their respective stalls into the corral where hay awaited, she tried to sort out what had happened and where it could lead.

Tigers didn't change their stripes, and playboys didn't suddenly become monogamous. And a Taylor didn't fall in love with a McKenna and vice versa. So if this was just a casual relationship, what would be the fallout when it ended? To her ranch? To her heart?

Me too.

Could there be a future for them? Or was she just spinning a fairy tale, a fantasy, and nothing more?

If only she knew more about Cody. What was important to him? What were his dreams? Why hadn't he married yet? And just what did *more* mean?

The last horse she turned out was Custer, and just as she unhooked the lead from his halter, she spotted a rider on a paint horse coming up the driveway. She stepped out the corral's gate. The sun was already warming the air, which was filled with the familiar scents of earth and manure. She latched the gate just as Cody slid off Comanche.

Leading his horse, Cody walked toward her with that easy, loping gait of his, as if he could handle anything. And he likely could. What she wouldn't give to bottle up his self-confidence and take a drink when she needed it. Like now.

He looked good in dry clothes and a fresh cowboy hat, this one in white, and a smile that could charm a snake out of the grass. If only things were different. But they weren't different, and she needed to remember that…always.

"Everything okay?" he asked when he was within speaking distance.

A pickup truck had pulled into the makeshift gravel lot by the barn. She'd have to make this quick to avoid being overheard.

She nodded. "And with you?"

"I'm good. Better than good." His smile broadened, and she felt that little flutter in her stomach as he strolled closer.

He stopped a foot before her, and she felt the warmth of his hand as he rested it on her shoulder. "Today is only a half day for me, being it's the holiday weekend. You have any plans for the rest of it?"

She had the ranch management system to update, food shopping for when her mother returned, and the horses to take care of at the end of the day.

She looked into his blue eyes, filled with expectation. "No."

"Good. I'd like to show you the Cross T. Then maybe we can come back here to be alone."

He wanted to show her the Cross T? She nodded her agreement.

In the distance, a truck door slammed shut, and he glanced over his shoulder as Jim Smith approached. "We'll figure out the particulars. If anyone asks, I left my truck here because I had to move some cattle at my ranch yesterday, so I rode my horse home."

Jim Smith, the manager of the breeding program, was almost upon them.

"Tonight, one way or another, we'll be dry, in a soft bed, and things will be even better." His eyes positively sparkled in the sunlight.

She was in such trouble.

* * *

"So this is the Cross T?" Cat had been surprised when he'd mentioned showing her his ranch. And she was eager to see it. Eager to know more about this cowboy who caused her heart to race and her mind to go blank whenever he was near.

Jace, he'd explained, would be out on the range checking on the cows about to give birth. Duane didn't usually work on weekends, and the house would be empty for the afternoon. She'd followed over in her own car so no one at Pleasant Valley would get suspicious.

"Where's Mikey today?" she asked.

She was flattered that he had offered to show her

his ranch. As if he wanted her to know more about him. As if he wanted a deeper relationship.

Was it crazy to hope so?

"Out with Jace. Sadie, his mother, is out there too."

Cat looked around at the barns and corrals and the small hodge-podged ranch house that Cody called home. The buildings were modest in comparison to Pleasant Valley, but well kept. Three horses grazed in the corral. The scene looked bucolic by any standards. No one would guess the Taylors faced bankruptcy.

"Come on," Cody said, stretching out his hand for hers.

She felt the power of his fingers as she clasped them, and together they strolled toward the fences.

"I want you to meet the future of the Cross T." His voice held pride.

He unlatched the corral gate, and they stepped inside. All three horses raised their heads, undoubtedly curious about their visitors. One of the horses whinnied.

"That's Gun Smoke, mother of Smoking Gun. Smoking Gun is to the left of her. The one to the right is another brood mare we are hoping to breed when we have the stud fees."

The two-year-old gelding stared at her with intensity, as if he was scrutinizing her as much as she was scrutinizing him. His lines were beautiful. He was a bay horse with a full black mane and tale.

"So what are your plans for him?" And for us?

Cat had sworn she would not mention their future together, that she would relax and see where things went. But she wasn't sure she was a woman who could "just relax" anymore. Being lax had gotten her into one life-altering situation already.

"My plans *were* to get him ready for showing in a three-year-old futurity. His bloodlines are good, and he's already shown himself to be intelligent. He'll make a great cutting horse. Maybe even show worthy. And he could command a lot of money if he shows as well as I think he will. But reality is, I haven't had much time to work with him, and it's likely, given our situation, that I'll have to sell him soon." Cody shrugged, but it didn't hide the deep disappointment in his voice.

"I thought working at Pleasant Valley was helping."

Cody looked down at her. "It helps, but not enough."

The Taylors must be more deeply in debt than she thought.

"But you'll get something for him regardless, right?"

"A lot less than if I could wait. He was to be the seed money for stud fees and brood mares. That plan has been blown to bits." He tugged the brim of his hat down, shading more of his face, and turned away from her and the horses and toward the gate. Likely so she couldn't see his disappointment.

But she felt it.

She knew how it felt when life threw you a curve and there was no one to pick up the bat and help. She wanted to be the one to help him. She wanted him to be the one to help her.

If he gave her even a little encouragement...

They walked together out of the corral. He secured the gate before they continued toward the house. Cat looped her arm through Cody's and rested her hand on his forearm. He patted her hand as if for reassurance. Being connected felt right.

"And here is home," he said as they mounted the wooden steps to the porch. Though no doubt an older house, there was no peeling paint or rotted floorboards. Everything was meticulously maintained... by people who cared.

Without bothering with a key, he turned the knob and pushed the unlocked door open. "Hope you don't mind the mess. We've been baching it."

Cat stepped into a small living room with hardwood floors, a tan rug, and furniture that looked a decade too old. A big-screen television, a tad on the small side for the size of the room, was parked on a wooden cabinet at the far end. A couch covered in brown coarse-grained fabric was placed perpendicular to the television, while two recliners sheathed in faux leather were opposite, both chairs angled toward the TV. Other than a wayward napkin and an empty plate on the end table, the room was relatively neat.

Cody gathered up the napkin and plate. "You want a beer? Water? Coffee?"

"Water is fine," she said. She felt like a teenager at her boyfriend's house while his mother was at work. And just as awkward.

Not that she wasn't happy to see where he lived, but it seemed a little surreal. Maybe because she was a McKenna, he a Taylor.

"Have a seat. I'll be right back." Cody strode into the next room that, from the sight of a white refrigerator she'd glimpsed through the doorway, was undoubtedly the kitchen.

Cat settled on the couch and took a moment to look around. Family photographs cluttered the top of a cabinet. A ranch scene hung on the wall between the two chairs. She moved to look at the photos. They were mostly of Jake and Cody, on horses, riding a tractor, in their baseball uniforms, and one of all four of them. Cat studied the family photo. Cody looked like his father. Jace was a combination of both parents. In the photo, Zeke Taylor looked the picture of health—broad shoulders, tall like his sons, a cowboy hat on his head, and a pair of blue eyes she recognized. Cody's mother looked more fragile, thin, but pretty with a head of thick brown hair.

Cat heard dishes clanging. And something else. Something from outside. Maybe Jace was back already. She hurried to her seat on the couch.

A cabinet door slammed. A faucet was delivering water.

And then the front door flew open like a storm had battled it. Cat stared, thunderstruck. Cody sauntered in holding a beer bottle and a glass of water...and nearly dropped them both.

"What is *she* doing here?" Mamie Taylor cried.

Seeing his mother standing in the doorway sucked the air right out of Cody, like a vacuum hose was hooked up to his mouth. Mamie was in jeans and a short-sleeve shirt, and her hands were firmly planted on her narrow hips. She looked from Cody to Cat and back again to Cody.

"I asked you, what is *she* doing here?"

Cody took a dry swallow. "Cat McKenna, this is my mother, Mamie Taylor."

"I know who she is. I asked you what she is doing here." Mamie talked slowly, distinctly.

"I invited her," Cody said. He walked over to Cat and placed the glass of water on the coaster on the end table and stole a glance at her. Cat looked like she was staring down the barrel of a rifle.

"Why? If you are planning to sell this ranch to the likes of her, Cody Taylor, think again," his mother bellowed.

He turned around to face his mother. Anger stormed across her face and churned her features. He took a sip of beer. He should be used to facing turbulence. Unfortunately, this hurricane was named Mamie.

"No such plans.

"I come home on this long holiday weekend to help clean up the place and surprise my boys, and I find...her." Mamie waved her hand at Cat. "Why is she here?"

"Maybe you'd better sit down, Mom."

"No thank you. I have a feeling I'm better off standing." She crossed her arms over her chest.

Cody glanced at Cat. The color had drained from her face, and she sat on the edge of her seat, as if she was ready to bolt.

"I'm working at Pleasant Valley. Cat hired me on as the ranch foreman. I've been working there since you've been gone."

Mamie shook her head. "I hear the words, but I can't comprehend the meaning. Why in the Lord's good name are you working for the likes of them"— she pointed at Cat—"and not working at the Cross T? Is this some plan to ruin us faster?"

She'd sucker punched his heart with that accusation. "I'm trying to save this place. Not only is Cat McKenna paying me a good wage, she's paying for one of her hands to work here with Jace while I help her out."

Mamie raised a trembling hand to her head. "And why would she do that?"

"I needed to hire someone who knows ranching and can teach me about running an operation like Pleasant Valley, Mrs. Taylor. And Cody seemed the best person to help me. That's all there is to it," Cat said. Her eyes were wide, her voice at least an octave higher.

Might as well take the whole plunge.

"That's not all there is to it. We're dating."

Mamie glanced from Cody to Cat and back again. "The hell you are." This time Mamie sat down in the recliner. "No son of mine will ever date a McKenna. Nor work for one."

Cody walked over to his mother's chair. At the moment, he'd prefer to face a grizzly than his mother, but if there was ever a time to cowboy-up, it was now.

"I'm a grown man. And head of this family. And I'm working at Pleasant Valley to save this ranch. I've been able to make regular payments on the mortgage and a few of the medical bills. We need the money. And I will continue to see Cat."

His mother looked fragile sitting there, hunched over hugging her belly like she had a stomachache. She raised her face to look at him. The disappointment in her eyes was palpable. "I don't condone it. None of it." She turned to Cat. "I ask you, Miss McKenna, to please leave my house and stay away from my son. You are not welcome here. I don't know what your game is, but…"

Cat rose.

"You don't have to go, Cat," Cody said.

"I understand your feelings, Mrs. Taylor…" Cat said, looking eager to leave.

"Do you? I don't think you understand anything about feelings, Miss McKenna."

"I assure you, I do. And I am sorry to be the cause of any strife between you and your son. We didn't plan any of this. Not the job. Or…our attraction to each other. But I will respect your wishes."

Cat moved toward the door. Cody intercepted her. Placed his hand on her forearm.

"I'll see you tonight."

Cat shook her head.

"Yes, I will. I'm not quitting you or Pleasant Valley." He kissed her on the forehead and opened the door for her.

"Good-bye, Mrs. Taylor," Cat said before she scurried out like a deer that had a reprieve from a mountain lion.

Cody closed the door behind her.

"That wasn't right," he said, sitting across from his mother, who was hugging herself like she was going to fall apart. "I know what I'm doing."

She looked at him, the pain written on her face. "Do you? The last time you helped that girl, you nearly got accused of rape. Next she'll be accusing you of stealing from her."

Cody thought about the night before when she'd come looking for him out in the pasture. But that was before they'd made love. Before she'd told him she wanted more.

"As Cat said, neither of us planned this attraction to each other. It just happened."

"It happened because you were working together. I just can't understand what you were thinking. What would your father have said?"

"I'm hoping he would understand that I am doing what I have to do to save this ranch. She needed help. We needed money. She's willing to learn and pay for it."

"As long as you teach her."

"She made me an offer I couldn't refuse."

"And trapping you into marrying her is part of that, is it? Seems she tried that before, and it didn't work. The man was too smart for her."

Calling little Jake a trap seemed mighty harsh. "No one said anything about marriage. Neither of us are looking for that from the other."

"No? She needs a husband to run that ranch and a father for that boy of hers. Seems you fit the bill on both counts."

"I am not marrying anyone." Reality was reality—he was broke, in debt, and would be lucky if he ever got out of it.

I want more. Cat McKenna was likely looking to marry. And the idea it would be with someone else rankled.

"So just fornication, is it? Scratching that itch?" Her nose wrinkled in disdain. "Is that what you were going to do today? No one here and you were going to have at it? In my house? In your father's house?"

"I wanted to show her Smoking Gun. She was curious about the Cross T. And believe it or not, I'm proud of this place." He'd wanted Cat to understand where he came from, what he was, and why Cross T mattered to him as much as Pleasant Valley mattered to her. Maybe more, considering he loved ranching. And she didn't.

Mamie rose from her seat. "I'm cleaning." She wagged her finger in his direction. "You're right. You're an adult. I can't make you quit your job any more than I can make you stay away from her. But if you have any shred of decency, any respect for me as your mother, you will not bring her into this house again for any reason. Promise me that."

Cody took a deep breath. "If that's what you want." If he needed any reinforcement that there could be no future with Cat McKenna, he'd just gotten a full dose of it.

Cody walked out the front door in time to see Cat's car winding down the driveway, away from him, away from the Cross T. And felt the ache of loneliness.

Despite his mother, he couldn't give her up. No more than he could give up the Cross T. Not without a fight. How this had happened, how a cowboy like him had fallen for a princess like her, was the wonder. He was in love with Cat McKenna. The one woman in Wyoming he couldn't have and shouldn't have fallen for.

Chapter 21

In her comfy alma mater sweatshirt and black yoga pants, Cat sat alone in the living room and stared at the television, airing a rerun of *Friends*. One of the many episodes where Ross and Rachel should be together but timing and circumstances, family and friends, were keeping them from their happily ever after. Which never came, she reminded herself.

The incident with Mamie had unnerved her, but it also brought a much-needed dose of reality. There could never be a future with Cody Taylor. Even if she loved him.

The precise moment when and how she'd fallen for him eluded her. Whether it was when he first praised her for herding the cattle, or while he was teaching her son T-ball or fishing, or as he showed off Smoking Gun and shared his dreams for the future, or when he stood up to his mother, or as he made volcanic-erupting love to her—or all those things. Regardless, she'd developed feelings beyond the physical call of lust. Strong feelings. Deep feelings. Forever feelings.

I'm not quitting you or Pleasant Valley.
But nothing could come of it.

So why was she looking at the clock and wondering if he would come tonight? Betting he wouldn't, hoping he would. It was already past seven and no sign of him. No text. No phone call. Had his mother gotten to him after she left? And wasn't that for the best? Her own mother would react exactly like Mamie.

As a mother herself, Cat didn't want to be responsible for strife between a mother and her son. And for what purpose? For what could only be a fling? For what would certainly result in her heart being broken? Not worth it. For either of them. And maybe Cody realized that.

The doorbell's ring sliced through air.

Cat's heart hitched as she padded to the door.

She took a deep breath and opened it. Cody stood there with a crooked smile as he leaned against the doorjamb, his black cowboy hat on his head, black T-shirt stretched across his muscular chest, and jeans hugging his legs, looking like a fantasy man, her fantasy man.

"You shouldn't have come," she said, though every inch of her was happy he had.

He frowned, stepping past her into the hallway even though she hadn't invited him in. He grabbed her arm and turned her to face him. "I had to come. 'Fraid you might have been scared off by my mother." His smile held a dare.

"We are not going to work." She said it for him as much as for herself.

With his free arm, he pushed the door closed. "We are already working."

He pulled her, and she stumbled only to be

278

righted by large hands that crushed her to him as his mouth slanted over hers with a savageness that both scared and elated her. She ran her hands up the side of his warm neck. He tasted like coffee and sex.

The kiss deepened, taking the breath from her and vaporizing her willpower while he slid his hands under her sweatshirt and up her sides to her bare breasts. His groan filled the air as his cool hands cupped her breasts, and his thumbs brushed her nipples, causing an eruption of tingles through her body.

She fed him kisses—of need, passion, want, desire, lust…and yes, love.

He groaned again, this time deeper and fuller and pulled back to look at her. His eyelids were heavy with lust, and he looked like someone who had just woken up. "I want you. Now."

Any thought of resistance had fled the moment his lips touched hers. She nodded as she started to unbutton his shirt.

"Not here. In bed. A soft bed with sheets."

Holding his hand, she led him up the stairs at a running pace, turned left into her bedroom, and pulled him onto the bed. Willpower was so overrated.

Cody flung his cowboy hat over the bed and kissed the side of Cat's neck. She tasted sweet, smelled like flowers, and had nothing on under her sweatshirt. The bed was big, the cover was soft, and the shades were drawn so only shadowy light remained. Just enough that he could see still see her.

"Take this off," he whispered as he kissed the belly button of her flat stomach.

He was with his princess, and he was going to

make the most of it. He'd sensed her resistance when he'd walked into the house, but the moment they'd kissed, he knew she was his, for the night at least.

Only he wanted more. Didn't mean he could have more. But he wanted to give her everything. How he'd gone so butt over heels for her he wasn't sure. But somewhere between showing her how to ranch and kissing the daylights out of her, he'd fallen in love with Cat McKenna, complications and all.

He wanted to know if there was any chance for a debt-ridden cowboy. Even a slim one. Did she feel the same way? Could she ever imagine?

He was acting like a lovesick bull…and he didn't care. Not one wit.

She looked at him coyly as she lifted the sweatshirt over her head, leaving him eye level with a pair of nicely rounded breasts, palm sized and perfect, just like she was. He slid his mouth onto a nipple while he slid his hand under the waistband of her yoga pants and inside her panties, where she was warm and wet.

"These too," he said, indicating her pants, before turning his attention to the other breast.

His groin throbbed, his erection strained against his jeans, and lust seized his balls.

She slid the pants and panties down to her knees. He pushed them the rest of the way. Tugging them off her feet, he scrunched up the clothing and threw it toward the door.

He turned back to a totally nude Cat McKenna.

Her shiny brown hair cascaded down past her smooth shoulders, almost covering her beautiful breasts that glowed in the gray light like full moons.

Stepping closer, he perused past her tight waist and flat stomach, to the mound that held her very core, to the long legs that dangled over the side of the bed. Tonight she was his. His to please and pleasure. And he intended to do a lot of both.

"Now it's time for me to see you," Cat said, sliding her palms up his tight skin, over the ribbed flesh of his abdomen that peeked out of his opened shirt, across the muscles of his chest, to his broad shoulders. She pushed the shirt off his shoulders, and he slipped out of it with ease. Balling it up as he had done her pants, he threw it in the same direction.

Her gaze flitted over taut skin, rippling muscles, brown nipples, and washboard abs, which she knew he had gotten through honest work, not courtesy of some gym membership. Cody was authentic from his hat to his boots and every blessed thing in between.

"Everything," she said, greedy to see all of him.

In the line shack, there hadn't been room to move, much less view. But she knew by touching him, by feeling him throbbing inside of her, that he was a magnificent specimen of a man.

He didn't have to be asked twice. He unbuckled his belt as fast as a tie-down roper removing his hooey. In rapid sequence he unzipped his pants, toed off his boots, and stepped bare assed out of his clothes. And what a nice ass it was. Round and firm and supported by a pair of stalwart, hair-brushed legs. He turned around, and she had to clamp her mouth shut to keep from exclaiming.

His large, plump erection jutted toward her as if it was a divining rod looking for water and she was its oasis. Before she could reach out and touch, he was covering her with his warm body, feeding her kisses, and stroking her skin.

For one night she would pretend it was forever.

He made love to her in that bed. Hurried, frenzied, and out of control And later in the kitchen against the counter from behind, bending her over, slapping against her, cupping her breasts and shouting her name when he came. And then in bed again, this time slow and tender, his kisses languid, his thrusts controlled and rhythmic. And all three times, he'd driven her to climax. He'd driven her crazy.

As night lumbered on, they lay there exhausted until he turned toward her, propped his head in one hand, and covered the rise of her hip with the other one.

"Tell me your dreams."

"My dreams?"

"What do you want? You told me in the bar you wanted a good man. What makes a good man for Cat McKenna?"

You. "I don't know."

"You seemed pretty sure about things the other night."

She bit her lip. The other night, she hadn't been sure about anything, including Cody Taylor. "I guess I want what most women want. A man who loves me and my son. A man who can respect me as well as laugh with me. And if he's a good rancher for Pleasant Valley, my problems are solved."

His fingers traced the seam of her mouth, leaving a trail of heat and want. "That would be one lucky man."

"What are your dreams, Cody?"

"You."

Her thoughts scattered at his answer, and she was left trying to put them back together. "Me?"

"I won't lie to you by saying I can offer marriage. I can't, no matter how much I might want to."

He wants to?

He swiped her nose with his finger. "I have no money and a ton of debt. I can't support a wife. Even if you would have me." He stared into her eyes. "It's a dream, I know."

Having perched on the rim of uncertainty, her heart took the plunge. But should she tell him? It was so early in their relationship...and yet it wasn't. She'd been with him every day. She knew him better certainly than she had Jake's father. And he was talking marriage. Not a one-night stand, but marriage. If only...

"I'd have you, Cody Taylor." She rejoiced at the smile that filled his face, but at the same time she felt a profound loss knowing it could never be. "If we could find a way."

"Our families aren't going to make that easy. Nor the legacy of our ancestors. And then there is money. I have none. And I'm not going to live off yours. Hell, your father would likely rise from the dead if he thought that was happening."

"I have a little money of my own squirreled away. Money I inherited outright when my father died. It's a little over five grand, but it's mine. It could be our start in life."

And there was the offer to sell Pleasant Valley. It could be the answer to their problems. She could open a preschool and help pay the bills.

"I wouldn't take any money from my wife. I'm

not that kind of guy." His finger traced a line down the side of her neck, across her collar bone, down her arm.

Wife? That word resounded in her ears and traveled straight to her heart.

"It would be our money."

"You'd be using money from the sale of Pleasant Valley to pay off Cross T's debt instead of investing in your boy's future. I can't let you do that. It's not fair to you, to Jake, or to Pleasant Valley."

She cupped his cheek with her free hand. "It isn't fair to kill dreams before they've had a chance."

He turned his head to kiss her palm. "It's good to have dreams, Princess. And it's good to know that our dreams have a lot in common. But the reality is, they are just dreams. We can't change the hand that we've been dealt."

"But if we can figure out a winning way to play it…"

"That's what I love about you, Princess. You don't give up."

What he *loved* about her? She felt like she was flying. His gentle kiss on her forehead made her ache.

"Maybe we should start acting like a couple and test out the waters," he said and pulled her tight against his rock-hard body. "If you're game, so am I."

It was shortly before dawn that he kissed her good-bye and told her he'd see her in the evening. As she listened to him drive away, she wondered what would happen when her son and mother returned. When the gossips rang the telephones of the town, as surely they would now that his mother knew. When the world judged their relationship.

And for the first time in her life, Cat McKenna didn't care.

Chapter 22

Sunday, Cat didn't see Cody until after dinner, and it began and ended pretty much like the previous evening. They'd talked again about their dreams, about the obstacles of family and money, about testing the waters. They had done a good job of identifying the problems and a poor job of finding solutions.

He hadn't told her he loved her. But he didn't have to. She hadn't said the words either. But they were planning for a future. Together.

Before he left, he'd made her promise she would come to the town's parade on Monday morning, and here she was standing on the corner of Main Street, occupied by Miller's Feed Store, having recruited Cyndi Lynn to stand with her as the participants passed by.

Main Street had been closed off to provide the parade route from the municipal building to the gazebo at the edge of town. Where vehicles had parked on slants in front of buildings, people now sat on lawn chairs or stood, American flags in hand, to wave at the small floats, high school bands, and baton twirlers. Smells of popcorn and hot dogs from the food truck parked on the side street mingled in the fresh air, and

Cyndi Lynn had bought a bag of popcorn, even though it was ten in the morning.

Dressed in jeans, a tight T-shirt, boots, and a hat, Cyndi Lynn wore the uniform of everyone else who lined the street, Cat included. She'd thought about a nice sundress, but since she had been up at dawn to clean the barns and feed the horses and would have to do it all over again in the evening, she'd decided to stop fighting the fact she was a rancher. For now and into the foreseeable future.

"So," Cyndi Lynn began. "Rumor is that you are seeing Cody Taylor now." She popped a kernel of popcorn into her mouth.

No sense trying to obfuscate what everyone knew. And besides, Cody said they were a couple now and should start acting like it. "We're...dating."

"Want some?" Cyndi Lynn held out the bag.

Cat shook her head. Her mother would find out as soon as she returned home, no doubt. One more day of freedom from judgment.

"Have you two, you know?"

Not a question Cat wanted to answer. Or explain. "You and Jace seeing each other?"

Cyndi Lynn actually blushed. "That was just bad judgment on my part. If I haven't already apologized, I am sorry I made you go home by yourself."

"No biggie."

"Here comes the National Guard," Cyndi Lynn said and began waving her flag. "Love me some soldiers."

Next, the men dressed as Union soldiers made their way past the crowd, followed by several Girl Scout troops. The Grange members rode by in trucks, one dragging a float. One Grange member was wheeling himself down the route in a wheelchair, a small dog on his lap. A number of vintage cars followed, along with a motorcycle group throwing candy.

Cat scanned the crowd. No sign of Cody. Why had he made her promise to be there?

On the opposite side of the street, a little farther up, Cat spotted Mamie Taylor. She wore a blue print cotton dress, and the breeze blew wisps of hair around her bun. She was talking to Joanne Littleton.

All the world would soon know something was going on with Cat and Cody.

Determined not to let it bother her, she looked back at the parade. A group riding horses were coming down the road—the horses prancing as if aware of their moment in the spotlight. Various riders zigzagged the street, handing flowers to family members. Giving a flower to a loved one was a tradition with this group.

Cody was in the lead, Jace a row back. In all there were about ten riders, two up front and then two rows of four across.

Cody looked in command sitting atop Comanche. Her heart swelled, and she wondered how she would ever be able to put the genie back in the bottle.

He passed his mother with an acknowledging nod. Behind him Jace rode his horse over to the side and presented Mamie with a pink carnation. Another rider broke rank and presented a young girl, presumably his daughter, with a yellow carnation. And so it went.

But her focus was on Cody with a red carnation in his hand.

He looked in her direction, tipped his hat, and guided his horse over to where she stood.

"Hey, Cyndi Lynn," Cody said as he pulled on the reins to stop his horse. "Hey, Princess." He stretched out his hand to Cat, a hand that clasped a red carnation. "For my princess."

Cat's heart fluttered like a sparrow trapped in a cage, even as her cheeks heated. She took the flower, their fingers touching. With a wink and a nod, horse and rider resumed position at the head of the line, and Cat felt like soaring.

"Well, shut my mouth," Cyndi Lynn clucked. "Looks like more than dating to me, and you two have definitely done the deed." Her smile was smug. "My mother bet me that the rumor wasn't true. Looks like I've won."

There was no hiding now. Cody Taylor had singled her out with a red carnation for all in the town to see. And her mother would know it all in less than twenty-four hours.

* * *

"Cody, Cody, Cody." Jake ran up the path to the barns, waving his hands as he shouted, in case Cat and Cody, who stood talking, couldn't tell he wanted their attention.

Cat had been expecting her mother and son Monday afternoon with a mixture of apprehension and eagerness. She'd missed Jake and, if truth be told, her mother as well. But she dreaded the inevitable confrontation about Cody and selling the ranch—and she wasn't quite sure which would be worse.

Dressed in jeans and a plaid shirt, Jake looked like a miniature Cody, sans cowboy hat.

Cat's heart squeezed.

Lydia trudged after Jake. Her slow movements and bent posture testified, Cat was sure, to her mother's fatigue. It was a long drive from Montana, and having a four-year-old in the car surely hadn't made it feel any shorter.

Cat opened her arms, but her son blew right past her straight to Cody, who scooped up Jake.

"I got a fish the first day. And then"—he looked down at his fingers and counted on them—"and then four more." His face was flushed and his eyes bright, and he was focused on no one but the man holding him.

"That's great, partner."

"And we saw cowboys. And they had horses. Neither Danny or Tommy have a horse. Only me." He shook his head. "I was the only real cowboy in the bunch."

"Everything was Cody on this trip," her mother said, coming up alongside her and keeping her voice low as Jake prattled on about fishing and horses, streams and mountains. "I think you have a real problem there," she said, pointing her chin in Cody and Jake's direction. "One you better nip in the bud right now."

"How am I supposed to do that? He works here." Not that she had a mind to put a stop to anything regarding Cody. Having spent the last couple of nights in his arms, she'd reached the point of no return. She'd resolved to let fate lead her to wherever she was supposed to be.

"Exactly. You need to hire someone else pronto. Right after branding wouldn't be soon enough. Or you'll regret it." She looked over her daughter, as if checking for something. "Both of you."

The gossip brigade had reached Lydia.

* * *

Dinner with her mother and Jake had been noneventful…except for the scowls her mother sent her at every opportunity. As Cat cleaned up the dishes and then readied Jake for bed, she tried to steel herself against the upcoming lecture.

Despite his mother's disapproval, Cody hadn't wavered and, in fact, had made their relationship very public. She wouldn't waver either.

As she read Jake a bedtime story about a cute bear and his mischievous friend, the fox, her thoughts drifted to Cody. To what he was doing at that moment. To how they could make this work going forward. Answers eluded her.

Coming down the stairs she heard the voices of commentators from the evening news drifting out of the living room. Part of her wanted to run right out the front door, and part of her wanted to get it over with. She'd faced worse. She'd faced Joe McKenna and asked to come home. She could do this.

Taking a deep breath, she entered the living room.

Her mother, sitting on the couch with her feet up, raised her gaze from the newspaper, slid her eyeglasses down her nose so she could get a better view of Cat, and, with the remote, turned off the television.

Cat sat in the club chair and decided to plunge in. "You've heard."

"First you hire the man against my good judgment. Now you're dating him?" She looked over the metal rim of her eyeglasses as she clasped her hands in front of her like she was afraid that if she didn't, she'd use those hands. "Rumors are flying that it is more than that. I pray they are wrong. I thought you'd have learned a thing or two from the last time you slept around with a man."

Her mother had a way of putting things that left Cat feeling like a scolded child.

"It's true. Cody and I are seeing each other."

Her mother's hand flew to her forehead, and she rubbed her temple. Fatigue showed on her face. "And he gave you a flower. In front of his mother? In front of the whole town?"

Her mother said it as if Cat should be ashamed. She wasn't.

"I leave for a few days, and suddenly you're copulating with a member of the one family in the country that would offend your father. That's why you're doing it, you know. Whether you realize it or not, that's why you are doing it." Her hand moved to her chest and rested above her heart. "Question is, why is he?"

"I am not doing it to hurt my father." That was just too ludicrous to contemplate. "First, Dad isn't here to be hurt. Second, your generation had decided to keep up this feud. Cody and I have moved on. And the fact he could after the court ruling says a lot about his character." She ran her fingers through her hair, trying to dispel the rapid beating of her heart. "Having worked together, we've gotten to know each other. And we like each other. He's a decent, upstanding man who is helping me out…"

"For a princely sum of money. And so you've decided to trust him not only with the ranch but with your heart?" Lydia shook her head, like she was lecturing Jake. "Don't you realize that money is the attraction for him? He doesn't have any. You do."

Her mother's words couldn't have stung more if she'd slapped Cat. "I'm glad you think I have so little to offer a man that he needs to have an enticement to date me."

Lydia scowled as she righted herself, placing her feet squarely on the floor so she sat facing Cat. "You are a fool for a good-looking man, Catherine Ann McKenna. And he's going to make a fool out of you. You wait and see." She shook her finger in Cat's direction. "And don't come running to me for sympathy. I'm done with cleaning up after you mess up."

If Lydia thought her threats would cow her daughter, she was sorely mistaken. Instead, fury pounded inside Cat like a barreling storm.

"Is that what Jake is—a mess you helped clean up?"

"Don't go twisting my words. I love my grandson, and you know it." Her mother rubbed her temple. "I don't want Taylor working on this ranch. It was a mistake, and this is the price I'm paying for it."

She was paying a price?

"Cody is staying as the ramrod. Daddy's will put me in charge of running the ranch. If you want to exercise your right as trustee to withhold funds and throw us into bankruptcy, you can do that. But you can't decide who I hire. Or, given I am twenty-five, who I date. Or who I marry, for that matter."

Her mother's mouth opened as she clasped the area near her heart. "You wouldn't. You can't be that serious about him."

She could be very serious about Cody if their respective mothers weren't obstacles.

"I'm done discussing Cody. There's a matter about the ranch we need to discuss."

"More bad news?"

"Depends on what you think of an offer we've had to sell the ranch." Cat explained the terms of the offer and laid out the pros and cons.

"You aren't seriously considering selling Pleasant Valley, where your family has ranched for over a century? The ranch your son is due to inherit? The ranch your father literally worked his heart out for to preserve for your son? I swear, Cat—you are trying to give me a heart attack."

Cat took a swallow. "Kyle thinks we should do it."

Lydia's hand shook as she brushed it over her legs as if smoothing out invisible wrinkles in her pants. "And what do you think?"

"You actually want to know? Considering your lack of respect for my judgment, I'm surprised you care what I think." Her mother's criticism burned.

Lydia's eyes narrowed. "Don't be peevish, Cat. It doesn't suit you. What do you think?"

Cat thought about the money, the preschool, the ability to be free of responsibilities. She thought about the generations of McKennas who had worked

Pleasant Valley and built it into one of the larger ranches in Wyoming. She thought about her son and where it would be best for him to grow up and into a man. She tried not to think about what this would mean for her future, or lack thereof, with Cody.

"That we shouldn't sell."

Her mother sat back against the sofa. "Well, at least we agree on something."

"A very important something. If you're sure, I'll telephone Kyle in the morning and tell him the news."

Lydia nodded her assent. "But promise me you'll think about what I said regarding Cody Taylor. As a mother now, you should know that when I tell you things that are hard to hear, it's because I'm trying to protect you." Lydia rose from the couch, newspaper in hand, as if she was leaving. "Think about getting yourself a new ramrod. Before you and my grandson get too attached to a man who could never give Pleasant Valley his best effort and who is too poor to ever make an honest woman of you."

Chapter 23

Two men leaned against the driver's side of the black BMW. One dressed in a long-sleeved white shirt, tie, and dress pants, his jacket neatly hung on the hook in the backseat. The other was dressed in a plaid shirt, jeans splattered with dirt, and work boots. A rickety old pickup truck sat a few yards down the dirt road.

"The old lady won't budge. I've got to get the daughter to change her mind. Rumors have her falling for this guy. We take out Cody Taylor, she's not only going to be devastated, she'll have no one to run the operation, and I'm betting she'll be ready to sell," the man in the white shirt said. "Especially when we up the offer."

"But I think she was with Cody that night."

"Even better. Your friend is going to say he was out there to meet up with Cody. And Cody acted like he wasn't part of it by going after you two because she was with him. I've got it all planned out. Don't worry."

"You're sure you can protect my partner? He won't do any time? Have any record?" The man in the plaid shirt didn't like putting his rustling partner in the middle like this, but a lot of money was being offered. Half paid now. Half when the real estate deal closed.

"As long as you're sure your partner doesn't know about me." The guy in the suit scrunched his eyes and smoothed back his hair. The guy looked nervous, and he never looked nervous.

The man in jeans shook his head.

"Good. I've fixed it with the sheriff. There is a plea agreement ready for your partner to sign. All he has to do is testify against Cody Taylor," the guy in the shirt and tie said.

The guy in jeans rubbed his hand across his stubbled chin. It was risky. And wrong. He didn't enjoy fingering an innocent man, but Cody had been a burr under his saddle since the man had arrived at Pleasant Valley. And it was a lot of money, money that would allow him to quit and move closer to his daughter. His arthritis was so bad, most days he couldn't walk. And his friend needed the money just as badly as he did.

"It's risky, but I'm in. Branding is taking place on Thursday."

"I'll be there. With the sheriff."

* * *

They began arriving around seven the morning of the branding, filling the large pasture with pickups and horse trailers. Cowboys, mostly neighbors, dressed in chaps, their boots jangling with spurs, and hats shading their eyes, unloaded their horses or simply milled around by coffeepots that had been set out on banquet tables covered in checked plastic-coated cloths. Plenty of pastries and homemade breads were on hand for hungry helpers.

After setting two new breads on the table, Cat stood with Jake and watched the chaos unfold. She'd thought about sending Jake to his preschool, but Cody had persuaded her that Jake should get a dose of the ranch life he'd be leading if he chose to keep Pleasant Valley, and Cat was happy to ditch the hour round trip it would take to get him to his school.

"Stay close to me," Cat cautioned her son.

Jake nodded, but his good intentions were shelved the moment he saw "Aunt" Mandy disembarking from a shiny silver pickup. He ran across the yard and right into her arms.

Cat walked over, happy to see Mandy, who also brought along her husband, Ty Martin, and brother, Tucker Prescott. Mandy's family, along with Libby and her husband, had agreed to help out today, and Cat was anxious to talk to her girlfriends.

"How's my best little guy?" Mandy cooed, bending down to get her kiss from Jake.

"It's branding day!" Jake exclaimed.

"I know, and Uncle Ty and Tucker are here to help," Mandy said, motioning to the two handsome men flanking her. Ty was tall, dark, and handsome, and Tucker was blond, blue eyed, and dreamy. Both wore chaps over their jeans, Tucker's being a little more decorative than Ty's, and their chambray shirts were different tones of faded.

"Is Delanie coming?" Jake asked.

Mandy smoothed down Jake's hair. "I don't think so. She'll be in school today, but I hear her daddy is coming."

Cat's son's smile was replaced by a frown. He had enjoyed playing with Delanie, Mandy's niece by way of her brother-in-law, the few times they'd met.

"Mommy let me miss school. I'm going to help!"

Everything her son said could be punctuated by an exclamation point.

Mandy stepped forward and gave Cat a quick hug as she whispered in her ear, "Where's Mr. Taylor?"

"He's out rounding up the rest of the cattle to drive them in." She'd gotten up early in order to see him off. And sneak a quick kiss behind the hay bales.

"I can't wait to see him after all this time."

"Who are you talking about?" Ty asked, coming up alongside the two women and giving Cat a peck on the cheek.

"My new ranch foreman. He's a neighbor, but our families have been having an old-fashioned feud for over a century now. So it's kind of ironic that he's working at Pleasant Valley."

Ty's eyebrows peaked. "Sounds like there is more to this story. I'll have to get the details later."

Tucker stepped forward. He was tall, lanky, and good looking.

Cat couldn't ever remember seeing Tucker without a smile on his face. He'd eschewed the rodeo business for riding in rodeos. Good natured, low keyed, and a charmer, that was Tucker Prescott.

"Haven't seen you since their wedding," Tucker said, giving her a peck on the other cheek.

"It has been a while."

The crunch of tires on gravel signaled the arrival of another helper. A tall, taciturn, dark, and roughly handsome man who looked similar to his brother, Ty, only with more chiseled features, stepped out of a battered gray pickup. Trace Martin was taller than his brother and more weathered and should make any girl's heart skip a beat. That Trace hadn't done much to Cat's heart was disappointing for her friend, Mandy, who had hoped the two would pair up.

Cat did admire all Trace had been through, but the man was as reticent as a bat in daylight, and Cat liked a man who spoke his mind. Like Cody.

"We'll help him unload the horses," Ty said and motioned Tucker to follow.

"I want to help," Jake said.

"You stay with me. Trace will be over here when he is done, and you can ask about Delanie. I don't want you under feet when they are unloading horses."

Jake scowled with a child's exaggerated disgust, but he stayed put as Mandy's husband and brother walked toward Trace's trailer.

"So anything more to tell about Cody? It's clear you didn't fire him," Mandy said, swatting at a horsefly.

"I'll tell you everything when Libby gets here. No sense in saying it twice." She turned toward an RV parked near the pasture. "Let's leave the men to unloading the horse, and we'll head for some shade under the food trailer's awning," she said, mindful of Mandy's expanding stomach and the sun, already warming up the morning.

Libby arrived soon after with her husband, Chance, and seven-month-old, Shane. Chance was a bronc rider, but May was generally a slow month, and though he wasn't used to heelin' or headin', he came along to offer two extra pair of hands to work the branding iron.

Once horses were unloaded and tied to the fence posts, the party headed over to coffeepots and goodies, Chance pushing Shane's stroller over uneven ground.

Libby and Chance's son was a bruiser, at least relatively speaking. Petite Libby was already worried that she wouldn't be able to carry him if he got much bigger. Cat knew Libby would have another year, minimum, of back pain to look forward to.

Jake was awed by the little tyke and insisted on helping Chance push Shane's stroller over the gravel.

"Someday I'm going to be a big brother," Jake said as the men grabbed cups for coffee. "Right, Mommy?"

Cat forced a smile. "I hope so," she said, even as she doubted it would come true now. A cowboy named Taylor owned her heart, and there didn't seem to be any path to a future. Cody had told her they'd find a way, but seeing how each of their mothers had reacted to their relationship, Cat was convinced it was a long shot.

She just wasn't ready to give up.

A low rumble sounded in the distance, and Cat shaded her eyes to see. "They're coming now," she said and pointed. In the lead position was Cody, with Jace on the other side of the herd, and the rest of the ranch cowboys fanning out behind them as the cattle rumbled toward the open pasture gate manned by Will Springer.

Branding day had begun.

Before the operation started, Cody rode over to say hello to Mandy and introduce himself to Libby. He shook hands with Ty, Trace, Tucker, and Chance and seemed right at home with Cat's friends' husbands and kin. It wasn't long before roles were sorted. Giving in to Jake's pleas, Cody had lifted Jake up and placed him in front of him on Comanche so Jake could have a bird's-eye view of the proceedings before Cody took his turn.

Under the rays of the morning sun, pairs of cowboys on horses took turns cutting the calves from their mothers' sides and roping for the branding iron. Cat was in the thick of things, along with a few of the older men, handling the vaccinations, while Tucker and Chance and some neighboring cowboys worked the branding irons. Libby and Mandy watched in lawn chairs from the safety of the other side of the fence and tended to baby Shane. The smell of charcoal and hide scented the air as the sounds of lowing and mooing added to the din. It was organized chaos.

Cat had been pleased to see Cody pointing out things to Jake, no doubt explaining what they were doing and why they were doing it, and probably giving him some tips on how to do it. It warmed her heart the way Cody made time for her boy, whether it was T-ball, fishing, or cowboying. And Cody seemed to enjoy it almost as much as Jake. If only…

A little after ten, it was time for Cody to take his turn at roping, and he set Jake down by Cat. With a wink and a touch of his hat, he went to work. She escorted Jake to the sidelines and stood by her friends. Though Ty and Trace had done a good job of roping, it was clear that Jace and Cody were the experienced team, used to working together. The movement of their horses looked as graceful as a timed ballet, and the branding pace quickened due to their expertise.

Cat felt a surge of pride as she watched Cody

skillfully maneuver his horse and rope the calves in efficient fashion.

"So that's him," Libby said. "He's not only cute, he's got a nice way about him. Relaxed and confident."

Cat sighed. That about summed up Cody.

"And back in the day," Mandy said, rubbing her rounded tummy, "just about every girl in Cat's high school was in love with him."

Libby giggled. "So tell us, Cat."

Cat looked down at Jake, who was mesmerized by all the action. She'd give them the shortened version.

She filled them in on the stakeout and the rustlers, leaving out the part about shots being fired. "And that night, a spark was ignited, and it's turned into a roaring fire. For both of us."

Mandy rose and stood close to her friend. "Finally!"

"But I'm falling for him. We're falling for each other."

"That's wonderful," Libby said.

"Not if one of us is a McKenna and the other is a Taylor."

Mandy frowned. "If he can forgive you taking his land, what is the problem?"

"Our mothers, mostly. And the fact he's in debt and pride won't let him take on responsibilities he can't meet."

Libby nodded. "Pride can be a difficult thing."

The sound of a bell from the vicinity of the RV traveled down to the pasture. Time to get lunch on the table.

Casseroles of every description lined the portable banquet table. A huge pot of chili anchored one of the ends. Potato, macaroni, bean, and other assorted salads filled out the menu. And this was just for lunch. Tonight would be a barbeque at the house.

Cat, Jake, her girlfriends, and their husbands and brothers, as well as Cody and Jace, sat at one of the portable picnic tables set up near the old RV her mother used to handle the food. In their chaps and cowboy hats, the men looked like something out of the Old West, and Cat could almost imagine what it must have been like over a century ago when the first branding would have taken place.

Were Taylors at that first McKenna branding, before all the trouble had started? What would her ancestor think of Taylors being here now?

She glanced at Cody, surprised to find he had been watching her. Her heart practically blossomed under his gaze. He was working hard for her. For Pleasant Valley. And she was lucky to have him in her life. Even if it couldn't be permanent. She was willing to take whatever happiness she could find.

"Look, Mommy," Jake said, pointing toward a police car that halted at the far end of the makeshift pasture parking lot. Another car pulled in alongside it. "The policeman came."

"What the…" She turned for a better view. Getting out of the car was Kyle Langley dressed in a suit, and stepping out of the police vehicle was Deputy Sheriff Brian Morris in his uniform, looking too somber for good news.

Chapter 24

"Kyle, what a surprise," Cat said as her lawyer drew near. The deputy sheriff seemed headed for the other side of the table, where most of the men sat. She rose from the picnic bench. "Is it business or curiosity that brought you out here?" Although Cat couldn't fathom what business would involve the sheriff, or engage her lawyer's curiosity, for that matter.

Kyle stopped next to the food truck and kept his eye on the deputy sheriff, who had leaned over between Cody and Jace and was talking in a low voice. Every head had turned, and all talk had ceased as Cody leaned in to catch the deputy sheriff's words.

Cat walked over to Kyle. "What's going on?" she asked. Something wasn't right. Something didn't feel good.

Kyle pointed his chin in the deputy sheriff's direction. "He's here to arrest the person who has been rustling your cattle."

"Who?" A feeling of pure dread clamped down on her chest like the jaws of a giant alligator had just found dinner.

"Your ramrod, Cody Taylor."

Cat heard the words, but her mind, her heart,

refused to comprehend them. Instead, she stood frozen in place, along with the half-dozen or so people still at the table, and her mother, who stood in the doorway of the RV.

Cody rose from his spot on the bench and extricated himself from the confines of the picnic table.

"You can't take him. You have no proof. And you have no proof because he didn't do it," Jace said, his voice raised so that everyone could hear.

But the deputy sheriff was doing it.

"It's all right, Jace. It's a mistake. I'll get it cleared up," Cody said, looking straight at Cat.

She met his gaze, held it. But she couldn't move.

It wasn't true. She knew it in her heart. But her mind was churning.

The deputy sheriff's hand was holding Cody's elbow as they walked past the men at the picnic table, past the neighbors who had been talking just a minute ago but now stood in silence. Everyone was frozen in place, including Cat.

"Where is Cody going, Mom?" Jake said, his voice holding a child's worry.

Cody passed by, his gaze never leaving her face until he was headed toward the waiting patrol car.

Something kicked in, like a sudden electric surge. "Wait," she called. "You have the wrong man." She felt Kyle's hand on her arm as if trying to tether her.

The deputy sheriff stopped and looked back, not releasing his grip on Cody. "I have a man in custody who has sworn that Cody Taylor paid him to rustle your cattle, Ms. McKenna. That's enough to warrant an arrest."

The ground seemed to shift under her feet. She

felt dizzy as she watched the back of Cody as he was led away.

"But I saw them. The rustlers. I was with Cody when we saw them," she said, but the deputy sheriff didn't turn around, and neither did Cody.

"I'll explain everything," Kyle said.

Cat looked at Kyle, who still rested his hand on her arm. She looked back at Jake, who seemed about to cry. He may not understand what was going on, but anyone, even a four-year-old, could see it wasn't good.

Jace rose. "I've got to go. We'll collect our horses tomorrow, if you wouldn't mind caring for them overnight." Without waiting for an answer, Jace followed Cody.

Like a starting gun to a race had been fired, everyone started talking at once. Cat was only vaguely aware of Libby and Mandy hugging her, and their husbands and brothers crowding around her. But Kyle Langley's hand was still holding her arm.

Will had offered to supervise the rest of the branding operation, and Tucker and Chance took Cody and Jace's place once horses had been found for them to ride. The neighbors banded together to finish the operation, and Mandy and Libby promised to help with clean up. There would be no end-of-branding barbeque back at the ranch house, and no one, it seemed, had a heart for it anyway.

Cat, her mother, and Jake had ridden back to the house in Kyle's car, and nary a word was spoken by the adults in consideration of Jake's tender ears. It didn't stop the questions tumbling out of her son's mouth, questions to which she had no answer. At the house, Cat had slid a DVD into the DVR and promised her son she'd be back in to explain it all, even though she didn't have a clue how she could explain the unexplainable.

Her mother joined Kyle and Cat in the study, and Cat tried to settle her emotions so she could understand what had just happened. Her mind just couldn't wrap around it. She knew it couldn't be Cody rustling her cattle, yet the damning testimony of someone she didn't know had accused Cody. Why?

"Tell me what is going on, Kyle," Cat said, not sure she could believe any of what she would be told if it meant Cody Taylor was being charged with rustling her cattle.

Kyle settled into the chair behind the desk and crossed his arms over his chest. "Ray Spencer came into my office today to work out a plea deal. He wanted out of the rustling business. As you may know, he has just gotten his divorce, and he's decided he wants to go to Montana, but Cody was apparently putting pressure on him to stay and threatening to tell the authorities it was Spencer rustling your cattle. Spencer decided his best bet was to turn in Cody in return for dropping any charges against Spencer. So far, Spencer has refused to name the second man, but I'm sure the sheriff will get it out of Cody." Kyle leaned forward. "I think Cody's brother could be that second person."

"I knew it. I knew we couldn't trust him," Lydia cried, jumping out of her chair. "He took this job for one reason—easier access to our herd. He was never interested in helping us out." Her hands were on her hips, and a self-righteous expression was on her face.

Cat felt...numb. She didn't want to believe it. But it was hard to argue with an eyewitness accuser who just happened to be Cyndi Lynn's ex-husband. Still, there must be an explanation. There had to be.

"I'm sorry, Cat," Kyle said. Why didn't he sound more sincere?

"She's always been gullible," Lydia chimed in. "And it's brought nothing but problems."

The charge washed over her, dampening her spirit. She'd heard it too many times before. It was all her fault. She had poor judgment when it came to people, to men.

But when Jake's father had turned away from her, it hadn't come without warning. She'd known something wasn't right from the beginning. She just hadn't wanted to believe it. When she finally had to face the truth, it was a truth that made sense of a lot of things.

Cody rustling her cattle made no sense. The night at the line shack, his interactions with Jake, his lessons on ranching, his pointing out the stolen cattle in the first place, his lifetime of doing the right thing, including protecting her at that party after high school…that wasn't the MO of a cattle rustler.

Her mind joined with her heart in fighting the urge to believe in his guilt, even with the facts shoved in her face. It couldn't be true. If it was, everything she believed in would be suspect. Everything.

"Can I see Cody?" If she could just talk to him.

"No," Lydia said with enough force to blow down a house.

"I wouldn't advise it," Kyle said in a more even tone. "Let the law handle this, Cat. If he is innocent, he'll be able to prove it, and it might be all over in a day. If he's not, well then, he'll likely be in jail until there is a trial. I doubt they'll be able to raise a bond, much less bail."

Bail? She hadn't thought about Cody having to remain locked up. "If he has to stay in jail until he's proven innocent in a trial…it will bury the family. They will have to sell the Cross T." She felt the pain skip from her heart to the pit of her stomach.

"He's not innocent, Cat. Did you hear anything Kyle said?" Her mother's voice dripped with disgust.

She heard, but hearing was not believing.

"This might not be the best time to bring it up, but the consortium interested in buying Pleasant Valley upped their offer." Kyle named a price ten percent higher than the initial offer. "I think you two should give it serious consideration. If nothing else, the events of today prove that running Pleasant Valley is perhaps more of a challenge than either of you have the wherewithal to meet. And however much Cody may have contributed to running the place, as opposed to stealing from it, he's not going to be able to contribute any longer, nor would you want him to. If we can complete this deal by the time the calves are ready to ship, you'll get the proceeds from the sale of your stock and from the sale of the ranch, giving you a nice tidy sum. I can help structure it so we can lessen the tax burden and still provide a nice trust fund for your son, and as I told you, Cat, I would be supportive of investing in a preschool or something similar. I know you'd rather work with children than cattle."

That had been true once, but she wasn't sure it still was. If it meant working with Cody, she preferred raising her son on the ranch to anywhere else.

But if it had been an unrealistic dream before, Cody's arrest made it an impossible one. How had her world turned upside down in just a few minutes?

She looked up. Her mother's expression was one of resignation, even if there were tears forming in her eyes. "Maybe we should consider it. An operation like Pleasant Valley might be too much."

"You mean especially if you can't trust my judgment."

"I mean it is too much for you." Lydia's jaw clenched like she was trying to keep her real thoughts from coming out. Cat could only imagine what those thoughts were.

* * *

"Cody Taylor, someone to see you," the guard said.

Cody sat on the edge of the hard plastic chair in a large cell filled with other men on hard plastic chairs. Waiting was the name of the game in the holding pen. Waiting for a court-appointed lawyer's counsel to accept whatever the prosecutor was offering, waiting for a family member to tell you this was all a mistake, waiting to be moved inside to the actual prison.

Cody had tried not to let the cinderblocks, the bars, and the dozen or so characters right out of one of those cable news lockdown shows unnerve him, and so far, he'd been winning that battle, but the fight was just beginning.

"There's no one I want to see."

He'd already been visited by his brother and Melissa Meyer, accompanied by his new lawyer, Gavin Heely, who was a criminal defense attorney in Melissa's firm. And it would be too soon for his mother to have made it from Laramie, even if she had decided to leave work, which he prayed she wouldn't. He'd tried to persuade his brother to delay telling her, but given his cousin Michael, the detective, had already contacted Jace having heard about the arrest, Jace wanted to be sure he was the one his mother heard it from.

His new lawyer hadn't minced words. The prosecutor's case against Cody was based on Ray Spencer's word that Cody had organized the rustling. Gavin would press them to produce evidence rather than just one guy's testimony, and they would try to paint Ray as an unreliable witness. They needed to find the second man Cody had seen rustling the cattle, because Spencer wasn't talking, and the prosecutor seemed satisfied with bagging the supposed ringleader.

Cody didn't know who was paying Spencer to create this lie. All he had were suspicions with no proof and that no one was likely to listen to. Locked up, he wouldn't be able to find out. His bail was set at $50,000—as if he'd murdered someone—and there was no way they could raise even a tenth of that for a bond, as required by any bondsman. And worse, Jace had been questioned by the deputy sheriff as to whether Jace was the second man that night.

"She's insisting. Claims she's your sister. She don't look like you though. She said you had different fathers."

His sister? Could be Cat. Did he want to see her? It had been nothing short of humiliating to be walked out in front of friends and neighbors, and worst of all little Jake.

But the look of disbelief in Cat's eyes had eaten at his soul.

Cody shook his head. "I don't have any sister."

Chapter 25

Cody was free…at least for the moment. Somehow his family had arranged bail. He felt the weight of obligation. He owed a lot to Aunt Lucille and Uncle Tom beyond just the money.

As he stepped into the waiting area, he was relieved to see his brother. Jace wrapped his arms around Cody in a bear hug and just as quickly released him. They'd never been a hugging family.

Neither brother spoke until they were inside the pickup cab, Jace at the wheel. He didn't start the engine.

"Who sprung bail for you?" Jace said.

"I was going to ask you. Thought maybe it was Aunt Lucille."

"Don't think so. Uncle Tom was trying to gather as much money as he could through the family, but as I recall, they were about fifteen hundred short of the ten percent needed for the bail bondsman."

"I don't have a clue who would have that kind of money. Didn't they say at the jail?"

"All I got was a call from that Gavin guy's office. Said your bail had been posted by a bail bondsman and someone was to come get you. That's all the information they gave."

"Whoever it is, we have no way of paying them

back, and I don't like being beholden. But I am sure glad to be out."

Cat was the only one he knew who might have access to that kind of money, and based upon the look on her face when they led him away, he doubted she would be putting up any money to save him.

Cat and he had started to talk about a future, even if it was only in "what-ifs." And the kicker was, he'd fallen in love with her against his own instincts and the wishes of his family.

With someone pointing the finger at him, he couldn't blame her if she believed he was guilty, though it hurt more than he could say to know she thought him a thief, to know that she'd had to watch as he'd been led away by a deputy sheriff in front of family, friends, and neighbors, accused of stealing from her. She must think one more man in her life had betrayed her, and that ate at his very being.

She deserved better than that. Better than him.

Somehow he had to find a way to prove otherwise. Not just for his reputation. But so he could look her in the eyes again and not see her pain. There might not be a future for the two of them, but he needed her to see that she wasn't wrong about him, for pride if no other reason.

Jace started the engine. "Me too. Calving season has begun. Got the first two newborns today. Duane is out there by himself."

It would be good to get to work and take his mind off of this horror he'd fallen into.

"Any others look ready to birth?"

"Looking at their udders, I'd say at least one more could happen today."

Cody looked out the dirt-spattered window as Jace turned onto Daley Street and headed out of town, past the low buildings and bungalows that dotted the prairie landscape.

"You should know," Jace continued. "Mom's been cursing the McKennas every which way since she heard. She's on her way down here. At least she won't have to visit you in prison."

"It was a detention center, but yeah, I'm thankful for small favors." And really big ones, like getting bailed out. "I don't know how we'll pay back whoever paid that bail bondsman. Or pay for the lawyer. Or pay the bills, now that I'm not pulling in a paycheck."

Jace turned onto the highway. Prairie opened up on both sides of the road. Cody drank in the sight of wide-open spaces. He would lose everything. Whether he got convicted or not.

"We'll have to sell for sure, now."

Cody leaned his cheek against the window. Jace had stated the inevitable, but it was still a bitter pill.

Cody felt about as low as a snake's belly in a wagon rut as he watched the tears roll down his mother's face. She'd left work and taken the hour-and-a-half drive expecting to find her son in prison. She'd found him at home, but it hadn't stopped the tears from flowing.

"I told you she was trouble. From the very first I told you."

Nor the recriminations about Cat McKenna.

"She had nothing to do with this. Spencer turned me in. I haven't even seen the guy in months. I don't know what the hell is going on." Cody felt like a

314

mouse in a maze. Every time he thought he'd found a clear path to resolving the family's troubles, it turned out to be a dead end—and now a fatal end because there was no way he or the rest of his family would recover from this.

He was facing a felony offense with up to ten years in prison, and he hadn't done anything to warrant it. Yet it would be his word against another guy's, and he doubted Cat being with him that night would save him. First, she might not testify in his defense if she believed he was behind the rustling, and second, even if she did, it wouldn't negate the accusation against him. They'd just say he had to change his plans when Cat showed up.

He laid his hands upon his mother's back as she bent over in the small chair, rocking back and forth as she cried.

"Where are we going to get money for the lawyer?" she asked, her voice low and muffled.

Cody had been thinking about it all the way back to the ranch. It would ruin him, but it could spare his mother and brother.

"I'll take a plea deal if they offer it."

Jace sat up, and his mother jerked to attention.

"Like hell you will," Mamie said with a resolve that humbled him. "You are innocent, and I'll sell everything I have to prove that. It's bad enough the McKennas took our water and will likely take our ranch, but I'll be damned if they will take the Taylor good name."

"We could sell Smoking Gun," Jace offered.

Cody nodded. That was the least they would have to do. "And we'll likely have to sell the ranch." That was the sane thing, though it meant the end of his dreams and his family's. It meant the end of any hope, small as it had been, for a life with Cat and Jake.

Standing accused, even if he didn't do the crime, he'd never be able to face her. And she would be left believing he did it. That hurt worst of all.

Cat sat at the desk in the study, the contents of her father's strongbox, where he stored all the family's important papers, strewn across the desktop. She had finally gotten around to going through her father's papers, as Cody had once suggested.

She and her mother had decided, after much discussion, to accept the consortium's offer. What they hadn't decided was where they would go now that they had options. Maybe Colorado. Maybe Montana, where Cat's aunt and uncle lived.

She picked up a piece of paper, examined it, and placed it in its proper pile.

She glanced at her phone. It had been days since Cody had been led away and she had posted bail from her meager savings, wiping out her personal bank account. She was convinced he was not involved with rustling her cattle, just as she knew sitting in jail would cost him—ranch-wise and emotionally.

Cody was a proud man. Proud of his reputation. Proud of his ethics. This accusation had shredded it all. She wanted to help him. She wanted him to know she didn't believe it. But he wouldn't see her. Had refused to see her at the detention center, although he knew it had to be her asking to visit. And when she'd texted him that first day to see if he'd been released, he'd typed one word: *yes*. That was it.

She'd texted after that asking to meet him. Silence.

Likely he blamed her. Only she had nothing to do with it.

Her mother was as certain of Cody's guilt as she was that God listened to her prayers every night. And Cat had kept her silence about paying for the bail bond, equally certain Cody was not guilty.

He wouldn't have spent that night in the line shack with her if he had been guilty. He wouldn't have filled her head with possibilities if he was guilty. He wouldn't have cared so much for Jake. If Cody was guilty, she might as well crawl in bed, pull the covers over her head, and never come out again, because it meant that she was wrong about everything in her life.

The truth was she loved Cody Taylor. Loved him for his integrity and grit, loved him for the care he'd shown her son, and loved him for having faith in her abilities despite the odds.

But regardless of the legal verdict, there could be no future for the two of them. He obviously blamed her for his predicament, and the animosity between the Taylors and McKennas had only escalated. Even neighbors were now divided into Taylor and McKenna camps.

And if it could never be, she needed, for sheer sanity's sake, to move on emotionally and physically. Selling the ranch was part of that moving on. But before she did, she planned on finding out the truth about who was rustling her cattle. How she was going to do that, however, hadn't come to her yet.

If she was selling the ranch, she wanted to be sure what it was she was selling. Cody's insistence that the ranch wasn't being sold for ranching had left her unsettled. So she had rummaged through various McKenna family birth certificates, marriage licenses, BLM leases, and the original deed to the ranch, yellowed and creased, as well as recent land surveys to try to understand what mineral rights she owned in addition to the land.

There were papers for equipment, cars, and trucks. There were expired leases from when Pleasant Valley had leased mineral rights to the company that had pumped those three now-abandoned oil wells in the north pasture, depleting them of their black gold. But no geological survey.

She fingered a trifold packet of papers. Could this be such a survey?

She unfolded the papers. The letterhead of the first sheet bore the name of Kyle Langley's firm. Her gaze darted to the bottom, where Kyle's signature was scrawled. She scanned the date and did the math. Sixteen months ago. Before her father had died.

She read it. Kyle was urging her father to take the offer.

She shuffled to the second page. It contained an offer from LEW Consortium. For a million dollars less than they were now offering her. She read further, right to the paragraph about what they were going to do with the land. The words *wells*, *fracking*, *natural gas*, and *horizontal drilling* stood out like neon lights on a billboard.

LEW Consortium was going to frack the abandoned wells and begin horizontal drilling for natural gas. Everywhere. They had included copies of their geological studies, and the letter referenced the fact that Pleasant Valley had unfettered access to water.

Natural gas. Fracking. She didn't know much about it beyond a few stories in the local press claiming depleted water supplies or spoiled wells as a result of fracking, which apparently required tons of water to execute.

She sat back and closed her eyes.

If she sold to LEW Consortium, she likely would be sealing the fate of Pleasant Valley as a ranch...and probably the Cross T as well, if the water got depleted or contaminated. And contrary to what Kyle Langley had led her to believe, he knew what LEW Consortium planned to do with the property. Why hadn't he told her? It was things like this that seeded her unease with her lawyer.

One more complication amid a beehive of complexity.

Opening her eyes, she went over to the printer/copier and made copies of the letter. She needed to confront Kyle with this information. What he hadn't disclosed probably wasn't illegal, just unethical. After Cody had shared his skepticism, the uncomfortable feeling that something wasn't quite right with this offer had grown. And now she knew why.

If it is too good to be true, it probably isn't true.

She tucked the original letter back into the fireproof strong box and stuffed the copies into the pocket of her jeans. Even though drilling and fracking were upsetting uses for the land, after all that had happened, could she afford to reject the offer out of hand? It might take years to find a ranch buyer for

Pleasant Valley. And the challenge of managing Pleasant Valley alone was overwhelming. She wasn't certain she could find another experienced ramrod quickly. Besides, she didn't want to ranch without Cody by her side. The only thing that gave her pause was the effect it might have on the water for the Cross T.

Only she'd learned just yesterday that the Cross T was up for sale. That fact had spread like a spark hitting gasoline. No doubt legal fees on top of all the other debt had necessitated the move. Her heart hitched at the thought of what this was doing to Cody. His dreams, his life, were crumbling around him, and he didn't want any comfort from the owner of the ranch that had been the wrecking ball. Even if it hadn't been her fault. Even if she believed in his innocence.

Not knowing what documents she might need in the future, she clipped together the papers of each organized pile. She found an envelope for the deed and recent surveys, the same survey that had been the basis for the adverse possession claim. As she stuffed the deed into the envelope, a yellowed sheet stuck out. She pulled the paper out.

The aged paper had formal writing, but it was the signatures that snagged her attention. The first one was Alistair McKenna, the second Emma Taylor, the date 1909, and witnessed by a Woodrow Stanton. The paper read:

I, Emma Taylor, agree to allow Alistair McKenna access to the body of water known as Crystal Creek, which resides on my land per the deed titled Cross T Ranch and situated ten feet from the southern border of the ranch known as Pleasant Valley per deed of said ranch, for the sum of one dollar per year for ninety-nine years for a total of ninety-nine dollars, paid in full at the signing of this lease.

The subsequent pages were copies of the deeds for the Cross T and Pleasant Valley, clearly showing Crystal Creek on Taylor land.

She reread the paper. Could this mean that her ancestors had leased the land and the water rights from Cody's ancestors? She rubbed her temple.

And if that was the case, that would mean the ten years needed for an adverse possession claim hadn't been met. Making her claim invalid.

Had her father known this? And not said anything waiting for the ten years to be up? It would explain why nothing had been mentioned about boundaries and water when the ranch passed to her father.

She took a hard swallow as she carefully folded up the faded lease and placed it in the envelope.

Pleasant Valley no longer had a right to that water.

Without access to water, Pleasant Valley could not survive as a ranch.

Without access to water, LEW Consortium could not carry out fracking.

Pleasant Valley was essentially worthless land.

Her mind raced with possibilities. She could lose the consortium's offer and decimate the value of Pleasant Valley if she disclosed this lease. She could also save the Cross T. Maybe she could negotiate water rights with Cody and pay him for access for water—but would the Taylors be of a mind to grant water rights to the McKennas for any price now?

And what if she didn't disclose this lease? What

if she left it in the envelope until ten years had passed, as her father probably intended, or destroyed it? Could she live with herself? Could she rationalize that she was doing this for her son? For his future?

She needed to talk to Kyle Langley and find out if the lease was even valid and why he hadn't disclosed to her the intent of LEW Consortium.

Anxiety roiled her stomach and pricked her limbs as she watched Kyle read over the copy of the lease document, a document that could change her fortunes forever, and not in a good way. He sat on the corner edge of his uncluttered desk, one foot on the floor, the other leg dangling over the side, paper in his hand.

When Kyle's customary frown deepened and his mouth flat-lined, Cat braced for bad news. But when he looked up from the paper, he shrugged.

"I wouldn't be too concerned," he said.

"Really? But wouldn't this negate the adverse possession claim?"

"If it was valid, the clock would start from the end of the lease, and you wouldn't yet have reached the ten-year minimum."

Just as she'd feared.

"But if it was recorded and therefore official, I would have found a record of it, and I didn't. And we don't know if money ever changed hands. Certainly if the Taylors had such a document, they would have produced it. They didn't." Kyle slid the paper onto his clean desk. "I'd just ignore it."

Ignore it? She'd been worrying about the consequences of this document since she found it. And if it hadn't felt right taking Cody's land when she thought she had a legal claim to it, then it certainly didn't now, when there appeared to be much more to the story.

Kyle rose off the desk. "If you want, I'll keep this and look into it some more, but I doubt I'll find anything. If you get me the original, it may help with my research."

She nodded, though she had no intention of giving him the original. Especially given her next topic.

"And I also found this." She pulled from the folder a copy of the letter from Kyle to her father and the original offer the letter referenced.

"Why were you going through all these old records?" Kyle asked as he took the papers from her hand.

"Just cleaning up the office. Since we were thinking of selling, I thought I would make sure we had all the proper papers."

He frowned. "*Were* thinking of selling?" He scanned his letter and raised his head. "Yes, I sent this to your father. And yes, I knew about the offer and what they wanted to do with the land. I was prepared to tell you before you officially accepted, but because as trustee I do think this offer should be accepted, I wanted to be sure you and your mother were interested before I explained their purpose."

That sounded good, but it didn't convince her. Kyle had always been a little too slick for her liking. "I haven't told my mother yet. I don't know if mining on our land, drilling on our land, would be acceptable to her."

"Then you could wait years for a buyer who

actually wants to ranch it." Kyle's tone was matter of fact, but he squinted his eyes.

"I know that without water rights, ranching would be impossible, but if you find out that this lease is valid, would a company intent on fracking still be interested?"

"No. To do natural gas exploration or open up old oil sites, the fracking process requires water. Maybe more so than even ranching. If you didn't have access to water, your land, the ranch, would be pretty much worthless for anything. But as I said, I wouldn't be worried about the water rights based on a document more than a hundred years old and never filed. Your access to Crystal Creek has been legally affirmed."

Cat rose. She had some difficult decisions ahead of her. But that certain something about Kyle made her feel he wasn't the one to help her with those decisions. She hoped her judgment was not failing her, had not failed her.

"That's good to hear, but I'd feel better if you did some investigation."

"It would help if I had the original. And in the meantime, I wouldn't mention this to anyone. Not your mother, and certainly not anyone friendly with the Taylors. No one."

"Let me know what you find," Cat said, not committing to anything.

Chapter 26

Sitting atop her horse, waiting for Cody to arrive on his side of the creek, it felt like a gymnastics team was performing in her stomach. Questions rolled through her like a tumbler on steroids.

Was she doing right by her son? Would she ruin any chance for the sale of her property? Was she doing this because she wanted Cody to love her? Or because it was the right thing?

Her mother would surely throw this in her face as one more example of her impulsive and destructive behavior. Lydia would see this as a betrayal. And maybe, when Cat's son grew up, he would too.

When had doing the right thing gotten so hard?

When had knowing what the right thing was gotten so hard?

He was coming into sight, riding his paint horse, sitting tall in the saddle. She drank in the sight of him like a woman lost in the desert. It had been weeks since the deputy had led him away. Days since she'd confronted Kyle, who told her in no uncertain terms to let it go.

And weeks since she'd realized she'd loved him.

The cruelty was she still loved him. Accusations and all. And she wasn't sure she would ever stop loving him.

Cody wished he were anywhere but coming to see Cat. Life was too complicated now for him to give in to the feelings that swamped him every time he thought of her. He should be consumed with calving at the Cross T and figuring out a future for his mother and Jace—one that wouldn't include the ranch, or him if he went to prison.

But Cat had sounded desperate on the voice mail she'd left for him. And he'd responded via text that he would meet her by the creek where she first asked him to work for Pleasant Valley—a fateful request that had brought him to the accusations that now sealed his ruin. Because he was sure that whoever was really behind the rustling, and he had his suspicions, was intent on also ruining Pleasant Valley. The rustling had been part of the ruination—getting rid of him by pinning the rustling on him was the other part.

He couldn't fathom what Cat had to say to him, but he had to resist any notion they could find happiness in the unlikely event she still cared. There was a good chance he was going to jail. People in these parts didn't like rustlers, and even a hint of such activity was enough to earn most people's condemnation. Even if he beat this charge, the animosity between the two families had only increased. Why should she trust him? And what if she believed he was guilty, as they had an eyewitness who said he was?

Still, as he drew near and saw her atop her horse Custer, he couldn't help the surge of feelings that promised to upend him if he wasn't diligent. He'd fallen in love with Cat. Fallen in love with her tenacity, her princess ways, and her little boy.

For a few brief moments, he'd let himself imagine life with Cat as his wife and Jake as his son, and that had made his fall from their grace even more severe and bitter.

The thought of Jake growing up thinking Cody had done him and his family wrong ate away at his soul like maggots on a carcass.

But there she sat, shifting in her saddle, brushing back her hair, as she often did when she was nervous.

He stopped at the edge of the stream and motioned to her to cross. There was no way he was setting foot on Pleasant Valley land while he stood accused of stealing from them. No way.

Cat slowly walked Custer through a shallow part of the creek. She grasped the horn of the saddle as the horse climbed the small embankment.

Cody waited, seemingly calm and collected, but he was watching her with an intensity that caused her stomach to flutter. It all had to be a lie, a false accusation, made for reasons that eluded her. Otherwise, everything she thought she knew about people, everything she thought she knew about herself, was wrong.

His gaze swept over her like a cold wind, bringing a similar chill despite the growing heat of the day.

Seeing him up close, her first thought was how haggard he looked. Dark smudges of fatigue encircled his eyes, his hair was tousled, and his clothes were rumpled like he'd been disturbed from sleep. She would bet he hadn't been sleeping but working, probably most of the night, delivering calves. Delivering calves for a ranch that he would no longer run.

"You said you had something important that I

needed to know?" His hands, crossed at the wrist, casually rested on the horn of the saddle, belying the alertness with which he watched her.

No *I've missed you* greeting or *It's good to see you* welcome.

She took a swallow. What happened next would change her fortunes and those of her son's for eternity. But there was no turning back. It was the right thing to do. The only thing she could do and still look herself in the mirror.

"It's good to see you too, Cody. How have you been?" she asked. If only he would say a word to let her know he'd been at least thinking about her.

"As well as I can be under the circumstances. Six cows gave birth just this morning. Tell me what brought you here, and let me be on my way."

His words bit like a frenzy of horseflies. She didn't need any more proof that whatever feelings he'd once harbored for her had been destroyed by these allegations. Maybe it had all been a mirage, a house of cards, with no real substance if those feelings could be dispatched so quickly.

She took a deep breath. "I've found something, something important, among my father's papers."

"About your mineral rights?" he said, obviously referring to his earlier insistence that she investigate the reasons behind the offer for her land. And he'd been right. "Why tell me?"

"Because while I did find information about the mineral rights, I also found new information about water rights."

His right eyebrow quirked. That had at least gotten his attention.

She dug into her pocket and extracted one of the copies she made of the lease. Leaning across the saddle, she held it out to him.

He looked her over, as if he was trying to decipher something, but took the paper from her hand, brushing his fingers over hers as he did so. Even that simple touch made her ache inside.

Cody scanned the paper. Words like *Crystal Creek*, *water rights*, *lease*, and *southern border* jumped out at him. He reread it more carefully and slowly. His pulse increased, and his breathing sped up. He looked up from the paper and into a pair of apprehensive eyes.

"You know what this could mean?" It could mean everything to him. It could mean that for once in his life, things could go in the direction of the Taylors. It could mean his family would be saved from ruin, even if he was not.

She stared at him, her vulnerability written across flushed cheeks and a trembling lip. "That my claim isn't valid. And my land is worthless."

She did know. And the thought that she knew and still came to him with the information made him want to scoop her up and kiss the daylights out of her, made him want to hold her in his arms and show her how grateful he was, made him want to show her how much he loved her for the sacrifice she'd just made. For him. The thought was sobering.

"And yet you brought this to me, the guy accused of robbing you."

"You should know my lawyer doesn't think this is valid," she said, ignoring his comment. She shaded her beautiful eyes from the afternoon sun. "My lawyer says that he didn't come across any record of it when his firm did a search for the adverse possession suit, and therefore he thinks it was never filed."

"You showed it to Langley?" That was unfortunate if his suspicions were true.

"I wanted to get his opinion on the legality of the document." She brushed her hair back from her face. "And you were right. That consortium wants my land for natural gas exploration, not ranching. They corresponded with my father before his death. Before I found this, we, my mother and I, planned to sell them Pleasant Valley."

She'd always been stubborn and persistent, and that was what he'd liked about her. But now she was going to sell Pleasant Valley—for mining. The idea brought a lump to his throat.

"Why?"

"I fooled myself into believing I could run the ranch because it was easier than facing a decision to sell. With all that's happened…" She closed her eyes as if she was trying to block it all out. "It isn't worth fooling myself anymore."

"Regardless of what has happened, Cat, you were becoming a good rancher. You would make it ranching. I'm sure of it."

Her lip trembled more visibly. Made him want to pull her off that horse, wrap his arms around her, and make her his. But then he'd be the one fooling himself.

"Without water rights, there is no Pleasant Valley. I guess that is why there was a ninety-nine year lease, or at least they thought about one. For not much money. Apparently the Taylors and the

McKennas weren't always feuding."

"If this is valid, we could work something out if you wanted to keep the ranch." Although it wouldn't be easy to get his mother to agree after all that had gone on now and in years past.

If he'd known about the lease six years ago, his family could have been collecting money from the McKennas, and they might not have had to take out a second mortgage.

But Cat was right—the lease he held in his hand could be worthless.

She shook her head. "I think it's best if the McKennas move on. And maybe you can keep the Cross T and lease the water rights to someone new, someone without our history. At least I hope you will consider leasing those rights, because our land is likely worthless without them."

And she wanted to move on without him, even if she did believe he was innocent. Not that he blamed her.

"Won't matter. We have to sell the Cross T. I've already sold Smoking Gun."

It had hurt more than he'd thought to load that young gelding into someone else's trailer. It would have happened eventually, but at least he could have taken pride in the type of horse he'd helped Smoking Gun become. Instead it felt like just one more he'd betrayed. The look in Smoking Gun's eyes as the horse had resisted loading had wrenched Cody from the inside out.

But he'd done what he needed to do. And the little money he got for the horse was sorely needed. And Cat was doing what she needed to do…without him.

"Not Smoking Gun. He was the future of the Cross T. He was your future."

"The Cross T has no future, not with Taylors running it anyway. Jace and my mother will be leaving the town."

None of them could stand to stay anywhere near the Cross T and watch as someone else ran the operation and worked the land. Land that would always be Taylor land, in their mind anyway.

"And you?" she asked. Was she welling up? He hoped not. It wouldn't do either of them any good.

"One way or the other."

Cat shook her head. "If you are found innocent, you won't need to leave. Leasing the water rights would give you extra income."

At one time that could have been enough. "The accusations have driven the final nail in the coffin. Accusations don't have to be true to ruin a man."

"I know they aren't true. Others know it too."

She still had faith in him. The knowledge warmed him like hot brandy on a cold night. Not that it would affect the future. He'd faced the fact he could be convicted even though he was innocent. The law wasn't always perfect. Justice wasn't always served.

"What makes you so sure?"

"Because if you rustled my cattle, nothing else makes sense." She shifted in her saddle. "When I found out Jake's father was married, suddenly everything made sense. His reluctance to talk about the future, his disappearance most weekends, the calls he'd take outside or in another room. But why would you take the time to school me in ranching? Why would you have taken an inventory count or mentioned the possibility of rustling? I would have been perfectly content to believe it was my mismanagement that was diminishing the herd. And why would you take the time to teach Jake about fishing or T-ball if you didn't want to be part of Jake's life, if just as a neighbor?"

Jake. The idea that Jake would think Cody had betrayed him, betrayed his family, was almost more than he could live with. "You know I wanted to be more than just a neighbor to Jake. To you." The words cost him, but he might never have another opportunity to say them to her. Might never have another opportunity alone with her.

A tear escaped down her cheek. "It just wasn't meant to be, you and me." Several more tears followed.

Cody nudged his horse closer, reached over, and swiped his thumb across her soft cheek. "We would have been good together, Princess. If life had given us half a chance."

Just touching her again brought feelings that overwhelmed him.

She turned her face into his hand, and her lips caressed his palm, reminding him of what it meant to hold her, kiss her, be with her.

He leaned over. Cupped her chin. Their mouths met, and a deep need surged through him. Their tongues mated as the kiss deepened.

This could be the last time he would ever kiss her, and he wanted her to remember his kiss. His touch. He wanted her to remember him.

They tortured themselves for a few more seconds before Comanche shifted his weight, probably annoyed Custer was so close. Reluctantly, Cody pulled back.

There was no future.

"Thank you for this, Cat. I know how much it cost you."

"Not as much as all of this has cost you," she said.

Cat McKenna had been loyal to him to the end.

* * *

Lydia paced across the kitchen floor like a caged tiger, and just as angry.

"I can't believe you did this. I can't believe you did this behind my back." The words, laced with condemnation, were voiced barely above a whisper.

"When is Cody coming over, Mommy?" Jake asked from the perch of his booster seat at the kitchen table.

Kyle Langley had called during dinner, and her mother had answered. And then all hell had broken loose. Cody lost no time filing to reopen the adverse possession claim against his ranch. And Kyle, as their family lawyer, had been notified. The offer from LEW Consortium had been withdrawn.

"He's very busy, Jake." Cat hadn't broached the subject of Cody, but that didn't prevent her son asking the same question several times a day.

Lydia stopped, facing Jake. "He's never stepping foot on this ranch again. Not while we're here."

Jake frowned. "Why? Why can't he come over, Grandma?"

Because he's a...."

"Mom," Cat said as sharply as she dared. She leaned her elbows on the table and clasped her hands in front of her.

"He needs to know the truth."

"And when we know the truth, I will tell him. Until then, nothing else is to be said." Cat pushed her half-full dinner plate to the side. She had no appetite.

"He needs to know so he doesn't believe everything some lowlife tells him."

Like her mother thought she did.

"Tell me, Mommy." Jake climbed down from his seat.

"I'll take you to ride your pony." Anything to change the subject. And get out of the house.

"You've ruined us, Cat McKenna. And your son's future. And for what? Because some man paid you a little attention. And stole from you."

"Run outside, Jake. I'll be there in a moment."

The prospect of riding his pony worked as she'd hoped. Jake fairly flew out the door. Cat rose from the table and faced her mother. Lydia's hands were on her hips, her jaw was tight, and her eyes held pure fire.

"I did the right thing according to my standards."

"Was it the right thing to conceive a child out of wedlock?"

The thunder of humiliation mixed with the lightning of anger. "Think what you like about me. But what is done is done."

"The ruination of this family, of your son's future. The destruction of the McKenna legacy. The end of Pleasant Valley. I hope your righteousness will keep you warm at night." With that, Lydia turned and left Cat standing in the kitchen. Alone.

* * *

It had been two weeks since she'd showed Cody the letter, and she'd heard nothing from him—at least not directly. Her mother treated her like Hester Prynne and Benedict Arnold rolled into one.

Running the ranch with Will instead of Cody was an exercise in frustration, and every day confirmed her need to sell the ranch. Only there were no buyers. Not with the water rights situation unresolved.

In between her lawyer's recriminations (he'd barely stopped short of calling her an idiot), he'd advised her that a hearing had been set for the adverse possession claim for September in light of new evidence and that LEW Consortium had withdrawn their offer due to this question of water rights. If she lost her case, she'd have to fire sale her cattle…all of them.

So far, no one had guessed that she had posted bail, and she hoped it could stay that way. It would just be one more thing her mother and Kyle would chastise her about. In her heart she was glad she had posted bail, glad she had given Cody the lease despite the chaos that had ensued.

Jake continued to ask after Cody. Her heart might be breaking, but so was her son's. And there was nothing she could do about it.

Her mother had accused of her of being impulsive, of not thinking with her head, and those were probably true.

Kyle had said he didn't think they would get a fifth of what the land was worth without water, because if Cody's counterclaim prevailed, someone would have to pay an awful lot for access.

The last time Cat had felt this isolated and alone was when she was pregnant with Jake.

As much to keep her mind occupied on something other than Cody Taylor and the problems of Pleasant Valley, Cat spent what little free time she had searching through trunks in the attic for clues as to why Emma Taylor granted such favorable terms to Alistair McKenna. Her diligent efforts were rewarded one day, not too long after she'd given Cody the letter.

Alistair McKenna kept a journal of sorts about ranching in the new country. He was just twenty when he staked his claim in the 1880s, and he wrote about mundane things like the weather, crop planting, type of cattle, etc. But somewhere around his twenty-fifth year, he noted something unusual. Something about the young Mrs. Taylor. Something about her querulous husband and her having two young sons.

Alistair was married at the time, and Cat couldn't say the notations were of a romantic bent, but she thought it odd.

A year later in the diary Alistair mentioned losing his wife in childbirth and being left with a young baby boy to raise. A few more pages and he referred to the young widow Taylor.

Cat continued paging through, looking for mention of the widow Taylor. From what she could piece together, the widow Taylor helped Alistair McKenna raise his son, and Alistair McKenna helped the widow Taylor raise cattle, *despite the animosity of her boys.*

Rumors persisted, Alistair noted, so there could be no mingling of McKennas and Taylors.

There was more to the story, Cat was sure. But

the journal ended abruptly six years after the man had started it and just a few months after both Alistair and Emma had lost their spouses. She did know that years later Emma Taylor formally granted Alistair McKenna access to Crystal Creek for ninety-nine years, or at least intended to. But it didn't answer the question of the feud, or what the rumors were and why they prevented the "mingling" of Taylors and McKennas.

Chapter 27

Late one afternoon Will Springer stood at Cat's door, hat in hand. They'd only recently turned the bulls out, and Cat feared something untoward had happened with the cattle. Seemed these days, every day brought another problem.

"I need to talk to you, Miss McKenna. Alone." He shifted his wary gaze down the hall.

"Just me here, Will. My mother's gone to pick up Jake," she said. "Come in. We can talk in the study."

"Can I get you some coffee? Water?" she asked after Will followed her into the room.

"Nothing, thanks. What I have to say won't take long. But I need your word that no matter what I tell you, you won't hold me responsible. You won't press charges." His narrowed-eyed gaze unnerved her.

"Press charges? Why would I press charges?"

"Promise me."

"Does this have something to do with Cody?"

Will nodded. "I knew your father a long time and worked for him for five years. That should count for something."

If Will had something that would help Cody, she was willing to agree to anything, with one exception.

"As long as it doesn't involve anyone getting killed or injured, I promise."

"No, ma'am. Not yet at least."

Cat's breath hitched at the last comment. "I think I'd better sit down for this." She slipped into one of the club chairs. Will sat in the other.

He twirled his hat in his hand, just like Cody had once done.

"I'm all ears, Will," she prompted.

"This ain't easy. I'm not proud of what I'm going to tell you, but you need to know. Cody Taylor needs to know."

"Wouldn't it be best to go to the sheriff then?"

"I don't think the sheriff is going to promise he won't prosecute me."

"You've been rustling my cattle?"

Will nodded and rubbed his hand across his mouth as if trying to wipe away a bad taste.

Cody had tried to warn her, tried to tell her. But she wouldn't listen. She didn't want to believe it. But like with Jake's father, it made sense of a lot of things. Like why Will hadn't been more proactive. And then there was the bandanna.

"Why?"

"Because someone else, not Cody Taylor, paid me a lot of money."

She felt both elated and queasy at the knowledge.

"I've known it wasn't Cody Taylor. I just didn't know how to prove it or who it was. He thought you were involved though."

"He was getting too close to the truth. That's why he pinned it on Cody."

"Who? Spencer?"

"No, Langley."

Cat took a gulp of air, filled her lungs, and breathed out.

"Explain."

"Langley is the L in LEW Consortium. He wanted Pleasant Valley so he could drill for natural gas. Apparently, there is a huge reserve under this here ground. And he paid me to make things go south at the ranch to force you to sell. Rustling cattle was part of it."

"And not moving my cattle so they'd get scours and assorted other problems was the other part?"

Kyle Langley had wanted to destroy the ranching operation so that Cat and her mother would sell it to the consortium, his company. Everything made sense now. His urging her to sell. His anger about the water rights. His failing to disclose the purpose of LEW.

Greed was at the heart of it. Not only Kyle Langley's greed, but her father's. He failed to disclose that the lease had run out when he must have known, hoping to run out the calendar and when ten years had passed, file for an adverse possession claim. Only he had died before those ten years, and she had filed the claim, prematurely, as it turned out.

"Yes, ma'am."

"Why? Why did you betray me? Betray my father?"

"Your father...excuse me, ma'am, was a sonavabitch to work for."

Cat could almost laugh if it wasn't all so terrible.

"And me?"

"You didn't have a clue what you were doing. The ranch was going to go down anyway. I just

341

hurried it along a little. And hell, you were going to get a huge sum for this here ranch. I didn't feel bad about any of it."

That was a rationalization if there ever was one.

"But you've accused an innocent man? He might have been sent to prison."

"I've nothing against Cody Taylor except he was getting in the way of Langley's plans and therefore in my way. You see, for my assistance, I was promised a lot of money when the consortium bought your land. But now that it ain't happening, Langley told me I'm getting nothing. And that's not right. I was planning to go to Idaho to be with my daughter. I could retire on what he'd promised me. My arthritis is so bad I can hardly get out of bed in the morning. I'm too old to be doing this kind of work. But I ain't got nothing but Social Security to live on, and not much of that, having worked under the table for most of my life."

"And so you are ready to turn in Langley." No honor among thieves, and clearly Will thought he was the aggrieved person in all of this. Not Cody and not Cat McKenna. "And Ray Spencer is in on this too, I guess."

"He needed money. Got into a bad thing with those painkillers. They're prescription, but they cost a lot, he tells me. I fed him the lie about Cody being behind it. He thinks that Cody is the guy. Through me, Langley offered him a tidy sum to come clean to the sheriff and arranged for immunity for his testimony against Cody. Got to hand it to Langley. He's smart."

Her mind was churning along with her stomach. "How do we free Cody though? Will you come forward?"

"Not unless you get me the same deal as Spencer—immunity. And a little bonus would be nice for my retirement."

Cat blanched. "I'm pretty sure that paying you for testimony isn't legal, or shouldn't be. But I can try to get you immunity." Though how she would do that without Kyle's help, she wasn't sure. "Give me some time to work this through though."

"Langley wants me gone. I think my staying around is getting him nervous. I told him to pay me what he promised, and I would be gone, but he's refusing. He thinks he's got me over a barrel because he will just tell Spencer to finger me as the second man. That's why I'm telling you. I can't go to jail. I wouldn't survive with my arthritis. All I want is to be with my daughter in Idaho. I never asked for all of this."

But by his actions, he had asked for it. He'd stolen from her, decimated her herd, colluded to send an innocent man to jail, ruined her chance at happiness, and caused her to put her ranch up for sale, a ranch that had been in her family since Alistair McKenna. And yet Will Springer acted like the injured party.

She resisted the urge to tell him off. Instead she took a deep breath, counted to three, and agreed to get back to him in twenty-four hours.

* * *

Things happened quickly once she'd gone to Cody's lawyer, Gavin Heely. Being a criminal lawyer, Gavin knew just what to do and how to approach the sheriff. And the sheriff knew just how to handle Kyle Langley—who was currently sitting in the detention center awaiting bail. No doubt he had the assets to post bail soon, but the thought of him, in his suit and tie, sitting in the holding pen with the criminal element of Rawlins, Wyoming, warmed her heart.

Her mother sat across from her in their living room as Cat explained everything, sheer disbelief on Lydia's face.

"Kyle Langley was stealing from us. Cattle? He doesn't even have a ranch."

Jake played behind the couch with his plastic blocks. Cat wished she didn't have to discuss it with Jake in the room, but it was too early to send him to bed, and maybe her mother was right. He might not understand everything now, but he needed to know the truth.

"It was part of his plan to decimate the herd so we would be more amenable to the offer from LEW Consortium. And it pretty much worked if it hadn't been for that lease I found and giving that lease to Cody so he could reopen the case. Without clear rights to water, LEW had to withdraw its bid, causing Langley to renege on his promise of money to Will Springer, leading Will to come clean about who really was behind the rustling. In exchange for immunity, of course." She didn't mention that she'd also agreed to pay Will through December if he would testify and leave Wyoming. She'd done it to assure Cody would be cleared.

"I just can't believe that Kyle Langley would do something like this. He's been our lawyer for years. And Will. I guess I really didn't know the man."

"Shows that we can all get it wrong when it

comes to judging a person. We ignore the signs and believe what we want to be the truth. You ignored all the good signs with Cody. I ignored all the bad signs with you-know-who."

Her mother settled back into her chair. "I guess I owe that boy an apology. Do you think he will lease us the water rights if that lease is valid?"

She hoped so, because it was looking more and more like she'd have to stay and ranch unless she sold the land for a mere pittance of what it had been worth. "I don't know, but if he does, I don't think we can expect the deal that Alistair McKenna was able to get from Emma Taylor."

Her mother smiled. "Seems like there was something there between those two, maybe some unrequited love or something. It'd be interesting to know more."

Unrequited love. Like her love for Cody. She hadn't seen him since that day at the creek. He'd sent a text a day or two ago telling her not to sign any papers selling the ranch until he saw her. No worries there. Without rights to water, there were no takers anyway.

But he hadn't named a date or time for them to meet, and she'd heard nothing else since.

"Maybe."

Her mother looked over at her. "It wouldn't work out between you two. I might apologize, and I will when I see him, but I hear from Joanne Littleton that Mamie was ready to shoot you on sight for getting her boy mixed up with Pleasant Valley. With you."

"I imagine that's true." She could hardly forget her reception from Mamie when she'd been at the Taylor house.

"We McKennas and Taylors just aren't made to mingle," she said, borrowing a word from Alistair's journal. "Do you think he might want to buy Pleasant Valley?"

"Just because he's free doesn't mean the Taylors suddenly have money. I expect they are just as in debt now as they were before Cody went to jail. Maybe more so, given the cost of his lawyer." He'd had to sell Smoking Gun, and Cat knew how much that horse meant to him. And he'd told her he'd have to sell the ranch regardless.

"What about us, Cat? If we can't sell the ranch and we can't get water, what will happen to us?"

"I haven't thought that far ahead." She'd done nothing but think that far ahead, and she couldn't offer her mother much hope.

How had this happened? Why had Alistair McKenna staked a claim without access to water? There were some springs on the property, but it wouldn't be enough to keep a few thousand head of cattle, or to support a fracking operation, or a housing development.

She'd have to draw down the herd and give up her BLM leases. But that left a whole lot of land she'd be paying taxes on but couldn't use.

"Well, we need a plan. And soon," Lydia said.

"The Taylors haven't cut off our water yet." She could hope, yet what would that mean for the Taylors? Or for the McKennas? After seeing Cody at the creek, she didn't think she could sell to any fracking organization even if she did have water rights. And yet she didn't want to ranch. Not without Cody by her side. Heck, she didn't want to do anything without Cody, only that wasn't an option.

"You'll have to find another lawyer. Maybe that lease won't prove binding," Lydia said.

And pay him or her with money that would soon be in short supply.

"The fact that they've set another court date based upon that lease says they must think it has merit. And until we know about the water situation, we can't really make a move," Cat said. "But I have faith. We've had this land for over a hundred years. Alistair McKenna found a way. We'll have to at least try."

Chapter 28

From his post at the grill, Cody watched his mother dole out helpings of her famous potato salad and special coleslaw on this July Fourth weekend. They'd had a regular celebration with him, the guest of honor now that the charges had been dropped. Aunt Lucille and Uncle Tom had come down to the ranch for the weekend, and even Michael had gotten two days off from "detecting" in order to join in.

Cody should have felt as happy as a goat in garbage, but he couldn't get his encounter with Cat out of his mind. Truth was, he couldn't get Cat out of his mind.

Giving him that old lease could likely save the Taylor spread from extinction while costing the McKennas their ranch. What she had done was honorable, but he wondered if she would regret it the day she signed over her deed to someone else. And he couldn't imagine how little Jake would feel ten years from now when he would understand the implications of what his mother had done.

Jake wouldn't grow up to think Cody a rustler, for which Cody was grateful, but he wouldn't blame the kid if he felt cheated, if only by fate.

Cody turned the six steaks on the grill. Steaks were the second course. The ribs he'd finished grilling just a few minutes before were almost gone.

"Save a few ribs for me," he called just in time as his mother swatted Jace's hand going for a refill.

The sad thing was now, more than ever, he loved Cat McKenna. He loved her from the top of her stubborn head to the tips of her painted toes. He loved her girly ways and her stick-to-itiveness. He loved the way she was always brushing her long hair back from her face, the way she sat a horse, and the way she bit her lip when she was unsure of herself. He wanted to take care of her, see that no one took advantage of her ever again—and certainly no man. And he wanted to call Jake *son*. That little boy with his gumption and his guts and his can-do attitude had wrapped his hand around Cody's heart.

Yet an ancient feud of which no one alive knew the origins and which had been going on far too long was standing in his way. If he let it.

His mother was smiling and joking as she presided over the picnic table, looking ten years younger than she had on the day his father died or the day he had come home from jail. Her plate was piled high with food, testifying that her appetite had returned, and Cody hadn't detected any signs of drinking.

Things were looking up for the Taylors. But at what cost?

"Penny for your thoughts, cuz," Michael said as he ambled over and handed Cody a bottle of cold beer. Michael looked like his father—tall, stocky, built like a bull. A year older, Cody used to wrestle Michael

349

when they were younger, and Cody would always get pinned. Hadn't done much for his ego.

"Happy to be here." And that was the truth of it.

"Amazing that the McKennas' lawyer was behind all this."

"They still have to prove it in court, but I'm no longer a suspect."

"The thought of you in the pen had us all scrambling to cough up the money," Michael said, tipping back his bottle for a sip. "Who did post bond for you?"

Cody shook his head. "Don't know. Would like to find out. I'd like to thank whoever it was."

Michael frowned. "Well, it had to be someone with money, and ready money. You really don't know?"

Cody had his suspicions, but he hadn't been able to get the words out to ask her, and he wasn't sure she would tell him anyway. She'd already done so much to help him, and what had he done for her?

"Not a clue."

He knew what he wanted to do. Marry her. But it would likely tear apart his family. Jace would probably be okay with it, but his mother would never accept Cat as her daughter-in-law. Not to mention the fact he was broke.

Michael tipped his bottle again and then wiped his mouth on his sleeve. "I can try to find out. I know some bail bondsmen that might be able to help."

"I'd be grateful."

Michael looked down at the smoking grill. "Don't cook the juice out of those things. You know we like 'em still kickin' in this family."

Cody looked down at the expanding blackness of the meat. Might be too late.

"Where's your brother? He just ran out after dinner without a by-your-leave." Mamie pulled out the kitchen chair and sat down under the dim light of the small lamp that sat on their kitchen table, a just-made cup of tea in her hand. It was close to midnight, and Cody was riding in the July Fourth parade tomorrow, as he had done for Memorial Day. The flowers were in his truck, but he still wasn't sure if he would use them.

"We have some cows that haven't calved, so he and Michael are checking on them before we call it a night. Aunt Lucille and Uncle Tom okay in my bedroom?"

Michael was sleeping in Jace's room, and Cody, despite being the guest of honor, was sleeping on the sofa.

Mamie placed her cup of tea on the table. "Of course they are. It was nice of you to give up your room. Your aunt and uncle have been so wonderful to me." A smile bloomed on Mamie's face, erasing the care-worn years. "I don't know where I'd be without them. Certainly not working at a real job in Laramie."

"You seem happy there."

"I am happy there," she said, rubbing her hand over her face. "I miss the ranch though. I miss you and Jace. I'm just so happy that both my boys are working on the ranch as intended."

Cody understood what was left unsaid: *Instead of working at Pleasant Valley.*

"We still have a lot of debt to clear." He didn't want to blurt out his plan, even though how he said it likely mattered less than what he was about to say.

"We'll pay it off. And we'll do it with grass-fed cattle and McKenna money for that water. They can't

ranch without water. Your father must be doing a jig."
A rare chuckle escaped his mother's lips. "Calving
season has gone well, hasn't it?"

Cody couldn't dispute that. They'd only lost two
calves, and calving season was almost over. If his
father hadn't gotten sick, going grass-fed might have
saved the ranch all on its own.

"We have to somehow prove the validity of that
old lease. I'll have to get started looking through the
ranch's papers after the parade tomorrow." Even with
the lease, he wasn't sure they could keep the ranch, but
at least water rights gave him hope.

His mother reached across and rested her fingers
on his arm. "I'll help. I just know it is all going to turn
out okay. I can't believe fate would be cruel enough to
dangle this lease in front of us if it wasn't for real."

"You know we wouldn't have a prayer of keeping
the ranch if it wasn't for Cat turning over that old
lease." And Pleasant Valley could be in just as bad of
shape as the Cross T was as a result.

"It was the right thing to do. People shouldn't get
made out to be heroes for simply doing the right thing."

"Her lawyer told her it likely wasn't valid, so she
would have been within her rights to just forget about it."

His mother took a huffy breath. "If you want me
to say I'm grateful, I am. Grateful the girl had a
conscience, unlike that father of hers. He probably
knew the lease had run out and never bothered to tell
us, hoping in ten years to file that adverse possession
claim. Joe McKenna knew your father wouldn't have
granted him any rights without a hefty payment, and I
hope you will follow that same road."

Not exactly.

"I'm not going to gouge the McKennas simply because we can. Cat McKenna has been good to me, good to the Taylors. I'm hoping to return the favor." And a whole lot more.

"Where is all of this talk about the goodness of Cat McKenna leading? Because there are some facts you are forgetting—like the fact that for several years the McKennas have been using land they knew wasn't theirs and they were no longer entitled to use. The fact that she took you to court to press a claim that essentially stole our land from us. The fact that she was so easily misled by that crooked lawyer of hers. The fact she was willing to sell her land to a company that was going to initiate fracking, which would probably have poisoned a creek that wasn't even theirs, and even if it was theirs, she would have sold it knowing it would have ruined us."

"Our property was already for sale by that time. She's done right by us." And he wanted to do right by her.

"Why are you are working harder than a prairie dog digging tunnels to paint a glorious picture of Cat McKenna?"

Cody took a deep breath. "Because I am in love with Cat. And I am going to ask her to marry me. And I'm not sure she'll say yes unless you can accept her as your daughter-in-law."

Shock blasted across his mother's face like an exploding cannon ball. She stared at him. And stared at him. She touched her hair and smoothed it back. And stared some more.

Lifting her teacup to her lips, she took a sip and carefully rested the cup back on its saucer with a shaky hand.

"I have worried from the moment I saw her in my house that you would be bewitched by that pretty face. And you've never been able to resist a woman in distress. But I felt strongly that with all that the McKennas have done to the Taylors over time— draining our water during draughts, spreading lies about how we are bankrupt before your father ever got sick, humiliating your father at Grange meetings with his condescending manner, not to mention the fact that the Alistair McKenna who signed that lease is the one our family accused of killing Emma Taylor's husband all those years ago—that these actions would keep you from succumbing to your baser instincts, because that's all it is, son, lust. And then when you got arrested, I was sure that if there had been something between you, your arrest would surely kill it." A tear slipped down her face. "How can I do what you are asking of me? Accept her as my daughter-in-law? How do you know she feels the same about you?"

Cody rubbed his chin. "I don't. But I'm hoping to persuade her."

She folded her hands in front of her. "You told me not so long ago that you would never marry. That there wasn't enough money to support a wife, much less a family. That lease wouldn't change things all that much. You said so yourself."

Here was the hard part. "I love her. But it is no lie that together, Cat and I will have the best spread in Wyoming. Separate, neither of us has much."

Cat stood on the sidewalk by Miller's Feed Store, Jake's hand firmly in hers, and shaded her eyes from the noonday sun as she looked down the road. She could make out a slow-moving car headed their way. The July Fourth parade was beginning. Her mother stood on the other side of Jake, talking to Joanne Littleton in low tones, no doubt about recent events, since the whole town was buzzing about rustling, Kyle Langley, how the Taylors really owned Crystal Creek, and how the McKennas were selling their worthless land as a result.

Cat wondered about Cody's cryptic text message. Cat wondered about Cody. She hadn't seen him since that day at the creek, and he'd moved lightning fast to request a new hearing on the validity of the lease.

She was sure it was valid. And she had faith that if they couldn't sell their land—and there had been no takers since news of the lease had surfaced—that Cody would lease her the land and the water rights. She just wasn't sure under what terms. After all, he would have to get his brother and mother to agree, and though Jace seemed a reasonable sort, Cat wasn't so sure that Mamie Taylor would forgive all that had occurred at the hands of the McKennas.

As it turned out, Mamie Taylor was directly across the road, with a woman who could have been her sister, and a man of similar age, along with a rather handsome young man around Cat's age. Family, she imagined. No doubt Jace and Cody were riding in the parade again, as they had Memorial Day. She wondered how she would react when she saw him. Or how Jake would react.

"When is it going to start, Mom?" Jake said, tugging on her arm in his excitement.

"The car with the mayor is heading this way, Jake. See," she said, pointing.

"I want to see the cowboys. You think Cody will be riding in the parade?" He never stopped asking her about his favorite cowboy. It broke her heart to have to tell him she didn't know when he'd see Cody.

"I think he might. He rode in the Memorial Day parade." She still had the flower he'd given her pressed between the pages of a book.

Her mother's language had softened on the subject of Cody, but until the water lease was settled, Lydia held fast to the view that McKennas and Taylors didn't mix. Not that it mattered. Cody hadn't said one word about any future together. And why should she be surprised? It had been a dream, a fragile one at best, before his arrest. Now it all seemed to have evaporated.

"Look, I see the fire engine," Jake said, jumping up and down with the unbridled enthusiasm of an almost five-year-old.

It didn't stop her heart from aching for Cody. It didn't stop the fantasies of a future together rolling around her head whenever she had a moment to herself. And it didn't stop little Jake from wanting his best bud back.

The veterans were next, and Jake returned their salute. Behind them was a contingent from the air force base, riding on a flatbed truck that contained an old prop plane. The men looked great in their uniforms and threw candy out to the crowd whenever they spotted a child. Jake scooped up a handful of wrapped chocolate bars while asking for her help.

She obliged, though she stuffed more than a few in her jean shorts pockets, out of sight. As she bent down to grab the last one in their area, she heard Jake squeal. She looked up in time to see the parade of horses coming in their direction, Cody in the lead on Comanche, between two riders holding American flags. Her heart beat hard against her chest, and she felt the pull of love as the horses and riders pranced toward them.

Cody sat tall in the saddle, cowboy hat on his head. He wore a black shirt and jeans, and she thought he never looked so commanding—and he was staring right at her. Jake jumped up and down like he'd never seen Cody on a horse, and her own heart kept time with her son's leaps. It was a moment before she spotted the bouquet of red roses across his lap and a small cowboy hat nestled on the saddle horn.

"He's heading for you," her mother said in her ear, a noticeable scowl in her voice.

It did appear that way.

She glanced across the street. Mamie Taylor's frown was deeper than a plowed field's furrows, and her mouth had flat-lined like it had been crushed by a brick, an odd reaction to her son's appearance.

* * *

"Is that her?" Michael, her nephew, asked.

Mamie could only nod as she watched her son head toward a life-altering mistake. Her only hope now was that Cat McKenna was as duplicitous as she thought and would reject her son after leading him on. And painful as a rejection would be in front of the whole town, at least it would be final, for no man, and certainly not a man like her son, would carry on after being subjected to such a public humiliation.

"She's a beauty," Michael commented.

And that was what had turned her son's head, and all it was. He was blinded by a pretty face and couldn't see the content of her character.

"And she must love him a lot to do what she'd done."

Mamie's frown deepened. "Handing him that lease that proved we owned that land all along?" she scoffed.

"No. Putting up money to pay the bond fee for a man accused of robbing her. Guess she had faith in him despite what everyone was telling her. That takes love."

Mamie's heart cracked. She felt a little shaky. "Are you telling me it was her that bailed him out?"

"Got it from the bail bondsman himself."

She took a steadying breath. "Does he know?" she asked.

"Not yet. He asked me to find out though. She'd asked the bail bondsman not to make it public, but as I'm in the force, he didn't seem to have any qualms telling me."

Mamie closed her eyes and opened them again. She looked over at Cat McKenna, who was staring at Cody as he approached, like he was the second coming, hope shining in the girl's eyes. Her little boy, a cute tyke, Mamie had to admit, was bouncing like he was getting a visit from Santa Claus.

"Maybe the McKennas have a conscience after all, and guess the ranch can afford it." And she'd find some way to pay them back because she would not be beholden to that family.

"He said it came out of her personal bank

account. I don't think the ranch had anything to do with it. And you know she doesn't get that money back, even though he was freed."

Cat McKenna really did love her son.

* * *

Cody couldn't take his eyes off the woman and little boy who had stolen his heart. If he wasn't in some parade, he'd have galloped over, swept her up, and carried her away like men did in those old-time westerns. Instead, he kept his horse front and center and his focus on the woman he wanted to call his and the little boy jumping up and down at her side. As they had in the Memorial Day parade, each cowboy had a flower to give that special someone in his life. Only Cody had a bouquet of a dozen red roses and a child's cowboy hat in his lap.

As he neared, he took a deep breath, listened to the resounding beats of his heart, and nudged his horse into a trot toward the sidewalk where she stood.

Dressed in a T-shirt, denim shorts, and a pair of flip-flops instead of cowgirl boots, her toes and nails painted bright red, her hair loose and long, she looked more girly girl than cowgirl, and he loved every inch of her. And he was counting on her feeling the same.

He'd noticed Lydia McKenna staring at him with something akin to apprehension in her eyes. Both mothers would be an obstacle, but if Cat said yes and Jake agreed, no one else would matter—at least not for him.

He reined Comanche to the corner near Miller's Feed Store, next to the crowd of people that included

Cat and Jake, and dismounted with the bouquet in his hand. The troop passed, the clacking of horses' hooves reverberating in Cody's ears. Jake grabbed him around the knees in a hug as he reached up and got the child's cowboy hat off the saddle horn. Placing it on Jake's head, he declared, "A cowboy needs a real cowboy hat, partner."

Jake grabbed the brim of the hat, pulled it down on his head, and beamed a smile in Cody's direction. "Thank you, partner," the little tyke drawled and then hugged Cody around the knees again. "I've missed you."

"I've missed you too, Jake. But give me a minute with your mom, and it may come out all right."

After Jace presented a flower to their mother, Jace trotted over, as planned, to hold Comanche's reins, and Cody was freed to stare into a pair of brown eyes brimming with what he hoped was love. Around them, a circle of people drew closer. Out of the corner of his eye, he spied his mother crossing the street, a pink rose clutched in her hand. He had to hurry.

He bent down on one knee and looked up at the woman who held his happiness in her hands, and the crowd formed a circle around them.

"Cat McKenna," he began, surprised his voice was strong and steady, since he felt neither of those things, "I am here today because I love you. I love your tenacious spirit. I love your hopeful optimism. I love your never-quit attitude and your willingness to sacrifice for those you love. I love every inch of your frilly, fancy self. I love you as a mother to your wonderful son, as a rancher trying to do the best for your land and herd, and as the woman who did what was right even though it cost her. Together we are stronger than we will ever be apart—and I mean that in every way. Will you marry me and give me the honor of calling you my wife and Jake my son?"

"I'm going to get a dad," Jake yelled and hugged Cody's neck from behind, almost climbing on his back.

Cody held up the bouquet of roses. Tears fell from Cat's lashes as she vainly blinked them back. She looked back at her mother.

Was she going to tell him no? Had he misread her heart?

He raised his gaze to take in Lydia. She also had tears in her eyes. "Go ahead," she urged her daughter. "Follow your heart. It's clear he loves you."

Cat reached out and took the bouquet, handing it right back to her mother. Cody rose, and in that split second Cat had her arms around his neck and was squeezing him tight as she whispered yes over and over in his ear, while Jake clung to his knees.

The crowd clapped its approval, a crowd that he realized included his mother.

Cody Taylor was a happy man.

The wedding was a hasty affair, kept simple and small by both desire and necessity, since Cat was afraid their mothers might have a change of heart if the couple waited too long. It had not been easy for either Lydia McKenna or Mamie Taylor to reconcile themselves to being in-laws, but the women had at least been trying as they worked out who would cook what for the affair that was held at Pleasant Valley for just a handful of family and friends. Cat had been afraid they'd come to blows when pot roast was discussed. Each thought theirs was the best before it was decided that both women could offer up their classic dishes.

Cat had eschewed an engagement ring, settling instead on the couple getting a simple pair of gold bands for the wedding. She'd told Cody she had no need for a ring that would spend most of the time in its box, since wearing a diamond ring around cows and bulls, among manure and hay, wasn't practical. She knew he'd be relieved, since there was still that mountain of debt to clear up.

They had settled on what to do with their land interests. Cat had given up any claim to the land in question, and Cody and Jace had agreed to a reasonable water access lease for Pleasant Valley for another ninety-nine years plus back payment for the years the lease wasn't in force. The new lease relieved them of going through an expensive trial. It was clear the land was always meant to be Taylor land. Cat had never felt right taking the land to begin with.

The wedding went off without incident, both mothers bringing their best manners to their children's wedding. Jake was ring bearer, and little Delanie Martin was flower girl. Jace was Cody's best man, and Mandy Martin was matron of honor. Libby and Cyndi Lynn were bridesmaids, and Chance Cochran and Ty Martin were groomsmen, and a great time was had by all the attendees, which also included Cody's aunts and uncles, his cousin Michael, who seemed to be quite taken with Cyndi Lynn, the Littletons and the Logans, as well as neighboring ranch families, who all seemed interested in being part of Carbon County history when the Taylors and McKennas broke bread together.

When she'd presented her wedding gift to her groom, he whooped and hollered, almost spooking Smoking Gun. The horse, she told him, represented their future together.

Two months later Cat sat atop Custer and watched as the culled herd of over fifteen hundred head was loaded up for market. Prices were up, and Pleasant Valley would actually make a profit—under her watch. She couldn't have done it without Cody by her side. And she didn't want to do it without her handsome husband.

Cody supervised the loading, while Jake nestled in front of him on the paint. He was gesturing to Jake, explaining something about the herd to her boy, now their boy. The adoption papers had been filed.

Cody had a rancher's heart, and he certainly had this rancher's heart.

Dear Readers,

I hope you enjoyed this book as much as I enjoyed writing Cat and Cody's story. Please consider leaving a review on the book's page on Amazon's website. This helps increase visibility of the book so other readers can find it. All you need to write is a sentence or two. It means the world to authors to know what readers think of their books.

If you haven't read them yet, Cat's girlfriends Libby and Mandy have books of their own in the Hearts of Wyoming series. **Loving a Cowboy** is Libby and Chance's story and the first book in the series, and **The Maverick Meets His Match** is Mandy and Ty's story and the second book in the series, though you do not need to read these books in order.

The Loner's Heart will be coming out in 2017, where Mandy's single brother-in-law, Trace, finds himself attracted to a most unlikely lady. Can he convince her to change her life and become his wife and mother to little Delanie?

Weigh in on whose story you would like to see in subsequent books by sending me an e-mail or commenting on Facebook. Would you like Jace to find love and success on the rodeo circuit? Does Cyndi Lynn need her own happily ever after? What about that heartbreaker Tucker Prescott from **The Maverick Meets His Match**? Or Doug Brennan, Libby's brother from **Loving a Cowboy**?

You can keep abreast of what is happening in the Hearts of Wyoming series by signing up for my newsletter at http://www.annecarrole.com.

In the Hearts of Wyoming series there are lots of characters who need a second chance at finding their true love!

Hugs,
Anne

Hearts of Wyoming series
Book 1: Loving a Cowboy
Book 2: The Maverick Meets His Match
Book 3: The Rancher's Heart
Book 4: The Loner's Heart (coming 2017)

About the Author

I have been creating stories since I first wondered where Sally was running to in those early reader books. One of three sisters, I was raised on a farm where we had horses, dogs, cats, rabbits, hamsters, chickens, and anything else we could convince our parents to shelter. Besides reading and writing romances, you might find me researching Western history, at the rodeo, watching football with my hubby, in the garden, or on the tennis court. Married to my own suburban cowboy, we are the proud parents of an awesome twentysomething cowgirl and a cat with way too much attitude.

I'm also the founder of the Western romance fan page: www.facebook.com/lovewesternromances.com.

I love hearing from readers. You can friend, follow, or find me on:

Facebook: http://www.facebook.com/annecarrole.com
Twitter: http://twitter.com/annecarrole
Web: http://www.annecarrole.com (where you can also sign up for my newsletter)

Titles by Anne Carrole

Hearts of Wyoming series
Book 1: Loving a Cowboy
Book 2: The Maverick Meets His Match
Book3: The Rancher's Heart
Book 4: The Loner's Heart (coming 2017)

Novellas
Falling for a Cowboy (short contemporary Western)
Saving Cole Turner (short historical Western)